# A GALAXY UNKNOWN

# MILOR!

## Book 5

### BY

# THOMAS DEPRIMA

Vinnia Publishing - U.S.A.

# Milor!
A Galaxy Unknown series – Book 5
Copyright ©2003, 2012 by Thomas J. DePrima

ISBN-10 : **1619310104**

ISBN-13 : **978-1-61931-010-0**

2$^{nd}$ Edition

Amazon Distribution

*Cover art by:* Martin J. Cannon

Appendices containing political and technical data highly pertinent to this series are included at the back of this book.

To contact the author, or see information about his other novels, visit:

*http://www.deprima.com*

Many thanks to Ted King for his technical expertise and encouragement, and to Michael A. Norcutt for his suggestions, proofreading, and for acting as my military protocol advisor.

And kudos to my artist, Martin Cannon, for the fantastic cover artwork that features Lord High Space Marshall Gulqulk of the Milori Emperor's Imperial Cruiser Reguffa.

## This series of novels includes:

*A Galaxy Unknown…*

A Galaxy Unknown
Valor at Vauzlee
The Clones of Mawcett
Trader Vyx
Milor!
Castle Vroman
Against All Odds
Return to Dakistee

## Other series and novels by the author:

*AGU: Border Patrol…*

Citizen X

*When The Spirit…*

When The Spirit Moves You
When The Spirit Calls

A World Without Secrets

# Table of Contents

# Chapter One

~ January 11$^{th}$, 2275 ~

The sound of his footsteps echoed hollowly off the dark gray granite walls of the grandiose palace and raced fleetingly ahead of his shadow as he walked in determined silence. Magnificently attired potentates and prime ministers eyed him jealously from oversized portraits lining the hallways. Their time had faded, and Nadeil Marueck now held the high office of Prime Minister on Arrosa. He had steadily climbed— some would say clawed— his way up during decades of government service, and he now stood at the pinnacle of political accomplishment on his home world. The planet still supported a royal family, but the king and queen functioned merely as figureheads to an adoring populace. Marueck held the real strings of power, and he held them tightly lest someone as ambitious as he try to wrest control from his vise-like grip.

As he entered the large outer office with his usual arrogant gait, the people hoping for an audience rose quickly from their seats. Without so much as a glance in their direction, he crossed the room and disappeared into his large and lavishly appointed inner office. Pausing briefly to prepare a steaming cup of gyxorna from a beverage synthesizer, he continued on to his desk and sat down in the ostentatious chair that was just one more symbol of his supreme power. The seat back rose at least two feet above his head, strongly but silently proclaiming its occupant to be a person of unparalleled importance. It's not that the sixty-three-year-old ruler was short. At four feet, five inches, he was actually taller than ninety-seven percent of a planetary population where the average height for males was three feet, one inch. Arrosian women, at an average of three feet, five inches, were usually taller than their spouses. Marueck just felt that the stately chair made him seem even taller and more imposing to those privileged enough to visit his office.

Marueck prepared his mind for the day ahead while he sipped his gyxorna and listened attentively to his computer as it read off his appointments. Suddenly he yelled at the computer to stop, put his cup down so quickly and forcefully that the beverage sloshed over onto his desk, and jumped to his feet.

"Mirva!" he yelled in a loud and angry voice as he strode purposefully into the outer office to confront his secretary. "I told you I didn't want to see that idiot Tiksetti under any circumstances. Why is he listed on my appointments schedule?"

"I'm sorry, Prime Minister, but the king made the appointment for Professor Tiksetti. I couldn't very well say no to His Majesty."

"You can and will when I've given you instructions contrary to one of his eccentric whims. Now contact Tiksetti immediately and inform him the appointment has been cancelled."

"Yes, sir. Right away, Prime Minister."

As she stretched out a hand towards the com unit on her desk, the entire room suddenly shook violently. Plaster dust fell thickly from newly opened cracks in the ceiling and filled the office with a dense, choking white cloud that all but obscured visibility. Decorative objects, dislodged from the walls, crashed noisily to the floor. Having again jumped to their feet in the presence of the Prime Minister, visitors waiting in the outer office were sent stumbling into one another before falling. Marueck, unable to keep his footing, wound up sprawled on the floor like the others.

As the shaking ended, Marueck got to his feet and staggered to the doorway leading to his inner office. Pushing open the door, he saw that his massive desk was now a dozen feet closer to the door than it had been just minutes earlier. The wall immediately behind his desk was completely gone. Large chunks of masonry, wood, and plaster covered the floor and everything else in the room. The blast had pushed his magnificent chair against his heavy desk with sufficient force to smash the chair to kindling. The room was in total disarray.

A breeze, flowing in through the new floor-to-ceiling hole, prevented plaster dust from settling and kept loose papers swirling about the office. All color drained from Marueck's face as he stared at the carnage. If he hadn't lost his temper and rushed to the outer office, the blast would surely have killed him.

Brandishing laser weapons, several bodyguards burst into the outer office from the corridor and ran to the Prime Minister, identifying the plaster-dust-covered, ghost-like figure solely by his height. Fearing there might be additional danger, they grabbed his arms and pulled him away from his position by the inner office door. One guard then cleared the way ahead as the others half pushed and half dragged Marueck out of the office to a special elevator. Within minutes, the prime minister found himself down in a bunker deep beneath the palace. A number of other ministers and deputies were likewise collected and brought down to the War Situation Room.

"What's happened?" Marueck demanded of the young officer in charge of securing the room as he shook his head to dislodge some of the plaster dust that caked his hair.

"We don't have all the details yet, Prime Minister. We know there was a large explosion outside the building near your office, but we don't know what exploded. It could have been a missile, a mortar round, or a transport bomb. We're still investigating the matter. Colonel Dejemnik ordered that you and the other ministers in the palace be brought here until we can determine if there's any additional threat."

Marueck paced the underground room restlessly until word came that there didn't appear to be any additional danger, then walked from the room with a trail of ministers behind him. The lift only accommodated six at a time, leaving room for just two others in addition to Marueck and his three main bodyguards for the first trip. Pulling his Minister of State Security and the Minister of Intelligence into the car, he nodded to a bodyguard to close the door.

"Listen to me, both of you!" he said loudly and emphatically as the lift began to rise from the underground cavern. "I want to know who is responsible for this within the hour! I'll expect you to report to me by then! Understand?"

Both men nodded vigorously. No one said no to Prime Minister Marueck when he was in this kind of mood, regardless of how absurd his command. As the lift stopped spasmodically at the main floor of the palace, Marueck stepped out, followed by his three guards. Walking directly to his offices and finding only his secretary in the outer office, he said, "Cancel all my regular appointments for the rest of the day."

"Yes, sir. I reached Professor Tiksetti and told him I had to cancel his appointment. He said he had just heard about the explosion on the news and asked when he might reschedule. I told him I would call when you found time to see him."

"Good. Of course I don't expect to ever find the time."

The door to his inner office opened suddenly. Several maintenance workers emerged, steering 'oh-gee' dump carts loaded with pieces of broken building materials. Inside the office, bots were still sweeping up and filling more carts. Security forces observed all work and ensured strict adherence to security procedures for the loose papers and documents.

Marueck walked into the office and observed the cleanup effort. Other maintenance workers soon arrived and began directing bots tasked to cover the hole with temporary prefabricated wall panels. Marueck, still covered in white plaster dust, quickly tired of watching the banal activity and walked to his quarters in the palace to take another shower and change into clean clothes.

When Marueck returned to his office an hour later, the maintenance people were just finishing up, and his Security and Intelligence ministers were waiting nervously to give their reports. He motioned to them to follow him into his inner office and take seats in the informal conference area. He paced the floor in silence until the last of the maintenance people left and the door to the office closed.

"Well, Minister Lisaul?" he said, looking at the Minister of State Security.

"Excellency, the blast was caused by a ground transport filled with explosives. The explosion left a crater over two meters deep, and there is little left of the vehicle altered to appear like one of our own grounds maintenance vehicles, but we're attempting to learn its origins.

"We found the real transport parked at the recycling plant, and our investigator discovered the body of the driver beneath a tarp in the rear. Someone murdered him a few hours before the incident, and whoever took his place appears to have been an exact duplicate. The impostor even knew the names of the guards on duty at the gate and joked with them before driving to a place opposite your office. He must have known you were in the building and normally at your desk at that hour. But on the off chance that one of the visitors in your outer office notified the perpetrator of your arrival this morning, we're— *interviewing* them. It appears the bomber was able to walk off the grounds in all the confusion. That's all we've been able to learn so far. My people are continuing to follow up leads."

Marueck nodded and looked at the other man. "Anything to add, Minister Deruuw?"

"My people are tracking down all known and suspected dissidents. No one has claimed credit for the attack yet, but as soon as they do, we'll move in and arrest everyone associated with that group. We'll find out who perpetrated this attack, but it will take some time. In the meantime, security has been doubled and everyone entering the grounds must now submit to the retinal test we've only required of people entering the palace."

"A little late for beefing up security."

"We've never had an attack on the palace grounds before, and the ID badge was always adequate. I apologize and offer my resignation, Excellency."

"I'll tell you when I want your resignation, Deruuw. Right now, all I want is the head of the individual or individuals behind this attack on my person. But make sure we've drained every bit of useful knowledge from the head before separating it from the body. Understand?"

Both men nodded and replied, "Yes, Excellency."

# Chapter Two

~ January 14<sup>th</sup>, 2275 ~

Jenetta Carver stepped from the lift and walked confidently towards her offices in the Headquarters section of Stewart Space Command Base, cheerfully greeting everyone she passed. As always, her passage generated stares from base personnel, resident civilians, and visitors alike. The stares weren't because she had a face and body like that of Aphrodite, nor even because of her five-foot, eleven-inch height. Well, perhaps some were, but most were for the pair of huge cats that walked with her, one on either side. Black as space, with large yellow eyes that seemed to glow, their gaze was usually more than enough to halt any pedestrian in his or her steps.

The huge cats never strayed more than half a meter from Jenetta's side unless she was threatened. Should that unusual situation arise, the virtually identical pair of hundred-sixty-pound Taurentlus-Thur Jumakas would whirl to face the threat, prepared to spring at the potential attacker. Only one person had been foolhardy enough to attack Jenetta since she'd acquired the pair in a deal with an Alyysian trader. He had died violently, within minutes, from the trauma of having his throat ripped out by Cayla, while the powerful jaws of Tayna snapped the arm holding the laser pistol. At the time, there was some speculation about whether he had died from asphyxiation or loss of blood as his carotid arteries continued to flood the deck until his heart stopped.

Although she appeared to be only about twenty-one years of age, Jenetta wore the four wide gold bars on each shoulder that proclaimed her a captain in Space Command. Moreover, she was the base commander at this vital military installation.

Housed inside a giant asteroid almost five hundred light-years from Earth, Stewart Space Command Base was hundreds of light-years from its nearest counterpart. In permanent orbit around a Type F5 blue/white MMK class IV star with an asteroid belt but no planets, the asteroid shell protected the base from both enemies and natural celestial phenomena.

How one so young as Captain Carver appeared to be had reached such an elevated position in Space Command is a story in itself. Appearances aside, Jenetta Carver was actually thirty-eight years of age. As base commander of a StratCom-One designated base, a position heretofore only occupied by two-star admirals, Jenetta's supreme authority extended for hundreds of light-years in every direction from Stewart SCB. Her position even permitted her to overrule the patrol routes and mission orders established by Space Command HQ for any ship in the sectors of space she administered, with the understanding that such overrides must be proven to have been 'correct and proper actions' during a subsequent review. In the words of one junior officer, she was the "closest thing there is to God within four hundred light-years."

Jenetta reached her office suite and entered with her cats as the doors opened automatically. "Good morning, Lori," she said to her chief aide, Lieutenant Ashraf.

"Good morning, Captain," her aide said, smiling. "You look very cheerful this morning."

"I am, Lori, I am. I received a very important communication from Space Command Supreme Headquarters just before turning in last night."

"Yes, ma'am. I saw the secure message entry in your queue."

"Would you arrange for all senior officers on duty to come to my office this afternoon at 1500 hours?"

"Of course, Captain. Is there a topic which they should be prepared to discuss?"

"No, it will just be a quick meeting to announce what I learned from Supreme Headquarters."

"Very good, Captain."

Lieutenant Ashraf wondered about the content of the secure message but knew that if the Captain wanted her to know, she would have informed her. Although her position required her to know the details of most communications, some remained sealed until Captain Carver chose to reveal them.

Jenetta turned and walked into her office. The large cats hadn't moved from her side during her discussion with the Lieutenant, but once behind the closed door of Jenetta's enormous private office, they headed for their favorite resting spots. From their vantage points near the side walls, they could see everything in the room but were barely noticeable unless they moved. They had already spent an hour in the base gym running alongside Jenetta as she enjoyed her morning workout, so they were content to relax.

Jenetta prepared a steaming mug of rich, black, Colombian coffee at her beverage synthesizer before moving to her desk. The floor-to-ceiling SimWindow behind her desk was displaying an image of the large colony at Terra Meridiani on Mars, and she changed the view to see a real-time image of the base's port. Special sensors and cameras mounted throughout the large cavern altered what would to the naked eye appear like a dark void into an image that made the sixty-kilometer by thirty-kilometer interior of the asteroid look like the well-illuminated interior of a giant warehouse.

Although the outside wall she faced was constructed of reinforced building materials many meters thick, the 3-D SimWindow made it seem she was looking out a window made of ordinary plate glass. Moreover, she could zoom the image to show any part of the port from any angle.

Jenetta sipped at her coffee while watching the activity for a short time, then took her seat at the desk and began going through the morning's accumulation of messages and reports. She had completed reading everything in her queue, marked most for filing, and responded to others that required a response by the time her first appointment arrived. So began a day filled with numerous meetings.

Jenetta worked until the lunch hour and then left to take her daily walk through the civilian concourse where she'd stop at one of the many restaurants to have lunch. Other people on the concourse gave her a wide berth because of her cats, although most everyone knew they weren't a danger if Jenetta wasn't threatened in any way.

Virtually every sentient species known to the Galactic Alliance visited the base at one time or another. Even Pledgians, the small, round, furry creatures with stick-like arms and legs, and eyes mounted on stalks that could rise up a full meter from the top of the creature when it had need to be vigilant, were seen frequently. At rest, the arms, legs, and eyestalks disappeared into the creature's body, leaving only a furry gray, medium green or magenta ball visible.

Stepping into one of the newest eateries, a Nordakian restaurant, she was seated immediately once the owner and staff could be coaxed to rise from their knees. If her status as base commander wasn't enough to guarantee special treatment, then her status as a Nordakian Azula and Lady of the Royal House of Nordakia would have guaranteed it in any Nordakian business. Nordakian males, normally between seven and eight feet in height, were required to drop to one knee and bow their heads while saluting by holding their clenched hand to their chest when meeting a member of the royal family or the Nordakian nobility. An azula was the approximate equivalent of a duchess in Earth nobility, and the added distinction of being a Lady of the Royal House ranked her just below the royal family. Her estate on Obotymot, a colony planet of Nordakia, encompassed all thirty-six million hectares of the Gavistee Peninsula.

Although born on Earth, Jenetta held dual citizenship as both a Terran and Nordakian, and had been officially commissioned a captain in the Nordakian Space Force years before achieving that rank with Space Command. The citizenship, commission, and investiture as a Lady of the Royal House were rewards for services performed for Nordakia while functioning as acting captain of the freighter that had rescued her from a ten-year slumber in an escape pod. Most of her estate was a reward for restoring to the Nordakian people an original edition of the book that defined their religion. As their liege, she was legally responsible for the well-being of all people on the peninsula, although she had never even visited the estate. It was just one more responsibility heaped upon the shoulders of someone already responsible for billions of GA citizens.

After enjoying a bowl of queelish, a Nordakian vegetable stew for which she had developed a fondness, Jenetta tried to pay for her meal. The owner adamantly refused to take payment from Jenetta. She was forced to stop offering and graciously accept his generosity. Space Command had very strict rules about accepting gifts but permitted officers to accept food gifts up to a value of ten credits from any company, organization, or individual in any GST week. The Nordakian Space Force also permitted officers to accept small gifts of food, with the proviso they not exceed a value of fifty credits in any lunar cycle. Since the queelish was just a quarter-credit, it easily qualified for exemption from both services. However, after returning to her office Jenetta would note the small gift in her official daily log so no charge of impropriety could ever be levied. It was so much easier when merchants let her pay, but she always had to follow the most diplomatic course.

Speaking in Dakis, the language of Nordakia, she thanked him for extending the hospitality of his establishment. The owner beamed and told her she was always welcome as he pressed his closed hand to his chest and bowed his head. Jenetta smiled and touched her flattened, open hand to her chest with her palm parallel to the ground. Her cats fell in alongside her as she turned to leave.

Just before 1500 hours, Jenetta stopped working and began welcoming her senior staff to her office. By 1500, the entire on-duty staff of senior officers had assembled, and Jenetta spoke into her com unit. "Lori, would you come in here for a minute, please?"

The five-foot, eight-inch officer, with collar-length, raven-colored hair, almond-shaped eyes, and olive skin, walked in and moved to face Jenetta, who was standing in front of her desk. "Yes, Captain?"

"The room shall come to attention," Jenetta said loudly.

The seated officers stood up, and all came to attention as Lt. Ashraf's large, chestnut eyes opened a little wider.

Jenetta's cats that had been sitting comfortably in their favorite spots also stood up, trying to determine if there was a threat to their mistress. They were usually relaxed in the presence of anyone wearing a Space Command Uniform.

"Lieutenant Lori Elaine Ashraf," Jenetta said, "by order of Space Command Supreme Headquarters, with approval by the Galactic Alliance Council, you are immediately advanced to the rank of Lieutenant Commander." Jenetta produced the appropriate insignia from a box on her desk and replaced the lieutenant insignia Lieutenant Ashraf was wearing on each shoulder as she said, "These were my first Lt. Commander bars, pinned on me by Admirals Holt and Margolan at Higgins SCB. If there's any luck left in them, may they share it with you as you work to achieve your personal and professional goals."

Taking a step back, Jenetta saluted the newly promoted officer as she said, "Congratulations, Commander."

Lieutenant Commander Ashraf returned the salute and, although speechless for a few seconds, finally found her voice and said, "Thank you, Captain."

"The room shall be at ease," Jenetta announced loudly.

The other officers crowded around Lori to congratulate her on her promotion before starting to drift out and back to their jobs. No one ever objected to being called together for such short ceremonies because everyone appreciated receiving such recognition in the presence of their peers.

After the room was empty of other officers, Lieutenant Commander Ashraf said, "Thank you, Captain. I didn't expect this to happen so quickly. You only mentioned it a few weeks ago."

"You earned it, Lori. You've done a wonderful job as my aide, and I've appreciated all your hard work and dedication."

"It's an honor to serve in your command, Captain. Oh, you have a visitor waiting."

"Who is it?"

"An Arrosian freighter captain. He's been waiting for another ship to arrive and accept his cargo, but they haven't shown up. Neither are they responding to hails. He's concerned."

"Send him in, Lori."

"Aye, Captain."

A minute later, a diminutive ship's officer entered Jenetta's office. She'd prepared herself and was able to suppress the smile she always felt when seeing an Arrosian or Selaxian. Their small size made them seem like children, and Jenetta idly mused if Nordakian males felt that way about Terrans. Her small, belt-mounted translator device would immediately adjust to his language when he spoke. It would then send a properly translated signal directly to her CT. The miniature cranial transducer, mounted subcutaneously against the outside of her skull behind her left ear, would make it sound as though someone was standing next to her, whispering the translation directly into her auditory canal.

"Good afternoon, Captain," Jenetta said.

"Good afternoon, Captain Carver. I'm Captain Oluthru of the freighter *Gastrime*. Our registry is Arrosian. I'm sorry to take you away from your busy schedule."

"Not at all, sir. How may I assist you?"

"My crew and I have been waiting here for over a week to meet another freighter from our home world so we might exchange cargos. We would add their cargo to the cargo we've already collected for our run to Dixon, and they would take that part of our cargo destined for Arrosa. We've tried to contact the *Hunaray,* but they aren't responding to our hails."

"And you're afraid the *Hunaray* has met with harm?"

"Yes, as each day passes our fears increase."

"When did you last have contact with them?"

"About three weeks ago. They expected to be here to greet us when we arrived. And, as I said, we've been here for a week now."

"If they expected to be here within two weeks from their last transmission, they couldn't have been more than seven light-years away."

"Even closer. Their top speed is Light-150. Since Arrosa is eleven light-years away and they were halfway here, they must have been within five and a half light-years of the base. In light of the violent acts being perpetrated on my world, I'm worried the *Hunaray* may have met an untimely fate."

"What violent acts are being perpetrated against your world?"

"Why, the acts of terrorism, of course."

"Oh, I hadn't heard."

"Surely you must have seen something on the news."

"No, nothing. Nor have I heard anything through official channels. How long have the attacks been going on?"

"Almost a year. We've been away during the entire time, but we've received a steady stream of messages from our relatives back home. I can't believe you haven't heard anything."

"There hasn't been anything on the news channels or in my briefings from Space Command Supreme Headquarters. I know Arrosa petitioned to become part of the Galactic Alliance following the recent expansion that moved the boundary out a hundred parsecs, but we haven't established formal diplomatic contact yet. As I'm sure you're aware, we were formerly unable to do anything within the Frontier Zone except respond to pleas from ships under attack or in need of emergency assistance, and Arrosa was on the farthest edge, almost in open galactic space. Now that your planet is included within regulated GA space, we can help, but we're still only permitted to assist planets that specifically request our help. Otherwise, we're prohibited from becoming involved in their internal affairs."

"It's not just an internal affair. Everyone is pretty sure the attacks are the work of the Selaxians."

"The Selaxians? Aren't they your brethren?"

"They *were* our brethren, Captain. We haven't been brethren for over a hundred years since they began a war for independence. We speak a common language, of sorts, although colloquialisms and slang have crept into each of our languages over the past century. There are times, on space stations, when I overhear Selaxians speaking and can't figure out what they're talking about. I understand the words but not the meanings. It's like listening to my kids talk with their friends."

"Yes, I've heard of such situations in other cultures. I'm afraid I don't know very much about the politics on your respective planets. I wasn't even aware of your war."

"It wasn't *our* war," the captain said angrily. "It was *their* war. We founded the colony, transported the settlers, helped them build their towns and establish their civilizations in the wilderness of a hostile planet and then they *rebelled*. They said we weren't treating them fairly. They claimed they didn't have any representation in the Dregma. They even alleged that they didn't have the same rights they'd enjoyed while on Arrosa."

"I see. Did they?"

"Of course."

"How many representatives did they have in your Dregma?"

"Uh, I'm not sure."

"Did they have *any*?" Jenetta asked innocently.

"They must have."

"Why?"

"Why?" Captain Oluthru repeated, as though confused that such a thing would even be questioned.

"Yes, why must they have had representation? You said 'no representation' was one of their grievances."

"Every citizen on Arrosa is represented in the Dregma. It's the law on Arrosa."

"But the people on Selax weren't on Arrosa. Perhaps no one had ever been appointed to represent their issues. Perhaps that fact left them open to abuse and unfair treatment at the hands of those who should have been helping and guiding them."

"I'm sure they had representation," Captain Oluthru said with more than a hint of irritation. "Of course it all happened before I was born, but they taught us in school how we tried everything possible to maintain good relations with the colonists, and it still wasn't enough to keep them from rebelling. We generously bought everything they produced, but they claimed that the prices we established weren't allowing them enough to live. We generously sent them the products from our factories and farms, and they dressed up like pirates and destroyed the shipments without even paying for them. We did our absolute best to restore civil law and order, but they fought the poor soldiers we graciously allowed them to house in their own homes so they'd have immediate protection. Many troops were killed during a decade of fighting because the Selaxians fought like barbarians and terrorists instead of fighting like real soldiers. Finally, we pulled our troops out and left them to fend for themselves. We expected them to turn on each other next, but somehow they restored law and order and built a stable society. It was a miracle they survived without the firm pressure of our gentle, guiding hand.

"Anyway, during the past half century, we've begun to trade with them again. Their space program is still in its infancy, and we've refused to assist them in that endeavor, but they're as bright and resourceful as Arrosians. They now have a small cargo fleet able to traverse the mean fifty-two-million-kilometer distance between the orbit paths of our planets. They haven't built anything that can travel outside the solar system yet, but they've been hiring on with freighters servicing the planet and it's only a matter of time before they buy Light Speed technology or develop something on their own."

"Thank you for the brief history lesson, Captain," Jenetta said. "It was most enlightening. So who and what do you think is behind the recent acts of terrorism?"

"I suspect it has something to do with Isodow, a moon that circles Selax."

"Why?"

"A team of surveyors from our planet discovered rich ore deposits there a few years ago. A mining consortium has begun to mine the ore."

"And why is that a problem?"

"Selax claims the moon is their property simply because it revolves around their planet. Have you ever heard anything so preposterous? They're not even capable of mining the ore. If we don't mine it, it doesn't get mined."

"Perhaps the Selaxians feel their space program is reaching a point where they'll be in a position to mine it in a few years."

"We never ceded rights to the moon when we gave Selax its independence. It's ours now, just as much as it was a hundred years ago when we claimed it. We have the rights of first claim."

"I see. And you feel that this disagreement over the moon is responsible for the terrorism. Do you also think the missing freighter is part of this dispute?"

"What else could it be?"

"There are many possibilities. Perhaps it's Raiders, or perhaps it's simply a mechanical problem."

"Raiders are indeed always a possibility, although Space Command has really trimmed their operations in recent years, but I haven't heard of a Raider attack in regulated Galactic Alliance space since they tried to recover this base from you. And mechanical problems that disable both a ship's engines *and* communications are highly unlikely."

"Not so unlikely as you might think. A prototype ship I commanded suffered a massive electrical problem that disabled both our control of the ship and our IDS communications. It took weeks to get the com systems working again so we could signal for assistance."

"Yes, it's possible. But not likely."

"I'll alert our ships on patrol between here and Arrosa to be on the lookout for the *Hunaray*. If we learn anything, I'll see that you're notified immediately, Captain."

"Thank you, Captain," he said, as he stood to leave. Almost apologetically, he added, "Sorry for bending your ear."

"Not at all, Captain. As I said, I found the information to be most enlightening. I find it amazing that your government has managed to keep such a tight lid on the news of the terrorist attacks. But until a formal request for assistance is made to the GAC, there's nothing I can do. That is, unless it has moved off-world, as you believe. But even if that's the case, my intervention is limited to extra-world activities."

"I understand. I hope you can help me with the *Hunaray* problem though."

"We'll do our best. Good day, Captain," Jenetta said, extending her hand down to Captain Oluthru.

* * *

Everyone already in the council chamber jumped to his or her feet as Prime Minister Marueck strode in intently. Moving to his customary place at the center of the large table, he took his seat, allowing everyone else to sit down again without waiting for further permission. The people in the room were all senior members of the government, except for a chief aide here and there, and were used to commanding respect and obedience within their own sphere of influence. But this was the Prime Minister's circle.

Marueck cleared his throat and began his prepared statement. "My fellow ministers, for more than a year our home planet has been under increasing attack by terrorists. The recent attack on my person clearly shows that the terrorists have become emboldened by their successes. Our security forces have been unable to uncover the people behind the attacks or even to identify any of the attackers. After placing explosives, the terrorists either detonate them from remote locations or escape in the confusion caused by the explosion. No claims of credit or demands for political change have been sent to us, so we're unsure of the motives behind the attacks. In the absence of precise information, we're speculating that the Selaxians are responsible. The ownership of Isodow has been a hotly contested issue for some time, and while it's inconceivable to many of our citizens that the Selaxians would engage in such provocative action, we must remember that we fought a long and bloody war with our cousins just over a hundred years ago. The close trade relations and decades of peace our planets have shared mustn't sway us. We must begin planning our response to these unprovoked attacks."

"Prime Minister, are you suggesting we preemptively attack Selax?" Minister Lisaul asked in horror.

"I'm only saying that we must develop plans for such an attack so we'll be prepared once we finally have proof of their duplicity."

"But Prime Minister," Minister Deruuw began, "we've found absolutely no evidence to suggest Selax is behind, involved in, or even knowledgeable about these attacks. If we begin developing an attack plan, word could reach them."

"So much the better. They'll know they'd better cease these attacks immediately or face our devastating weapons. I want a plan developed that will lay waste to their entire planet. We didn't have such weapons a century ago, but we do now. We'll show them how Arrosians respond to acts of terrorism."

# Chapter Three
~ January 17<sup>th</sup>, 2275 ~

The small transport ship slipped into orbit around Scruscotto without incident and established an orbital track for landing. The ship carried no special markings but was easily recognizable to anyone who'd seen it before. Patched repeatedly through the several decades of its existence with whatever materials were at hand when repairs were necessary, its appearance was— distinctive. Functionality came first, beauty came— well actually, beauty never figured into it at all. Functionality was first, last, and always.

With no planetary approach or departure control, near misses around Scruscotto were more common than anyone liked to admit. When departing the colony after their last visit, the *Scorpion* had just barely avoided becoming a large smear on the front of a three-kilometer-long freighter entering orbit. It had taken all the expert piloting skills of Trader Vyx, the *Scorpion's* captain and pilot, to keep the ships from colliding. When the desperate maneuvers had been completed, a mere dozen meters had separated the two ships.

The descent to the surface was peaceful enough as Vyx piloted the small ship to the Weislik Space Port. The slight semblance of traffic control at the various space ports that dotted the surface was helpful. Each port would queue takeoffs and landings at its own location, and it made things quite a bit safer in sub-orbital flight. No one wanted a hundred thousand tons of wrecked spacecraft landing on their town or, worse yet, their home. Larger freighters naturally remained in orbit and allowed their space tugs to ferry the containers of cargo up from and down to the surface. Ships that broke up due to collisions in orbit were less of a concern to the planetary inhabitants because there was always someone ready to salvage them before their orbit could destabilize enough to present a danger. Of course, there was always the peril of being struck by small fragments not collected during the cleanup, but the mining planet was huge and sparsely populated, so the chances were small that any individual would be struck.

Vyx allowed his ship to settle gently on a cushion of 'oh-gee' waves at the assigned landing pad. He cut the engines and permitted his almost six-foot body to slump in the pilot's chair, sitting quietly for several minutes as the tension drained.

It was always like this on worlds without coordinated planetary approach or departure control. His two associates knew better than to waste effort trying to talk to him. Until the stress had drained from his system, he wouldn't respond to queries.

As undercover agents for Space Command, Vyx, Byers, and Nelligen worked in environs where Space Command officers rarely traveled. As a line agent, Vyx performed jobs requiring quick wits and even quicker reflexes. Byers and Nelligen, officially listed as information agents, normally worked at menial jobs and collected interesting tidbits of information they overheard for later transmission to the Intelligence Section at Higgins Space Command Base. Stationed on the Gollasko Colony when Vyx arrived there to perform a mission, the pair had found themselves caught up in Vyx's plan to intercept a large cache of illegal arms after the GA border expansion. The trio had then moved into the new Frontier Zone together to complete Vyx's original assignment.

Since completing their mission just a couple of months earlier, the three men had been without any specific assignment, so they traveled back to Scruscotto with a twofold purpose: they wanted to clear up a little side business related to the mission, and they needed to reestablish themselves in the criminal world.

*   *   *

Originally, the Galactic Alliance territorial delineation was a cylindrical area with a diameter of five hundred light-years. It extended through the center plane of the Milky Way galaxy for a distance of five hundred light-years above and below.

In 2203, the Galactic Alliance had expanded their borders by one hundred parsecs, except where other nations had a prior claim to the space. Additionally, the new territory now included *all* space within the cylindrical boundary, meaning everything above and below the Milky Way median plane. This 'border space' was intended mainly to act as a buffer with other nations.

Immediately following the first expansion, almost sixty-one percent of the Galactic Alliance still bordered on space unclaimed by any nation. Shortly thereafter, the Kweedee Aggregate had expanded its own border to include all space up to the new GA, but this still left the GA with more than forty-seven percent of its territory bordering on open, unclaimed space.

Insufficient resources meant Space Command could not adequately patrol the newly claimed territory, so while they responded to calls for emergency assistance there, they didn't maintain any official bases in the area and never overtly enforced the laws of the Galactic Alliance. The resulting lawlessness was responsible for the territory becoming widely known as the Frontier Zone.

When a criminal organization known as the Raiders had become so powerful that they threatened the safety of citizens in 'regulated GA space,' Space Command was finally allocated sufficient funding for the ships and resources they needed to clean up the nucleus of GA space. The efforts of Captain Jenetta Carver had been so instrumental in driving the Raider Organization to its knees that in 2273 the Galactic Alliance Council, believing they might finally be able to offer protection to the planets in the Frontier Zone, converted the former Zone to 'regulated' space and immediately laid claim to an additional one-hundred-parsec-wide swath of previously unclaimed space, thus establishing their lawful claim before any of their neighboring empires, kingdoms, dominions, confederations, or coalitions could. With announcement of the expansion, every criminal in the 'prior' Frontier Zone had immediately begun moving their operations to the 'new' Frontier Zone.

*   *   *

"I'll pay the landing fees and pad rent, then meet you at the Weislik Grand," Vyx said to Byers and Nelligen. "One of you arrange to restock our food stores and the other can arrange for three rooms."

"I'll handle the food shopping," Nelligen said immediately, hoisting his tall, thin frame out of the copilot's chair he had been occupying.

"Oh no, you won't," Byers said, leaping up from the jump seat behind Vyx and using his shorter, slightly over-weight body to block Nelligen's exit from the bridge. "We'll do it together or I do it alone. My stomach can't tolerate all that hot food you buy."

"Okay, we'll both do it. Let's go. We'll book the rooms first."

Before exiting the ship, the three operatives donned the special equipment that would supplement the oxygen each individual could gather from the thin atmosphere on their own. Terraforming efforts had so far created a basic atmosphere, but only long-time residents had become sufficiently accustomed to forego special apparatus. Contained in a soft bag about the size of a newborn infant, the unit drew oxygen from the atmosphere. A small tube clipped to the wearer's nose and released the accumulated oxygen as needed. Unless overexerted, the release was minimal.

The planet's slightly lower gravity added a spring to Vyx's step as he walked to the spaceport's office. As always, all eyes in the room carefully watched the business transactions of newcomers, making mental notes of everything they saw or heard. Vyx recognized several faces among the half dozen or so species and nodded to them as he left. The paid watchers at the spaceport already knew his face, and several hurried to pass on the information that the lean, mean-looking Terran with dark brown hair, brown eyes, and deeply tanned skin was back.

Vyx took his time walking to the hotel and found that Byers and Nelligen had completed making arrangements for the three rooms before he arrived. After registering his thumbprint, he went upstairs to take a long, hot, relaxing shower. When Byers com'd his room later, he agreed to meet his two associates in the lobby and they went in search of a place to eat dinner.

Real Terran beef was a delicacy on Scruscotto where the usual steak was a cut of Cheblookan daitwa, a sort of domesticated horse-like creature found in a nearby system. After enjoying a genuine slab of beef, they had the waitress clear their dinner dishes and bring fresh tankards of a local ale. They were on their third tankard when the individual they were seeking finally arrived. The Wolkerron spotted them immediately and approached the table.

"Welcome back to Scruscotto, gentlemen," the tall, thin, Hominidae-like creature, with a long, yellow face and large black eyes said. "I'm surprised to see you back so soon."

"Have a seat, Ker," Vyx said, using his foot to push the chair opposite his away from the table. After the Wolkerron had taken the proffered seat, Vyx asked, "Are you surprised to see us so soon or just surprised to see us?"

Ker Blasperra was instantly on his guard. The tone in Vyx's voice was ominous. "Why, to see you *so soon*, of course," the Wolkerron said pleasantly, offering what passed as his specie's equivalent of a grin but which looked menacing to the uninitiated. "How is it you're back here *so soon*?"

"Shev Rivemwilth decided to alter the arrangements of the contract after we had loaded my ship with his ordnance. He stole the ship and marooned us at his former base."

"I find that information most shocking, gentlemen. Shev Rivemwilth has always conducted his deals with honor. If your claim is accurate, this will seriously damage his reputation."

"His reputation is no longer of concern to him. The survey team of a mining operation rescued us, but Shev Rivemwilth didn't fare as well. It seems I neglected to tell him about the timed explosive charges aboard my ship. Two weeks after he left us stranded, the ship was depressurized and Shev Rivemwilth died, along with his entire crew. He apparently couldn't suck vacuum any better than he could judge Terrans. Space Command discovered the ship floating dead in space. They've seized the ship and the cache of arms, and blamed the theft of the vessel on Rivemwilth. Case closed."

"You set explosive charges aboard your own ship?" Blasperra asked incredulously.

"Of course. When I'm aboard, I reset the timer every so often, but since I wasn't there, the timer ran all the way down. The Light Speed engines were immediately taken off-line, all interior doors were opened wide and locked into position, and dozens of tiny explosive charges, sufficient to evacuate the air before anyone could suit up in EVA suits, ended Shev Rivemwilth's career. I had removed the control chip from all of the emergency rebreather masks just before we reached the RP because I didn't trust that ugly toad."

"Very clever, Trader, very clever," the Wolkerron said somberly. "You're as dangerous an opponent as I've heard."

"I always cover my bases, Ker. I may not be around to exact revenge personally, but it will *always* be exacted. Unfortunately for Shev Rivemwilth, he didn't learn that lesson until it was too late."

"So I see. Are you available for new business then?"

"Not until we settle our old business."

"Our deal called for payment after a year and a half."

"The deal was that when the job was complete, you'd transfer the entire amount into whatever account I named. The contract is complete. In fact, Rivemwilth owes me about fifty million credits more. That's my estimate for the value of the ship he stole from me. I'll settle for the five hundred thou now and figure out how to get the rest later."

"Trader, be reasonable. The money is invested and I can't withdraw the funds without losing all the interest it's already earned."

"That's too bad. I guess that as Rivemwilth's direct repre- sentative, his treachery will affect you also. At least you're alive— so far."

Blasperra swallowed nervously. "I don't think I can even get the credits right now."

Vyx narrowed his dark brown eyes and fixed them on Blasperra, giving him a silent, withering look. Blasperra began to look exceptionally nervous. "I'll tell you what," Vyx finally said, "tell me where Rivemwilth's new base is, and I'll wait for the full year and a half."

"Why, I don't know. Rivemwilth didn't trust me any more than he trusted anyone else."

"Don't give me that. You wouldn't have represented him without knowing all the facts."

"For an Alyysian of Shev Rivemwilth's reputation— and, shall we say, volatile nature— I— made certain exceptions."

"If you don't know precisely where it is, you know approximately where it's located. Now either give me the information or get our money by tomorrow."

Blasperra sat looking nervously undecided for a few seconds. "You're absolutely certain Rivemwilth is dead?"

"I am. You can verify that yourself if you have any contacts inside Space Command, although I'm sure they've disposed of his desiccated corpse by now."

"Alas, Space Command is not an easy organization to penetrate."

"Then you'll have to take my word. My reputation among our *brotherhood* is as good as Rivemwilth's ever was, probably far better. *I've* never cheated a fellow trader or client."

"I've heard nothing but positive things about you, your associates, and your deals," Blasperra said. After another short pause he added, "Since Shev Rivemwilth is no longer with us, I guess I won't be betraying a trust." Lowering his voice, he said, "All I know for certain is that his new base is located in the Rhoitter system. He did mention once that it was on a moon similar to the one where his old base was located. I might know someone who can give you more information, but it will cost you." Blasperra stopped and immediately put up his hands when Vyx's expression changed. "Not for me, Trader. I arranged for the construction crews Rivemwilth ferried to the moon, and although he never allowed them to know where they were, the foreman might be able to describe the moon or perhaps the planet it orbits because extensive exterior work was obviously required."

"Who is it?"

Blasperra wrote some information on a piece of paper and slid it over to Vyx. "I trust you won't be expecting the five hundred thousand credits until the original term is up?"

Vyx looked down at the paper, then back at Blasperra. "I always stand by my deals."

Blasperra smiled with relief. "You're an honorable trader. If you need something to do after satisfying your quest, I'll find you a good deal. There's always plenty of work for people who can be trusted." Blasperra stood up, bowed slightly and left the restaurant.

It took three days to track down the construction foreman who'd supervised the work at Rivemwilth's new base. The operatives found him working on a project for a mining company at another settlement. Vyx confronted him in a local bar after the construction crew had finished for the day. After hearing what Vyx was seeking, the man told Vyx in very explicit terms where he could go. But when Vyx held up a thousand-credit note, the man's eyes lit up. As he reached for the bill, Vyx yanked it away.

"The information first, Darrigo."

"I can't," the foreman said as he looked greedily at the money. He was almost as big as Vyx and looked nearly as mean, but he was out of shape, having spent too many nights drinking his dinner in whatever miserable hole of a town his company had sent him to. "Rivemwilth would kill me."

"He won't be killing anybody; he's dead. His ship lost atmosphere while he was transporting his arms cache to the new base. Having a second heart didn't help him this time."

"He's dead?"

"Yup."

"And you figure to help yourself to his base?"

"That's none of your business. You only have to tell us what you know."

"Uh, I'll tell you for a piece of the action. I want ten percent."

"Ten percent of what?"

"Ten percent of whatever deal you've got going."

"Okay, you can have one of the empty storerooms in the new base instead of the thousand credits."

"Empty?"

"Yeah. Space Command found Rivemwilth's transport and confiscated the entire arms inventory intended for the new base. As far as I know, the base is totally empty."

"Then what do you want with it?"

"That's our business. Do you want the thousand credits or not?"

"Nobody's going to pay a thousand credits for nothing."

Vyx put the thousand credits bill back into his pocket. Darrigo's eyes followed it until it disappeared from sight.

As Vyx stood up and prepared to leave, Darrigo said, "You'll never find it without my help."

"Yes we will. You see, we know the system where it's located, and we know the way Rivemwilth liked to hide his base entrances. We'll find it. Your information could have saved us weeks of mapping effort though. Good-bye, Darrigo."

"Wait a minute," Darrigo said. When Vyx ignored him, he said louder, "Just hold on a second."

Vyx stopped moving away and turned to face the construction foreman again. He waited a few seconds and then said, "I don't have all day."

Darrigo looked up at him. He had bits and pieces of information, but didn't know in which system the base was located. Here was an opportunity to sell something that wasn't of any use otherwise, and he didn't want to lose the opportunity. "Okay, I'll sketch out the landscape as it appeared from the flight bay doors. The bay is in a cliff wall at the end of a long, narrow canyon. We constructed a camouflaged roof that extends out several hundred meters from the flight bay. I never got a look from elevation, but you could see a purple planet twice a day as the moon revolved." He pulled a flexible drafting tablet from his coat, unfolded it, and drew a sketch of what he had seen of the location.

Vyx studied the sketch for a few minutes, then looked intently at Darrigo. "If this isn't accurate, I'll be back to collect this money, even if I have to take the value out of your hide. Rivemwilth was a pussycat compared to me when I've been cheated." He linked his viewpad to the drafting tablet and uploaded the image before he tossed the thousand credits bill onto the table. It disappeared into Darrigo's pocket so fast it was little more than a blur.

"It's accurate. Just scan the surface until you see those three key peaks I've drawn. You can't miss it after that."

The three operatives ensured the ship was fully provisioned, then prepared to leave Scruscotto immediately. It was important to get to the base before anyone learned of Rivemwilth's death and beat them there. As often happens on such planets as Scruscotto, a couple of dozen travelers, marooned due to a lack of funds, begged for a ride off the rock. Vyx told them it wasn't possible because they wouldn't be stopping at any inhabited planets before returning to Scruscotto. A few looked at him in disbelief but all stopped pestering him.

Traffic was light when they completed their preflight and lifted off in the early, pre-dawn hours. They didn't experience any near misses with other ships during this departure, and they collectively breathed a sigh of relief as they reached orbit.

As soon as the navigation computer acknowledged the course data, they departed the planet. Vyx intentionally set a course that led to a system well away from his real destination in case anyone was watching. In a few days, if they determined that no one was following, they would change course again and head towards the Rhoitter system. Their journey would take months of travel much further into the Frontier Zone than Vyx had ever ventured and then possibly that much time again to actually locate the base.

Vyx found himself wishing the small ship was just a little larger because the bickering between Nelligen and Byers never seemed to cease, and there was no place in the crew quarters area where he could find any peace. Vyx felt sure it wasn't just the food that gave Byers stomach problems, but he also knew that neither of the two would have it any other way. He decided to fashion a comfortable spot in a secluded area of the cargo hold where he could relax and be alone to read.

# Chapter Four

President Tasenal plopped tiredly into the rear seat of his limo for the ride back to his residence after attending one more in a long line of political fundraisers for his upcoming election campaign. His chief aide, noticeably absent for the past hour, climbed in beside him.

"Sir," the aide started as soon as the door closed, "our intelligence service reports that Arrosa is planning an attack on our planet."

"What did you say?" the President asked incredulously.

"Our intelligence people on Arrosa report that the Ministry of State Security is developing a plan for an all-out attack on our world."

"With absolute certainty?"

"Yes, sir, with absolute certainty."

"When is this attack set to begin?" the president asked nervously, his normally ruddy complexion having turned ashen grey. At four feet, two inches, he towered over most of his people. The fifty-two-year-old politician hadn't entered the political arena until he was thirty-six, but his popularity had helped him climb swiftly through elective offices— so swiftly, in fact, that this was his first time seeking reelection to a previously held office.

"Unknown, sir. No date has been established."

The president took a deep breath and a little color began to return to his face. "Perhaps it's just an exercise such as when we develop plans of defense and counterattack."

"Our people assure us it's much more than that. They claim the plans are a response to the terrorist attacks Arrosa has been suffering. Apparently Marueck believes us to be responsible."

"That's ludicrous— isn't it? I haven't authorized any such attacks. Tell me honestly, Uthey; is it possible that any of our people are involved?"

"I have absolutely no knowledge of anyone from Selax being involved, sir, but I can't guarantee that no Selaxians are culpable. Tempers are still running pretty hot over the Arrosian theft of our moon's ore. It's possible that some extremist group made up of Selaxians might be carrying out these dastardly attacks, but I know of no organized plots within the government."

"I need more assurance than that, Uthey. I want an immediate and thorough investigation to determine if any-one— I repeat, anyone— on Selax has the slightest involve-ment. Get onto it."

"Right away, sir."

\* \* \*

Jenetta had just begun her workday when the message from Space Command Supreme Headquarters arrived. Even with the three-light-year-per-hour speed of IDS communi-cations, it had taken a week for the message to arrive. Jenetta tapped the play button and then had to lean forward to complete the retinal scan that would permit decryption of the message. The image of Vice-Admiral Raymond Burke, the three-star admiral responsible for Space Command bases, appeared once the computer had confirmed Jenetta's identity.

"Hello, Captain. I trust this message finds you well and the base situation quiet and stable.

"The Galactic Alliance Council has received an urgent appeal from the planetary government on Selax, which claims to have incontrovertible proof that the planet Arrosa is plan-ning to attack them. As they're now located within Galactic Alliance regulated space, they've petitioned for full member-ship and are requesting that the GAC step in and protect them from their solar system neighbor.

"Space Command is powerless to take action before Arrosa actually commences an attack, so the Admiralty Board would like you to contact the two chief planetary officers and see if you can't defuse the situation. You have the authority as Stewart SCB base commander, and thus the supreme military authority in your sectors of space, to take whatever action you deem appropriate to stop hostilities if diplomatic solutions fail. But I'm sure you understand that military force is only acceptable as a final option.

"A diplomatic team charged with setting up a permanent mission on Stewart, plus embassies on dozens of planets in your sectors, was dispatched several months ago, but their transport won't arrive there for more than a year. The entire team is currently in stasis sleep and so is unaware of the situation. You'll have to handle this matter on your own until they arrive.

"Forward your reports of any contact with these parties directly to my office. Good luck, Captain.

"Raymond A. Burke, Vice-Admiral, Space Command Supreme Headquarters, message complete."

The screen went blank and Jenetta grimaced. "Just what I need— two neighboring planets with a common ancestry who can't resolve their own problems peacefully."

The missing freighter still hadn't been located. Now officially listed as missing, patrolling Space Command ships were on notice to look for it or any sign of debris.

Thanks to the briefing by the freighter captain, Captain Oluthru, Jenetta felt she had a solid feel for the situation in the Weitack solar system. She sighed and tapped a button on her com unit.

"Lori, see if you can find contact addresses for the chief government officials on the planets Selax and Arrosa, please."

Jenetta returned to her reports as the com unit on her aide's desk beeped and the message appeared on the screen. Lt. Commander Ashraf stopped what she was doing and immediately began searching the computer for contact information. Since the planets were eleven light-years away, any communication to the planet would take hours to reach them, and replies would naturally take just as long. Not finding any communication addresses in the base computer for the chief executives and not wishing to waste time following a single trail of referrals that might take days to yield results, Lt. Commander Ashraf sent simple queries to all the addresses in the base computer that held some promise of reaching someone in a key position.

By late afternoon, Lt. Commander Ashraf's efforts had produced a message from the Selax Department of State that included an address purported to be that of the president's personal secretary. She immediately forwarded the message to Jenetta, who was still in her office.

When Jenetta noticed the message pop up on her com unit, she saw an opportunity to take a break from writing reports. Straightening her tunic, she sat erect in her chair before tapping the record button.

"Message to President Bezeel Tasenal, Chief Executive of the planet Selax. Begin message.

"Hello President Tasenal. I'm Captain Jenetta Carver, base commander of Stewart Space Command Base. Space Command Supreme Headquarters is concerned with the situation described in your communication to the Galactic Alliance Council. They have asked me to look into it. I assume Arrosa hasn't yet initiated any hostilities and that the threat still exists. Please let me know how we might be of service to you. You understand, of course, that I cannot commit military resources unless and until hostile activities actually commence. Perhaps both parties should meet in a neutral location to discuss their grievances. I suggest that Stewart might be the appropriate venue for such a conference. I shall await your response before contacting Prime Minister Marueck.

"Jenetta A. Carver, Captain, Base Commander, Stewart Space Command Base, message complete."

Jenetta sat back in her chair and viewed a replay of the message before transmitting it unencrypted. It was highly unlikely that the Selaxians would have Space Command diplomatic decryption codes yet since they hadn't been officially welcomed as an Alliance member.

Among the numerous messages waiting for Jenetta when she arrived at her office the following morning was one from the Deputy Prime Minister of Arrosa, who said he would gladly forward any message to the Prime Minister. Another was a reply from President Tasenal of Selax. After preparing a mug of coffee, she sat down to view the President's reply first. Because the language translator was operating, his lip movements didn't match what Jenetta heard.

"Greetings, Captain. I was most pleased to receive your message. Your fame has naturally preceded you and we're delighted you'll be involved in this process. Arrosa hasn't yet initiated any hostilities, but we're fearful that they could attack us at any time. There's no doubt their weapons technology is far superior to our own and they could easily devastate our planet.

"Our information is that they suspect us of being behind a series of terrorist attacks that have taken place on their planet during the past year. They believe we're striking back because of a dispute over ownership of our moon. I can assure you that although we resent the theft of resources from Isodow, my government has no involvement in or knowledge of who might be perpetrating the attacks. We've conveyed that information to the office of the Prime Minister of Arrosa.

"If someone *is* carrying out these attacks in our name, they must be stopped before Arrosa attacks my planet. The only way to accomplish that might be to settle the dispute over which planet actually owns the moon that orbits Selax. What I would ask of you is that you arbitrate the dispute and settle the issue. I'm sure my people would abide by whatever decision you, as a representative of Space Command and the Galactic Alliance, might reach.

"Bezeel Tasenal, President of Selax, message ended."

Jenetta continued to stare at the empty screen long after the message finished. She didn't feel equipped to handle a dispute between two worlds, a task normally reserved for diplomats, judges, and lawyers. The trouble was, as base commander *she* was the only GA diplomat presently on Stewart. And until both parties formally became members of the Alliance, no involvement by GA judges and lawyers was permissible.

After thinking the matter over for some time, she called the senior officer in the Judge Advocate General's office.

Captain Donovan wasn't in his office so Jenetta asked his aide to locate him and have him come to her office as soon as possible.

Donovan arrived out of breath in twenty minute's time. He knew that when summoned to the base commander's office, he shouldn't waste time getting there.

Alerted to his presence in the outer office, Jenetta told Lt. Commander Ashraf to send him in.

"Come in, Captain," Jenetta said as Donovan entered her office. "Make yourself a beverage and then please have a seat."

"I'm fine, Captain," he said as he sat down. Perspiration dotted his brow.

"Captain, we have a serious problem."

Captain Donovan suddenly looked like a little boy caught with his hand in a cookie jar. "Uh, we do, Captain?"

Jenetta was amused by the expression, but didn't mention that or let her face reflect it. "Yes. Space Command has requested that we intercede in a dispute between two planets in this sector. There's a risk that if the situation is allowed to continue unabated, the stronger of the two might attack their neighbor." Captain Donovan's face had relaxed when he realized the problem wasn't with him. Jenetta thought an attorney should have a better poker face.

"Which planets are we talking about, Captain?"

"Arrosa and Selax," Jenetta replied, "in the Weitack system. It's roughly eleven light-years from here."

"And what is the dispute that requires our intervention?"

Jenetta related everything she had learned about the situation, beginning with Captain Oluthru's background information.

"It sounds like there are still some hard feelings over past events," Captain Donovan commented.

"Yes, they've only had a hundred years to get past it. Since their average longevity is almost that of Terrans, there must still be some people on both planets who were alive during the war and perhaps even fought in it."

"Anyone from the generation who actually fought in the war, or their immediate descendents, might be hard-pressed to forget the grievances," Captain Donovan said.

"It'll be our job to help them finally put it into the past, at least as far as this matter is concerned."

"It's too bad the diplomats won't be here to assist. It'll make your job as arbiter that much more difficult."

"*My* job? I'm not a lawyer," Jenetta said. "You're the senior JAG officer. I'd like you to handle it."

"I'm sorry, Captain, but as base commander and the senior military authority in this part of space, you're the only one who *can* legally do it. My staff and I can advise, but we can't sit for a flag officer or, in this case, the senior military commander. While I can sit as judge for most military and civilian trials, you're the only one who can adjudicate a general court martial for an officer, capital offenses committed by civilians, or Galactic Alliance proceedings. "

Jenetta grimaced. "I was afraid you might say something like that."

"Sorry, Captain. Those are the regulations."

"I understand, Captain," Jenetta sighed. "I'll let you know when I've learned more about this situation so you can advise me on Galactic Alliance law and legal precedents. Dismiss-ed."

Captain Donovan stood up and turned to leave, then stop-ped. "Excuse me, Captain. Where would this arbitration take place?"

"I've suggested that Stewart might be a suitably neutral place."

"It would be," he said, nodding, "but it might be prefer-able to conduct the sessions aboard a battleship posted in the Weitack system. At least you'd be able to prevent access by both support and dissension groups. Here on the base, they'd have access to common areas and could potentially clash."

"You have a point, but if I'm to be the arbiter, I have to conduct the sessions here. Travel time by the *Chiron* is ten days. I couldn't afford to be that far away if trouble were to occur here. Base security will have to keep protestors and supporters apart."

Captain Donovan nodded. "Good luck, Captain."

"Thanks. I suspect I'll need all I can get."

After spending another hour thinking about the situation before composing a message to the Prime Minister of Arrosa, Jenetta finally straightened her tunic, faced the video unit squarely, and tapped the record button.

"Message to Prime Minister Nadeil Marueck of the planet Arrosa. Begin message.

"Greetings, Prime Minister Marueck. I'm Captain Jenetta Carver, base commander of Stewart Space Command Base and the military commander for the sectors of space around your planet. Space Command Supreme Headquarters is concerned with the situation that seems to be developing between your planet and Selax. While we maintain a strict policy of non-intervention in the internal affairs of any planet within GA regulated space, maintaining the peace *between* planets is one of my prime responsibilities. I'd welcome the opportunity to open a dialogue with you regarding the dispute over the moon that orbits Selax. President Tasenal has requested our involvement. He asks that we mediate the matter. Naturally, we'll be happy to comply, and I hope that both parties will submit to binding arbitration.

"I look forward to hearing from you, Mr. Prime Minister.

"Jenetta A. Carver, Captain, Base Commander, Stewart Space Command Base, message complete."

Jenetta immediately recorded a second message.

"Message to the captains of all military ships assigned patrol duties in the sectors surrounding Stewart Space Command Base. Begin message.

"Captain, a potentially dangerous situation is developing in the Weitack System where a dispute over ownership of the moon orbiting Selax might escalate quickly. The superior military power is Arrosa, and it's feared they might begin hostilities without warning. I request that all ships whose patrol route takes them to the vicinity of that solar system make their presence known by passing close enough to Arrosa to be identified by the Arrosian Space Control System. I don't anticipate any hostilities directed towards our ships, but I want the Arrosian authorities to understand we're never very far away.

"Jenetta A. Carver, Captain, Base Commander, Stewart Space Command Base, message complete."

Unlike the messages sent to the two planetary chief executives, Jenetta encrypted this latest message before sending it.

It took several days for a reply to arrive from Arrosa. Jenetta got her first look at Prime Minister Marueck after tapping the play button on the com unit.

"Greetings, Captain Carver. Thank you for your concern, but the situation in our solar system is an internal matter and we demand that Space Command not get involved. We're fully capable of resolving our own disputes.

"Nadeil Marueck, Prime Minister of Arrosa, message complete."

Jenetta didn't require time to think about her reply. A more forceful message was obviously called for. She tapped the record button.

"Message to Prime Minister Nadeil Marueck of the planet Arrosa. Begin message.

"Hello, Mr. Prime Minister. Thank you for your reply. Again, I want to state that Space Command will not interfere with the internal affairs on your planet. However, I would be remiss if I didn't remind you that your laws and military powers end at the apex of your planet's sensible atmosphere, established as one hundred kilometers above the planet's mean surface. From that point outward, all actions become subject to Galactic Alliance law. As the military commander in this sector, I have no choice but to involve myself in the affairs of any planet that elects to launch aggressive acts offworld. Since you apparently choose not to participate in binding arbitration, or even to present your side of the issue, I must advise you that the final decision could easily go against your interests, and your people might be forcefully removed from the moon orbiting Selax."

"Jenetta A. Carver, Captain, Base Commander, Stewart Space Command Base, message complete."

Jenetta reviewed the recording to see if she appeared too harsh. She wished to appear firm but not insensitive. Satisfied with the recording, she transmitted it. Quickly reviewing events in her mind, she decided there was nothing more to be done unless or until Arrosa agreed to arbitration or launched a pre-emptive attack against its neighbor. "Wouldn't it be wonderful if nothing happened until after the diplomats arrive?" she murmured.

# Chapter Five

The delectable aroma of fresh fried chicken filled the small room adjoining the galley as Byers placed the large dish of breaded, steaming cutlets on the dining table. They were real cutlets, not synthesized versions. As Terrans had spread throughout Galactic Alliance space, they had brought chicken embryos in small stasis chambers along with them. It was now difficult to find an inhabited planet in Galactic Alliance space where Terran chicken was not readily available at very reasonable prices. "Dig in guys. I used my mother's special seasoning recipe for the coating this time, just for a little variation."

Vyx and Nelligen each took two pieces, adding them to the plates already filled with mashed potatoes, broccoli, and creamed onions."

"There's a distinct advantage to having a former short-order cook among the crew," Vyx said.

"True," Nelligen said as he liberally coated everything on his plate with red and black pepper. "It's just a shame his stomach is so bad that he has to make the food so bland."

"I could serve you up a bowl of molten lava and you'd complain it wasn't hot enough," Byers quipped.

"I think it would be hot enough— and maybe just a little bit less gritty than your mashed potatoes," Nelligen shot back.

"Just load them up with red and black pepper. Your palate will never know you're not eating something five days old that you found in the waste disposal can and warmed up," Byers said to the person he loved to harass more than any other he'd ever known. It was a friendly harassment though, and both loved the constant repartees.

"Speaking of hot things," Nelligen said to Vyx, "just what are we going to do at Rivemwilth's base? Might we be flying into a firefight with nothing to gain? We've gone along with you because you always seem to have a plan, but isn't this a wasted trip?"

"I really don't know," Vyx responded in all honesty. "We won't know until we get there. I know that Rivemwilth had an arms cache with him on Gollasko and that he evacuated it from the planet after the borders shifted and he needed to get out before Space Command ships arrived. It would have been foolish to add it to the arms he already had at his old base. I'm betting he sent them on ahead in his small transport, along with everything else it could carry since we didn't find any ships in orbit around the moon. It's also possible he was keeping his ship parked somewhere else in the solar system, intending for it to join the *Maid* for the trip to the new base. When the *Maid* lost atmosphere and Rivemwilth died, the crew of the small transport might have taken off for parts unknown, along with their cargo of arms. But we won't be able to start piecing the story together until we reach the base."

"What if the base is full of his people?" Nelligen asked.

"I admit it's a possibility. He had quite a number of Tsgardi working for him, and none of them were at the old base. Since we're in the new Frontier Zone, we can't depend on Space Command to come to our rescue, so we'll just have to be extra careful."

"Great," Nelligen said. "We might be walking into a firestorm of laser pulses."

"If anything, it would probably be a flurry of lattice tubules. But that shouldn't concern you guys. I'm the only line agent here, so I'm going in alone. If anything happens to me, you guys just take off again and get back to Scruscotto. Blasperra will have the five hundred thousand credits ready and you can set up shop on the planet with enough credits to enjoy life until Space Command gives you new assignments."

"You mean you just want us to leave you there and forget you?" Byers asked.

"Only if something happens and I can't get back to the ship. There's no sense in you two getting hurt needlessly."

Byers and Nelligen exchanged looks. They ate the rest of the meal in silence. It was the best meal Vyx had had aboard his ship since they joined him.

*   *   *

"Captain," Lieutenant Commander Gage, manning the tactical console on the bridge of the GSC Battleship *Thor*, called out, "our sensors just produced an anomalous reading. We passed an object that shouldn't be there."

"Where was it, Commander?"

"About ninety thousand kilometers off our larboard beam."

"What can you tell me about it?"

"All I can say is that the object was several kilometers in size and wasn't producing an energy signature. There's nothing listed in the navigation hazard database, and we were in and out of sensor range too quickly to collect data."

"Helm, come about."

"Aye, Captain," the helmsman called out.

"Tactical, pass the location information to navigation. As soon as we're back in sensor range, get me everything you can on that contact."

"Aye, Captain."

"Com, alert the crew to prepare for a General Quarters announcement."

"Aye, Captain," the com chief said as he deftly tapped the contact switches that would issue a GQ standby announcement. "The crew has been alerted, sir."

Throughout the ship crewmen were busy stowing or locking down everything loose enough to present a hazard during an action, but no one was hurrying to battle stations yet.

The *Thor* was on routine patrol, so it was required to check out all such anomalous readings. The computer already contained basic information on every nebula, star or star cluster, planet, moon, and comet in the sector, as well as data on most asteroids larger than a baseball, and was programmed to register anything the ship encountered that was inconsistent with that data. It was the job of the science ships to conduct detailed investigations of celestial phenomena, but all ships were required to note and report on anything that might affect interstellar navigation.

Traveling at Light-337, the *Thor* had gone many billions of kilometers past the object in the minutes it would take to reverse its course. If the object had been in their path, the collision avoidance system would have shut down the Light Drive immediately.

The *Thor* returned to the vicinity at Light-337 and then slowed to Plus Ten (a hundred kilometers per second) as it closed to within twenty-five thousand kilometers. As soon as they were in sensor range, the tactical officer had begun an active scan of the object.

"It's a ship, Captain," Lieutenant Commander Gage called out, "about three kilometers in length. It appears to be a freighter. Confirming that now, sir. From the configuration data, it's definitely a freighter. It's not under power and is barely moving."

"Armament?"

"It appears to have twelve laser arrays in cargo link sections."

"Com, try to hail her."

"Negative response, Captain," the com operator said a few minutes later. "They aren't answering my hails."

Captain Payton thought for a few seconds before saying, "General Quarters. We don't want to get caught with our pants down."

Laser gunners and torpedo guidance specialists previously alerted by the standby announcement now hurried to their battle stations in fire control centers located along the center axis of the ship, while other crewmembers hurried to assigned posts or safe rooms. The computer confirmed that all crew-members were where they should be as the ship came within range of the freighter.

Payton ordered the *Thor* to remain ten thousand kilo-meters from the apparently derelict freighter while a full platoon of Marines disembarked in two Marine Armored Transports. Five Marine fighters would provide additional protection while the status of the freighter was determined.

"No sign of exterior hull damage," Lt. Commander Pincus, the *Thor's* second officer in command of the investigative team, reported. "It looks like we've found Arrosa's missing ship. We're preparing to board."

The large monitor at the front of the bridge showed an enlarged view of the area outside the flight bay where Marine personnel would attempt to gain access to the freighter. The exterior lights from the two MATs illuminated four EVA-suited team members as they left one of the small ships and approached the freighter. They succeeded in opening an airlock hatch to enter the ship and disappeared inside. Several minutes later, a flight bay door opened so the two MATs could move inside. While the fighters continued to circle the freighter helically, the flight bay door closed and the bay was pressurized.

The tactical officer on the bridge of the *Thor* changed the view on the monitor from the image produced by the MATs exterior cameras and sensors to a grid of individual images received from the helmet cameras of Marines inside the freighter. The atmosphere in the ship was still intact, but the temperature was below freezing, so the squad members wearing EVA suits were the only ones authorized to move about inside the ship until the temperature rose. Dispatched to engineering with orders to stabilize the life support functions aboard the freighter, they hurried off.

Crewmembers on the bridge of the *Thor* watched and listened as Pincus issued orders and team members spoke about encountering frozen bodies sprawled in grotesque positions. Their helmet cams produced high res images of the scenes they witnessed.

After reaching engineering, the EVA-suited team located the life support computer console and reset the temperature, but it would take an estimated twenty minutes for the internal temperature in corridors and key areas to rise above a point where exhaled breath didn't condense. The higher temperature, between seven and eight degrees Celsius, would help keep the video lenses from fogging over when the Marines left the shuttles, although the lenses were built to minimize such problems. Pincus ordered that none of the EVA-suited team members were to leave the engineering area until the rest of the platoon was available to participate in the mission.

When the temperature had risen to an acceptable minimum, the Marines removed their EVA suits. Outfitted in lightweight battle armor, the platoon moved through the corridors as the ship's temperature slowly rose to normal levels. They continued to encounter thawing bodies at irregular intervals.

"*Thor*, are you receiving these images?" Pincus asked.

"Affirmative, Commander," Captain Payton said. "We see the bodies."

"They all appear to have been shot by laser blasts at close range. Definitely small arms fire, most likely pistols. Moving on."

As the team moved towards the bridge, they encountered more and more bodies of deceased crewmen. Upon entering the bridge, they found the thawing bodies of the ship's senior officers.

"*Thor*, it looks like everyone on board is dead, but I'd like to make a full sweep of the ship, including the cargo containers. I could use another platoon of Marines for the search and some engineering techs to check out the ship. The commissioning plate on the bridge confirms this is the Hunaray."

"I'll send over your additional personnel, Commander," Payton said. "We'll need complete records for the investigation into this incident, so do it by the book. Let me know if you need anything else."

"Aye, Captain."

Payton looked at his first officer and nodded. Commander Dansiger knew the signal meant he should see to assigning the needed personnel.

Dansiger walked to a computer console at the tactical station and checked the duty roster before issuing the orders. Meanwhile, Payton had gone into his briefing room to compose a message.

* * *

Jenetta had been in conference with several of her senior officers when the message arrived, but she noticed it as she checked her schedule after the meeting was over and the officers had left. She tapped the play button and sat back to see what Payton had to say.

"Good afternoon, Jen. We've found your missing freighter, the *Hunaray*, named on the posted alert. We're approximately four light-years from the base. Our preliminary investigation indicates that those still on board died from laser fire at close range. My Marines are presently searching the entire ship to see if they can locate the killer, or killers, but we don't expect to find anyone. The internal temperature of the vessel was below freezing when we arrived. Why, we don't know. A *Hunaray* crewmember trying to oppose the killer may have lowered it, or perhaps there was some other motive. Whatever the reason, we have a perfectly preserved crime scene at this point. We'll try to determine if any shuttles or tugs are missing. The cargo sections appear intact, so this doesn't appear to have been a Raider attack.

"William E. Payton, Captain of the GSC *Thor*, message complete."

Jenetta debated whether to notify the Arrosians immediately or wait until she had more information. Since all aboard seemed to have been murdered and there wasn't anything the Arrosians could do to help, she decided to wait.

"Message to Captain William Payton, GSC *Thor*. Begin message.

"Thank you for your preliminary report, Bill. As soon as your investigation permits, please tow the freighter to Stewart, or bring it here under its own power if the power systems are undamaged. Place the link sections in one of the 'cargo farms' outside the base, and bring the freighter inside after inspection by the HazMat and BioAgent teams. I hope you'll be able to identify each of the dead crewmen and discover if any are missing.

"Jenetta A. Carver, Captain, Base Commander, Stewart Space Command Base, message complete."

Arriving at work the next morning, Jenetta discovered a new message from the Thor among the dozens of others awaiting her attention.

"Hi, Jen," the new message from Captain Payton began. "We've completed our investigation and the search of the ship. We've accounted for all crewmen listed in the computer; however, one person listed as a passenger is missing. The individual's name is Xamto Paluuk. We're also missing a space tug. All shipping sections are present and the cargo appears to be intact. I've put my first officer in command of the freighter, and we're underway for Stewart with the freighter operating under its own power. We should be there in ten days.

"William E. Payton, Captain of the GSC *Thor*, message complete."

Jenetta sat up straight in her chair and tapped the 'record' button on her com unit.

"Message to Prime Minister Nadeil Marueck of the planet Arrosa, with a copy to Captain Oluthru of the freighter *Gastrime*. Begin message.

"Mr. Prime Minister, it's my sad duty to report to you that one of our battleships, the *Thor*, has come across an Arrosian freighter adrift in space. Since Captain Oluthru of the freighter *Gastrime* reported the *Hunaray* as missing, I've had my ships looking for any sign of it. It's been determined thus far that all crewmen died by close-range laser fire at the hand of an unknown assailant or assailants. The ship and cargo appear intact. A space tug is missing, along with the sole passenger named in the computer files, a Xamto Paluuk.

"I've ordered that the ship, found just four light-years from Stewart, be brought here so a full investigation can be conducted. Since the crew died while the ship was in interstellar flight, Space Command must conduct a full investigation, but we'll welcome a representative from your government to function as liaison. The ship will arrive at Stewart in about ten days, and you will receive a full report upon completion of our investigation.

"I offer my condolences to the families of the crewmen aboard the *Hunaray*."

"Jenetta A. Carver, Captain, Base Commander, Stewart Space Command Base, message complete."

\* \* \*

When the message from Captain Carver arrived, Marueck was tempted to ignore it, only because he was still angry about the previous message that essentially promised retaliatory military action if Arrosa moved against Selax. But it would have been stupid to ignore a message from the GSC military commander in this sector, and Marueck hadn't achieved his position by being stupid.

After listening to the message, he picked up the nearest item— a solid globe of crystal presented by a visiting dignitary from a remote province. He hurled the fist-sized ball at a wall with all his might. The crash brought a guard stationed outside the door rushing into the room with his pistol drawn. Seeing no danger other than the Prime Minister cursing like a madman as he paced around the office, he immediately withdrew.

Marueck, after calming down enough to talk, called his Minister of State Security.

"Lisaul, contact the rest of the council and get everyone up here. The Selaxians have struck again. Now they're attacking our freighters in space."

Marueck continued his rant for the first ten minutes of the council meeting. He finally took a deep breath, sat down, and said, "I want each of you to tell me what you're doing to combat this menace."

Each minister talked about the problem, how it affected his department, and the measures he had enacted to prevent attacks or find the offenders. At the end of the presentations, Marueck was no more satisfied than he had been at the start. He stood up again.

"I will no longer tolerate these attacks from the Selaxians. I want a plan to take the war to them— one that won't bring Space Command down on our heads. Any suggestions?"

"Terrorist attacks, such as the ones *we're* being subjected to," Minister Deruuw, the Minister of Intelligence, suggested.

"Good!" the Prime Minister shouted as he immediately embraced the idea. "Very good! How will you go about it?"

Surprise at being designated to plan and carry out the attacks made Deruuw fumble for words. "Well— well— it will take a while to implement. The information agents we've worked into their society are having greater difficulty securing classified data since the Selaxians learned we were formulating attack plans. They have no doubt heightened their vigilance. We'll need to plant new agents— agents capable of carrying out the attacks."

"How long?" Marueck demanded loudly.

"We should be able to begin activity in six months to a year."

"A year?" the minister shouted. "Not good enough. By then our citizenry will be calling for my head. We need something now."

"There might be something we can do to slow or even stop the terrorist actions on Arrosa," the Minister of Protocol said musingly.

"What? What is it? Speak up, Petliop."

"We could enter into formal negotiations over ownership of Isodow. That might be enough to stop the terrorism and give Minister Deruuw a chance to infuse his people into Selaxian society."

"Are you mad? We can't risk losing Isodow through the ruling from some— some— alien."

"I'm not talking about negotiations involving Space Command. I mean direct negotiations with Selax. We publicize it heavily all over the planet and drag out the talks endlessly. When Minister Deruuw's people are in place, we declare an impasse and break off the talks."

Marueck thought the plan over carefully. "I like it. Very good, Petliop. We'll do it. Prepare press releases immediately."

"Hadn't we better contact the Selaxians first?" Deruuw asked.

"I don't think that's necessary," Marueck said dismissively with a wave of his hand. "They'll jump at any opportunity to avoid an attack by us. I'll contact them, of course, once we release the announcement to the press. We must be seen as reaching out first."

\* \* \*

President Bezeel Tasenal read the message aloud several times. Selax and Arrosa were close enough to allow direct calls, but the two chief executives had never spoken directly. Written messages allow opportunities to craft a masterful document steeped in subtleties. The cabinet members at the large conference table listened carefully to every single word.

"Any thoughts?" President Tasenal asked after the third reading.

"Marueck is after something," one member said.

"I agree," another said, "he's not really interested in having a meaningful discussion and settling the issue. I believe he's only interested in halting the terrorist attacks, and he believes this is the means to that end."

"You think he'd risk giving up control of our moon to stop the attacks?" President Tasenal asked.

"No, sir," another said. "He's probably only using this as a ploy to buy time to find the attackers. He believes the terrorism will cease if he appears to be engaging in meaningful dialogue. He'll eventually find some excuse to break off the talks, but not until he's gotten the time he's seeking."

An aide interrupted the meeting just then when he entered and handed the President a note. After reading it quickly, he said, "Prime Minister Marueck has released a press statement in which he announces that Arrosa and Selax have agreed to open a meaningful dialogue over ownership of Isodow and its resources." He put the paper down and looked at the cabinet members. "He apparently feels we're not in a position to refuse."

"I can't believe he released that statement before we even responded," a cabinet member said.

"Why not?" another asked. "He knows we can't refuse. If we do, it'll look like we were behind the attacks all the time. And if we try to back out now, he really gets the moral high ground."

"Perhaps we can swing Marueck's announcement to our advantage," the President said, "and teach Marueck that two can play the game of releasing press statements without first getting agreement from the other party."

\* \* \*

Prime Minister Marueck was having dinner when an aide brought him the news bulletin. The press service was reporting that Arrosa and Selax had agreed to work out the issues over ownership of Isodow. Marueck thought the article was simply a report written from the press statement released by his office and he was about to put it down when he saw a quote attributed to President Tasenal. It read, 'The President reports that at the invitation of Captain Jenetta A. Carver the talks will be conducted at the Stewart Space Command Base. They will be conducted under the rules of binding arbitration and both parties have agreed to abide fully with the impartial decision of the Galactic Alliance representative.'

Marueck's face became a mottled red as he jumped up from his chair. Ripping up the bulletin, he swept his arm across the table, sending the dishes, silverware, and everything else crashing to the floor as he bellowed at the top of his lungs.

*   *   *

The *Hunaray*, under the temporary command of Cmdr. Dansiger, moved into line for inspection after dropping off its cargo sections. There was only one other ship waiting for clearance to enter the port and the teams had already been aboard her for a couple of hours, so the wait shouldn't be more than half a watch.

As it turned out, an inspection team arrived in less than a half hour. The special team had been waiting for the arrival to speed the Arrosian ship through the process. When declared free of hazardous materials and bio-toxins, it continued into the asteroid port. And no sooner had it docked than another team of investigators boarded. The new team, all forensic specialists, would thoroughly check the ship, its logs, and the bodies of the dead Arrosian crewmen. Commander Dansiger and his small team were relieved from their temporary duty assignments and told to return to the *Thor*, which had docked earlier since it didn't need inspection clearance for entry to the port.

As Commander Dansiger walked through the airlock, he encountered Captain Carver standing on the docking platform. Dansiger stopped and saluted.

Jenetta returned his salute and said, "How was the trip, Commander?"

"Uneventful, ma'am, with the *Thor* right next to us. I'm glad it's over though. Ten days in a Munchkin Land ship is about as much as a full-grown Kansas boy should have to take," the six-foot-tall officer said, smiling. "We had to bunk on the decks because there wasn't a bed over a hundred forty centimeters long on the entire ship. We couldn't fit into the seats so we had to disassemble the sides, leaving only a tiny base to perch on and a short back against which to recline. We had to stretch out our legs in front of us because we couldn't raise the seats high enough to be comfortable. We ate our meals standing up or sitting on the floor, and most of us whacked our heads on doorways or overhead conduits at least several times a day. We're about the same height, Captain, so if you're ever invited to travel on an Arrosian ship, I suggest you pass."

Jenetta smiled. "Thank you, Commander. I shall remember your advice. Did you ever find any trace of the missing passenger?"

"Negative, ma'am. He must have bugged out as soon as he'd done the deed. He could have made it to Scruscotto or another planet in the Frontier by now."

Jenetta nodded. "That's very true. He could be a long way from here. Thank you, Commander."

# Chapter Six
~ May 10<sup>th,</sup> 2275 ~

Three months passed before Arrosa finally announced that their delegates would soon leave for Stewart Space Command Base to begin arbitration talks over the ownership of Isodow. The Prime Minister had delayed as long as possible and finally only named a delegation when enormous crowds of citizens began to protest in the capital over the inability of the government to stop the increasingly violent acts of terrorism being experienced all over the planet. As soon as the date was set for the talks to begin, the acts of terrorism began to slow. This was sufficient proof for the Prime Minister of Selax's responsibility, but the process had begun and he would have to send the delegation as promised.

\* \* \*

As the GSC battleship *Chiron* prepared for a six-month patrol, Jenetta and her sister Christa met for their last dinner before deployment. The *Thor*, having just returned from patrol, would now remain in port to provide security for the base in place of the *Chiron*. For more than six months while the *Chiron* had been in port, Jenetta and Christa had dined together as often as possible. Even on those evenings when Jenetta was entertaining the senior staffs of newly arrived ships— her custom since she had first become base commander at Dixon, the nearest base to Stewart SCB— Christa had had a standing invitation to the evening meal if she was free. For this final dinner, the two women were alone in the base commander's private dining room.

"Have you heard from mom?" Jenetta asked.

"I got a message two days ago. You?"

"The same. I got messages from Billy and dad yesterday."

"Ditto," Christa said. "It's great that dad's so happy with his new command. He was lost when he was playing golf every day. I'm glad they raised the mandatory space retirement age to eighty-five. Dad was much too young to be forced out when he was just sixty-five."

"Mom sounds sure he'll opt for base duty when he reaches eighty-five instead of retiring again. She thinks the extra fifteen years of duty will be better for him and keep him out from under foot at home."

"I wonder how we'll feel when we reach that age," Christa mused.

"That's a long way off. You and Eliza are only five-year-olds now. You have almost ninety-five more years to go before you reach mandatory retirement."

"The only advantage of being clones. With stasis time now discounted when computing mandatory retirement, you only have seventy-one more years. What will we do with our other four-thousand, nine hundred years?"

"We don't know for sure we'll live that long," Jenetta said. "Arneu only said we *might*."

"So far, everything else he said has come true. With soft tissue injuries, we heal ten times faster than other Terrans, alcohol has virtually no effect on us, our bodies have developed into a man's vision of a sexual goddess, and we haven't appeared to age a day since they experimented on you. I'm glad you were cloned *after* the DNA recombinant process so that Eliza and I inherited the same modified DNA."

"I've spent a lot of time thinking about how I'll handle near immortality if it does happen."

"Me too," Christa said as she sighed.

"It's distressing to think we'll still be around while our family and friends leave us at a hundred forty or maybe a hundred fifty. Think of the generations we might see born and then have to watch die."

"It's too depressing. I get depressed even thinking about mom and dad not being here, and they should be around for at least seventy more years. Do you think our offspring, if we *have* offspring, will have our modified DNA?"

"I don't know. We'll just have to wait and see. I know that when testing to determine lineage they always try to match a child with the mother instead of the father. There seems to be a closer bond with matrilineal DNA. Here's an interesting thought for you. Since our DNA keeps us looking like we're twenty-one, what do you suppose the situation with offspring would be? Would a child always be the size of a newborn? Would it ever physically mature?"

"Perhaps we're getting ahead of ourselves. Our chosen profession is about the most dangerous job there is. We may not live long enough to become near-immortals."

"At least there are three of us with my DNA. One of us should survive long enough to bear children."

"Not at the rate we're going. Eliza and I are just five, but you're approaching forty in chronological years and you're still a virgin."

"I spent almost eleven years in stasis, so I only think of myself as twenty-nine."

"I wonder, would you still be a virgin if you were stationed at Higgins?"

Jenetta reflected for a minute before speaking. "I really don't know. I had begun to think Zane was my true love, but he never even returned my last message. I think he was disconcerted when I made Commander ahead of him. Now that I'm a Captain, I doubt we'll ever get together."

"It's inexcusable that he never called, but he wasn't right for you anyway. You know that he tried to date Eliza while you were away?"

"What? She never told me."

"She didn't want to hurt you. She refused his advances, of course, despite the fact we both inherited your feelings for him. She said he told her he never tried to hide the fact that he dated other women while you weren't in port."

"We never discussed it, but I assumed he wasn't monastic during my absences. We weren't *engaged* after all."

"You're better off without him. It's time to find somebody new."

"It's difficult, being the supreme military commander for this part of space. Regulations prohibit fraternization between officers and enlisted personnel, and I can't have a relationship with an officer under my command. I'm certainly not attracted to most of the alien species that live on the base, so that leaves the merchants on the concourse or the freight-haulers passing through."

"The merchants I've met here are only interested in one thing— amassing as many credits as possible."

"And the freight-haulers are only here for anywhere from a day to a month and then gone for a couple of years, possibly much, much longer."

"They're definitely not good material for a long term, intimate relationship," Christa giggled.

"There's not even time to *begin* to develop a real relationship. It looks like a series of one-night stands is all we can hope for."

"Speak for yourself, sis."

"What? Have you found somebody?"

"Well— remember that I'm not hampered by all that gold you carry around on your shoulders."

"Come on, give. Answer the question."

Christa giggled. "Okay, there is a certain Lieutenant(jg) aboard the *Chiron* that I've sort of been seeing."

"What does 'sort of been seeing' mean?"

"When you're too busy in the morning, he and I exercise together after my watch and then have breakfast. He's on second watch."

"Is he cute?"

"Dreamy. And he wants to get together, but I've held him off so far."

"Don't wait too long or you'll wind up like me."

"Stop it. You make it sound like you're going to die a virgin. You're going to look like a twenty-one-year-old goddess for possibly five thousand years. There's no way you'll die a virgin."

"Perhaps not, but I've felt that way at times. Every night I go back to my apartment alone and talk to my cats. Remember our school teacher, Mrs. McBride? She once told us she had eighteen cats. She was a spinster."

"Just be careful if you do bring somebody with you someday. Your cats might misunderstand the passion." Christa giggled.

Jenetta had to giggle also. "You mean that the claw marks on his back won't all be from my nails?"

"And the bite marks won't be from your teeth."

The two sisters broke into a fit of laughter that lasted several minutes.

The Selaxian delegation arrived at Stewart aboard the GSC destroyer *Ottawa*. Selax didn't yet have faster-than-light ships and the Arrosians had refused to carry Selaxians on any of their ships since the *Hunaray* incident. It turned out, Jenetta learned, that the missing passenger from the freighter had carried a Selaxian passport disc.

Jenetta greeted the delegation at a conference room especially prepared for the arbitration sessions. The conference table was horseshoe shaped, and while the floor-to-table height at the center of the horseshoe was seventy-three centimeters— the proper height for Terrans— platforms built along either extension provided a table-to-floor height of only forty-one centimeters, the height found throughout the *Hunaray*. Chairs, also constructed to agree with sizes aboard the freighter, had been especially prepared to suit the physical attributes of the delegation members.

The Selaxian delegation was extremely pleased with the arrangements and thanked Jenetta profusely for being so understanding of the physical differences between humans and their species. They said they'd had a difficult time aboard the *Ottawa* despite Captain Crosby's indisputable attempts to make their stay as comfortable as possible.

"I'm sorry he couldn't be more accommodating," Jenetta said, "but we have quite a bit more flexibility on the base. Your accommodations have likewise been altered to conform to your physical requirements using measurements taken from the living quarters aboard an Arrosian freighter."

"Your consideration to our needs is most appreciated, Captain. I'm surer than ever that our President made a wise decision when he appealed to the Galactic Alliance Council for assistance. We know you'll be a fair and impartial arbiter on the matter of Isodow."

"I'll do my best to render a fair and equitable solution. I hope you'll feel the same afterwards."

"More than anything else, we wish to avoid war with Arrosa. We're ill-equipped to defend ourselves against their superior weapons. Will Space Command enforce the decision you issue?"

"We'll enforce any decision reached as a result of the arbitration, and we'll do everything possible to see that Arrosa doesn't commence hostilities if the decision goes against them."

"That's all we wish for, Captain."

\* \* \*

The terror attacks had slowed on Arrosa, but they didn't stop. It was as if the terrorists were warning Arrosa not to stall or delay the talks on Stewart. With hundreds of people dead and thousands wounded all over the planet, Prime Minister Marueck continued to promise that they would find the perpetrators and bring them to justice. But after a full year they were no closer to finding the guilty parties than they had been at the beginning.

The hundreds of people arrested had to be released as their alibis were verified. Travel restrictions, imposed in an effort to reduce the terrorist activity, only seemed to be infuriating the general populace. Checkpoints throughout the major cities caused massive traffic bottlenecks, and tempers were constantly flaring. It was not an easy time for citizens or politicians. If it weren't for Space Command's regular presence in his solar system, Marueck would have already declared war on Selax if for no other reason than to divert attention from his administration's failure to find the terrorists.

Selax, on the other hand, was as calm as any inhabited planet ever became. Arrosa's intents had gradually leaked from government sources and the newspapers had inundated the planet with sensational headlines for a few weeks. When no attack materialized and the government didn't activate reserve forces or issue warnings to be prepared, the issue quickly became a non-issue. The people went about their lives with the comfortable feeling that Space Command would protect them from outside attack.

The complacent attitude on Selax infuriated Marueck all the more. His planet was practically operating under martial law while those responsible were going about their lives as if nothing was wrong. His only consolation was that Deruuw continued to infiltrate agents into Selaxian population centers.

# Chapter Seven
~ May 29th, 2275 ~

Of the twenty-six moons in the Rhoitter solar system, Vyx, Byers, and Nelligen were quickly able to narrow the search to one. Only one planet appeared as purple, and that planet only had two moons. Further, only one of the moons made two full revolutions each day. If the information from the construction foreman was accurate, the base had to be located somewhere on its surface, and the information would be worth every credit Vyx had paid for it.

They first made several quick passes through the entire solar system, looking for any signs of orbiting ships. Finding none, Vyx had the ship's computer begin a search for a narrow canyon that opened towards three peaks as drawn by the foreman. Then it was just a matter of sitting back and waiting while the ship's computer mapped the surface of the moon from high orbit.

The computer signaled when it had completed mapping the entire moon. It was nothing like the incredibly detailed mapping work survey teams performed since the agents were only trying to locate very prominent features. Of three possible locations, Vyx picked the one that most closely resembled the map drawn by the construction foreman.

"This is a very likely candidate for the canyon we're looking for," he said to Byers and Nelligen, "but the only way to find out for sure is to go down and take a look. Nels, you'll take the copilot chair. Get out fast if I can't handle whatever we find."

"Right. We'll zip out if we lose contact or if you tell us to git."

After plotting a descent path with the navigation computer, Vyx engaged the system and sat back. The small freighter began dropping from orbit upon reaching the designated start point. Vyx would allow the ship to handle the approach unless something unexpected happened, but he'd take manual control for the final hundred meters of descent.

Vyx set the small freighter down about five hundred meters from the wall at the end of the chasm. The hundred-meter-high roof, anchored to the rim walls on each side of the long dry canyon, was just as Darrigo described it. Viewed from above, the camouflaged roof looked like the surface of the moon. Any ships parked beneath the cover because they were too large to fit inside the flight bay would be invisible from above the mountainous terrain. Vyx donned an EVA suit and stepped into an airlock after double checking the signal from the com system with Nelligen.

Byers and Nelligen watched Vyx's bouncing progress across the surface of the two-fifths-gravity moon. Reaching the flight bay wall, Vyx entered an outer airlock door immediately next to the flight bay door. Both Nelligen and Byers tensed as he disappeared from view.

Vyx waited until the airlock completed its cycle and then stepped into the flight bay. The surprisingly large area contained neither tugs nor shuttles, giving Vyx hope the base was deserted. Although there was atmosphere in the bay, he remained in his suit. If there *was* someone hiding, the individual could open the flight bay doors at any time and Vyx would find himself out on the moon's airless surface.

Crossing the bay, he cautiously entered the airlock that led to the main corridor. He hadn't gone more than a dozen paces in the corridor before two Tsgardi stepped out from a doorway with lattice pistols leveled at his midsection. He immediately froze, remembering an almost identical scenario in Rivemwilth's old base. At that time, he'd been one of the defenders as Tsgardi tried to enter the base. The Tsgardi hadn't survived the encounter, and he knew his own current chances in the bulky EVA suit were somewhere between slim and none.

Lattice weapons had long ago been outlawed by the Galactic Alliance, but they remained the favored personal weapon of Raiders and other criminals because they could be fired aboard ship with the certain knowledge that they wouldn't puncture a titanium hull. Like laser pistols, they used energy in place of chemical propellants, but they fired an actual projectile rather than an energy beam. Each six-centimeter-long projectile, consisting of four narrow pieces of flat spring-steel, appeared like a circular latticework tube. Loaded under great pressure into hundred-round magazines, projectiles were stored in compressed form. When pulled into the chamber, it instantly expanded to its full twelve-milli-meter diameter. The leading edge was as sharp as any straightedge razor. Spun by a rifled chamber, the fired projec-tile bored through whatever it struck like a drill bit. Since it wasn't attempting to push its way through the material, as a lead projectile would, it didn't require nearly the mass or velocity. Rather, it cut its way through like the narrow blade of a filleting knife. Where a laser pistol sealed the wound as quickly as it made it, the lattice pistol left large gaping holes that allowed a person's life force to bleed out in minutes from wounds in what should be non-vital areas.

Vyx bent slowly and put his laser rifle on the deck. This was no time for foolish bravado. Straightening back up, he removed his helmet. The Tsgardi facing him weren't wearing protective suits, and with the airlock door sealed behind him, there wasn't any danger he would suddenly find himself sucking vacuum.

The Tsgardi, a warlike race from a planet a thousand light-years beyond the new Galactic Alliance frontier, more closely resembled tall, skinny, upright Terran baboons with dark grey fur, than humans. Most often found in the employ of the Raiders or other criminal types, they enjoyed free movement in Galactic Alliance space unless a specific indiv-idual was guilty of committing a crime. Even so, they were only rarely seen anywhere except in the Frontier. Operating in the circles he did, Vyx had had run-ins with them before.

"I didn't know Shev Rivemwilth had left anyone here," Vyx said, smiling. Byers and Nelligen could hear his every word because he was wearing the headset.

"I remember you," the closest one said. "You're Trader Vyx. You should have died on Gollasko."

"Perhaps. But Recozzi's cousin wasn't fast enough."

"Bresozzi wasn't his cousin. He was his brother."

"Ah, that clears up the question of the family resemblance."

"Shev Rivemwilth ordered us not to kill you or you'd be dead already. What are you doing here, Terran?"

It was obvious they were unaware of Rivemwilth's death. If he let on, they'd probably open fire immediately. "Shev Rivemwilth didn't tell you? I'm the one who contracted to move all the ordnance from the old base to this one."

"We haven't heard from him in almost a GST year. He told us he was expecting a freighter and would be leaving soon. He doesn't like to transmit messages because he's afraid Space Command can track the signals."

"The Shev has always been extra cautious. Space Command can't follow a signal if there isn't one to follow."

"You still haven't told us what you're doing here."

"I'm here to wrap up my deal with the Shev."

"I've seen your ship. You couldn't get one percent of our stockpile into it."

"The *Scorpion*? That's true; the *Scorpion* is far too small. I sent the *Maid of Mephad*."

"That's a Raider ship."

"*Was* a Raider ship. Space Command took possession when they seized Raider Eight and it became Stewart SC Base property. I stole the *Maid* from Stewart during the first few months when everything was in total confusion there, so it's my ship now and I contracted with Shev to use it to move his ordnance."

"What was the contract amount?"

"Five hundred thousand credits through Ker Blasperra on Scruscotto."

The two Tsgardis lowered their weapons slightly and Vyx took his first real breath since walking in. The place reeked of Tsgardi. He hadn't noticed it before then.

"The Shev hasn't arrived yet. Come back in a month."

"A month? It took me four months to get here. This is the date I arranged with the Shev. He should be here at any time."

"If he's supposed to be here, than he must be in the Frontier Zone. Why don't you try calling him?"

"He said he was changing his frequency and scramble code after we completed our arrangements. He said he'd call *me* after he arrived here if I wasn't here waiting for him."

"That's another thing," the leading Tsgardi said, raising his lattice pistol again. "The Shev hasn't trusted anyone with the location of his base before."

"We have a unique arrangement. I trusted him with my new ship worth fifty million credits anywhere in the Frontier, and he trusted me with the location of his new base. Anyway, he considers people who contract with him to be his employees. It's not like Space Command would come here, even if they knew exactly where it was."

The Tsgardi thought for minute and then lowered their pistols all the way. They were ferocious fighters but not great thinkers.

"You can stay if you brought your own food. We're running low and can't feed you from our supplies."

"No problem. We have plenty on our ship. I'll be happy to share it with you."

The pistols came up again.

"We? I thought you worked alone?" one of the Tsgardi said.

"I used to. But new opportunities have required I take on associates and employees. I couldn't have stolen the *Maid* and piloted both it and the *Scorpion*, could I? I have two of my people with me and I sent another half dozen with the *Maid* to help with loading the ordnance."

The Tsgardi were completely confused and off guard now. "Tell them to bring some food in with them," one of them said. "Anything real. I'm sick of synthesized food."

Vyx made a big deal of appearing to turn on his headset. "Hello, *Scorpion*, this is Vyx. Do you read me?"

"I hear you," Nelligen said.

"I've encountered some of Rivemwilth's men in here and they've invited us to stay until he arrives, but they're low on food. Move the ship in beneath the camouflaged roof so it can't be spotted from above and bring enough food supplies for—" Vyx looked over at the Tsgardi who had done all the talking. "How many are you?"

"Just us two."

Into the headphone mike, Vyx said, "Bring enough food supplies for us and two Tsgardi for a week. Vyx out." Vyx made a movement that would make it appear as if he was turning off the headphone, although he didn't. He wanted Nelligen and Byers to hear everything that went on in case the Tsgardi had lied.

"Open up the flight bay and my men will come in with a freight sled full of food supplies," Vyx said.

The Tsgardi who appeared to be in charge nodded to the other one, who then moved to the flight bay control room. Vyx followed him and watched through the control room window as the flight bay's two doors opened wide. They looked on as the *Scorpion*, visible in the canyon outside the base, lifted off slightly and moved closer. Vyx cringed as the ship wobbled slowly on its cushion of 'oh-gee' waves and came within a whisper of brushing the canyon walls a couple of times. He let out a loud exhale when it at last came to a rest just outside the doors. The ship was too large to enter the base, but there was still adequate room for a shuttle or tug to squeeze past and enter because Nelligen had landed it very close to one side of the canyon. Vyx wondered if that was intentional or inadvertent.

It was another hour before Byers and Nelligen had finished loading a freight sled with food, donned their EVA suits, and left the Scorpion. By then Vyx had pretty much confirmed there weren't any other Tsgardi in the base. He'd asked to use the bathroom and been escorted to the living quarters area, and then, surprisingly, had been left alone. After removing his suit, he'd used the facility and then exited into the corridor. He'd left his EVA suit in the bathroom but strapped on his laser pistol. There wasn't any sign of the Tsgardi who had escorted him to the bathroom, so he used the opportunity to look around. He found the crew quarters and saw that only two beds were unmade, although the room stunk as if ten thousand Tsgardi were staying there. Quickly searching each of the other rooms in the area, he didn't find any evidence of additional minions. This was going to be easier than he'd anticipated after first stepping from the airlock.

Vyx walked back to the flight bay where the two Tsgardi were watching Byers and Nelligen moving towards the bay through the bay's control room window. Vyx assumed that the second Tsgardi had left him alone so he could verify they weren't about to be overrun by men from Vyx's ship. He couldn't both watch Vyx and cover the base entrance with his companion.

The flight bay doors closed as Byers and Nelligen moved inside. As the bay was re-pressurized, the Tsgardi opened the cargo door airlock to allow the opposed-gravity sled easy access to the mess hall corridor. Crossing over the threshold of the flight bay, the sled dropped almost to the floor before the auto adjust controls managed to raise it to the proper height again. With the entire base surfaced with gravity plating, any area was adjustable from three g's all the way down to weightlessness. It was currently set to one g, except in the flight bay where moon-normal gravity was in effect.

Vyx waited until everyone was in the mess hall and Byers and Nelligen were out of the line of fire before he made his move. The Tsgardi were at the freight sled pawing greedily through the fresh food supplies.

Pulling his laser pistol, he said to the two Tsgardi, "Okay boys, put your hands up. Nobody has to get hurt today."

Tsgardi are frequently too dumb to surrender, even in the face of insurmountable odds, and these two were no exception. Both reached for their lattice pistols and tried to pull them. Vyx, left with no other choice, fired his laser pistol into the chest of each. He was close enough to wound them, but if they had tried to pull their weapons with a laser pistol already pointed directly at their midsections, they would have continued to fight until they were dead.

As the two Tsgardi crumpled to the ground, Byers, still in his EVA suit, screamed, "Dammit Vyx, give us some warning next time."

Even without the headset, Vyx would have heard Byers. He had screamed so loudly that his voice had passed through his helmet. Thankfully, the headset electronics prevented volumes high enough to damage hearing, and Byers' voice came through just higher than normal speaking levels.

"I didn't have a chance. I wanted to take them alive. With their arms full of food, I thought this would be my best opportunity. There's just no predicting what Tsgardi will do. They should have surrendered. I had them covered."

"No Tsgardi is ever going to be a Nobel Laureate," Nelligen said.

"What I can't figure out," Byers said calmly, having removed his helmet, "is how they ever could have developed faster-than-light-speed spacecraft or even solar system space-craft."

"They didn't," Vyx said. "They captured a group of peaceful explorers who visited their planet. After learning how to operate the spacecraft, they imprisoned the travelers, then used the ship to invade the Flordaryns' home planet and enslave the people. The Flordaryn world is only thirty-six light-years from the Tsgardi world and was within the borders of the first territory the Tsgardi established. The enslaved Flordaryns are now forced to build ships and weapons for the Tsgardi."

"Where'd you hear that?"

"From a Tsgardi named Recozzi who I arrested a few years ago. He felt like bragging while I was transporting him, so he told me the whole story. They're proud of the fact that they don't have to do any scientific work or learn any science; they just steal everything they need or want. They stole lattice technology from another race they conquered once they had interstellar travel capability. We're lucky their world is a thousand light-years away from our outer border. They're a very family-oriented society despite their brutality, and we're too far away for them to mount a concerted attack against our territory. They only have Light-225 capability so it would take five years for a battle group to reach GA space, and they'd have to be gone from their families for at least ten years, not counting the years the war would take. The ones who do come here are mostly criminals or outcasts who can never return home, but we also see a few die-hard warriors who come on 'a mission.'"

"I'm going to put my helmet back on if I have to stand near these Tsgardi much longer," Byers said, wrinkling his nose. "My eyes are starting to tear up."

"It's not just in here; their smell has permeated throughout the base. But you should put your helmet on anyway. You and Nels take the bodies outside the base and cover them with some loose rocks near the canyon wall. I'll see if I can get the air filtration system cranked up a notch or two higher, and I'll take their bedding and stuff to the laundry."

"Are you planning to stay and inhabit this place?" Nelligen asked.

"For the present; we can discuss our plans after we clear some of the stench out."

By the time Byers and Nelligen had returned, Vyx had cleaned the bedding the Tsgardi had been using and all the clothing he found in the dormitory-style bedroom. When the pressed and folded items slid from the laundry equipment, they still bore the smell, but they were marginally better than the air in the base. Nothing would resolve the airborne stench. Their one hope was that the air scrubbers could clear the odor sooner rather than later.

"Okay, what now?" Nelligen asked.

"Let's have dinner, and then we'll take a look through the storerooms and see if there's any ordnance here."

"And if there is?"

"We take it or destroy it so no one else can get their hands on it."

"Then we leave?" Byers asked.

"I've been thinking about that during our trip. Space Command is going to need some outposts in the new Frontier Zone. If this base is constructed anything like Rivemwilth's old base, it's almost impregnable. We're buried inside a mountain with a very well-camouflaged entrance, and thanks to Rivemwilth's occupation and natural paranoia, almost nobody knows the location."

"So you're saying we should stay here?" Byers asked.

"I think we should stay for at least as long as it takes to get an answer from the Intelligence Section. I'll send a message today asking for their decision. That means we'll have to stay for at least two weeks— maybe longer if they have to think about it for a while."

"I don't think I can stand this smell for two weeks," Byers said.

"It's not nearly as bad as your feet just after you remove your shoes," Nelligen quipped.

"And it's not as bad as your breath after you've been eating that flamethrower chili you make, but I don't have to like it."

Vyx grimaced, decided that a reasonable discussion period was over, and turned to look through the food supplies for something quick and easy to make. Byers brushed him away and began sorting out the stuff so he could start dinner. Vyx hated to cook, so he allowed himself to be shooed away and left to check out the communications room. Sitting down at the console, he recorded a message to the nearest Chief Intelligence Officer— Captain Kanes at Higgins SC Base— then transmitted it. Nelligen came in just about the time he was done and announced that dinner was ready.

"Looks like the same setup Rivemwilth had at the other moon base," Nelligen said as he looked around.

"Except this one hasn't been destroyed."

"Yeah. Send the message?"

"Yup."

"Let's go have dinner."

Byers had prepared some kind of pasta dish with pieces of what appeared to be clam meat mixed in. It was tasty and a lot better than anything Vyx would have made for himself. If he continued to hang around with these guys, he was going to start putting on weight. He thought, facetiously, that in a few years he could look like Byers. *No,* he decided, *wouldn't happen.*

After the meal was over and the dishes cleaned up, they took a tour of the various storerooms in the base. They found a decent amount of weapons and ammunition in the first two storerooms, and Vyx felt sure it had to be the sample merchandise from Gollasko. Judging from the amount and variety, it probably also included some from Rivemwilth's old base. Vyx's only remaining question was this: Where is the ship that brought it here? It was unfortunate the Tsgardi had decided to go for their weapons. They could have provided useful information.

The rest of the storerooms were empty except for the last. Upon opening the door, Vyx's jaw dropped as he looked inside. Ten steps from the door, chained to a ring in the floor, were two naked Terran women.

The two young women pulled away from the three gawking strangers who stood in the doorway, at least as far as the chains on their ankles permitted. They were fearful, but they didn't scream. They had apparently been prisoners long enough to know the futility of— and punishment for— screaming.

Vyx entered the room and approached the women. "Who are you?"

The women stared back, unable to comprehend the reason for the question. The older of the two, all of about twenty-six, said quietly, "We haven't received our new identities yet. I'm Slave 65. She's Slave 66."

"What are your real names?"

"Those *are* our real names."

"I mean the names you had before you were taken."

"I can't say."

"Why not?"

"Because our masters beat us if we use them."

Vyx took a good look around the room. There was a bowl with water and another which appeared to have traces of dried food. A tall bucket had to be serving as a chamber pot, judging from the smell that wafted around the room. Turning to Nelligen, Vyx said, "Nels, see if you can find a pair of bolt cutters in the tool room we passed."

"How about just using the keys?" Nelligen asked, pointing to a hook on the wall just inside the door where a small ring of keys hung. He took the ring down from the hook and tossed them to Vyx.

Vyx stooped down and tried several keys until he found one that released the leg irons for both women. Neither moved when released. They just sat on the floor, watching Vyx warily.

"Okay, ladies, you can get up now." Vyx said as he stood up.

Both women got to their feet, never taking their eyes off Vyx.

"Follow me," he said.

Leading the little group to the dormitory room showers, Vyx picked up a couple of bath towels from a stack near the entrance and tossed one to each of the women.

"Get cleaned up and then we'll talk. I'll want your real names so we can notify the proper people that you've been rescued."

"Rescued?" the one who had identified herself as Slave 65 asked apprehensively.

"Rescued," Vyx confirmed.

"Where are our masters?" Slave 66 asked.

"The two Tsgardi we found in here are relaxing peacefully under a pile of rocks out on the surface of the moon."

"What do you mean?" Slave 66 asked, confused.

"He means they're dead," Slave 65 said.

"Is that right? They're dead?" Slave 66 asked.

"Yes. They refused to surrender even though I had them covered with my laser pistol."

Slave 66 began sobbing and dropped to her knees as she buried her face in the towel. Vyx stood there looking confused and wondering why she'd be crying over the monsters who had kept her naked and chained to the floor.

Slave 65 stooped and put her arms around the younger woman. Looking up at Vyx and seeing the expression on his face, she said, "She's not crying out of grief but out of relief. They treated us like dirt. She'll be okay in a little while."

Vyx nodded. "We'll leave you alone to get cleaned up."

The Tsgardi clothes Vyx had taken to the laundry were the only clothes he had seen in the base, so he left them outside the shower area while the two women bathed. He was glad now that he hadn't followed his original instinct and shoved them down the waste disposal chute instead of into the laundry chute. He returned to the mess hall to give the women privacy to dress.

When the women didn't appear after an hour, he went back to the dormitory. He found them sitting on a bed, covered only by towels.

"Aren't you hungry?" Vyx asked.

Both nodded.

"Then why are you sitting here? Get dressed and come to the mess hall."

"You didn't leave any instructions for us. We didn't know what you wanted us to do."

Vyx smiled sadly. It might take awhile for them to recover from the slave mentality to which they had succumbed. Pointing to the pile of Tsgardi clothes, he said, "I cleaned those earlier. They're the only clothes I've found in here, so I guess they'll have to do. Use what you can and then come to the mess hall. Byers is waiting to start cooking a special meal for you, so I'll tell him to start now. Come when you're ready. Turn left in the corridor, walk until you smell food cooking, then follow your noses."

"What should we call you?" Slave 65 asked.

"I'm Vyx. We'll talk after you've eaten."

The two women ate furiously but not a great amount of the spread Byers set before them. Months of meager rations had shrunk their stomachs. The one named Slave 66 made a sandwich for later, wrapped it in a couple of paper napkins, and then held onto it with her left hand like it was the last thing she'd ever receive to eat.

Vyx sat at the table drinking a cup of coffee and trying not to stare at the women. When they had finished and put their eating utensils down, he said, "The kitchen is always open to you. Feel free to come make yourself something to eat anytime you're feeling hungry."

Even that statement wasn't enough to make Slave 66 release her grip on the sandwich, so Vyx continued.

"Suppose you tell me your real names now and how you wound up chained to the floor in the base of a notorious arms merchant?"

"You first," Slave 65 said.

"Okay, my name is Vyx, Trader Vyx. That's Byers and that's Nelligen," he said pointing to his comrades. "We came here seeking a load of missing weapons stolen from Space Command. We found them in a couple of the storerooms. Now you."

"You're a Trader in illegal arms and you expect us to trust you?"

"We're the ones who freed you and fed you. That should be enough to learn what I asked."

"You might be trying to trick us. Maybe you're only pretending to free us."

"For what purpose?"

"I don't know."

"Did the Tsgardi know your names and how you wound up here?"

"Of course."

"Then what harm can it do to tell me?"

The two women looked at one another. Then Slave 65 said, "I'm Maria Elena Morales, and she's Sarah Lynn Hawkins."

"And what are you doing sixty light-years inside the new Frontier Zone?"

"We weren't in the Zone when we were captured. We were part of an advance survey team for Cestwidge Mining on the surface of a planet in the Argopp system when the Tsgardi landed near our camp. We tried to radio our mother-ship but we didn't get a response, and we didn't stand a chance against the Tsgardi by ourselves. We last saw the men in our party on the planet; I have no idea what happened to them. We were taken up to the Tsgardi ship and held in their brig for months, then transferred to another ship's brig and ultimately wound up here."

"The Argopp system? That's thirty light-years on the other side of the border."

"Yes, I know."

"How large was the ship that attacked your group?"

"I don't know. We never saw it except from the inside of their brig."

"Do you know its name?"

"No."

"Can you tell me anything that would be relevant?"

"We had a lot of different guards during the months we were there, and it was a long walk from the flight bay to the brig."

"So you're saying it was a big ship?"

"It must have been."

"How about the second ship?"

"We only saw two different guards while we were locked up. The brig was very close to a small flight bay only large enough for a couple of shuttles or tugs."

"That must have been Rivemwilth's ship. They apparently linked up with the Tsgardi transport on their way here. I wonder what happened to it after they unloaded you and the ordnance at this base. Did you overhear anything at all about their destination or purpose?"

"Nothing that made sense. They just said something about 'making the Arrosian delivery.'"

"Are you sure they said Arrosian?"

"Yes. But I don't know what they meant by it."

"Okay. What was the name of your ship, by the way?"

"The *Cestwidge Explorer IV*."

"Thanks Maria. I'm going to send a message about your being found alive and well. You'll either have to stay here with us until we leave, or they might possibly send a ship to pick you up."

"Who are *they*?"

Vyx smiled. "Space Command. I have a contact at Stewart."

"Shouldn't we leave here right away? Rivemwilth is expected at any time."

"Oh, don't worry about him. He made the mistake of cheating my associates and me. He won't be leaving the place where he is now. Contrary to what many authors have written down through the centuries, I don't think they actually let you leave hell."

# Chapter Eight

~ June 1st, 2275 ~

Jenetta was working in her office when an encrypted message arrived from Vyx. She put aside the portable view-pad and tapped the play button on her com unit as she leaned back to watch the communication. Vyx's face filled the screen as it began to play.

"Hi Captain. I'm transmitting this message from inside Rivemwilth's new base in the Frontier Zone. We discovered its location and traveled here to determine if any of the weapons he'd stolen had made their way here. We discovered a small amount I believe might have been the 'samples' brought here directly from Gollasko when he had to abandon his quarters there. We also found two Terran women chained to the floor in a rear storeroom. They've identified themselves as Maria Elena Morales and Sarah Lynn Hawkins, formerly of the *Cestwidge Explorer IV*. They claim to have been conducting a survey in the Argopp system when taken prisoner by Tsgardi eight months ago. They claim that after about three months in captivity aboard a transport, a smaller ship brought them here.

"I sent a report to Captain Kanes at Higgins regarding our discovery of this base, but he isn't aware of the prisoners because we hadn't yet discovered them at the time I filed. I see no real need to amend that report since it doesn't affect the query I posed. I asked if he'd like us to secure this base for use as an outpost in the Frontier Zone. We're sixty light-years over the border so the location might be useful, and I'm confident no one will contest the ownership with Rivemwilth gone. But now I'm also going to need a decision regarding these women. Will someone pick them up, or should I return them to Stewart? I'd appreciate any input you might offer.

"On a final note, one of the women overheard the Tsgardi referring to 'the Arrosian delivery.' She didn't have any information other than that, but it sounds like Arrosa was trading with Rivemwilth. The transaction might be perfectly legal, but I thought I'd mention it in case they had received any of the stolen Space Command weapons for which we can't account.

"Trader Vyx of the freighter *Scorpion*, message complete."

Jenetta's face reflected her intense concentration. She hadn't seen any reports about a missing survey ship in her sectors, and the Argopp system was clearly within her mission authority.

"So why didn't Cestwidge report the *Explorer IV* as missing when its absence was realized?" Jenetta asked herself aloud. "It has to have been noticed that the ship hasn't filed any reports in eight months. Or are the two women lying about their identities and circumstances?"

Sitting up straight, Jenetta recorded and sent her own message to Captain Kanes at the Intelligence Section. She then transmitted a message to Vyx, thanking him for the information and informing him that she would notify him regarding transportation for the women as soon as she reached a decision.

*     *     *

The delegation from Arrosa finally arrived at Stewart. As with the Selaxian delegation, Jenetta met them at the conference room prepared for the arbitration hearing. But unlike the Selaxians, the Arrosians had nothing but uncomplimentary things to say. They were unhappy about the shape of the table, they complained that the seats were uncomfortable, and they said the height of the table was unacceptable. Jenetta listened patiently to their comments.

"I'm sure all those issues can be easily remedied," she said. "If you'll select a chair you all find comfortable from aboard your ship, we'll duplicate it exactly. Or perhaps you'd like to provide your own chairs from your ship's furnishings? As to the height of the table, we matched the height of all the tables aboard your freighter, the *Hunaray*. We assumed that since this height was standard throughout the entire ship, it would be the norm, but simply tell us what would be acceptable and we'll adjust your side to that specification. The same will go for the shape of the table. Tell us what you desire and we'll do our best to accommodate you. I'm sure the Selaxians will go along with whatever table shape is decided upon because they're more concerned with the substance of the talks, and I'm quite sure the shape of the table hasn't even occurred to them."

"Are you implying that we're being unduly concerned over trivial matters?" the delegation leader, Minister Thulrys, asked angrily.

"I'm sure these matters are of great importance to you. I'm only trying to accommodate you at this early stage."

"Which means you won't accommodate us later?"

"I'm to be the arbitration judge. Once the hearing begins, it isn't my place to accommodate either side. You'll have every opportunity to present your case, as will the Selaxians. When both sides have made their case, I'll issue as fair and impartial a ruling as I can."

"I'm sure you will, Captain, if you haven't already made your decision."

"Are you suggesting I won't be impartial?"

"I'm sure your decision will reflect your true feelings."

*Real diplomatic double talk, steeped in ambiguity and innuendo*, Jenetta thought to herself. It was no wonder she tried to avoid politicians and diplomats as much as possible. Politics were present in every bureaucracy, but the Arrosian delegation seemed to raise it to a science. "No, Minister, it will reflect the most fair and equitable solution I'm capable of rendering. My personal feelings will have nothing to do with it. You may forward your table and chair specifications to my office. Commander Blake," Jenetta glanced at the commander briefly, "will escort you to your assigned quarters. I have many other things to complete before the hearing begins. Good day."

While the Arrosians continued to delay the start of the hearing by registering a series of complaints about the conference room, Jenetta continued her duties as before. She wasn't any more anxious to conduct the hearing than the Arrosians were to see it progress, but she knew of its importance. She placed Commander Blake in charge of making the conference room satisfactory, within reason. Although not permitted to enlarge the room or change the wall shape or ceiling height, almost everything else was open for discussion.

Jenetta finally received a reply to her message from Captain Kanes. She leaned forward for a retinal scan to begin decryption and then sat back to watch.

"Hello, Jen. I hope you're well. I bet those four gold bars on your shoulders are feeling pretty heavy these days, but hang in there; you're doing a great job. I know the Admiralty Board is delighted with your performance.

"In response to your inquiry about a ship called the *Cestwidge Explorer IV*, the company maintains that the ship is not missing. Further, they report that no employees are missing and that they have no record of employing anyone by the name of Maria Elena Morales or Sarah Lynn Hawkins. Payroll reports, filed for tax purposes with the appropriate governments, support that claim. According to its logs, the ship has never even visited the Argopp system. I've also sent that information on to Vyx in my message to him.

"Supreme Headquarters has decided to take advantage of the opportunity to turn Rivemwilth's base into an outpost. I'm sure Vice-Admiral Raymond Burke will be in contact with you.

"Good luck, Jen, and take care of yourself.

"Keith Kanes, Captain, Intelligence Section, Higgins Space Command Base, message complete."

Jenetta thought about the message and the meaning of the information, trying to piece things together. The women had obviously lied. The question was why. In the absence of additional supporting data or documentation such as fingerprints and retinal scans, speculation as to their identities and reasons for deception would be futile. It could simply be because they were wary of Vyx, or it could be something much more sinister.

Receipt of an incoming message from Admiral Burke interrupted Jenetta's reverie. She sat back to view the communication.

"Hello, Captain. I hope this message finds you well and the base situation quiet and stable.

"I know you have your hands full with the Arrosian matter, but we have another task for you. We've decided to expropriate the former base of the Alyysian arms dealer named Rivemwilth for use as our first outpost in the new Frontier Zone. Captain Kanes has assured us that you're familiar with the situation there. You're to appoint a staff to man the base, make whatever modifications are necessary for its use as an outpost, and provision it. Having an outpost which can serve as a supply depot sixty light-years inside the Frontier Zone will be extremely useful to Space Command.

"Good luck, Captain.

"Raymond A. Burke, Vice-Admiral, Space Command Supreme Headquarters, message complete."

Jenetta frowned. A permanent outpost in the Frontier Zone meant permanent responsibility to keep it manned, provisioned, and maintained. Normally, Space Command bases rotated outpost staffs every six months. But the remote location of this one would make that difficult. She would have to establish the rotation schedule as being one year, at least initially. At seventy light-years from Stewart, the round trip was five to seven months. Rivemwilth's old base, already converted for use as an outpost, presented no staffing problems because of its location within regulated space. Quartermaster ships could re-supply it on their way to Stewart, and ships on patrol rotated the staffs. But all ships sent to the new outpost would have to be warships because of the higher threat level in the Frontier Zone.

Jenetta sent a memo to the base personnel officer to begin working up a list of personnel for the first deployment. She would also have to reassign one of the ships already assigned to patrol duties. That would leave them one patrol ship short for four months, and they already had far too few for the territory they had to cover. But it was unavoidable. At least there were several additional ships on their way to Stewart, including the one carrying the diplomatic teams. It was unfortunate they were still months away.

# Chapter Nine
~ June 27th, 2275 ~

Vyx was thankful he viewed the message from Captain Kane in private. Over the past few weeks he, Byers, and Nelligen had become friendly with the two women and an atmosphere of trust had started to develop. In just the time it took to view the message, that all changed. If the women lied about their identities, their occupations, and the circumstances that led to their capture and enslavement, what else had they lied about?

Waiting until dinner before bringing up the subject, Vyx said, "Oh, Maria and Sarah, I received a message today that Space Command has already dispatched a ship to pick you up. They've requested that we send them handprints and retinal scans because they've found dozens of people on Earth with the same names as yours and they don't want to contact the wrong families regarding your rescue. After we clean up we can do the scans and send them off."

The two women looked at each other and then Maria said nonchalantly, "Okay, Vyx."

After the meal, Maria tried to avoid having her handprints and retinal image recorded, complaining of cramps. But Vyx insisted, saying it would take only seconds to complete and then Maria could go to bed if she wished. Vyx completed the scans quickly and attached them to a message he had prepared earlier. After sending it off, he smiled at the women. "That's all, ladies."

"When do you expect the ship to get here?" Maria asked. She seemed to have fully recovered from the cramps.

"Oh, as early as tomorrow morning I guess. It might be two days though. The ship was already in the Frontier Zone responding to a call for help from a freighter with a temporal generator problem. They just have to divert slightly. You'll be on your way back to your lives with the mining company or your families real soon."

*  *  *

Maria shook Sarah's shoulder gently and the two women climbed out of the enormous bed in Rivemwilth's bedroom they had been sharing since regaining their freedom. They dressed quickly and quietly in the Tsgardi clothing they had been using and walked silently to the bedroom door. It was a little after 0300 according to the just barely visible chronometers in the very low illumination of the corridors.

Making it to the airlock that led to the flight bay, the two women donned EVA suits they found hanging in lockers there. Byers' suit was much too large, so they used Nelligen and Vyx's suits. Although those suits were too large also, they only had to wear them long enough to get to the *Scorpion*, parked beneath the overhanging roof right outside the airlock.

With the oversized suits sealed and tested, they engaged the door opening mechanism of the airlock. Both immediately froze as the door rolled back. Vyx was standing there inside the airlock with his laser pistol drawn.

What happened next surprised even Vyx. He would never have believed that anyone could move that fast in a bulky EVA suit, but Maria managed to execute a spin and kick that sent the pistol flying from his hand. Unfortunately for her, the weight and bulkiness of the suit made her fall victim to the simple laws of physics. Sir Isaac Newton's first law states that a body at rest tends to remain at rest, while a body in motion tends to remain in motion. She lost her balance when she tried to stop, and the action of her spin caused her to keep turning. She crashed into Sarah, who was standing next to her, and both women crumpled to the deck. Vyx had recovered his weapon by the time the women had disentangled themselves and managed to stand up. He stepped back out of range of any more kicks.

"I'm impressed, Maria. That was a very bold move for someone who seemed so thoroughly subjugated. Overall, it's been quite an acting job. Now, remove our EVA suits. We have something else you can wear."

Removing a small remote control from his pocket, Vyx pressed a button that initiated an emergency alert condition in the facility. Ten seconds after the alert lights started flashing and klaxons began to sound throughout the base, Byers and Nelligen came running down the corridor in their underwear.

Vyx watched the two women with his pistol drawn while Nelligen attached the leg irons to their ankles. They were now back where they started when the three agents found them, except they had pillows and blankets this time. Vyx permitted them to keep the Tsgardi uniforms they had been wearing after he searched them for possible weapons or anything they might use to free themselves.

"This should prevent you from trying to leave again tonight," Vyx said, yawning. "I thought you'd never make a break for it. I was getting pretty sleepy waiting for you. I'm going to catch some zzz's now. We can all have a nice talk later this morning. Sleep tight."

The two women stared down at the floor and never uttered a word. Instead of putting the keys onto the hook inside the door, Vyx dropped them into his pocket and left the room. Nelligen and Byers followed, turning off the lights as they left.

Sleeping until after ten a.m., Vyx showered and shaved before joining Byers and Nelligen in the mess hall.

"How did you know they'd try to escape last night?" Byers asked.

"I told them a ship was arriving to pick them up today. That had to make them believe it might be their only chance to get away."

"Why did they have to get away?" Nelligen asked.

"Space Command checked out their story. Cestwidge denies having any employees unaccounted for, denies that anyone with the names the women gave us have ever worked for the company, and denies that the *Explorer IV* has ever been to the Argopp system. Everything the two women told us was a lie."

"What's the truth then?" Byers asked.

"I don't know. I've sent the handprints and retinal scans to Kanes, but we'll have to wait until we hear back. There's no sense asking the women. They'd only spin some other yarn."

"Then the ship isn't coming today?"

Vyx smiled. "No. That was just a lie I used to get them to make their escape attempt immediately, if that was their plan. I didn't want to spend the next two months sitting in the airlock each night. That's how long it will be before a ship will arrive here to officially establish this as an SC outpost."

"I still can't understand why they didn't tell us the truth," Byers said.

"We'll find out eventually. Until then they stay chained up. Even if the Tsgardi smell is starting to dissipate, this base loses all of its appeal if we have no transportation off. There's a comfortable feeling in knowing the *Scorpion* is ready to lift off at a moment's notice."

\* \* \*

A little more than two weeks later, a message arrived from Captain Kanes at Intelligence. After viewing it, Vyx asked Nelligen and Byers to bring the two women to the communications room.

When they arrived, more than a bit grungy and disheveled from having spent the previous two weeks chained to the floor, Vyx tapped the play button again and leaned in for the retinal scan. The image of Captain Kanes appeared on the screen.

"Hello Commander. Using the scans you forwarded, we've been able to identify the two women. It turns out they're ours. The brunette is Lieutenant Brenda Cardiz and the blonde is Lieutenant(jg) Kathryn Earlich. We haven't heard from them in almost a year. Their last known location was the Duzzero colony on Ferdic Three. They were working the same case as you from a different angle. You should allow them to make their reports and then accord them all the courtesy normally afforded fellow agents in a secure location.

"Keith Kanes, Captain, Intelligence Section, Higgins Space Command Base, message complete."

Vyx turned to face the two women, who had stood quietly listening to the message.

"You're a Commander in Intelligence?" Brenda, formerly known as Maria, asked with surprise in her voice.

"Lieutenant Commander Victor Gregorian at your service," he replied. "You could have saved yourself two weeks of discomfort if you'd been a little more honest with us."

"How were we supposed to know that all of you are work-ing for Intelligence?" Brenda asked. "As far as we knew, you were just traders in illegal arms. We never actually saw the bodies of the Tsgardi you say you killed. It could have all been a ruse to get us to reveal our true identities, and the ship coming to get us might have been another Tsgardi vessel. Knowing how few Space Command vessels are on patrol in the Frontier Zone, it was a little too convenient that one would suddenly be available to pick us up with just a few days' notice. What would you have done in our place?"

Vyx scratched his chin. "The same thing I guess. It's a good thing I was able to stop you from making it to my ship."

"Why? The SC ship would have picked you up."

"My ship is booby trapped. If you had somehow managed to get past the entry hatch explosive charges, trying to acti-vate the ship's launch controls would surely have blown you and it into a thousand pieces."

The women stared at him impassively.

"The Space Command destroyer *Ottawa* should be here in six weeks to set up this base as a Space Command Outpost. You can grab a ride back with them when they leave."

"Where are you going?"

"We'll be heading back to Scruscotto. We'll wait here until the *Ottawa* shows up though."

"You don't have to stay on our account."

"We're not. We're staying here because those are our orders."

Brenda nodded. "Can we take showers and put on clean clothes before making our reports?"

"Suit yourself. You have the run of the base again. But please don't try to get into my ship. I'd hate to see you splat-tered all over the moon's surface almost as much as I'd hate to lose my ship."

After a good night's sleep in a bed, the women were in better moods. They began opening up now that they knew they were in the company of fellow agents.

"You said you killed Rivemwilth," Brenda said. "How?"

"I didn't say I killed him. I said he made the mistake of cheating my associates and me, and that he was in hell. I've established myself as an unsavory but reputable member in the criminal circles. I had contracted to move his arms cache to this new base from the old one. We borrowed a large transport from Space Command at Stewart, telling Rivemwilth I had stolen it during all the confusion at the new base. Space Command had installed a special tracking device so they could follow us out of sensor range. Upon receiving a call from me, they were to move in and take the ship. I'd removed all the detonators from the torpedoes so they couldn't explode, and the laser arrays would short out after a couple of shots.

"Everything was going well until Rivemwilth double-crossed us and left us marooned at his old base with all the com gear destroyed. He only got two weeks into his trip before the explosive charges I had rigged let go. They shut down the light engines, locked all the airtight doors wide open, and blew a couple of dozen holes in the hull. Everyone on board was incapacitated in minutes. They died of asphyxiation a few minutes later. Space Command moved in and took the ship after observing it sitting in space for a month, but it was a month too late for those aboard. Rivemwilth's body has been positively identified."

"Then you really do booby trap your ships?"

"Of course I do. If I'm not around to stop them, anyone attempting to steal a ship of mine won't get very far. They may not even get inside the doors. Now, how about telling us about you?"

"As Kanes said, Kathryn and I were working the stolen weapons case. We were in Duzzero following the trail of a crate of laser rifles allegedly sold to a particularly nasty character named Nuxxisty, a Cheblookan. He was looking to foment a tiny rebellion on his home planet because of an excessive property tax bill on his ranch that resulted in it going on the auction block. We intercepted him before he could return to execute his plan and we recovered the rifles. During the interrogation, he gave us the name of the seller and we moved in, but they had a lot more help than Nuxxisty had told us about. They took us down, and we found ourselves in the brig of a Tsgardi transport when we awoke. The rest of the story we told you is true. They transferred us to a small ship and brought us here. I imagine they intended for Rivemwilth to interrogate us and then sell or turn us over to the Raiders as slaves. Rivemwilth's delayed arrival and your timely arrival saved our skins."

"You're sure the transport was Tsgardi? Not just a ship with Tsgardi working on it?"

"Oh, absolutely. There was junk piled everywhere in the corridors. No captain, except possibly a Tsgardi, would ever allow that. Tsgardi never throw anything away if it has the remotest possible value."

"I wonder what a Tsgardi transport ship was doing near Ferdic Three. They rarely come into normal GA space unless they're on a mission."

"They were probably dropping off the crate of rifles. Ferdic Three isn't that far inside the border."

"An entire transport vessel to drop off a crate of rifles? Times aren't that tough. It has to be something much larger. If they dropped off the rifles, it had to be just a side errand."

"There haven't been any raids in normal space since the Battle for Stewart, and most people think the Raiders are gone for good. Space Command has even mothballed Carver, according to what you've told us."

"The Raiders aren't gone for good; they've just gone underground for a while. I doubt that we'll ever be able to eradicate them completely. And if we did, some other criminal group would simply spring into existence to take their place. Except in outer space, nature abhors a vacuum. The Raiders have merely returned to their old businesses of drugs, gun running, prostitution, and slavery. They had grown so large fifteen years ago that piracy had become not only possible but a logical extension of their growth. But by becoming such a serious threat to interstellar commerce and passenger traffic, they made themselves a prominent target. And by becoming so active, they lost their ability to hide effectively. We were able to find their fleets and some of their bases, and destroy them. Just for the record, by the way, Captain Carver isn't mothballed. She's the supreme military commander for this entire region of space. She's the one who dispatched the destroyer to make this an outpost."

"You know what I mean. She's stuck in an office now, piloting a desk."

"It was Captain Carver who sent a ship to pick us up after we were marooned at Rivemwilth's old base. She was only able to do that because of her position. But sending the battle-ship after us left the base's protection fleet short-handed when the Raiders attacked Stewart. By the time we got there, the battle was long over, but it could have ruined her career."

"Yes, we've heard your story of how she directed the battle and destroyed twenty-six Raider ships with just two warships in port and two that she was able to recall from patrol duty."

"I would hardly call that being mothballed."

"But she's stuck aboard a base like an old, impotent admiral."

"I know she'd rather be commanding a battleship, but like all of us, she follows orders, and the powers that be want her at Stewart. Don't underestimate what she can accomplish while flying a desk in an office. Captain Kanes is over four hundred fifty light-years away, yet we do his bidding."

"I just hope I never get to a point where I have to ride a desk all day."

Vyx smiled. "It's unlikely we will. Field agents never integrate back into the formal command structure very well. After graduating from the Academy, we spend our years being totally reliant on our own wits, reflexes, and fighting skills. At most, we can share our little world with a few others cut from the same bolt of fabric. But we wouldn't last a week saluting and following inane military protocols on a base or even on a warship. Besides, few of us live long enough to require a change of jobs."

* * *

The mood relaxed considerably now that no one had to be on guard constantly to protect their cover. It was only a matter of waiting until the *Ottawa* arrived to take over responsibility for the base. Byers and Nelligen spent their time in the mess hall, playing cards and harassing one another, while the two young women spent their time altering the Tsgardi uniforms to fit them better or exercising to keep fit. Vyx spent most of his time reading in a comfortable spot he had put together in one of the rear storerooms using several blankets from the dormitory. He also spent a couple of hours each day exercising, usually before the others were even up. His favorite exercise was running around one of the empty storerooms. He was surprised one morning when Brenda suddenly appeared next to him as he ran. They jogged without talking for over an hour until Vyx stopped to take a rest and cool down. Brenda stopped as well.

Once they were breathing normally, she said, "I wondered where you sneaked off to every morning."

"I don't sneak. I get up early, dress, and come here to exercise."

"Alone?"

He shrugged. "I'm used to working and being alone. I never worked with partners until this past year, and that was accidental. We just sort of fell in together because we were all leaving Gollasko after the borders changed. That and we were still involved in the stolen arms case."

"But even during the day you spend your time alone, locked in that storeroom. What do you do all day?"

"I read. I love to read, and it's something you can really only do alone unless you just happen to be with other people who are also reading alone. Noise is a distraction so I go to the storeroom. I haven't ever locked the door."

"What do you read?"

"Almost anything that's interesting, but I have a decided preference for fiction. I often reread the old classics, such as those by Shakespeare, but I'm not stuck on that period. Of course there have been relatively few great works created since the start of the twenty-first century, but the nineteenth and twentieth centuries were rich in great literature."

"I never would have thought that of you. I would have pegged you as a two-fisted loner who enjoys spending his spare time sitting in the corner of a bar, nursing one drink all night."

"You're not too far off. Except I occasionally enjoy several beers with dinner when I'm not actively working a case."

"No, I was way off. You're just in a profession that *requires* you to sit in bars nursing one drink all night. Maybe you should have majored in Literary Science."

Vyx smiled. "I did. When recruited for the Intelligence Section while at the Academy, I pictured myself reading reports and compiling data for more reports. They pictured me a bit differently."

"What now?"

"Now? Now I'm going to take a shower and have breakfast."

Brenda had been moving slowly closer as they talked. She put her hands on his hips and said, "Alone?"

Vyx shrugged. "I'm used to working and being alone."

"But this isn't work. How do you feel about showering alone? It's a more efficient use of water to wash two bodies at the same time."

"Oh? And do you know where I might find someone else who also needs a shower right now?"

"I might," she said, moving her body suggestively. "Let's walk to the shower room and we'll see what we can come up with."

Vyx continued to spend his days reading alone. Brenda also began to read alone, by his side. They could have read together, but their tastes in reading material were somewhat different. While he preferred plays and novels, she couldn't get enough poetry. Fortunately, the *Scorpion's* computer contained enormous quantities of both. Vyx downloaded a large selection of works into a holo-magazine cylinder for Brenda.

Twice as long as the thinner, ten-centimeter holo-tubes used for data, the three-centimeter-thick holo-magazine cylinders were extremely sturdy and lightweight, while offering better image resolution. Even at twenty centimeters, the composite-material tubes were very portable and updatable in minutes from files contained in a computer. Pressing a recessed button activated it, and a page of text and images rose up from the length of the cylinder. The reader could then twist the end of the cylinder slowly until they found something of interest. Although providing a much larger image than a viewpad, the tube didn't offer interactive computer capability.

Vyx and Brenda were each enjoying an afternoon reading session when the alert lights began blinking and the klaxons began bleating. Vyx was on his feet and halfway to the door before his holo-magazine cylinder stopped skidding across the floor. Brenda wasn't more than two steps behind as he raced through the corridors. When they reached the communications room, they found Nelligen buckling on his laser pistol.

"What is it?" Vyx shouted over the noise from the klaxon.

"Sensors have picked up a ship in orbit, and someone appears to be hailing us."

"I take it that it's not the *Ottawa*?"

"Right the first time. It's a small transport, not a large destroyer."

"It might be Rivemwilth's men returning," Vyx said.

"That would be my guess since this base is so secret, but it might also be an innocent prospector or survey team. Except— why would they be hailing us?"

Vyx spun on his left heel and raced towards the flight bay. Nelligen watched for a second with a confused expression on his face, and then followed Brenda, who was already running after Vyx.

Vyx was pulling on his EVA suit when Nelligen arrived outside the airlock next to the control room. "Where are you going?" he shouted over the sound of the klaxon.

"Until I know differently, I'm going to assume the ship is Rivemwilth's. When Rivemwilth buried us alive in his old base, I swore I would never allow that to happen again. The *Scorpion* is all prepped and will be ready to lift off in minutes. You guys remain here."

"You're just going to leave us here?" Brenda screamed, trying to make herself heard above the din.

"You're infinitely safer in here than outside. There's only one entrance, making this place easy to defend, and you have plenty of weapons in the storerooms. Space command has precise directions on how to locate the moon and the base. If I just leave the *Scorpion* where it is, they'll blast it to pieces as soon as they descend to the surface. Maybe I can get away and get them to follow me. I'll head towards Stewart and, if I get lucky, I'll meet up with the *Ottawa*. If Rivemwilth's men don't follow me, I'll swing around and be able to attack them from the rear."

Vyx pulled on his helmet and activated the suit's seal. Turning without another word, he entered the airlock to the flight bay while Nelligen and Brenda hurried to the control room window. They watched as Vyx crossed the bay and entered the airlock that led outside to the moon's surface. Byers and Kathryn rushed into the control room just as Vyx closed the airlock door.

"What's up?" Byers asked.

"Where have you been?" Nelligen asked angrily.

"I had to go to the can."

"I was washing my clothes again," Kathryn said. "I'm still trying to get the Tsgardi stink out of them."

"It appears that the rest of Rivemwilth's missing men have returned. We have to get ready to greet them. I'll head to the communications room and turn off the klaxon and warning lights. The rest of you better get to the storerooms and pick out some weapons. I'll join you there."


Firing up the *Scorpion*, Vyx maneuvered it out from under the concealing roof. After turning the ship, he punched a track to a low orbit path into the ship's nav computer. If he could achieve orbit, the ship's Light Speed drive would engage. But the Tsgardi, not having received a reply to their hails, were on alert, and the ship in orbit began firing its laser weapons at the *Scorpion* as soon as it emerged from beneath the camouflaged roof. Fortunately for Vyx, the gunners weren't tremendously skilled and most of the shots passed wide of the small ship.

Vyx achieved orbit and was just about to engage FTL when the *Scorpion* rocked violently. The emergency lighting kicked on as power fluctuated and then quit. Vyx was out of his seat in a microsecond, popping covers off panels and working furiously. He was able to restore most of the power, but the temporal field generator remained off-line. Without the ability to escape, there was only one option— fight.

Moving to the targeting computer, Vyx saw the Tsgardi ship coming up behind. They had stopped firing after he lost power and momentum, and he continued to monitor them in passive mode so as not to alert them he was preparing to fire. He knew he'd only have time for one shot before they threw everything they had at him. Firing without a targeting lock usually meant the gunner had one chance in a thousand of actually hitting his target, but Vyx had no choice. For their part, the Tsgardi were approaching his ship directly off the stern because it was the most vulnerable spot of any small ship. Large ships usually had rear torpedo tubes.

Time seemed to slow down immeasurably as Vyx waited for the Tsgardi ship to move to a position where he stood a chance of hitting them. He fixed a spot at which he intended to fire, but the Tsgardi ship began slowing before it reached that point. He cursed silently under his breath as he waited and prayed the ship would drift into the position he had selected.

The minutes seemed to pass like hours as he waited for the Tsgardi ship to reach the target point. Finally, it drifted into proper position. Pressing the control that would open the two hidden doors, he quickly fired once and then again. Two small torpedoes left their launch tubes a few seconds apart and streaked towards the Tsgardi ship. The Tsgardi must have spotted the launch because the helmsman suddenly pitched the ship to larboard and down to avoid the small torpedoes. The maneuver worked, and Vyx's first torpedo narrowly pass- ed over the Tsgardi ship's bow. Vyx was considering it lost when it suddenly exploded against the Tsgardi ship's stern. The explosion swung the ship around slightly just as the second torpedo reached it. The movement put the bow directly back into the path of the second torpedo. The effect of the helmsman's attempt to avoid the high-explosive torpedoes was inadvertently responsible for the strikes. Both missiles would probably have missed the ship altogether. Vyx smiled as the most forward frame section of the ship disintegrated into thousands of tiny fragments that glowed brightly for a second or two.

The damage to the stern had disabled the larger ship's main engines, and the damage to the bow destroyed their forward maneuvering thrusters. Because of the evasion maneuver, the ship was descending towards the moon without any way to stop or alter course. The *Scorpion* might be without engine power, but at least it was in a stable orbit. Vyx watched as the Tsgardi ship sank lower and lower towards the surface. While the moon had a low gravity, it would still exert an ever-increasing force over the ship as it neared the surface.

Vyx didn't believe that the damage his small torpedoes caused to the Tsgardi ship had incapacitated the gunners, but they were probably busy trying to save their skins. No more laser fire or torpedoes came in his direction as the disabled ship began to drop ever faster towards the surface. Once the Tsgardi accepted that they couldn't save their ship, they made a dash for their two small onboard shuttles.

Both shuttles made it out of the crippled ship, and then, surprisingly, three escape pods ejected as well. Vyx knew that if the shuttles made it down safely, the four agents in the base would have a real fight on their hands, so he targeted the shuttles and filled their engine sections with coherent light pulses from his laser weapons. Both shuttles, already in the grip of the moon's gravity, stopped moving under power and began to drop like the ship. It wasn't pleasant to fire on unarmed ships, but it was sometimes necessary in the fight for self-preservation, and this was one of those times. Vyx continued to watch as the main ship and the shuttles plummeted towards the surface and crashed, sending up great plumes of moon dust at each impact site. The three escape pods, not having soft landing capability, had automatically moved higher and achieved a stable orbit path around the moon.

With the excitement over, Vyx called the base.

"Nels here, Vyx. What's the story?"

"I engaged the Tsgardi ship and it's crashed onto the surface of the moon. I doubt there are any survivors aboard. They launched two shuttles, but I took them out also, and they crashed onto the surface as well. Three small escape pods made it into orbit, and I guess they can remain there until the *Ottawa* shows up."

"That's great. I guess we can stand down now. You're sure there's no additional threat?"

"Reasonably sure; the main ship spiraled in. The shuttles tried to glide in but instead crashed on the surface with great force. They're a very long way from the base, but keep an eye out just in case one of the Tsgardi survived. They're a pretty hardy species."

"We will. Are you going to return now?"

"I took a serious hit and my power systems are damaged. I have to see if I can make repairs to the *Scorpion* on my own. I'll let you know as soon as I figure out what the situation is."

"Okay, Vyx. And thanks."

"Vyx out."

"Nels out."

After several hours of trying to repair the small ship, Vyx admitted to himself that he wasn't going anywhere soon. He had thruster power, but that was it. He called the base.

"Nels here, Vyx."

"I've tried to repair the ship but I can't do it without some basic replacement parts that I just don't have. It looks like I'm going to be stuck up here for a while, like the Tsgardi in those escape pods. Life support is working fine, and between fresh food and emergency packs, I have sufficient food stores for a couple of years. I'm glad we stocked the base after moving in, so you guys should be in good shape also. I'll just wait for the arrival of the *Ottawa* from up here."

"You can't even land?"

"Not with any real degree of control. I have thrusters, but power to the opposed gravity system is out. At best, a landing would be a controlled crash. I'm sure the *Ottawa* will have the parts I need to get the *Scorpion* repaired well enough for us to get to a repair facility where I can have the temporal field generator and the sub-light engines overhauled."

"Okay, Vyx. Thanks for saving our bacon. We'll be here if there's anything we can do."

"Right. I'm going to send a message to the *Ottawa* and request their ETA. Vyx, out."

"Nels, out."

*  *  *

The reply from the *Ottawa* took more than eighteen hours. In the encrypted message, the captain informed Vyx that the ship expected to arrive at the moon in twenty-nine days. He also confirmed that the parts necessary for Vyx's repairs were available in the ship's stores and that they had a maintenance bay large enough to accommodate Vyx's entire ship. Working in a pressurized environment would make the repair work much easier and speedier. Working in an EVA suit made every task take three times as long.

The days passed quickly for Vyx as he settled down to await the arrival of the *Ottawa*. He had his books and everything else he needed for comfortable survival, but he found himself missing the warmth of Brenda's fine young body beside his as he read. He also couldn't stop thinking about her when he took his daily shower.

# Chapter Ten
~ September 19<sup>th</sup>, 2275 ~

"Captain, the head of the Arrosian delegation is here to see you," Jenetta read, as the message from her aide, Lt. Commander Ashraf, scrolled up on her com screen.

"Send him in, Lori," she replied.

Jenetta stood up to greet the Arrosian diplomat, who walked in and strode over to her desk.

"Good morning, Minister," Jenetta said.

"Good morning, Captain. I'm here to request that we begin the hearing as soon as possible. We can't wait any longer."

"Pardon me? You wish to start as soon as possible? But Minister, the Selaxian delegation and I have been ready for months. It's only your delegation's objections to the room design and furniture that's prevented us from starting."

"Are you blaming us for the delay?"

"Minister, every time we've asked you if you're ready, you've replied that the hearing can't begin until we correct some minor defect or other in the room. Right now, we're repainting the room to agree with the new table you demanded, which you insisted was necessary to complement the new carpeting you insisted upon."

"I demand that we begin by tomorrow or I'll file a formal protest with the Galactic Alliance Council."

Jenetta stared down at the minister for several seconds. Taking a deep breath, she suppressed an urge to tell the minister exactly where he could file his formal protest, along with an offer to help him accomplish the task. "We'll be ready, Minister. What time would you like to start?"

"The time you call ten a.m."

"Very well. The hearing shall commence at 1000 Galactic Standard Time tomorrow. I'll see that the Selaxians are notified."

Everyone who had ever worked with or for Jenetta knew of her habit of always arriving early at meetings. So when she appeared just seconds before the hearing was due to start, everyone noticed. Others may have credited a variety of reasons for this departure from the norm, but her intention was simply to avoid contact with delegates looking for a last minute opportunity to lobby for favorable treatment.

She had tried to clear her mind and separate herself from any preconceptions about the issues or resentments towards any of the delegates before her arrival. Captain Donovan of the JAG office and Commander Blake, who had been charged with preparing the room for the meeting, were standing by with their aides. The Selaxians had brought a few large boxes of documents, while the Arrosians had brought *stacks* of boxes filled with documents. Both societies had computers but still used paper as the only acceptable form for official documents.

Jenetta moved immediately to the chair at the center of the horseshoe-shaped table as she entered the room. After all the protests by the Arrosians and changes that saw the table shape change from horseshoe to oval, to square, to diamond, and to triangle, it was back to the original horseshoe shape. However, the platform for the chairs *was* two millimeters higher on the Arrosian delegation side than it had been when the delegation first arrived. Jenetta took her seat at the center of the table and pounded the gavel twice.

"All parties will please take their seats," Jenetta said.

Captain Donovan sat down on Jenetta's left and Commander Blake sat on her right. The aides took seats against the wall, a meter or so behind. Both the Selaxian and the Arrosian delegation took their seats after bowing to one another as a group. The bowing was apparently a custom on their respective planets when parties faced off against one another in court. Cameras, mounted in each corner of the room, recorded everything that occurred.

Once everyone was seated, Jenetta said, "This hearing to determine ownership of the moon known as Isodow, a natural satellite that circles the planet Selax in the Weitack system of Galactic Alliance regulated space, is now in session. As the supreme military commander in this sector, I, Captain Jenetta Alicia Carver of the Galactic Space Command, will arbitrate. Both parties have agreed to be bound by my decision on this matter, and my decision will be final with no avenues for appeal. I will allow each party to present their testimony in alternating half-hour segments and submit written evidence in support of their claim. Each party shall address its remarks to the arbiter. Should a party ask a direct question of the other party, they lose control of their time and may not interrupt until the second party has completed their answer, but if I feel that the second party is deliberately attempting to exhaust the half-hour time segment of the first party with their answer, I shall interrupt and give control back to the first party. The second party shall not attempt to answer rhetorical questions, and the first party shall refrain from asking rhetorical questions. The two parties drew straws before I entered to determine who would begin and the winner was Arrosa. The chief delegate from Arrosa is recognized for thirty minutes."

Jenetta pounded the gavel and a large chronometer on each wall began a thirty-minute countdown. The chief Arrosian delegate rose and began his opening remarks.

The delegates used the first day to relate their particular version of the settling of Selax and the history of their people. The delegates were true politicians and never used ten words when ten thousand would convey the same message. Owing to Jenetta's inexperience and the fact that it was only the first day, she allowed the delegates full rein. They used their full thirty-minute segments to expound the virtues of their own society while vilifying the other. Jenetta only stopped the proceedings three times when one of the parties or the other took exception to remarks and interrupted. She admonished the offender and restarted the proceedings.

At the end of the day, Jenetta adjourned the proceedings and scheduled them for resumption at 1000 hours the following day. Captain Donovan and Commander Blake followed Jenetta back to her office so they might discuss the hearing.

"You're letting them go too far afield, Captain," Captain Donovan said. "Keep them on topic. It's not necessary for you to hear about the hardships of the original settlers or the expense and difficulty of establishing a civilization out of a wilderness. It has no bearing on the case. You have the power to make them keep their statements relevant and material."

"I agree, Captain," Commander Blake said. "At this rate, they'll have us tied up here for a year."

"You're both right," Jenetta said. "I hesitated to keep too tight a rein on this first day. I hoped they would tire of the superfluous verbiage and redirect themselves to the matter at hand, but my leniency only seemed to fuel their desire to hear themselves talk. I'll maintain tighter control starting tomorrow. Have I committed any other errors?"

"Hearings like this are usually run rather informally, as opposed to the strict procedures used in a judicial court," Captain Donovan said. "There is no really right or wrong way. You decide what's proper and appropriate, as long as you treat all parties equally. In that respect I think you did well for your first day."

"Thank you, Captain. Let's hope I can keep the parties from dragging this out any longer than necessary."

Jenetta did a better job of narrowing the scope of topics discussed over the following days, but the hearing still plodded tediously along as the delegates took their turns talking throughout the day. Jenetta tried to focus all her attention on the speaker but found herself thinking about other station problems if the speaker digressed from the main topic. She looked increasingly forward to the end of the hearing. When the Arrosians began submitting their documents into evidence, Jenetta thought terminal boredom would set in. The normal rule of half-hour segments was suspended during the submittal as tens of thousands of pages had to be logged in for review. Jenetta's eyes crossed briefly as she thought about the work involved in reviewing the documents. They would first be scanned into a computer database and organized electronically rather than trying to examine each of the documents manually while translating them.

After the submission of all documents into evidence, Jenetta addressed the parties.

"It will take time for my staff to scan all the documents into the computer and verify the accuracy of the scans. Both parties will receive a complete set of the other's documents in electronic form so they may review them and be prepared to contest their content. My staff will translate the documents and we'll study each one for relevancy to this case. We shall adjourn until that phase of this hearing is complete, and both parties will receive twenty-four hours' notice before the hearing is set to resume."

Jenetta picked up her gavel. "I declare this hearing to be in recess." She pounded the gavel base once.

# Chapter Eleven
~ October 11<sup>th</sup>, 2275 ~

The *Ottawa* arrived at the moon on the twenty-ninth day following their message to Vyx. He was reading in the small lounge aboard the *Scorpion* when the ship's sensors detected the approaching destroyer and sounded an alarm. Dropping the holo-magazine cylinder he was using, he ran to the bridge. Once satisfied that the arriving ship was the *Ottawa*, he calmed down and hailed the ship. The image of Captain Crosby appeared on the front viewer in response to the hail.

"Hello, Trader. Has your status changed?"

"Hello, Captain. No, sir, my ship is still incapacitated."

"I'll send out a tug to bring you into our maintenance bay."

"I'm ready, sir."

"We're picking up emergency beacon signals from only two escape pods, not the three you reported."

"I saw three eject from the Tsgardi ship. Perhaps one's beacon failed or was deactivated by the occupant."

"Is it possible that one was already retrieved?"

"Unlikely. My sensors should have alerted me to the arrival of any other ships in orbit."

"We'll continue the search then. It shouldn't take us long to find the third pod. It may simply be on the far side of the moon right now. Prepare to come aboard. Crosby, out."

Vyx called down to the base and informed them of the *Ottawa's* arrival, although their sensors had already alerted them when the ship entered orbit.

An hour later, Vyx stepped from the *Scorpion*, now resting securely within the *Ottawa's* large maintenance bay. A Space Marine immediately escorted him to Captain Crosby's briefing room where the captain and his first officer were waiting.

"Come in, Trader," Captain Crosby said, waving off the security escort. "Welcome aboard. Allow me to introduce my first officer, Commander Upton."

"Good day, sirs. I'm happy to be aboard."

Gesturing to a chair, the captain said, "Please have a seat. Captain Carver briefed us on your situation before we left Stewart, and only Commander Upton and I know that you and your companions are with the Intelligence Section. The cover story is that you contracted to scout out possible locations for resupply depot locations in the Frontier Zone and that the Tsgardi henchmen of a deceased arms dealer attacked you when you accidently stumbled across a former hideout here. Everyone knows about the cache of arms brought to Stewart aboard the *Maid of Mephad*. We've located the third escape pod, by the way, and all three should be aboard soon. If you'll verify the coordinates of the new outpost, we'll send down the first groups."

"Of course, Captain. Someone should also visit the crash sites of the Tsgardi ship and shuttles just in case someone survived."

"We'll do that next. Tell us what's happened here since you arrived."

Vyx spent the next hour recounting the events since he, Byers, and Nelligen had located the base. He concluded by telling them of the fight with the Tsgardi ship.

"You have *rear* torpedo capability in that tiny ship?" Commander Upton asked incredulously.

"Yes. They're not the enormous torpedoes Space Command uses, but they're large enough to cause some serious problems to many of the ships I might encounter. The Cheblookan make them for their planetary defense fighters."

"They were apparently large enough to down the Tsgardi ship," Captain Crosby said.

"Oddly enough, the Tsgardi ship went down because of its attempt to avoid being struck. So that I didn't alert them that I was preparing to fire, I targeted them in passive mode. I'm sure they didn't expect such a small ship to have torpedoes, and I caught their laser gunners off guard. The helmsman nosedived the ship to avoid the torpedoes and that trajectory sent them towards the surface. The first torpedo passed over most of their ship and struck their stern, knocking out their sub-light engines, and the second torpedo took out their bow thrusters, eliminating their ability to correct their course and reestablish an orbit path."

"You must have surprised the hell out of them," Commander Upton said approvingly.

Vyx grinned. "I had the torpedo tubes installed when I first got the ship, figuring that an enemy would never expect it from such a small vessel. It took a tremendous amount of jury-rigging to get the tube racks mounted back there and keep them both hidden and isolated from the stern engine functions, but we did it. Their placement was the reason I named the ship *Scorpion*. A scorpion is most dangerous when it can use the stinger in its tail."

Vyx hitched a ride on one of the first groups of shuttles headed down to the base. The flight bay at the new outpost was large enough to accommodate four full-sized shuttles at one time.

As soon as the bay was pressurized and the crews had begun to disembark, the four occupants of the base hurried in. Brenda raced to Vyx and jumped up, wrapping her arms around his neck and her legs around his torso. Vyx stumbled backward a step before regaining his balance.

"I'm happy to see you also," he said calmly.

"I missed my reading partner," she whispered breathlessly into his ear. "Reading alone isn't as nice when you really are alone."

"I know," he whispered back. "Showering isn't as much fun either."

"Let's go work up a sweat so we have an excuse," Brenda said seductively.

"Later, after things are squared away here. There are going to be Marines crawling all over this barn for the immediate future. I don't think we'll be able to get a moment's privacy."

Byers, Nelligen, and Kathryn had also reached Vyx by then.

"Welcome back," Nelligen said, pumping Vyx's hand. "It's good to see you."

"Likewise," Byers said.

"Me too, Trader," Kathryn chimed in.

"I'm glad to see you're all okay," Vyx said.

"Thanks to you for taking out the Tsgardi before they could attack us here," Nelligen said. "We got ready for a war and then never saw a bit of action."

"That's always the best kind of disappointment," Vyx said.

"What's the deal now?" Byers asked.

"I only came down to get my things. Go pack your stuff; we're getting out of here today. The Marines are taking over and we have quarters waiting for us on the *Ottawa*. The *Scorpion* is also safely aboard the ship in a maintenance bay. A couple of engineers are already looking at the *Scorpion* with anxious eyes, and I want to get back before they start making repairs. I completely disabled both explosive charges just in case they can't wait for me."

"Where are we headed?" Kathryn asked.

"The *Ottawa* will be going back to Stewart after a two-month patrol here in the Frontier Zone. We might as well hitch a ride with them; it'll give me plenty of time to get the *Scorpion* fixed up. And since the *Ottawa* is a much faster ship, we'll probably arrive at about the same time as we would if we traveled directly there in the *Scorpion*."

"Sounds good to me," Nelligen said. "I bet I can find someone else aboard who likes spicy food."

Byers scowled. "Does everything have to revolve around your stomach?"

"Why not? It's central to my being. It's even centrally located. Look," he said, patting his belly.

Vyx just shook his head and started moving towards the base's interior with Brenda at his side and Kathryn following. With their audience leaving, Nelligen and Byers trailed along, still trading barbs.

After gathering the few personal items they had at the base, the five agents took the next shuttle up to the *Ottawa*. Ship's engineers and Space Marines would continue to prepare the new outpost for occupation. Once aboard ship, the agents were assigned rooms in the guest quarters section. Low-level security passes, typically given to SC civilian contractors, allowed them to enter most non-secure areas of the ship without an escort. As soon as they had settled in, the two women went in search of central stores to have some clothes made, while Vyx headed to the maintenance bay where he had put the *Scorpion*.

The bay was the largest on the *Ottawa* and was large enough to house half a dozen MATs, but if the *Scorpion* had been another five meters longer it wouldn't have fit. As it was, there was just barely enough room to move around outside the ship. Several ship engineers, not needed for work in the new outpost, were busy disassembling the hull plating and engine covers where the Tsgardi torpedo had damaged the *Scorpion*. Vyx had arrived back just in time to supervise the work, not that he wasn't grateful for the interest and help.

Vyx's preoccupation with making repairs to the ship sent Brenda, who wanted him to spend more time with her, into a mild state of melancholy. At dinner each evening he would again explain that they'd have months together later and that it was imperative he be heavily involved in the *Scorpion's* refit. Then he'd leave for the maintenance bay right after the meal even though he had already spent the entire day working on the ship. She understood, although it didn't lighten her mood.

The repairs to the *Scorpion* had become sort of like a pet project to the ship's engineers. After working with Space Command equipment all day, they couldn't wait to get their hands on a ship that appeared to have been constructed from a vast collection of incongruous components.

That assessment wasn't far off, which is why Vyx felt he had to be involved in all aspects of the repairs. The ship had been repaired dozens of times at different shipyards, most of which never seemed to have the proper parts. Rather than waiting months or even longer for a proper part to be located,

Vyx had authorized the use of somewhat similar parts. A couple of Marines passing by on roving patrol duty had the effrontery to question if the *Scorpion* had gotten to the moon under its own power or had been towed here.

\* \* \*

The *Ottawa* remained in orbit until the outpost was properly established and then left to begin the Frontier Zone patrol route assigned by Captain Carver. Although Supreme HQ normally established all patrol routes around Stewart, the *Ottawa's* role in establishing the outpost exempted her from continuing the prepared routing this time out. Their assignment from Captain Carver was to look around and record any ship traffic patterns they observed, but they weren't to engage in interdiction activities unless something unusual occurred. As always, they were required to respond to any distress calls that occurred within the sectors through which they would pass.

A week after leaving the moon, Captain Crosby sent for Vyx. Since the bridge was a high-security area, a Space Marine escorted Vyx from the maintenance bay to the captain's briefing room during the first watch.

"Come in, Trader," the captain said as he waved off the Marine escort. "Care for a beverage?"

"I'm fine, Captain," Vyx said as he plopped into a chair facing the captain without waiting for an invitation to sit. He nodded to Commander Upton, who was sitting in the other chair that faced the captain's desk.

"I know you're busy with your ship, so I'll come right to the point. Do you know anything about Milori?"

"Milori? I know they're probably the ugliest sentient species we've happened across since Terrans first moved off Earth, and that's saying something. Just looking at them makes my skin crawl. They're generally about the same height as Terrans, but covered with a dense brown, stringy hair that completely conceals their body. They have what passes for two arms, but their hands always remind me of crab claws, although the claws are reputed to be slightly flexible, like cartilage rather than bone. When the claws are wide open, two opposing digits, sort of like the thumb and forefinger on a Terran, are visible. I suppose the digits provide the dexterity needed by all higher life forms. What probably upsets Terrans the most is that they have four tentacles attached at their lower back. The long cloaks they wear completely conceal these appendages when at rest. But the tentacles can reportedly dart out and coil around you, then crush you to death, as would a boa constrictor on Earth. Their four eyes offer them superior peripheral vision, but they make them look like some kind of enormous insect. It's the eyes that make people refer to them as cockroaches rather than any other similarity. Generally, they make a Tsgardi look attractive."

"It sounds like you've met some of them then?"

"In a manner of speaking. I saw four of them in a bar during my first visit to Scruscotto awhile back. No one wanted to associate with them, and everybody was giving them a wide berth. They stayed in the bar for a while and then left. I was surprised to see them this far into Galactic Space, even if it is the Frontier."

"Would you recognize them again?"

"I really doubt it because they all look pretty similar. The ones I saw were all about the same height and had the same shade of brown hair all over their bodies. I'd probably have to see a lot of them before I learned what differences to look for. Why do you ask?"

"We have three on board. They were the occupants of the three small escape pods you saw leave the Tsgardi ship."

"Milori? In Tsgardi escape pods? Now *that* is unusual."

"Why so?" Captain Crosby asked.

"The Milori are a warrior civilization like the Tsgardi, but unlike the Tsgardi, they're reported to be quite intelligent. They'd never work for the Tsgardi, so they must have been passengers. But I can't see anyone trusting the Tsgardi enough to travel with them."

"Maybe they were prisoners?"

"No. If they were prisoners, they'd still be aboard the crashed ship. The Tsgardi wouldn't have taken the time to release prisoners from their brig in their scramble to get to the shuttles. Have you asked them what they were doing on board the ship?"

"Whenever I ask a question, they ask one also. I haven't gotten a single answer from them since they were brought aboard."

"What have you told them, Captain?"

"Nothing."

Vyx smiled. "Then that's your problem."

"What do you mean?"

"I've never spoken to one, but I've heard that if you want to get any information from a Milora, you must first tell him something he doesn't know. Each thing you tell them builds up a sort of credit account that they're obligated to balance out. They may not choose to answer your questions, but they legitimately cannot ask you any of their own until the account is balanced. If you haven't told them anything, the balance is equal and they can ask you anything they wish."

"That's the strangest thing I've ever heard."

"I didn't invent the system," Vyx said defensively, "I'm only telling you what I was told about dealing with them."

Captain Crosby smiled. "I'm sorry. I didn't mean to imply that your information was inaccurate. I only meant that their system is extremely odd."

"That it is, Captain. Why not try it? You have nothing to lose. Just don't give them any vital information they can use back on you. They're pretty tricky, I understand. Don't confuse them with the Tsgardi just because they're ugly as all get out."

"Would you like to sit in?"

"I'd better not. If they are the same Milori I saw on Scruscotto, they might recognize me and blow my cover. It's bad enough that so many Space Command personnel and Space Marines have seen me aboard the *Song*, *Thor*, and *Ottawa* in recent years."

"Okay. I'll let you know if your information was correct after I question them this afternoon."

Later that day, Captain Crosby, Commander Upton, and Marine Captain Porter, the senior security officer on the ship, confronted the first of the Milori prisoners in the interrogation room next to the brig. Although the prisoner spoke Amer, he demanded a language translation device before he would even sit down.

"I'm Captain Crosby. You're on the GSC *Ottawa*. We're a Space Command destroyer assigned with patrolling this part of Galactic Alliance space. This is my first officer, Commander Upton. That's Marine Captain Porter." *There, that's five pieces of information,* Captain Crosby thought to himself. *Now let's see if Vyx is right.* "What's your name?"

The Milora hesitated for a moment and then answered. "I am Uthqulk, first deputy negotiator to Commander Acoxxuz." The Milora answered in his native tongue, but each of the officers was wearing a translator device on his belt and heard the answers in Amer through his CT. Captain Crosby was pleased and felt that the Milora still *owed* him at least three answers.

"What were you doing aboard the Tsgardi ship?" Crosby asked.

Uthqulk didn't answer, but he also didn't ask any questions.

Normally, Crosby would have said something like, "Did you understand the question?" but he didn't want to use up his credits with insignificant questions. Instead, he asked, "Why are you working for the Tsgardi?"

Uthqulk stirred. Crosby knew he had reached him.

"Milori do not work for Tsgardi scum who will work for anyone who will feed them. A Milora would rather starve than take orders from Tsgardi or Alyysian swine."

"I thought your race was friendly with the Tsgardi?"

"They left us to die aboard their crippled ship. They refused to allow us into their shuttles. They threatened to shoot us with their lattice pistols if we tried to force our way onboard."

Crosby could see that Uthqulk was raging. His hair, matted down originally, now bristled all over his body.

"What were you doing aboard the Tsgardi ship?" Crosby asked again.

Uthqulk still didn't answer.

Captain Crosby decided he had used up his credits. It was time to provide more information. "You're being held in our brig for attacking a Space Command outpost and supply ship. The sentence for those crimes should keep you tucked safely away for the rest of my career in Space Command. You'll be a very old Milora by the time you're released."

"We had nothing to do with attacking your base or ship. We were merely passengers on the Tsgardi ship."

"Where were you when this ship picked you up?"

"We were on Bajurrsko, a mining colony."

"I'm familiar with it, but I'd never heard of any Milori visiting it before. I was told that you were on Scruscotto."

"We visited there briefly an annual ago. We came to negotiate a sale with an arms merchant and thought we might find him there. We returned to Bajurrsko when we discovered he wasn't there. It's perfectly legal, according to your Galactic Alliance laws. We represent a sovereign government engaged in fair trade."

"Why have you traveled more than two hundred light-years into Galactic Alliance space to buy arms? Your home planet is what, more than a thousand light-years from Bajurrsko?"

Uthqulk didn't respond right away, and Crosby had begun reviewing the exchange to calculate if his allotted questions now exceeded his answers when the Milora began to speak again. "We are always on the lookout for new weapons super-ior to our own. An Alyysian dealer named Shev Rivemwilth said he had weapons we'd be interested in."

"Rivemwilth hardly had anything worth traveling from your home planet for. You were tricked into traveling a very long way for nothing."

"We only traveled a fraction of that distance for weapons. We were already within this sector, looking to establish possible trade agreements with mining consortiums. This trip was merely a side activity. Shev Rivemwilth wouldn't give us the location of his base and insisted that he provide us with transport."

"Sorry. I'm not buying your story. You'll stay in our brig until I learn the truth."

Uthqulk looked at Crosby for a few seconds. "I demand to speak to my three companions."

"You only have two companions left. One died inside the Tsgardi ship when it crashed. His escape pod got stuck in the tube. Tsgardi don't make very good ship's engineers because they don't maintain their equipment."

The Milora bristled anew. "You lie," he shouted. "All my companions live."

"I have no reason to lie," Crosby said calmly. "Actually, you and your two companions got off luckier than the Tsgardi. They all died as a result of the attack on the small transport that was supplying our Frontier Zone outpost."

Uthqulk stirred again. "They told us that the ship they were attacking was leaving *their* base."

"They told you that our outpost was their base? That's very curious. I wonder exactly what they had intended for you? Did they intend to offer you to us? There's no bounty on Milori."

Perhaps the Milora felt that he had already given too much information away, and he refused to answer further questions. He didn't ask any either, so Crosby felt the credit was still to his side.

Over the next few hours, the interrogation team interviewed each of the other Milori. To keep the question and answer equation straight, Crosby was the only one to talk with the prisoners. He didn't get any new information from the others, but the information he did get seemed to verify what they had already learned. Since separate cells were always used to house prisoners, he had to assume that either the information was correct, or the Milori had some sort of telepathic capability. But if they had telepathic ability, they should have known that one of their numbers was missing.

Several days after the interrogations were completed, Captain Crosby sent for Vyx again to relate what he had learned.

"Thanks for your tip. Without it I wouldn't have gotten anything. I've added it to the files so other Space Command officers will be better prepared to deal with this species in the future."

"You're welcome, Captain."

"I've been in communication with Captain Carver and she's approved us altering our patrol route, so we're currently headed for Bajurrsko. She'd like you to go to the colony while we hold position outside the solar system. Our Milori claim they visited Scruscotto only briefly before returning to Bajurrsko. Your mission will be to learn everything you can about visits by the Milori and then report back to the ship. She's already sent a message to Captain Kanes requesting that you be allowed to perform the special assignment."

"That wasn't necessary. As Supreme Military Commander in this sector, she doesn't need permission to reassign me or the others."

"Your ship will be repaired long before we reach Bajurrsko. Is there anything else you'll need, Trader?"

"Nope. We'll deploy and get you the information you need, Captain. Bajurrsko is quite a ways into the Frontier Zone."

"Yes, almost a hundred twenty light-years. That's double the distance from the border to the outpost, and we'll have to watch our own backs from here on. There are no other Space Command ships this far inside Stewart's Frontier Zone sectors."

The repairs to the *Scorpion* moved along well. With all of the engineering talent available, Vyx was able to get a number of other things taken care of that had needed attention for some time, such as instrumentation calibrations and exterior sensor replacements.

With his ship repaired, Vyx was able to relax and spend time reading. Of course, Brenda was always by his side, also reading. They didn't use their time together just for reading though. There were also showers and other activities that happened naturally when two people who had developed a deep interest in one another spent so much time in close proximity.

# Chapter Twelve
~ December 16<sup>th</sup>, 2275 ~

"Captain, my people are demanding to know what's happening with the hearing," Minister Thulrys, the chief delegate from Arrosa, said obstreperously in Jenetta's office. "It's been more than two months since the recess was called."

With his first words, Jenetta's cats had jumped to their feet. They were eyeing the minister keenly. If he made any move toward Jenetta, they'd be on him in a second. Their quick movement and intense interest hadn't been lost on the minister, but it was several seconds before the implications of their actions dawned on him.

"We're still examining the tens of thousands of documents your delegation submitted. It takes time to translate them, ensure that our translation is completely accurate, and then fit them into the picture we're attempting to build. I understand that the terrorist acts have all but ceased on your planet?"

"Uh, yes, that's true," he said, lowering his voice. "There haven't been any acts we could attribute to the Selaxians in more than a month."

"I was under the impression that none of the acts could be attributed to the Selaxians. My information is that you don't have a clue as to who's really behind them."

"Uh, I misspoke. I meant that no acts had occurred in more than a month."

Jenetta nodded. Senior ministers and ambassadors didn't make such mistakes. It was just another attempt to sway her judgment against the Selaxians. "The process will take as long as it takes, Mr. Chief Delegate. As soon as the process is complete, I'll reconvene the hearing."

"Very well, Captain," he said calmly, eyeing one of the cats. "Good day."

"Good day, Minister Thulrys."

Jenetta turned to the SimWindow in her office as the Arrosian delegate left and the cats resumed their relaxed positions. Changing the image from a picturesque view of Niagara Falls to a live image of the port, she sipped her coffee and looked out at the activity. During the past month, three more Space Command warships had arrived in support of the new base and the territorial expansion. Space Command had been assigning as many ships as possible to the outer sectors since the expansion. Since this part of the border faced the center of the galaxy, it was receiving the most attention. And having a base in such close proximity to the Frontier Zone made it a prime location for homeport assignments.

Slightly more than half of Galactic Alliance space border-ed nations whose own internal conflicts or attitudes presently kept their attention focused inward. Since there was little threat from outside forces there, the older ships still being retrofitted were destined for service in those sectors. A num-ber of re-commissioned ships were already handling patrols, freeing the newer ships for reassignment to areas that were potentially more lawless and hostile.

The five Space Command warships presently sitting in the port were the most since the failed Raider attack aimed at retaking the base. A dozen of Space Command's largest and fastest quartermaster supply ships were presently unloading their cargos. The *Ottawa*, *Chiron*, *Asuncion*, and *Song* were all out on patrol activities, with the *Geneva* and *Thor* sched-uled to leave soon to begin their patrol routes. That would leave the most recently arrived warships, the cruisers *Romanov* and *Plantaganet*, and the destroyer *Beijing*, as security protection for the base while their crews rested and relaxed from their year-and-a-half journey to Stewart. The convoy bringing the new diplomatic corps was still months away.

SC-assigned personnel now filled most positions on the base, so personnel on loan from ships since the establishment of the base were returning to their ships. The concourse work was now complete, with more than half of all available retail space leased by operating businesses. The living quarters had been completely redecorated and furnished with repaired or new furniture. Freight hub operations were now running nonstop, and the 'cargo farms,' huge floating assembly points in orbit around the base, were always filled with cargo link sections awaiting pickup by freighters either headed towards the heart of Galactic Alliance space or into the Frontier Zone. The base never slept and rarely even seemed to slow down, even during the third watch. Jenetta's duties had shifted from refurbishing the base and creating a command and control structure to maintenance and control. Her days were busy but never very satisfying. At least she was now able to sleep through the night. Problems that required her immediate attention during the early hours had become rare.

*   *   *

Jenetta was working on her weekly report to Space Command when Lt. Commander Ashraf notified her that a Merchant officer, a Commander Michaels from a newly arrived freighter named *Attar*, was requesting an audience.

"Send him in, Lori," Jenetta spoke at her com. The message instantly appeared on Lt. Commander Ashraf's com screen.

As Commander Michaels entered the office, Jenetta smiled, stood up, and came out from behind her desk. "Hugh, it's great to see you again."

"Hello, Captain," he said, smiling. "You look wonderful. You seem to be a lot taller now, but you're still the prettiest GSC captain in the galaxy." At six-two, Hugh was almost three inches taller than Jenetta.

Jenetta's cats watched the stranger and their mistress embrace lightly but didn't stand up. They recognized that his voice and movements weren't signaling hostility.

"Thank you, Hugh. At least my rank is official now."

"I've never thought of you as anything but a captain, not since the day we met."

"That's not what you said in court, under oath," Jenetta teased.

"Well— well—" Hugh stammered, slightly embarrassed as he remembered the testimony he had given during Jenetta's court-martial. "It was only because of your apparent age when we first met, but I followed all your orders without question despite my initial uncertainty. Even later on, when you told me you were only an ensign in Space Command, I continued to think of you as my captain."

Jenetta giggled. "I know, Hugh. You always supported me, and I appreciated it. Don't mind my teasing. This is the first time we've been alone since the court martial."

Hugh smiled. "I don't mind. I'm glad to see that Space Command has realized what everyone else already knew, that you deserve to be in a senior command position."

Jenetta sighed. "I just wish I was aboard a ship."

"Have you requested a transfer to shipboard duty?"

"Space Command knows without my putting it into writing. Admiral Holt has fought to get a shipboard assignment for me, but the Admiralty Board has decided I should remain here for a full five-year duty tour. Perhaps after that I can get back aboard a ship."

"It sounds like they're grooming you for something else. Maybe they intend you to be the youngest admiral in Space Command history."

Jenetta chuckled. "I'd resign my commission and become a freighter officer like you if I thought that. I can't see flying a desk for the rest of my career."

"Don't resign your commission just yet. Freighter duty isn't all it may appear to be. It's true we spend our lives on ships, but it doesn't have the excitement of Space Command. We just fly from point A to point B, drop off some cargo, pick up new cargo, and then leave for a new point B. Since you wiped out the Raiders, there's not even the possibility of an attack to quicken our pulse. And now the company makes us spend half our passage time during long trips in stasis sleep so they don't have to pay us full wages for the whole period. They max out our load at ten kilometers every chance they have, even when it means discounting the rates and thus our bonuses."

"You're just trying to make me feel better."

"Maybe a little, but I'm serious about most of it. I've also heard that the freight companies are lobbying the Galactic

Alliance Council to increase the allowable length on any trip over a hundred light-years. They believe it's not a problem as long as the flight path doesn't take it through any inhabited solar systems. With increased loads, they wouldn't mind altering course a little to avoid any heavily trafficked areas."

"It would allow them to handle more cargo without increasing the crew complement, but it's hard to imagine that the GAC will allow it. Before Space Command established the limit at ten kilometers, our engineers performed extensive testing. They found that the linkage system just couldn't handle the constant stress of longer cargo loads."

"They're proposing a new link section made with alloys not available when the old system was designed and tested. Its strength is reputed to be greater by an order of magnitude."

"An order of magnitude? Are they proposing increasing the maximum length to a hundred kilometers?"

"No. I doubt anything like that would fly. I understand they've petitioned for fifty kilometers, hoping to get twenty-five. And I hear they're using the trip where you hauled a ten kilometer freighter, the *Klidestru*, with the *Vordoth* as an example of what's possible. Your length was sixteen kilometers and you didn't report any problems, according to the ship's log."

"That was under battle conditions. I only did it because it was an emergency."

"I understand. I'm only telling you what the freight companies are saying to the GAC."

"Great," Jenetta said sadly. "Space Command will never let me off this rock if they have to listen to a repetitious narrative on my violations of Galactic regulations while I served as a ship's captain."

"Oh, it's not that bad, Jen. Space Command understands you were operating under extraordinary circumstances with extenuating conditions each time you deviated from the regs. You wouldn't be where you are if they didn't have confidence in you. Look, I'm sorry for bringing it up. I didn't come here to depress you. I came here to invite you to dine with me tonight."

Jenetta pushed her previous feeling aside and smiled. "Love to. My dining room at 1800 hours?"

"Your dining room? I thought we might find a nice restaurant on the concourse. I heard that Gregory Harden has opened up a place here."

"If you'd prefer that, it's fine. I only thought we'd be able to speak more openly in the base commander's dining facility. No big ears straining to hear every word I utter."

"Hmm, I hadn't thought about it like that. I guess people here hang on every word you say because of your position."

"Yes, I normally only eat on the concourse when I'm dining alone."

"Okay, Jen. Your dining room it is. Should I come here or go directly there?"

"There. My aide can give you a map so you can find your way. I'll see that security passes you through."

"Great. I'll see you at dinner then."

"Okay, Hugh. I'm looking forward to it already."


Jenetta left the office early after rushing to complete her work. Hurrying to her quarters with her cats, she bathed and prepared for the meal as if it was a real date. The cats looked at her strangely when she chose to wear a skirt with her dress uniform. It was the first time she'd worn a skirt or dress since the party at the Nordakian embassy on Higgins years earlier. Since her body didn't permit any changes, she didn't have to worry about it not fitting. The cats sniffed at her as she put on her stockings, then settled comfortably to watch her continue her preparations. Because of the natural coloring 'programmed' into her DNA by the Raiders, she never had to make up her face, and she wore her hair short to make it easy to care for. Since trimming it from its required long length on Nordakia, it had never exceeded shoulder length.

Before leaving her quarters, she fed the cats. They tried to go with her as she walked towards the door, but she told them to stay, so they returned to their food bowls while she closed the door and walked anxiously towards the elevators.

Hugh was already in the dining room when she arrived. He stood up at her entrance and she saw that he had 'dressed' for dinner as well. There was no dress uniform in the merchant services, so he was wearing civilian clothes in place of the uniform he had worn earlier.

"You look great," he said. "I haven't had dinner with a woman in a skirt in over two years."

"Thank you. You look great also. I like your civvies."

Hugh looked down at his clothes and chuckled. "I don't get much occasion to wear anything except a uniform. We've been traveling for two years to get here, so my clothes are probably hopelessly out of fashion on Earth."

"The way fashion trends move these days, you'll probably be back in fashion by the time you get back to Higgins."

"Won't be the first time I skipped a whole fashion cycle while I was away," he quipped. "I think fashion reached its zenith, or perhaps its nadir, when body painting came into vogue a couple of hundred years ago. Now it's just the same old recycled looks every few years. There's only so much that can be done with clothing, and it's all been done many times over."

"As long as fashion like they had on Nordakia until a few years ago doesn't come into vogue, I can put up with almost anything."

"As I heard it, you completely changed the face of Nordakia."

Jenetta laughed. "All I did was present them with a computer core I acquired on Dakistee. They took it from there. I don't take any credit for the changes their civilization has undergone."

"Still, you were basically responsible for the changes. I'm beginning to think, like most other people, that you can change the galaxy."

"Me? Change the galaxy? I can't even get off this base."

"That'll come," he said, "and probably when you least expect it. Uh, I don't want you to think I'm changing the subject, but my stomach is reminding me I haven't eaten all day. What's for dinner?"

"I asked the chef to prepare prime rib. I remembered that it was your first dinner request after we escaped from Raider One."

"Prime rib? From real Terran beef?"

Jenetta smiled and nodded. "Of course."

His face lit up with a smile. "Great. I haven't had any in two years. The freight company doesn't believe in pampering its employees with such non-essentials as decent food, and we're a long way from Earth."

"An enterprising Cheblookan rancher had a dozen cows and two bulls brought from Earth about ten years ago. He'd tried to sell his Cheblookan livestock to visiting Terrans but rarely found any interest. I understand it cost him a small fortune to develop special stasis beds for the transport, but the animals arrived in healthy condition and have thrived on the planet. He runs them on the same pastureland as his domestic daitwa, and he's developed quite a herd already. I've contracted to purchase all the beef he'll sell us. We get about half of his annual output, with the rest going to contracts with meat suppliers on several planets. He only sells one mature bovine for every two calves born, so his herd continues to enlarge while providing him with a nice return. In the past few years, a number of other ranchers have followed his example and begun raising Terran cows and bulls. Eventually it'll be as easy to get a Terran beef steak out here as it is to get a Cheblookan daitwa steak."

"Have you ever eaten daitwa? It's extremely chewy and has a strange, greasy taste. I can understand why that rancher had trouble selling his livestock to Terrans. Ya know, I've heard that some people have an uncontrollable urge to whinny when they're done eating."

"I've tried it several times— the daitwa, not the whinny— but I don't like it. The only way I can tolerate it is when it's part of a heavily spiced stew. I usually stick with fish and vegetables. I've signed long-term contracts with several farm co-ops to produce Terran fruit, but it will take years for the apple, orange, plum, peach, and pear orchards to mature and begin producing fruit. We hope to have grapes and pineapples a little sooner. We're getting fresh Terran vegetables by the ton now because farmers can produce them in one growing season from seeds, and we expect to start receiving chickens and eggs in substantially greater quantities soon. Our main poultry producer has quadrupled his ranch size."

The mess attendant came in to inform Jenetta and Hugh that dinner was ready, so they took their seats and began their meal. During the meal, they talked about the times they had shared and the things they'd done since parting.

When the meal was over, Jenetta invited Hugh back to her quarters so they could continue to talk. As they entered the apartment, the cats immediately approached Hugh and smelled him.

"They won't hurt you," Jenetta said reassuringly. "Just let them smell you and they'll relax."

"I saw them in your office, but they didn't approach me."

"They're used to visitors there and don't get excited unless they perceive a threat, but I rarely have visitors up here so they're naturally a bit uneasy right now."

Hugh stood perfectly still as the cats circled him twice and then moved away. "They seem to have decided I'm not a threat." Glancing around the enormous living room where they were standing, he said, "Wow! This is fabulous. I had no idea base commanders lived like this. My entire quarters aboard the freighter would fit in this one room twenty times over."

"One of the Raider commandants must have had two executive apartments combined into one. I have two master bedrooms and a conference-room-sized office, plus a dining room, full galley, and steward's quarters, although I don't have a steward. I eat my meals in my private dining room, so that's been more than adequate. I didn't bother changing it back when we were redecorating the housing section. I thought that the admiral sent to assume command would appreciate the quarters as they were."

"But you turned out to be the admiral?"

"All the headaches but none of the pay," Jenetta said, smiling. "It's okay. I don't want to give them the idea that I might want to stay on here. Come take a seat and finish your story about your trip to Pelomious."

Jenetta moved to the large sofa and Hugh sat down immediately next to her. He put his arm on the backrest behind her and continued the story he had started just before they left the dining room.

"Next to Earth, it's the most beautiful planet I've been to. It has large oceans, tall mountains, and vast plains. Its waterfalls are legendary, and from space it looks a lot like Earth. It has abundant wildlife, none of which is sentient, although some of it is as dangerous as any found on Earth, but the main continent is pretty safe. It's surprising that there are so few settlers there. The government recently estimated the planetary population at just ten million. I guess that with its remoteness, the poor mining opportunities, and so many other planets to choose from, settlers haven't flocked there in great numbers yet. I've purchased a small section for myself. By the time I'm ready to retire, I should have it paid for."

"Retire? You're still young."

"Well, I'm not going to retire for a while yet, but I'm approaching fifty now. I have to start thinking ahead a little. Before I know it, I'll be a hundred and they'll be kicking me out of the way. Maybe I'll raise Terran cattle. As you've said, there's a market for beef out here."

"That takes a lot of space. How much land did you buy?"

"Just a small plot, about ten thousand hectares. But it's mostly grassland, and a river borders the land on one side."

"Small plot? That's a hundred square kilometers."

"It's small for Pelomious. You have to remember that it's very unpopulated. My nearest actual neighbor is about two hundred kilometers away. Hopefully that will change by the time I retire. And didn't I hear somewhere that you have a royal estate on Obotymot that's as large as Texas?"

Jenetta grinned. "It's not as large as Texas. It's only about the size of a combined Kansas and Oklahoma. And it presently isn't producing enough food to feed the small staff of my residence there. Perhaps one day it will be productive again, once the dirt kicked up into the atmosphere by the meteor strike clears. Do you really think you can settle down on a ranch after a life in space? My father retired a few years ago and he was going out of his head with boredom. Now that they've increased the mandatory retirement age, he's back in

Space Command as the captain of a re-commissioned cruiser on patrol in deca-sector 8667-3179."

"Being a freight-hauler isn't much better than being retired most of the time, but there are times when I actually feel useful. At least we're in space. It might be something for your dad to consider when he reaches 85."

"Mom's pretty confident that he'll choose to stay in Space Command until he reaches the new mandatory base retirement age of 100 if he can't be in space."

"If life gets too tame at Headquarters, he should consider short-haul freight operations. Are your grandfathers still working?"

"No. Mom and dad are both from Los Angeles. My grandparents all died in the great disaster of twenty-five. It's what prompted my folks to start their family earlier than they intended. They were going to wait until dad had reached the rank of lieutenant, but after the disaster they decided to go ahead right after he completed his training at the Warship Command Institute while he was still a JG. Billy was born a year later."

"I'm sorry you didn't get a chance to know your grandparents. Mine practically raised me because both my parents worked. Grampa Michaels always found time to take me fishing or to the spaceport to watch the launchings." He paused for a few seconds as he thought about growing up. "It's interesting that your dad returned to Space Command. They contacted me right after the expansion to see if I'd like to return to active duty."

"You weren't interested?"

"I was very interested, but I had just signed a new four-year contract with the freight company. They refused to release me and sent me off to Stewart for my next trip. Perhaps they thought I'd come to my senses if I had time to think about it."

"And have you?"

"I didn't share the opinion that I was out of my senses to begin with. Freight company owners think only of money and can't understand anyone who doesn't share their convictions."

"It comes in handy for those who buy enormous ranches on Pelomious."

"Yes, it does that," he said, smiling. "But I have fifty years to pay that off and sock away enough to live comfortably for my remaining years."

"Does that mean you're going to return to the service?"

"I'm seriously entertaining that idea. What do you think?"

"I can't really imagine doing anything else, even though I might grouse a little to family and close friends from time to time when I'm feeling bored with being posted on a base."

Hugh had been moving steadily closer as they talked for the past several minutes and Jenetta hadn't pulled away. Their voices had dropped considerably from normal conversational levels and neither was really concentrating on the topic. His face was now just inches from hers. Neither spoke for several seconds. Hugh closed the gap, simultaneously taking his arm down from the backrest and pulling Jenetta closer as their lips met.

# Chapter Thirteen
~ January 23rd, 2276 ~

Vyx carefully maneuvered the *Scorpion* out of the *Ottawa's* maintenance bay and set the navigational computer to take them to Bajurrsko. The destroyer would remain at its present position just outside the solar system while the agents traveled to the planet and attempted to learn anything they could about a Milori presence there. Vyx had decided that the two female agents should stay aboard the *Ottawa*. A quick mission to a dangerous environment with potentially hostile individuals was no place for women. But Brenda and Kathleen naturally objected and proclaimed their feelings in a most vociferous manner.

"This mission doesn't require any finesse," Vyx told Brenda. "We're going to hang around bars and question inebriated miners or anyone else we can bribe to secure the information. This colony doesn't see very many women, outside of those in the 'houses.' You and Kathleen would only distract them from thinking about Milori."

"What makes you think we can only do finesse?" Brenda questioned angrily. "We're agents, trained in the same schools as you and the others, and we can be just as hard as the situation calls for. The five of us can cover the colony a lot faster than just the three of you."

"Just because the Tsgardi overwhelmed us with a large force and took us prisoner doesn't mean we can't defend ourselves," Kathleen added.

Vyx took a hard look at the women and realized that perhaps he was being too overprotective. They were agents, after all, and women could often get men to reveal information they'd never give to another man.

He finally agreed to take them along on one condition. "You must be in visual sight of one of the guys at all times."

Both women agreed, reluctantly. They knew he'd refuse to take them along otherwise.

Bajurrsko was totally without any form of traffic control for arriving and departing spaceships. Thankfully, traffic was light compared to Scruscotto, so the danger was minimal. Usually called the Bajurrsko Colony because that was the name of the first settlement there, the planet was dotted with small mining operations and settlements. The first settlement, normally referred to by natives simply as 'The Colony' now, was still the largest by far.

Vyx set the *Scorpion* down on an empty pad at the North Spaceport. Ships belonging to mining operations mainly used the South Spaceport. The atmosphere on Bajurrsko, while marginal, was sufficient that they wouldn't need tanks or even breathing-assist equipment.

After Vyx had paid the landing pad fees and returned to the ship, they discussed the team assignments. Ore shipments from this region of the planet all left from the South Spaceport, and every mining company maintained a presence there. Because that part of the colony was mostly inhabited by miners, it had a greater density of bars. Vyx selected the south side for Byers and himself. Brenda, Kathleen, and Nelligen would make up the other team and cover the north half of the colony. Team members could operate independently if they chose but should never lose sight of one another. It was only mid-afternoon, but the bars would be getting busy as soon as the first shift in the mines ended. After strapping on their weapons, the agents left the spaceport in two taxis. Each agent had been instructed in how to disable the explosive charges used to protect the ship from unauthorized access.

Being so far inside the Frontier, Vyx didn't really expect to meet anyone he knew, but he recognized a Terran from the Gollasko colony in the first bar he and Byers visited. They had gotten a glass of ale at the bar and started to walk around the room when he spotted the familiar face. The man was sitting alone at a table, sipping frequently from a glass of ale.

"Meader, you old claim jumper," Vyx said. "You're a long way from Gollasko."

The man looked up and focused on Vyx's face for a couple of seconds. When recognition dawned in his besotted brain, he smiled. "I could say the same about you, Trader. Take a chair. What brings you to the most miserable hellhole in space?"

"The usual," Vyx said as he and Byers sat down at the table.

"Gun running? It's hardly profitable in a territory where Space Command doesn't enforce Galactic law."

"I trade other merchandise beside guns."

"What is it this trip?"

Vyx shrugged. "Let's just say I'm looking for Milori."

"Milori? There haven't been any Milori around here in five or six months."

"You saw them?"

"Yeah," Meader said, contorting his face into a mask of revulsion. "Ugly creatures! It's a damn shame they're too big to step on. Those tentacles of theirs really give me the creeps. Yuck!" He shuddered.

"Where'd they go?"

"I heard they left with some Tsgardi. There's another race the galaxy would be better off without."

"Did you hear where they were headed?"

"Naw. Don't care where they go as long as I don't have to look at 'em."

"Think you could find out?"

Meader's expression of disgust changed to one of sudden interest. "Why would I want to do that?"

"It might be worth your while."

"What's it worth?"

"Depends on the info. I'm interested in contacting any Milori, and I'll pay whoever can put me in touch with them. Let's say fifty credits if you can find out where they went and a hundred if you can find out where they are now."

"I might be able to find out something. Where are you staying?"

"On my ship, the *Scorpion*. It's up at the North Spaceport, but I'll be working the south side until I get a lead."

"Come back tonight. I'll have some information for you."

"For sure?"

"Pretty sure. I have to talk to a friend who mentioned something about them recently. I wasn't really listening closely at the time."

"Just give me his name. I'll pay you twenty credits."

"Wouldn't do you any good; he won't talk to you. I knew him for three years before he'd even tell me his damn name. Come back tonight."

"Okay, if I haven't learned what I want, we'll drop back."


Vyx and Byers went from bar to bar over the next six hours but didn't learn anything more than they had from Meader. Four Milori had been there six months ago, were seen talking with some Tsgardi, and then were gone. They heard the same story in half a dozen bars, but all it cost was a few dozen glasses of ale.

After eating a late dinner, they headed back to the bar where they'd seen Meader. He was sitting in the same chair at the same table, and from his condition it appeared he hadn't left the bar all day. Vyx sat down while Byers went to get three ales.

"Did you learn anything?" Vyx asked.

"Nobody knows where the Milori that were here went to," Meader slurred. "I checked around and that's gospel. But I did hear how you might contact some other Milori."

"How?"

"Five hundred credits," Meader said.

"Five hundred? I said fifty."

Byers arrived at the table and set the three glasses down.

"I want five hundred for what I know," Meader said stubbornly. "Otherwise, you'll have to travel a thousand light-years to see a Milora."

Vyx pushed one of the glasses towards Meader and took another for himself. After a long pull on the drink, he said, "You know for sure where they are?"

"I know fer sure where they were six months ago."

"Big deal; I know where they were six months ago also. They were here."

"No, not them. I know where the two Milori warships were six months ago."

"Warships?" Vyx said in surprise.

"Yeah. Two of their biggest destroyers."

"In the Frontier?"

"In the Frontier," Meader confirmed, nodding his head.

Vyx took another drink. "Okay, five hundred if they're still there. If they're gone, I'll be back to collect my money."

"All but fifty," Meader said.

"All but fifty if I can confirm they were there six months ago."

"My buddy says that last part won't be a problem."

Vyx dug into his pocket and produced five one-hundred-credit notes. He extended them to Meader, but didn't let go when Meader tried to take them. "I want everything you know. There won't be any more credits for additional information."

"You get everything I know."

Vyx let go and the five bills disappeared beneath the table. "We're listening."

"Okay, here it is. My buddy is a prospector, see? He was doing a little looking around on the second planet in the Elurra System. Said the place is hot as blazes. Anyway, these two Milori destroyers show up. His small ship was hidden pretty well so he hung around for a couple of days to see what was going on. He couldn't believe it when he saw the Milori start laying out a base on the planet. He decided to get out of there before they spotted him, so he jumped on his dune donkey and zipped back to his ship. Milori have a reputation for shooting first and questioning later."

"A base?"

"Yeah. They were bringing building materials down from the ships by the kiloton the whole time my buddy watched. When they started to erect buildings, he jumped on his dune donkey and got out of there. The Milori aren't the friendliest species we've met and my buddy figured they might not want anyone knowing they were building a major military base in the GA's Frontier Zone. He said he hugged the surface until he was on the opposite side of the planet before lifting off."

"Your buddy is smart."

"Dumb prospectors disappear quickly in the Frontier and are never seen again."

"You're sure it was in the Elurra System?"

"Yeah, that's what he said. The Elurra System."

"Okay, Meader. See you around."

"Uh, what is it you hope to trade to the Milori, Trader?"

"Milori? Who said anything about Milori?"

Meader looked at Vyx stupidly for several seconds before he understood. "Not me. I don't know anything about any Milori."

Vyx nodded and he stood up to leave. As Byers stood also, Vyx turned to Meader again and bent over. In a low voice, he said, "Your friend is smart. You be real smart too, and don't mention that planet to anyone. If the Milori hear you're talking about it, your life might not be worth a credit."

Meader looked at Vyx for a couple of seconds, nodded, and took a long drink from his glass.

The others weren't back yet when Vyx and Byers returned to the *Scorpion* so they did the preflight check on the ship and then relaxed in the lounge.

"What do you think?" Byers asked. "Was he telling the truth?"

"I think so. He knows that if I find out he lied, I'll be coming after him. I've worked hard to establish that part of my reputation. Everyone believes that if they cross me, they'll see me again, and it won't be pleasant. I'm considered to be a real bad-ass when crossed."

"Why would the Milori be constructing a military base in Galactic Alliance territory?"

"Don't know. Perhaps they found some rare mineral and are setting up a base to protect a mining operation."

"They're a long way from home."

"You mine ore where you find it," Vyx said offhandedly. "It's possible they're long gone already, or will be by the time we get there."

"You think we should go to the Elurra system? That's another hundred light-years into the Frontier. We're already a hundred twenty light-years from the inner border."

"I think it's important that we go see what's up, but the decision will be up to Captain Crosby, or perhaps Captain Carver. If we have to travel there in the *Scorpion*, it'll take at least a year for the round trip. In the *Ottawa*, it will only take eight to nine months."

"It would be a lot more comfortable in the *Ottawa*. The *Scorpion* only has four beds."

"If the *Scorpion* goes alone, the girls don't go with us. I'm sure Space Command has better stuff for them to do than take a year-long ride with nothing to do. SCI may not even want you and Nels to go. The *Ottawa* could drop you off near Scruscotto so you could get yourself settled in."

"Trying to get rid of us?" Byers asked good-naturedly.

"Not at all. I'm just weighing all the options and trying to predict what Space Command will choose to do. Personally, I've grown sort of used to having partners along."

"I have to admit that I've enjoyed our time together a lot more than any of the assignments I've had in years. I'm really going to miss the girls when they go. It's sort of been like having a family. They're like the daughters I never had."

"Don't get all maudlin yet. If the *Ottawa* receives orders to go to Elurra, we'll be together for a while yet."

"Yeah, you're right. How about something to eat? I could whip up some snacks."

"Sure. I could go for some more ale also."


Nelligen and the women didn't return for several more hours, and by then Byers and Vyx had fallen asleep in the lounge. They awoke as soon as the airlock began cycling and were waiting by the airlock with pistols drawn when Kathleen stepped out.

"Just me guys. Brenda and Nels are with me."

Vyx and Byers holstered their weapons. One never knew who would try to board one's ship when parked on a mining planet.

"I'm glad you're back," Vyx said as soon as everyone was seated in the lounge. "What did you learn?"

"It was the same story everywhere we went," Nels said. "Everyone has either seen or heard about Milori on the colony, but no one has seen them for six months. Nobody had a clue where they went, but a couple of people said they were last seen with some Tsgardi."

"Yeah, we got the same story," Byers said, "except Vyx met someone he knew and we bought some information. Five hundred credit's worth."

"Five hundred credits!" Brenda exclaimed. "Did it come with a map to a lost platinum mine?"

"Not a platinum mine, but it might be almost as valuable. A prospector friend of my contact was scared off a planet in the Elurra system when two Milori destroyers arrived and started constructing a major military base on the surface."

"Scared off?" Kathleen asked.

"My contact said the prospector figured the neighborhood had suddenly become a bit unhealthy. He didn't actually have any contact with the Milori."

"So what now?" Nels asked.

"We've already performed a preflight of the ship and we were only waiting for you to return. Let's head back to the *Ottawa* and turn the problem over to the brass hats. Okay?"

Vyx glanced at each agent and received a nod of agreement. He stood and walked to the cockpit. Brenda followed him there and sat in the copilot seat as he readied the ship for liftoff. An hour later they were away from the planet and headed for the *Ottawa*. At Light-187, they would dock with the ship in less than twenty minutes.

Once aboard the *Ottawa*, Vyx walked to the bridge and requested an immediate audience with the captain. The XO informed him that the captain had retired for the night and asked if the matter warranted waking him. Vyx answered that he considered the matter to be of vital importance, so the First Officer made the decision to call the captain. A sleepy voice responded to the hail.

"Captain, Trader Vyx has returned and requested an immediate audience. He says his information is vital."

The first officer listened to his CT for a few seconds, then signed off and said to Vyx, "The captain will see you in the office in his quarters."

"Thanks, Commander."

When Vyx reached the captain's quarters, the Marine sentry admitted him immediately. Captain Crosby, in his robe, was waiting in his office. "Come in, Vyx. I understand you have information that can't wait until morning?"

"I felt you should hear it right away and decide its importance. It might be very time sensitive."

"Very well; tell me what you've learned."

Vyx filled the Captain in on the events that had transpired since they left the ship and the information he had secured from Meader.

"And you believe this Meader?" Captain Crosby asked.

"I believe that he believes it. He didn't see the Milori personally, but if the prospector was being truthful, this might be very important. I've never heard of Milori warships entering Alliance space before."

"Nor have I," Captain Crosby admitted. "Very well, I'll compose a message and send it off to Stewart immediately. Is there anything else?"

"No, that's all of it, Captain."

"Then, goodnight, Trader," the captain said in a dismissive voice.

"Goodnight, Captain."


A response from Stewart took almost four days, not because Captain Carver was indecisive or needed to consult with Supreme Headquarters on Earth, but simply because of the distance. Stewart was a hundred thirty-six light-years away, and it took ninety-one hours for the messages to travel round trip.

Captain Crosby was just getting ready for bed when the Priority-One message arrived. He had it routed through to his office and sat down at his desk to view it. The image of

Captain Carver appeared on his com unit's screen as soon as he had lifted the cover and pressed the play button.

"Hello, Jeff. I've dispatched a message to Supreme Headquarters advising them of a potential hostile incursion by Milori warships into Galactic Alliance space. Should Space Command Supreme Headquarters feel differently, they'll no doubt issue a recall, but since it will take a couple of weeks to receive a reply, it would be advantageous to have you already under way. Please proceed at top speed directly to the Elurra system with the stated objective being an investigation of the reported incursion. Since the Milori will outnumber you, if the report is accurate, please exercise extreme caution. Good luck.

"Jenetta A. Carver, Captain, Base Commander, Stewart Space Command Base, message complete."

Captain Crosby contacted his Second Officer, who was the current watch commander, and instructed him to make for the Elurra system at top speed. The navigator had prepared the course several days ago on Crosby's instruction. Then Crosby sent an acknowledgement to Jenetta. With sleep tugging at his brain, he pushed the top of his com unit down and walked back into his bedroom. He hoped that thoughts of an encounter with hostile forces didn't keep him awake all night.

Crosby received confirming orders from Supreme Headquarters to investigate the situation in the Elurra system several weeks later. By then the *Ottawa* was more than fifteen light-years closer to the Elurra system than they had been when Crosby had received the orders from Captain Carver.

Vyx and Brenda had lots of time to spend together aboard the *Ottawa* because, as passengers, they had no duties. They passed their days working out in the gym, running on the track set up in a cargo bay, or simply reading as they lay together in the cozy area Vyx had prepared in the *Scorpion's* hold. Their retreat inside the small ship gave them the ultimate in privacy for whatever activity in which they chose to engage.

Byers and Nelligen spent their days playing cards in one or the other's assigned quarters, while Kathleen spent her time with one of the numerous admirers who happened to be off duty when she was in the mood for companionship. All five agents usually came together for their evening meal.

One hundred twenty-nine days after beginning their trek to the Elurra system, the *Ottawa* was nearing its destination. The ship's sensors had detected numerous other ships during their journey, but their mission parameters didn't allow them to deviate for any side trips to investigate. For all they knew, the other ships might have been the Milori warships they were seeking, but their orders were to proceed directly to the Elurra system.

Captain Crosby was on the bridge as they approached the solar system, although it was the second watch and the first officer had the bridge. As Commander Upton, occupying the First Officer's chair, ordered the ship slowed, Crobsy watched the front monitor from the command chair.

"Tactical, any signs of ships in this system?" Commander Upton asked.

"Nothing's under power, Commander. We'll have to get in closer for the sensors to pick up ships that might be in orbit around the planets."

"Commander," the com operator said, "I'm picking up com traffic. It appears to be coming from the second planet."

"Tactical, concentrate on the second planet. Helm, take us in. Light-37."

Both crewmen said, "Aye, sir."

A few minutes later the officer at the tactical station said, "I'm picking up the presence of multiple ships in orbit around the second planet. They match the configuration of Milori warships, according to the computer."

"How many ships, Commander?"

"I've identified eight so far— six destroyers and two cruisers."

Commander Upton and Captain Crosby exchanged glances.

"Sir, we're being hailed by one of the ships."

"By name?" Upton asked.

"No, sir. They're addressing us as 'the ship that has just entered the Elurra system.' The message is in Weutrak, the principal language used by the Milori."

"Tactical," Captain Crosby said, "how many ships have you identified in orbit now?"

"There are sixteen ships in orbit— eleven destroyers and five cruisers."

"Is that all?" Commander Upton asked.

"Affirmative, sir. That's all the ships in orbit around the second planet. And I'm not picking up any sign of others in the system."

"Helm, all stop. Leave our temporal envelope intact."

"I'll take the bridge, XO," Captain Crosby said. "Com, answer the hail and put it up on the main screen."

The image of a Milora appeared on the screen. Remembering the unique communication system used by the Milori, Captain Crosby said nothing. He simply stared at the Milora.

After several seconds the Milora said, "I'm Lord High Space Marshall Gulqulk of the emperor's Imperial Cruiser *Reguffa*."

"I'm Captain Crosby of the Galactic Alliance Space Command Destroyer *Ottawa*."

There was silence for several seconds as each officer sized up the other.

"Your ship is trespassing in Milori space," the Milora said. "I demand that you leave immediately."

"Actually, the reverse is true, Lord High Space Marshall. This system is part of the Galactic Alliance Frontier Zone. You're approximately a hundred light-years inside our border. You are the one who's trespassing."

"The Milori Empire doesn't recognize your claim to this part of space. You don't patrol it and you don't enforce your laws here. Therefore, your claim is invalid. The Empire has officially annexed this space."

"Really? Just when did this annexation occur?"

"The proclamation was made eleven of your Earth months ago."

"I'm afraid you were too late. The Galactic Alliance laid claim to this part of space more than four Earth years ago."

"Your claim was invalidated when we proclaimed ownership. Leave now and we won't destroy you. And don't stop before you're across the Milori border."

"The Milori border?" Captain Crosby said.

"We claim all space up to the border with what you call your 'regulated' GA space. Immediately pull all your ships out of Milori space or we shall be forced to destroy them."

"Are you declaring war on the Galactic Alliance?" Captain Crosby asked.

His question went unanswered as the screen suddenly went blank.

"I guess the discussion is over," Captain Crosby said. "I guess I was asking more questions than giving answers."

"The signal was terminated at the source, Captain," the com operator stated.

"Captain," the Lt. Commander at the tactical station shouted nervously, "sensors show that six of the ships have started to move." A couple of seconds later, he added, "Now eight are moving, sir."

"Helm," Captain Crosby said calmly "get us out of here. Top speed. Take us back towards Stewart."

"Aye, Captain."

"We're running away, sir?" Commander Upton inquired calmly.

"Shakespeare wrote, 'The better part of valor is discretion.' I don't think it wise that we remain and take on this entire Milori taskforce by ourselves. My first responsibility is to apprise Space Command of this situation." Captain Crosby stood up. "Tactical, are those ships still following?"

"Aye, Captain. I picked up thirteen ships maneuvering to leave orbit before we were out of range."

"How many actually followed us?"

"Unknown, Captain. They fell into line behind one another. I can only see one ship on our sensors. They're emitting a signal that's confusing the DeTect system. It can only see a long blur behind that first ship."

"That's one of the Milori tricks," the captain said to his first officer. "When in pursuit they travel in a straight line so the quarry is never sure how many ships are still engaged and they emit electromagnetic signals that blur the DeTect beams. It might be all sixteen or just one. Let's think of it as sixteen and keep plenty of distance between us, Commander."

"Aye, Captain. I'll keep our speed at one hundred percent."

"Carry on, Commander," Captain Crosby said as he strode towards his briefing room.

News of the confrontation with the Milori spread rapidly throughout the ship. When Vyx learned of it, he hurried to visit Captain Crosby.

"Come in, Trader," the Captain said from behind his desk in his briefing room.

Vyx walked over and, without an invitation to sit, plopped into a chair. "I understand we ran into an overwhelming force of Milori ships?"

Captain Crosby nodded. "Eleven destroyers and five cruisers. I guess that qualifies as overwhelming."

"And they're behind us now?"

"As far as we know; I think it better we not stop to count noses."

"A wise decision, Captain," Vyx said, grinning. "But as long as they're on our six, we can't stop and investigate any other situations."

"That might be the intent. The Milori commander has ordered us out of the Frontier Zone. The ship or ships on our six might just be a sort of escort. Perhaps they don't intend to engage us as long as we keep moving at top speed. They haven't tried to close the gap, but we're not outdistancing them either. Our database doesn't include any information on the speed capability of Milori ships."

"We've had very little contact with them before now. Our translator capability came from the Wolkerrons, or we wouldn't even be able to speak to them."

"We'll just keep heading for Stewart at top speed until we either reach the border or the Milori drop off our six. Just relax and enjoy the trip, Trader."

# Chapter Fourteen
~ June 10<sup>th</sup>, 2276 ~

Jenetta was just sitting down to dinner when she received notification via her CT that a Priority-One, Stage-One Emergency message was waiting for her. The status meant that she could only listen to it in a secure area, so she jumped up from the table and hurried to her office, leaving her mess attendant to stare after her in open-mouthed astonishment.

The message from Captain Crosby began to play as soon as she had completed the required retinal scan identification procedure.

"Jen, we've really stirred up a hornet's nest out here. We found eleven Milori destroyers and five cruisers in orbit around the second planet of the Elurra system. As soon as we arrived, they hailed us, told us we were trespassing, and ordered us out of *their* space. They're claiming all territory outside regulated GA space— in other words, our entire Frontier zone. Right now we're headed back towards Stewart at maximum speed with anywhere from one to sixteen warships on our six. We can't determine the number because the Milori pursue in a straight line to confuse their quarry. We know that at least thirteen ships were preparing to leave orbit when the chase began.

"From what I understand of Milori tactics, they'll pursue us right up to the border and perhaps beyond. I'm just hoping they don't have any ships positioned ahead of us to cut us off. We're prepared to deactivate our ACS system immediately if they attempt to stop us by cutting across our bow. I've sent a report to Supreme Headquarters and I included a copy of the bridge video log. I'm appending a copy to this message as well. I'll be grateful for any assistance you can provide.

"Jeffrey Crosby, Captain of the GSC Destroyer *Ottawa*, message complete."

Jenetta played the attached video log showing the communication with the Milori commander. There was no doubt in Jenetta's mind that the Milori were committing open acts of aggression against the Galactic Alliance by declaring their ownership of Galactic Alliance territory and hostile pursuit of a Space Command ship. She sat up straight in her chair and depressed the record button on her com unit.

"Priority One Message from Captain Jenetta A. Carver to the captains of all GSC ships in the sectors around Stewart Space Command Base.

"Captain, at this moment a fleet of Milori warships is pursuing the GSC Destroyer *Ottawa* inside the Frontier Zone. The *Ottawa* is racing towards Stewart with what we believe to be as many as sixteen destroyers and cruisers on their six. From statements made by the Milori commander to Captain Crosby, I'm assuming that the intentions of the Milori are hostile. Treat any contact you have with Milori warships with the utmost caution. We must be prepared to meet this threat when it arrives. On my authority, I'm ordering the immediate return of all ships to Stewart SCB. Please keep the contents of this message secure until we verify the intentions of the Milori.

"Jenetta A. Carver, Captain, Base Commander, Stewart Space Command Base, message complete."

The Priority-One status would ensure that the captain was notified immediately, regardless of how he or she might otherwise be occupied. Jenetta also marked the message as a Stage-One Emergency notice. Calling up a map of the sub-sector containing the Elurra system, she studied it for a few minutes before composing a message to Space Command Supreme Headquarters. Her second message about the Milori was an assessment of the situation and notification that she was recalling all ships on patrol. By issuing the recall, she was overriding the individual patrol orders issued by Supreme HQ to each ship's captain, so it was important they knew of her action.

After sending off the message, she returned to her dining room to continue her dinner. Nothing more than what she had done was required or necessary at this time.

As she sat down at the table, the mess attendant hurried over with a fresh salad. She knew things had been going too well lately. She'd had a wonderful month with Hugh, followed by several months of relative calm. The terrorist activity on Arrosa had stopped, the delegates from Selax and Arrosa were actually being cordial to one another, and the document work for the hearing was almost complete. The JAG section had compiled a very short list of Arrosian documents that actually had any bearing on the case, and, best of all, a convoy of ships, one of them containing the new diplomatic corps for this sector, was set to arrive in a few weeks. Jenetta would still have to complete her duties as arbiter, but the diplomats would be there to help smooth the waters afterward.

The ships on patrol began to report in the following day that they had altered course for Stewart as soon as they received the message from Jenetta. The Command Center, knowing their location, speed, and destination, began tracking their progress. If a situation developed, Jenetta could divert them, but all ships were expected to be back at Stewart within a hundred eighty days. Traveling at maximum speed, the *Ottawa* wouldn't cross the border from the Frontier Zone for two hundred seventy-eight days.

Once an enemy commenced hostilities, it wasn't unusual to find military personnel waiting for a battle to commence, but nine months of waiting was a bit outside the norm. Still, there was little for Jenetta to do except plan and wait, and handle her normal duties. Three weeks after receiving the initial message from the *Ottawa*, Jenetta received a message from Admiral Richard E. Moore, Admiral of the Fleet, Space Command Supreme Headquarters. Jenetta completed the retinal scan and sat back to watch the message.

"Hello Captain Carver," the image of Admiral Moore said. "I've been following your career closely since I presented you with the MOH almost eight years ago. Your performance and dedication have always been of the highest caliber, and I'm proud to list you among my top officers.

"We've studied the vid log sent by Captain Crosby and we're in agreement with your assessment that the Milori pose an imminent threat to the sovereignty and security of Galactic Alliance territory. We've issued a general alert, and all warships within twelve month's travel time are under orders to proceed to Stewart at top speed. The *Prometheus* should be home shortly, and we expect that at least five additional warships previously reassigned to Stewart will arrive in time to join the ten currently based there with sufficient time to meet the Milori threat.

"An additional nineteen warships are now underway, including three Nordakian cruisers, but they aren't expected to arrive before the Milori reach the Frontier Zone border. The latter ships can, however, serve as a replacement force for lost ships should the Milori really choose to engage our forces.

"I won't minimize the danger you're facing. The Milori are a warrior race that prides itself on its battle readiness and capability. They are a far more dangerous foe than the Raiders or Tsgardi you've faced in the past, but with a fourteen-ship taskforce, increased by one when the *Ottawa* arrives, we feel the forces will be evenly matched. They'll have one more ship, but we'll have four battleships aligned against their destroyers and cruisers.

"As you're well aware, your post is normally held by a Rear Admiral, Upper Half. Despite your lower rank, we knew you were well suited to handle the job of establishing a new base, but we never anticipated you'd have to face such a threat as we now expect. A StratCom-One base commander is responsible for all military activity in the sectors where the base is located and is therefore in command of any assembled taskforce. But the Admiralty Board feels that more senior captains might have reservations about following the orders of a captain with much less time in grade— at least in a situation where the battle takes place well away from the base.

"A number of alternatives have been discussed, including the temporary reassignment of one of the more senior captains to base commander for the duration of the threat, but we were quickly reminded by Admiral Holt, who happens to be at Supreme Headquarters for a series of meetings, that we did that once before, and that we later regretted our hasty action. We promised ourselves never to embarrass you like that again.

"We've also discussed the appointment of one of the senior captains to the rank of Rear Admiral, Lower Half, but we know none of them wish to give up their ship, and the situation would mandate that they surrender ship command and accept a base posting at the end of the conflict.

"Our dilemma was resolved when Admiral Burke recalled that we still have a regulation on the books that allows for brevet rank, although we've never employed it. The military history of brevet appointments goes back many centuries, and the precise definition has varied considerably in the militaries of different Terran nations. Generally, it was of very limited duration and carried with it no increase in pay or privileges. Although its use has greatly diminished since Earth's World War I, Space Command regulations still allow for the temporary promotion of any officer holding a command position consistent with, or greater than, the duties and responsibilities of the higher rank, such as when a senior officer is incapacitated and a lower-ranking officer must permanently assume responsibility for the command. Space Command regulations provide that a corresponding increase in pay and privileges must be included for the duration of the appointment.

"Congratulations, Admiral Carver. Your brevet appointment was approved today by act of the Admiralty Board."

Jenetta's jaw dropped and her eyes grew wide. From the statements at the beginning of the message, she expected notification that someone would be assuming her role as Supreme Military Commander at Stewart. She expected Admiral Moore to announce he was brevetting one of the senior captains to admiral, temporarily, so he or she could revert to their former position after the conflict was over and retain command of their ship. But since the rank of captain was normally the most that any senior officer aboard a ship could attain, and since the Admiralty Board obviously didn't want to first appoint one of the captains to the position of base commander, replacing Jenetta, the ship captains weren't eligible for a brevet promotion.

"You'll retain your new rank for the remainder of your tour at Stewart. Until returned to your former rank, you're a fully authorized flag officer, one of just two hundred eighteen such authorized flag positions in Space Command.

"I have every confidence that you'll lead your taskforce to victory over the Milori. Good luck, Admiral."

"Richard E. Moore, Admiral of the Fleet, Space Command Supreme Headquarters, Earth, message complete."

Jenetta just sat in her chair staring at the Space Command logo on the com unit's vid screen. She didn't know whether to scream or cry. If the promotion were anything other than temporary, she'd already be transmitting a message in which she refused to accept it. A promotion had taken her from a posting she loved once before, and she didn't intend to spend the rest of her career behind a desk, a fate that all admirals in Space Command shared. But the more she thought about it, the more she realized it was an opportunity to get off the base for a while. The leader of a taskforce normally led from a ship, and as an admiral, she was empowered to appoint someone to replace her on the base for the duration of the conflict. She could even select which ship would serve as her flagship. It wouldn't be so bad after all, as long as the rank was only temporary.

She was still thinking about the possibilities when Lt. Commander Ashraf announced the delivery of a package to the outer office.

"What sort of package, Lori?" Jenetta asked.

"It's from central stores, but it's addressed to Admiral Jenetta A. Carver, Base Commander."

"Bring it in, Lori."

Lt. Commander Ashraf watched a minute later as Jenetta opened the small package, looked inside, and then dumped the contents onto her desk. A small pile of rank insignias bearing a single star for Admiral, Lower Half, skidded across the smooth surface.

"Have you been promoted, ma'am?" Lt. Commander Ashraf asked.

"Yes, Lori. It's just a brevet promotion for the remainder of my tour here. Either Admiral Moore or Admiral Burke must have arranged for this delivery. I just learned about it in the message from Admiral Moore."

"Then allow me to be the first to congratulate you in person, Admiral," Lt. Commander Ashraf said with a salute and a wide smile.

"Thank you, Lori." Jenetta said, smiling. "This promotion means I'll be going aboard a ship when the Milori approach. I'll have to find someone to take over in my absence. You'll need a replacement also if you wish to accompany me."

"Yes, ma'am. I absolutely do wish to accompany the Admiral."

"Okay, Lori. Prepare a list of candidates you feel would be best qualified to handle your duties in your absence. I'll interview them and make a decision."

"Yes, ma'am," Lt. Commander Ashraf said, still grinning.

Jenetta procrastinated for hours before sending messages to her family about the promotion. She didn't even change the insignia on her uniform until she returned to her quarters following dinner. By then, word had spread throughout the station. The clerk who'd filled the order for the insignia and forwarded the package had most likely told a few other crewmen, and that was all it took for the grapevine to swing into full operation.

She delayed the messages still longer by taking the time to change the rank insignia on the rest of her uniforms. She finally walked to the office that was a part of her suite. Sitting at her desk, she tapped the record button on the com unit.

"Message to Captain Quinton E. Carver, GSC Cruiser *Octavian* from Admiral Jenetta A. Carver, Stewart SC Base. Begin message.

"Hi, Dad. I wanted to tell you about my promotion before you heard about it from one of your buddies at Supreme Headquarters. I hope I'm not too late. Since you're way over on the other side of galactic space but still much closer to Earth than I, you may have heard already.

"I can picture you getting upset because you think I'll be stuck behind a desk now, but that's not the case. The rank is only temporary, so I guess I'll be credited with another first. I'm the first brevetted admiral in the history of Space Command, but I'll only retain the rank until the end of my tour at Stewart.

"The reason for the promotion is out of necessity, according to Admiral Moore. We know that an enemy force consisting of as many as sixteen Milori warships is headed this way. They've proclaimed ownership of our Frontier Zone and are currently pursuing the *Ottawa* after having ordered all Space Command vessels to leave or be destroyed. As base commander of Stewart, I'd naturally be in command of the taskforce preparing to meet the approaching Milori taskforce, but Supreme Headquarters feels that the captains may feel awkward taking orders from another captain with less time in grade during an engagement that occurs away from the station. By promoting me, Supreme HQ feels that the chain of command is more firmly established.

"Ships as far away as Dixon are being diverted to support the upcoming operation, so it may even have a ripple effect in your area. I'll continue to send weekly messages for as long as I can, but once we leave Stewart, outgoing com traffic will be limited to official communications only until after the operation is over.

"I love you, Dad.

"Jenetta A. Carver, Rear Admiral, Lower Half, Stewart SC Base Commander, message complete."

Jenetta then recorded a message to her mother but left out any mention of the upcoming operation. Instead, she talked about the things they were discussing in their regular weekly messages to each other after giving her the news of the promotion.

She also sent messages to her brothers and sisters. Since they were all in Space Command and three of them would actually participate in the operation, those messages were similar to the one that went to her dad. Lastly, she sent messages to her sisters-in-law so they wouldn't feel slighted, even though she knew her mom would be sending messages to everyone.

She felt better after sending the messages. Her oldest brother, Billy, still a commander and First Officer aboard the St. Petersburg, might experience some mixed emotions. On the one hand, he would be happy for his baby sister, but on the other, he might feel some jealousy since he was seven years older. Her three other brothers might also experience mixed feelings, but she knew her sisters would only be happy for her.

Jenetta's morning walk to her office always drew stares. But on this first morning after her promotion, passersby were staring at the shiny gold star on each shoulder that replaced her normal four gold bars.

The troop transport ship ferrying the diplomatic corps arrived a couple of days later with two quartermaster supply ships. But most importantly, the GSC battleship *Prometheus* was acting as escort to the convoy. Jenetta planned to visit the *Prometheus* as soon as possible, but a series of scheduled meetings prevented her from getting away. She was preparing to leave for the ship when Lt. Commander Ashraf messaged her.

"Admiral, the Captain of the *Prometheus* is here. He requests a few minutes of your time."

"Send him in, Lori."

Jenetta stood up as Captain Gavin strode into the office and came to attention in front of Jenetta's desk. He saluted as he said, "Captain Lawrence Gavin reporting to the Admiral."

Jenetta smiled and returned his salute. "Welcome back, Captain. It's wonderful to see you again."

Gavin let his smile break through the serious expression he had been able to maintain until then. "It's good to see you also, Admiral."

"Jen, please, Captain."

"Okay, but only if you'll call me Larry."

"Deal. Care for some coffee, Larry?" Jenetta asked, motioning towards the beverage synthesizer."

"I could use a cup." Gavin walked over and prepared a mug of coffee. "Anything for you, Jen?"

"Thanks, I'm set," she said as she sat back down behind her desk and picked up her coffee mug to take a sip.

Gavin came over with his prepared coffee and sat in one of the large, comfortable 'oh-gee' chairs that faced her desk. Getting comfortable, he said, "It seems to me that you were just a Commander when I left here."

Jenetta nodded and smiled. "You've been gone a long time."

"Only thirty-one months. We expected to be back in twenty, but protection of the diplomatic corps transport and two supply ships altered that. Our return trip took twice as long because of those damn supply ships. Their top speed is only Light-187. I'm sorry we weren't here for your fight with the Raiders."

"We could have used your firepower, but everything worked out."

"I read the report issued by Supreme Headquarters. Congratulations. You did a fantastic job, Jen."

"Thank you. We were only facing an undisciplined collection of thieves, murderers, and smugglers. Nothing like the enemy that's getting closer with each passing minute."

He nodded. "Yes, I wish we knew more about the Milori."

"I've studied everything I could get my hands on. One of our intelligence operatives had some interesting information about them, and Jeff Crosby filed a report about his interrogation of the three Milori he has in custody."

"How did he take Milori into custody? My briefing message from Supreme Headquarters indicated that the *Ottawa* was forced to run for it when the Milori started to maneuver their ships to leave orbit."

"Crosby's Milori were picked up three months earlier, floating in Tsgardi escape pods after our intelligence agent was forced to destroy the ship on which the Milori were passengers. The Tsgardi attacked his small ship as he left our new outpost in the Frontier Zone and he had no choice. But the presence of Milori in our territory made Jeff Crosby curious. When our agent reported seeing Milori on the Scruscotto colony a year earlier, Jeff requested a deviation from his patrol route to check out reports of Milori on Bajurrsko. I approved it, naturally. After arriving at the colony, our agent learned from a prospector that the Milori were constructing a military base in the Elurra system. I then ordered the *Ottawa* to proceed to the system and further investigate the lead. So, Jeff still has the three Milori in his brig, and it appears that they've become prisoners of war now."

"Have you prepared a plan for greeting the arriving Milori?"

"I have a few ideas for a warm welcome. The assembled taskforce will be comprised of fourteen ships. We'll have a meeting of all captains as soon as everyone is here. Anybody who's late will have to catch up. We can pinpoint exactly when and where the *Ottawa* will arrive with the Milori in hot pursuit and we have to be in position."

"Are you still expecting sixteen Milori ships, Jen?"

"We haven't received any news to the contrary, but it's possible some may have dropped out. We can really only be certain of one."

"I don't understand the Milori. They haven't even conquered the five hundred light-years of territory between our outer border and their previously declared outer border. Why would they attempt to expand their border by over eight hundred light-years when they know it means war?"

"Perhaps they're just trying to ensure that the Galactic Alliance doesn't expand any further. By claiming our Frontier Zone, they establish a new outer border for both themselves and us."

"They have to know we can't let this challenge stand. And I would have expected them to attack with hundreds of ships, not a handful."

"We might have surprised them by learning about their base in the Elurra system so early. The ships there might only have been an advance guard, assigned the job of setting up bases for the re-supply of their forces once their operation begins. We have to consider that additional ships may already be on the way from their home world."

"Then it's doubly important we meet this threat now and chase them out of our territory before they can marshal all their forces. Have you decided on a flagship yet, Jen?"

"I thought the *Prometheus* might serve that purpose, unless you have any reservations?"

"None at all; I was going to suggest it myself. It will be great having you aboard again."

"I'm really looking forward to it."

"Is there anything I can do to prepare for your reception?"

"Not just yet, except to have your gunners get as much simulator time as possible. We still have months before the Milori arrive, but we want everyone as sharp as possible."

"I've already had my First Officer step up the training time."

"Who's your First now?"

"Commander Eaton. Tim moved up from Second Officer after you became a captain. Space Command knew you wouldn't be coming back as my first officer, but I never expected to have you aboard as Admiral Carver."

"If it wasn't a brevet promotion, you wouldn't," Jenetta said, smiling. "The chore only fell on my shoulders because none of the captains wanted to give up their ships."

A strange expression came over Captain Gavin's face.

"What?" Jenetta asked. "What is it?"

"Is that what Supreme Headquarters told you?"

"Yes. Admiral Moore told me himself."

"Then it's not my place to contradict the Admiral of the Fleet."

Jenetta grimaced. "Come on, Larry. We've known each other for a long time. I've always felt that we were friends, at least as much as possible within the command structure."

Captain Gavin was silent for a full minute as he sipped his coffee and stared into the mug. "I've always felt that way as well." He took another sip and looked up. "Okay. I happen to know that Bill Payton of the *Thor* or Andy Novak of the *Asuncion* would give up their ship in a heartbeat for a star."

It was Jenetta's turn to be silent for a minute. "Do you think they'll resent my being promoted?" she finally asked.

"Human nature being what it is, I'd think there might be some small resentment, but I'd expect it to be directed towards Headquarters rather than towards you. They both know of your intense desire to be back aboard ship. They certainly won't think you've been playing politics to get the promotion."

"Do you think it will inhibit their performance in the upcoming battle? Will they follow my orders?"

"No, and yes. They're both excellent officers and they won't let their personal feelings get in the way of their duty. And if either does harbor any slight resentment towards you, I'm sure they wouldn't be the first. You've climbed through the ranks faster than anyone in the history of Space Command, Jen. You're what, forty-one now?"

Jenetta nodded. "I reached forty-one in May."

"No one has ever received their flag in Space Command before reaching their fifty-sixth birthday. Discounting your time in stasis, you're really only thirty, and you still look twenty. That's bound to create a certain amount of envy. But the measure of an officer is how well they keep personal feelings hidden and how well they keep them from affecting their performance."

"How about you, Larry? You're the senior captain among our forces. You should have received this promotion."

"I don't have any envy of your promotion, Jen. I've twice refused to give up my ship to accept flag rank. Until the border expansion, I was afraid I would only have a few more years left as a ship's captain. I'd assumed that I'd then either take a flag promotion or retire. But with the GSC rolling out the mandatory retirement age to eighty-five, I have another twenty-one years in space. I intend to remain as a ship's captain for every minute of it, and I couldn't be happier."

Jenetta grinned. "I know how you feel. My only excitement from the promotion came when I realized I'd be able to get off this base and back into space— for a while at least."

"I'm afraid you have the same sickness that infects most of the ship's officers and crews in Space Command. We're just never happy on a base or space station. But stick us inside a metal cylinder hurling through space faster than the speed of light and we're in our glory."

Jenetta couldn't help but laugh. "True, but I'd hardly call the *Prometheus* a 'metal cylinder.'"

"It's not inaccurate," Gavin said, chuckling, "when consid-ered in its simplest form, but it is a rather undignified way to talk about such an elegant ship. I'm glad he can't hear me."

"Larry," Jenetta said, getting serious, "if Space Command has two qualified officers out here who would eagerly accept a promotion to admiral, why do you think they pushed this promotion onto me?"

"I don't know for sure, but I can think of two logical reasons," Gavin said. "If they promoted Bill or Andy, the new admiral would be expected to assume command of Stewart immediately because once they had an admiral out here, they couldn't very well leave a captain in command of a StratCom-One base."

"That would have been perfect. I could have assumed the promoted officer's position aboard the ship until a permanent captain arrived in a couple of years."

"Yes, it could have worked out that way, but perhaps they really want *you* to remain in command here. You have a JAG section here. Is the top officer an admiral?"

"No."

"An admiral is always the top officer in a JAG unit on a major base such as Stewart. Only a JAG admiral can adjudi-cate certain types of cases."

"Or the base commander must assume that role."

"Exactly. And they haven't sent a JAG admiral here or appointed one from the JAG staff on the base because they couldn't have a flag officer reporting to a commissioned officer. The admiral would have to assume command of the base, *but* a JAG admiral *can't* be the officially designated commanding officer of a base, just as an admiral from the medical corps or the quartermaster corps can't be a designated base commander. A base commander, like a warship's captain, must come from the line officer ranks."

"So you think they've gone through all this to keep me on here as base commander?"

"They've had to deviate from the standardized base personnel configuration considerably to accommodate your remaining on as base commander while a captain."

"It makes sense." Jenetta sipped her coffee before adding. "I mean it makes sense as you describe the stratagem, not that it makes sense they want to keep me here."

"Didn't you tell me that Supreme Headquarters had wanted to keep you on Dixon for a full tour but that Admiral Holt managed to free you up?"

"Yes, I did."

"Well, perhaps they don't want to free you from here yet. You've done too good a job, Jen. They're bending over backwards to keep you here and in command for your entire tour of duty."

Jenetta sighed. "I've already resigned myself to remaining here for the entire five years. What's the other reason?"

"If anyone else was placed in command, there's no guarantee he'd follow your tactical suggestions in the upcoming fight. You have to admit that your tactics are always a bit— unique, and some officers have believed you to be a 'loose cannon' at times."

"Yes. After the Battle for Higgins, my dad told me that half the instructors at the War College felt that way."

Captain Gavin nodded. "The Admiralty Board obviously doesn't share that assessment. Brian Holt has told me you've impressed the hell out of them with your tactics. So they're showing unequivocally that they want Jenetta Carver leading this campaign, and they'll do whatever it takes to make that happen."

Brightening a little, she added, "Well, it will be great to be aboard the *Prometheus* for a while. It would almost be like a vacation if not for the Milori."

"Yes, that does dampen the mood a bit. If the Milori show up in force, I'm afraid that many of us may not be returning from this battle."

# Chapter Fifteen
~ July 16<sup>th</sup>, 2276 ~

With the Milori threat still seven months away and little to do in preparation for it this early, Jenetta turned most of her attention back to other base business. The Arrosian minister had begun to push for the hearing to continue, and the JAG section had completed the work with the submitted documents, so Jenetta sat down to review everything discovered to have a bearing on the case.

Far less than one percent of the material submitted by the Arrosians fell into that category, so it didn't take Jenetta long to complete her review. She then spent several days in virtual solitude while she reviewed the testimony and deliberated the case. Lt. Commander Ashraf refused all appointments except for the most urgent ones and carefully screened Jenetta's messages to keep her from being distracted while she wrote her decision. When she was done, she had the delegates notified that the hearing would continue the next day.

\* \* \*

The large conference room was SRO to hear the decision. Everyone immediately stood and remained standing until she had taken her place at the head of the horseshoe-shaped table. To begin the proceedings, Jenetta pounded her gavel twice. Glancing around the room, she saw a number of faces she didn't recognize. Jenetta's office had issued a number of press passes to journalists for the final session, but the new faces probably belonged to the recently arrived diplomats. Jenetta had reserved a block of passes for the new ambassador to distribute as he saw fit.

"The hearing to determine ownership of the moon known as Isodow, a natural satellite that circles the planet Selax in the Weitack system, is now reconvened. Both parties have agreed to binding arbitration. I, Admiral Jenetta Alicia

Carver, as the Supreme Military Commander of Space Command in this region, was accepted by both parties to perform as Arbiter. My decision will be final. There is no recourse for appeal.

"This hearing was begun many months ago, and each side was allowed ample time to present their case. In fact, I imposed no time limits and I hope both sides feel that they have had an opportunity to make their positions clear. During the past few months while the hearing was in recess, our JAG officers and personnel have meticulously examined every document submitted into evidence by both parties. I, personally, have read every translated document that the JAG office believes has a bearing on this case, and I've now reached my decision.

"One hundred eight years ago, by the Arrosian calendar, a civil war broke out between the Arrosians and the settlers on Selax. A bloody campaign ensued, and after years of fighting, both parties agreed to end hostilities. The Arrosian Dregma, the ruling council on Arrosa, formally proclaimed that Selax would receive its independence from the mother world. Representatives of both worlds worked tirelessly for more than a year to create a fair and equitable treaty. Elected representatives signed the document, and a long period of peace followed.

"The treaty very clearly spelled out the terms of the separation and Selaxian independence. However, no document can possibly address every single issue that might later arise. Isodow is such an issue. The treaty does not include it in the separation."

The delegates from Arrosa began to smile.

"But neither does it *exclude* it."

They stopped smiling.

"Neither in the formal treaty, nor in any of the documents submitted into evidence that represented the first ninety years of Selaxian independence, is the moon even mentioned. It was not until an Arrosian mining consortium began mining operations on Isodow that the issue arose. It is the position of Selax that the moon was not mentioned because they implicitly understood that it belonged to them, while Arrosa's position is that the moon was never ceded in the original treaty, nor in any subsequent treaties or negotiations, because they never intended to relinquish possession.

"I find merit in the positions of both parties. I cannot order the Arrosians to terminate their mining operations, but neither will I award the moon to Arrosa. When Arrosa gave independence to the people of Selax, there were half a dozen communications satellites in orbit around Selax. Arrosa placed them there when the planet was still a colony and never removed them. Ceded to Selax through default rather than formally in the treaty, it established a precedent that satellites are part of the property transferred to Selax. Isodow is nothing more than a very large, natural satellite. I rule that Isodow, and all satellites of Selax, are now and forevermore the property of the people and the planetary government of Selax.

"I further rule that Arrosa shall be permitted to continue its mining operations on Isodow without hindrance from the planetary government of Selax subject to the following conditions: 1) Arrosa's mining operations shall be limited to the immediate areas where they had already begun operations when this hearing began, 2) Their rights expire at each location once a year has passed without mining operations being conducted at said location, 3) They must negotiate to purchase, from the Selaxian planetary government, the soil and subsoil rights for any expansion of existing operations or any new areas they wish to mine, and, 4) The Selaxian government has the sole right to grant or withhold such rights, just as if the mining operation was taking place on Selax.

"I hope that both parties feel they've been treated fairly by this decision. This hearing is now concluded."

Jenetta pounded the gavel once, then stood as the chief delegates from both sides hurried towards her from opposite directions. The Selaxian delegate reached her first.

"Admiral, allow me to congratulate you on your recent promotion."

"Thank you, Mr. Chief Delegate."

"And let me also express once again how much we appreciate the key role that Space Command has played in resolving this dispute. We know how busy you are with other matters. The people of my planet will rejoice this day. The moon that we always knew was ours has been officially declared as such."

"I'm glad the matter was able to be resolved peacefully."

"As am I, Admiral," the minister from Arrosa said. He had reached her as Jenetta was speaking. "I applaud your decision. I know the mining consortium will be happy to learn that their mining rights have been guaranteed by Space Command."

"I'll be gratified if my decision helps keep the peace between your planets. You have so much in common that you should be close allies, both working to make better lives for your citizens. Until this matter arose, it appeared that you were well on your way to normal, friendly relations and extensive trade agreements."

"If Selax can rein in its radical element," the Arrosian minister said, "we can resume those relations."

"Selax has nothing to do with the terrorist activity on your planet," the Selaxian delegate argued. "Our intelligence services have not been able to find one single thread of evidence to support such a claim."

"Gentlemen," Jenetta said, "it's time to mend the small holes that have developed in the fabric of your relations. You should be working together to find the terrorists who perpetrated the dastardly acts of violence against Arrosa."

"Arrosa is determined to track them down, Admiral," the Arrosian minister said. "Eventually someone will foolishly want to talk or brag about their deeds, and we'll be there to arrest them."

"I hope so, Minister. Now, if you gentlemen will excuse me, I have to get back to the business of running this base."

"Thank you again, Admiral," the Selaxian delegate said.

"Our thanks also," the minister from Arrosa said, not to be outdone by the delegate from Selax. "Your involvement in this matter has been most appreciated. I hope the Arrosian government can someday repay your assistance."

Jenetta smiled and made her way through the group of Selaxian and Arrosian delegates that had assembled around her to listen. She shook all proffered hands and eventually made it clear of the group. Captain Donovan and Commander Blake were waiting to congratulate her.

"Wonderful verdict, Admiral," Captain Donovan said. "Both parties got what they wanted."

"Yes, the Selaxians got clear title to their moon and the Arrosians get to keep their present mining operations. I was afraid the Selaxians might try to demand part of the profits from the mining, but I think they're just satisfied that war seems to have been averted. And they have title to their moon."

"A decision worthy of King Solomon," Commander Blake said.

Jenetta smiled. "I'm sure Solomon would have discovered who was committing the acts of terrorism on Arrosa. With the decision rendered, we may never know."

"I don't know about that, Admiral," Captain Donovan said. "Those things have a way of leaking out eventually, even if it doesn't happen until someone seeks absolution on their death bed."

"Perhaps, Captain."

"Excuse me, Admiral," a voice said from behind Jenetta.

Jenetta turned around and found herself facing a distinguished-looking gentleman of about eighty years.

"I'm Ambassador DelCordia. I just wanted to introduce myself. I've tried calling on you at your office, but your aide said you couldn't be disturbed."

"How do you do, Mr. Ambassador? It's a pleasure to meet you. I'm sorry you were turned away, but I was working on this case and I told my aide not to disturb me unless it was an emergency."

"I quite understand, Admiral. I've spent the last several days watching the video transcript of this case. May I say that I think your solution to the problem is excellent? Further, both parties seem genuinely satisfied. I wish all disputes could be settled so elegantly."

"Thank you, Mr. Ambassador. Now that you're here to help us, I'm sure they will be."

"If you have some time in the next few days, Admiral, I'd like to introduce you to my staff before they begin leaving for their assignments."

"Yes, of course. But I'm afraid your staff will have to remain at Stewart for a while. I can't possibly spare any ships to take them to their assigned destinations." Lowering her voice, Jenetta said, "We're facing an imminent threat from the Milori Empire and all warships must remain at Stewart for the immediate future. All of this is confidential and I ask you not to repeat it lest the news create a panic. Additional ships have been dispatched to Stewart and should be available to deliver your people in about six to eight months."

"Six to eight months? I wasn't informed. What's the problem with the Milori? Is there anything my staff and I can do to help?"

"I'm afraid not, Mr. Ambassador. The Milori have issued a proclamation that our Frontier Zone is now part of their empire and have ordered us to withdraw all our ships immediately or face destruction. A force of warships has entered our territory and begun building support bases. The GAC has decided not to simply surrender the territory. I'm sure you'll receive official word very shortly. As to meeting your staff, how about tomorrow afternoon at two o'clock?"

"That will be fine. Should we come to your office?"

"My office is much too small to easily accommodate your staff. How about right here?"

"Excellent. Until tomorrow then?"

"Yes. Good day, Mr. Ambassador."

Jenetta smiled at Captain Donovan and Commander Blake, and then left the conference room. She probably had a hundred messages waiting for her since she hadn't responded to any over the past few days. Lori would have told her if any required her immediate attention.

Reporters, denied access to Jenetta while she was in the conference room, immediately surrounded her as she stepped outside. Remembering from an earlier time when she refused to comment that they would hound her until she gave in, she composed herself and smiled. Vid operators powered on their cameras and aimed them in her direction. Jenetta gave a short statement, repeating what she had said in the hearing. Following that, she answered questions, giving monosyllabic answers whenever she could. When the questions all started to sound like rephrased questions of ones already asked, she ended the interview and walked to her office. The thought running through her mind was that she should have brought her cats. They always had a rather calming effect on reporters— outwardly at least.

Jenetta spent all her work hours until her meeting with the diplomatic staff clearing up her messages. She even skipped lunch so her message queue would be clear before the afternoon meeting.

Just before two o'clock, she hurried to the conference center. She had expected to see only the senior staffs that would maintain the embassies on the various planets in the sector, but the Ambassador had brought everyone, including the clerks, who could fit into the room. When she entered, those with seats stood up, then everyone applauded as if she was the keynote speaker at a conference. She quickly formulated a welcoming speech in her mind, using a blending of all the welcoming speeches she had made in recent years. Ambassador DelCordia introduced her through a short speech about her accomplishments, although that was hardly necessary, and then gestured to Jenetta that she had the floor.

Over the next hour, Jenetta told the new arrivals about the base and the situation in the sectors of space considered part of her command. She then opened the meeting up to questions and spent another hour responding. The diplomats, already well briefed, asked very pointed questions. Jenetta answered to the best of her ability, but many questions concerned diplomatic issues that had never crossed her desk.

Once the question and answer period was over, the ambassador had each person come to the front of the room for a personal introduction. Jenetta smiled and tried to remember as many names as possible. She shook their hands and again welcomed them to the base.

She was glad and a bit tired when the welcoming ceremony was over and she could return to her office. With the arbitration hearing finished, she could now begin to concentrate more fully on the arrival of the Milori.

Jenetta spent the next morning in conference with Commander Barbara DeWitt, the senior officer of the Weapons Research section, and six members of her staff. The WR&D people would naturally take an active role in arming the ships for the upcoming conflict. Every ship had phased array lasers and torpedo capability, but special purpose ordnance was available in the armory. The armaments supply section only placed it aboard ships granted special approval.

Working together to plan for every possible contingency, they created a list of requisite weapons. The ordnance would be prepared, checked, and loaded aboard the ships before the taskforce left for the Frontier border.

* * *

Christa arrived in time for dinner with Jenetta on the day the *Chiron* returned to the base.

"Congratulations, sis," Christa said as they hugged. "I expected you to make admiral some day, but I wasn't expecting it quite so soon."

"Neither was I, but as I told you in my message, it's only temporary. I'll be a captain again when my tour is up. And I was as much as promised a ship by Admiral Holt when they stuck me here for five years."

"What's the big emergency? Captain Powers remained pretty tight-lipped about the reason for our return. Besides the Captain, I think only our XO knew."

"I'll tell you but you'll have to keep it to yourself."

"Where's the fun in that? Everybody's expecting me to bring back the scuttlebutt tonight."

"Christa, I'm being serious. We don't want to risk creating a panic among the civilian population on the station."

"Panic? Now you *really* have my interest."

"A fleet of Milori warships might be headed this way."

"Might?"

"We're only sure of one ship but feel confident there might be as many as sixteen."

"Why? We haven't had any problems with the Milori. Their empire's outer border is at least five hundred light-years beyond our ncw outer border."

"*Was* more than five hundred light-years beyond ours. They've announced they're laying claim to our Frontier Zone and everything between our territory and their old border. The Ottawa encountered sixteen warships in the Elurra System, and the Milori began pursuit after announcing to Captain Crosby the details of their claim. They've ordered all Space Command vessels out of *their* territory and back inside regulated GA space. They deny that our prior claim has any validity."

Christa made a whistling sound that dropped off quickly in pitch and volume. "That's an undeniable declaration of war."

"Exactly. Now you know why the *Chiron* abandoned its patrol and returned directly here. We're going to need every ship assigned to this base if the Milori intend to enforce their demand that we surrender our Frontier Zone."

"Yeah, and then some. We can't possibly defend the entire Frontier Zone against the Milori. We barely have enough ships for normal patrol duties inside the inner border."

"We'll do what we can with what we've got. We're not simply going to let an invading fleet take over. If we don't stand up now, they'll think they can take the rest of our territory whenever they feel like it. Appeasement doesn't work. We learned that on Earth a long time ago. Look what happened prior to World War II when Great Britain's Arthur Neville Chamberlain gave in to Hitler in hopes of averting a war. Each concession made Hitler more secure and made war more inevitable. Winston Churchill once said, 'An appeaser is one who feeds a crocodile, hoping it will eat him last.' These Milori interlopers cannot be permitted to believe their aggressions will succeed."

"When do they get here?"

"We still have several months before they arrive at our inner border. Preparations are already under way for a welcoming party. It'll be a warm reception."

*   *   *

For weeks, Jenetta was flooded with congratulatory messages regarding her promotion. It had taken many weeks for the word to circulate to the furthest reaches of the Galactic Alliance and for the messages to reach her. She normally would have spent time creating a custom response to each one, but she had so much to do that she just recorded a general message and appended a custom opening and closing remark. She naturally sent custom messages to family, very close friends, and important dignitaries.

When all ships based at Stewart, excluding the *Ottawa*, were back in their homeport, Jenetta called a meeting of all nine captains. They met in the large conference room located next to the base's Combat Information Center.

"Good morning, Captains," Jenetta said. "As we prepare to face a new threat, I'm glad you're here with me. The destroyers *Asuncion*, *Geneva*, and *Beijing*, cruisers *Song*, *Romanov*, and *Plantaganet*, and battleships *Prometheus*, *Chiron*, and *Thor* will soon be joined by the destroyers *St. Petersburg*, *Buenos Aires*, and *Cairo*, the cruiser *Mentuhotep*, and the battleship *Bellona*. This will constitute the entire Space Command taskforce assembled to meet the enemy. There are an additional nineteen ships underway for Stewart, but we expect they'll arrive too late for the confrontation. The *Ottawa*, as you all know, is bringing the Milori to the party.

"Over the past several weeks I've dispatched half a dozen small ships that will function as observation posts, and we've been in constant communication with Jeff Crosby on the *Ottawa*, plotting his course to Stewart precisely— *very* precisely. The ships we're using for observation posts were commandeered when we secured this base from the Raiders. They're of little use as fighting vessels because their hull protection is limited. We know that at least one Milori ship is currently pursuing the *Ottawa*, but how many other ships are still following is unknown because of the Milori tactic of following in a precise line behind the lead ship to confuse the quarry. My plan is to use the main weakness of that tactic against them.

"We're assuming that the lead Milori ship intends to follow the *Ottawa* right up to the border. If they assume we'll be there to meet them in force, their plan may be to split off the other ships in an effort to outflank us before reaching it. The observation ships are arraying themselves perpendicular to the *Ottawa's* current path, forty billion kilometers apart. Each will deploy four DDG satellites on either flank. That will extend their normal DeTect range from four to twenty billion kilometers. They'll be far enough from the course of the *Ottawa* that the Milori ships won't see them, but if there are Milori on the flanks, they'll show up on the DeTect systems in the observation ships. The way our OPs are spread out, we can watch a two-hundred-forty-billion-kilometer-wide swath of space across the path of the *Ottawa*.

"Here's the basic plan I've come up with. Computer, display the hologram you created for me earlier today, Carver-zero-one." An almost blank holographic projection appeared in the center of the table. It contained a single straight line in white. "This line represents the flight path of the *Ottawa*. Instead of meeting the Milori at the inner border, we'll meet them twenty light-years *inside* the Frontier. If we're lucky, we'll catch them well before they expect us and we'll have them off guard. The area I've chosen is consider-ably distant from any solar systems and well off the normal routes that commercial traffic follows. At best, it sees only sporadic traffic. We'll be able to identify any passing ships that might send a message, jam their IDS communications, and hold them until after the confrontation.

"In order to engage the Milori, they must be operating at sub-light speeds. To slow them down, we'll use the Raider hardware we acquired when we took this base. As you know, the Raiders would place electronic equipment in the path of freighters and passenger ships that would project an electronic grid over thousands of kilometers. The grid causes collision avoidance computers to believe there are hard contacts directly in the flight path. The computer then shuts down the FTL Drive to protect the ship. Using six of these electronic systems, we can create a narrow grid-work *cage* one kilometer wide by one kilometer high and two hundred kilometers long. Computer, show the first grid image." A boxlike grid work consisting of four very elongated sides appeared on the holographic image around the white line. A blue dot appeared on the white line, with sixteen yellow dots aligned in a row directly behind it. As they watched, the seventeen dots moved along the line until they were inside the grid-work box. "The *Ottawa* will be following a radio beacon signal that will take it through the precise center of the grid box. The Milori should follow directly behind. We'll activate the front end of the box as soon as the *Ottawa*, represented by the blue dot, approaches the front of the invisible cage. Computer, advance image." A grid appeared along the front and rear ends of the box. The *Ottawa* flew through the front-end grid as though it wasn't there. "The *Ottawa's* ACS will ignore the grid, but the FTL engines of the Milori should shut down immediately and won't reset because the six sides of the cage will appear to be solid to their anti-collision system. The Milori DeTect systems will 'see' the framework of the grid and show them that they don't even have room to maneuver.

"We'll be waiting out of sight, and I'll call for the surrender of the Milori ships. I really don't expect them to comply, but they'll be unable to engage their Light Speed engines if our information about their ships is accurate. The grid won't affect our ships because they'll be using a rotating frequency ship protection code calibrated to ignore it. The code used for this engagement will be 'Alpha Sixteen.'

"Despite what their systems are telling them, the Milori will probably attempt to maneuver using thrusters as soon as we've trapped them, or they may simply disengage their Anti-Collision Systems. But if they approach the sides of the cage, they'll discover the newly designed proximity fusion mines that we'll have laid along all four sides and both ends. Computer, insert the mines into the holographic image." The image lit up with innumerous red dots around all six sides of the grid-work cage. "The ends of the box won't be mined at first, but as soon as the Milori have entered and the grid box has closed, the new mines will quickly self-position to seal both openings. Our ships, including the *Ottawa*, won't detonate the mines because of the rotating frequency ship protection code, so our only danger will be from the Milori laser weapons and torpedoes.

"The Milori might try to target the mines in an effort to open a path out of the cage, but the new mines are coated in a black, energy-dampening material that doesn't reflect a sensor signal. They're almost impossible to spot in the blackness of open space. Besides, the Milori will be busy trying to avoid our fire while trying to target us. Our new mines are electronically linked. Their programming will automatically attempt to close any gaps opened in the barrier by detonated mines. We'll circle the cage, targeting the trapped ships until they surrender or can no longer return fire. But it won't be like shooting fish in a barrel because these fish will be shooting back."

Jenetta paused to catch her breath. None of the captains had yet said a word.

"That's the basic plan I've come up with. This is your opportunity to poke holes in it or present a better one. Anybody?"

"What happens if the Milori don't follow the *Ottawa* into the trap?" Captain Pope of the *Geneva* asked.

"My entire plan revolves around them adhering to their reported tactic of always following one another in a straight line until they encounter the enemy. This plan wouldn't work with any other enemy we've ever fought. And if they deviate from that tactic, we'll be left to fight them conventionally. Since the new proximity mines won't explode if our ships come close or even have contact with them, our goal will then become to draw or drive the Milori ships into and through the minefield, repeatedly if possible. They'll also have to contend with the electronic grid, which, again, won't affect our ships."

"What happens if the Milori drop back before reaching our position?" Captain Novak of the *Asuncion* asked.

"We change roles and pursue. Our goal is to drive them out of the Frontier Zone by whatever means necessary."

"Suppose their plan is to draw us into a trap, Admiral?" Captain Payton of the *Thor* asked.

"Every battle is fluid, and we'll have to adjust to whatever is thrown at us. We're all familiar with the quote by Prussian General Count Helmuth von Moltke that 'no plan survives contact with the enemy.' He also wrote, 'You may be sure that of the three courses open to the enemy, he will always choose the fourth.' I'm open to any other alternatives, and you've all had time to think about this. What would you do?"

"We could also seed the area along the cage sides with limpet mines," Captain Debra Goran of the *Beijing* said. "As we spring the trap, we activate the limpets. They'll then seek out the mass of any ship nearby and attach themselves. If the Milori still want a fight, we send the detonate signal."

"Yes, that could work," Jenetta said, as she thought, "but it might alert the Milori to the presence of the cage. The energy-dampening coating on the new one-meter mines gives them such a tiny footprint that DeTect equipment can't pick them up. The limpet mines are uncoated. Although small, they're identifiable on DeTect screens at close range. If the Milori see them and avoid entering the cage, our entire plan is ruined. I think we should stay with just the new fusion mines. Good idea, though. Thank you, Debra. Anyone else?"

"I like your plan, Admiral," Captain Gavin said. "It's very innovative for a battle in open space. I hope it works, but what if the Milori attempt to outflank us, as you speculated?"

"Same basic plan. We try to draw them through the minefield while engaging them. But if we can't trap them in the grid-work cage, I'm not expecting anything other than a real slugfest. Even if the trap is successful, we may only be able to destroy half a dozen of their ships with the mines. Eventually the surviving ships might get free of the entrapping minefield and do their best to destroy us. So we'll have to move swiftly and decisively while we still have them ensnared with limited maneuverability. The better-trained crews, as well as the better-armed and protected ships, will have the best chance of surviving this battle. I'm projecting possible losses of as high as fifty percent, but I don't believe there's any question about us winning the day."

"Only fifty percent?" Captain Powers said. "That might be a bit optimistic from what I've heard about *their* ferocity in battle."

"Perhaps. But I know that our people are the best trained in the galaxy. We'll be bloodied, but we'll win."

"The ships behind the *Ottawa* haven't closed on it," Captain Novak said. "Perhaps they don't want a fight. Perhaps they're only trying to chase us out of the Frontier Zone."

"The Frontier Zone is Galactic Alliance territory and we're not going to simply cede it to an invading force that has engaged in saber rattling. They might not have closed on the *Ottawa* because we all know the dangers of trying to destroy a ship traveling faster than light. If they attempted to pass the *Ottawa*, Jeff Crosby would simply have shut down his ACS, leaving the extremely dangerous maneuver of an envelope merge the only possible alternative. And with their tactic of following directly behind the leader, the slightest error in judgment could destroy their entire taskforce. I believe they haven't closed simply because they don't have an easy way of stopping the *Ottawa*."

"Admiral," Captain Powers said thoughtfully, "what if we don't send in the ships after the Milori are caught in your cage? Each battleship carries a hundred twenty-five fighters. Among the four battleships, we'll have five hundred fighters available, and the cruisers and destroyers can add another three hundred or so. Like our warships, our fighters would be safe from our minefield, so they could enter the cage and attack the Milori like a swarm of bees. If they can't get the job done with their lasers and rockets, we could then still attack with the ships while they withdraw."

Jenetta stared at the holographic image for a few seconds as she thought. "The fighters don't have much clout. If the Milori are as dangerous as everyone predicts, they might simply sweep the fighters away in the blink of an eye. I hate to think about wasting our people in a useless gesture. On the other hand, if the Milori see our fighters flying through the minefield without incident, they might begin to think it's now safe for them as well and do the work for us. Okay, we'll commence the attack that way and modify it if it's not sufficiently effective. Good suggestion, Steve. Any other ideas? Anyone?"

Everyone was staring at the holographic image as they considered various offensive tactics.

"Admiral," Captain Gavin said, "when we were trying to crack open Raider Three, Keith Kanes told us about a new weapon that had been developed but not tested. It was housed in a standard torpedo casing."

"You mean the WOLaR bomb?"

"WOLaR?"

"Weapon of Last Resort."

"Yes," he said chuckling, "that sounds like what was discussed."

"It's been tested and put into production. We have ten in our torpedo armory."

"Let's take a few with us," Captain Gavin said.

"It packs a lot of punch. There won't be much left of any ship that's hit, but we only have ten."

"What would happen if we fired one into the center of a group of Milori ships, not aimed at any ship in particular?"

"I see what you're getting at, Larry. If we could detonate it right in the center of the group, we might do quite a bit of damage. Of course, the enemy ships would have to be very close together for the weapon to have the desired effect. Any ship more than half a kilometer from the detonation point would probably only be scorched a bit."

"From everything we've heard, the Milori like to fight in ultra-tight formations, wingtip to wingtip so to speak. It sounds ideal for this weapon."

Jenetta stared at the holographic image. "We certainly can't fire them while our fighters are in there, and if we fire them before the action starts, every gunner in the Milori ships will be targeting them. As I see it, the entire taskforce would have to make a single pass first, firing as many torpedoes as possible to distract attention away from the special torpedoes fired by the last ship."

"We'll do quite a bit of damage with just our conventional fusion warheads during that single pass," Captain Yung of the *Song* said.

"Yes, it might soften the enemy up a little for the fighters. Perhaps we won't even have to use the WOLaRs. Okay, we'll make that single pass. Good suggestion, Larry. The *Prometheus* will take the lead, firing as many torpedoes as possible, followed by each of the other ships on alternating sides of the cage, also firing as many torpedoes as possible. The last ship will be the *Chiron*, and by the time it begins its pass, the space inside and outside the cage should be alive with torpedoes heading for their targets. The Milori will only have limited maneuvering room, and they won't be able to evade the torpedoes without running into the mines, so their gunners will be busy trying to knock down the torpedoes. The *Chiron* will carry all our WOLaR weapons in his stern tubes. As he commences his run, he'll fire everything from his bow tubes, then empty his larboard tubes. He'll mop up by firing from his stern tubes after passing and identifying the tightest clusters of enemy ships. We'll have to assume that things will be a bit chaotic inside the cage by then and the Milori will be trying to use every bit of the two-hundred-kilometer length to avoid our fire. As soon as the last WOLaR torpedoes have detonated, we'll send in the fighters to see if they can drive or draw any remaining Milori ships through the minefield."

Everyone stared at the holographic image in silence after Jenetta finished recapping the revised plan. Some were thinking about the plan, and others were thinking about the carnage that lay ahead.

After a couple of minutes, Jenetta asked, "Any other suggestions or questions?"

"What happens," Captain Novak asked, "if the Milori simply surrender after we spring the trap?"

Jenetta thought for a few seconds before responding. "The idea hadn't even occurred to me. Like the Tsgardi, the Milori are renowned for fighting to the death. It seems unlikely they'd surrender en masse like that without even firing a shot, unless the enemy they're facing has overwhelmingly superior numbers or strength. If they do, we'll have a real dilemma on our hands. How do we take thousands of Milori POWs into custody and what do we do with them afterwards? I really don't know the answer at this point, but I think the chance is so remote that we'll never have to worry about it."

Silence again descended over the room until Jenetta said, "Is that it? Okay, that's our battle plan unless the Milori do something totally unexpected. Brief your senior staffs and prepare your crews. Each ship will receive as many mines as it can carry in its holds and attach to exterior surfaces. We leave Stewart in six days. That will give us sufficient time to reach the selected battle site and deploy our mines. The *Beijing* will take responsibility for detaining any ships we encounter within a billion kilometers of our trap. The WOLaR torpedoes will be delivered to the *Chiron*, along with their share of mines. All ships will be fully provisioned before departure. A copy of the vid log from today's meeting will be sent to Supreme Headquarters and to each of the five GSC ships scheduled to arrive in time to meet the Milori so they can prepare for the engagement. Thank you for your input. Dismissed."

\* \* \*

The following days were extremely busy ones on the base. Jenetta named Captain Donovan from the JAG office to fill in as interim base commander during her absence. Although JAG officers were not normally included in the succession to base command, he was one of just two senior officers holding the rank of Captain— the other being a medical doctor. Donovan worked side by side with her for half of each day, with the other half spent preparing his own interim replacement in the JAG office.

Jenetta, always besieged for interviews by the press, allowed the new representative of a news service to visit her in her office. Expecting a request for an interview, she was prepared to put him off until after the conflict.

"Admiral, congratulations on your promotion."

"Thank you, Mr. Kelleher. I really don't have time for any interviews right now."

"I'm not here about getting an interview, Admiral."

"What is it you want then?"

"You'd have to be deaf, dumb, and blind not to notice that something big is coming down. I want my guys and gals to have access."

"That's impossible. We're going into a dangerous situation."

"What exactly are you facing?"

"I can't tell you that— yet."

"Whatever it is, you owe it to the people of the galaxy to have it covered by the press."

"Will you keep what I'm about to say totally confidential?"

"Yes, until whatever happens is completely over."

"Fair enough. I've estimated that we could suffer losses as high as fifty percent."

"Fifty percent losses? Where are you going?"

"To the border with the Frontier Zone, but I can't be any more specific than that."

"Is it the Raiders again?"

"I really can't give you specifics."

"Okay, but my request to have people aboard your ships still stands."

"Even knowing that some, possibly half, may not come back?"

"Even knowing that."

Jenetta thought about it for a full minute. If she refused, she would have no control over what stories they might send out and when. "Okay, with several conditions."

"Anything."

"First, you will not talk, announce, or notify anyone about anything concerning this operation until it's over. One word and I launch your people in escape pods where they'll wait until someone can get around to retrieving them. If the opposing force knows anything about our plans, it could jeopardize lives."

"Agreed."

"Second, all of your people will sign waivers before being allowed on a ship. The waiver will clearly state that the chances of returning alive are slim to none, and they fully accept all risk."

"Agreed."

"Third, no stories will be filed until my office lifts the restriction on transmissions. I'm not trying to control *what* you report, only *when* you report it. I can't afford to have the other side learning even the smallest detail about our deployment by intercepting a news broadcast."

"Agreed, with one condition. My people will have full access to the bridge and be able to film the action."

"One person only will be allowed on the bridge, and that individual will act like a spot on the carpet. The captain will decide where the person can stand and has the right to have the individual permanently removed from the bridge if he or she moves from that exact spot. And there will be no questions posed to anyone while the ship is at General Quarters. Your reporter is a mute observer, not a participant."

"Agreed, Admiral. How many ships will be involved?"

"Fourteen warships will be leaving from here. One ship is already involved and unavailable."

"Okay, I'll have fourteen people ready to go when the ships deploy."

"One last thing. You'll have a twenty-four-hour exclusive on all stories, and then all footage must be shared with all other news services that request it."

"You expect us to take all the risk and then share our news stories?"

"That's the deal. I can't provide room for all the news services so the one that gets the spot has to share. If you're not interested, I'm sure one of the other news services will take the deal and share with you a full day after *they* break the story."

"O-kay," he said reluctantly. "Deal."

"My aide will prepare the waiver forms and give you all the information you'll need. I suggest that you not tell your management about it because if they leak anything— anything at all— I'll have to consider it to be the same as if it came from you."

"I understand, Admiral."

\*    \*    \*

Jenetta was exhausted by the end of each day, and the stress of knowing that an invasion force was getting closer each minute was beginning to show on her face. She really looked forward to her evening meals with Christa and being able to unburden herself with someone she knew would never reveal a confidence. They naturally discussed the preparations for the conflict and tactics that could be used in every conceivable situation, but they also discussed other things.

"How's your young lieutenant, sis?" Jenetta asked after they had finished talking about the Milori.

"Adam is caught up in all the hysteria of the moment. Things were going great until we got orders to return to Stewart. Now, all he seems to think about is the Milori. He spends all his free time in the simulators."

"He sounds dedicated."

"Dedicated? He's positively fanatical about it."

"That's what we need right now. It's unfortunate that it's happening while your romance is still in the early stages. With any luck, we'll all make it through this and things can get back to normal."

"How about you? Heard from Hugh lately?"

"We exchanged messages at least once a week until he went into stasis sleep. We won't be able to speak for six months, but I've been continuing to send messages every week. He'll have a lot to watch once he wakes up."

"Then he doesn't know you made admiral?"

"No, he went to sleep a few days before I was notified. And by the time he awakens, we'll be on our way to meet the Milori and communications will be restricted."

"At least you had a full month together."

"Yes. And it was a wonderful month. It was the happiest time I've had since I set foot on this base."

"I'm surprised the cats took to him so well."

"It took them a couple of days to get comfortable around him, but after he moved into my quarters, they adapted quickly."

"They didn't attack him when you made love?" Christa asked, grinning.

"No, they seemed to understand that I wasn't moaning because of distress. They didn't try to bite him or claw him even once," Jenetta said, smiling. "I took care of those things myself." Looking melancholy, she said, "I was really sad when he left. It was as if a part of me was leaving. I didn't think I'd get that attached in just a month."

"When you're starved for affection, it doesn't take much to really wind you up. Also, Hugh was really your first attraction since the Academy. I remember how we secretly felt about him after escaping from the Raiders. It wouldn't have taken much back then to get us excited. I think that if Hugh hadn't dropped out of sight right after the court-martial, Zane wouldn't have stood a chance."

"I knew going in that we'd only have a month, so I shouldn't have felt so lost when he left, and it'll probably be years before we see each other again. His freighter will be underway for almost two years before they get to Dixon, and he has a second sleep period before they get there."

"I don't know which is worse, going in separate directions or being aboard the same ship in an upcoming conflict. If anything happens to Adam, I don't know what I'll do."

"The *worst* is knowing that I'm responsible for the lives of almost twenty-five thousand crewmen in the taskforce. If I make a mistake, I could be responsible for the biggest disaster in Space Command history. To make it even worse, if that's possible, there will be four Carvers in this fight. With you on the *Chiron*, Eliza on the *Bellona*, Billy on the *St. Petersburg*, and me on the *Prometheus*, I could be responsible for wiping out half our family."

"You didn't start this, sis. The actions of the Milori Empire have brought us to this point. I feel more comfortable having you lead this taskforce than anyone else I can think of because of your ability and because I know you won't unnecessarily risk anyone's life. What's more, I don't know of anyone on my ship who feels differently. Everyone is solidly behind you."

"I just hope I don't let everyone down. We're not facing Raiders this time around, and I'm sure we're not coming through this un-bloodied. I'll let you know just how guilty I feel after the battle is over."

*　*　*

The *Bellona* arrived at Stewart on the day before the assembled force was scheduled to leave. The victualing and armament crews worked nonstop so that it would be prepared to depart on time with the taskforce. Like the other ships, the hull was crammed with ordnance, and every possible location on its exterior hull had a mine attached. The *St. Petersburg*, *Buenos Aires*, *Cairo*, and *Mentuhotep* would have to catch up after they reached Stewart and were provisioned and armed.

Jenetta, Christa, and Eliza met in Jenetta's dining room and were able to enjoy their last evening meal together before departure. It was actually the first time they had all been together in four years. For a few hours, Jenetta was able to forget all her worries and enjoy reminiscing about past days with her sisters.

The taskforce ships began backing away from the airlocks inside the asteroid base one at a time and making their way outside where they'd form up for the trip. Jenetta had come aboard the *Prometheus* early with her cats and had been escorted to her quarters. Her new rank seemed to affect the crewmen and officers she encountered aboard the ship much more than she expected, even though she knew most of them from her days as the ship's First Officer. She thought it might be because crewmen so rarely ever meet an admiral, but more likely it was because of the power her lofty position bestowed. The officer at the airlock entrance, a lieutenant who had been aboard when Jenetta was the XO, went rigid with a salute when she entered the ship. She got him to relax a little after she returned the salute by engaging him in a brief conversation.

The largest suite in the VIP quarter's section had naturally been reserved for Jenetta. Although rarely used, it was the suite always reserved for admirals, prime ministers, or other top dignitaries. She would have preferred quarters on the bridge deck, but they were already assigned to the bridge officers. Security had established two Marine sentry posts outside her door, and a steward was waiting to welcome her. As a base commander, she was used to always having a sentry at the door to her offices and another outside her quarters, but she hadn't had a steward since turning command of the *Song* over to Captain Yung. She'd contented herself on Dixon and Stewart with having a private dining room, cook, and mess attendant.

Lt. Commander Ashraf's quarters were immediately next to Jenetta's, although her rank wouldn't have rated such spacious accommodations if she hadn't been the admiral's adjutant.

After settling into her quarters, Jenetta told her cats to remain there as she left for the bridge. As she entered from the corridor, someone said loudly, "Admiral on the bridge," and everyone not at a duty station came to attention.

"As you were," Jenetta said loudly. She continued over to the captain's briefing room and waited until the door opened.

Captain Gavin, sitting at his desk, stood up. "Welcome aboard, Admiral."

"Thank you, Larry. Are we about ready to get underway?"

"Commander Eaton is down at the airlock. We're just waiting for a final container of fresh food supplies to be delivered and then we'll button it up."

"Good. I'll feel better when we're finally away."

"Coffee, Jen?"

"Yes. I'll get it. How about you?"

"I'm fine, thanks."

Gavin sat back down as Jenetta went to the food synthesizer and prepared a mug of coffee for herself. When it was ready, she came back to the desk and sat down in one of the overstuffed chairs facing him.

"I feel extremely uneasy about taking every available warship with us," Jenetta said. "The base will be virtually unprotected, except for the transports and quartermaster's ships. I'd hate to try to fight a battle here with just them for my defense. I hope the ships behind the *Ottawa* aren't just a feint to get our warships out of the base."

"Some of the additional ships that Space Command is sending will be here shortly, and they'll assume protection duties when they arrive. In the meantime, the base will simply seal up if any hostiles approach. You have no choice other than to send every warship you have available to this confrontation. If we don't fight the Milori in a place of our choosing in the Frontier, we might have to fight them here. And fighting them here would put a lot of civilians at risk."

"I wish we had some Intel on the number of ships following the *Ottawa*. If the others have fallen back and are maintaining a parallel course more than a hundred twenty billion kilometers away in hopes of outflanking us, we could be doing all the preparation work for nothing."

"I think your plan is sound, Jen. Everything we've heard about Milori tactics indicates they don't fan out until they're almost at their destination. Reportedly, they've developed a special electronics system to keep each ship a precise distance so close to the ship in front of it that they appear as one ship on the sensors. And every ship is connected to the sensor system of the lead ship. If the lead ship detects an object in its path, the temporal envelopes of the trailing ships are immediately dissolved to avoid a collision."

"Hmm, that's interesting. That information wasn't included in any report I've seen."

"It wasn't in an SCI document. It was by a newsie who referenced an article in an Uthlaro military engineering publication. I'll send you a copy."

"Thanks, Larry. Let's hope the Milori make maximum use of that technology until we get them in our cage."

"As long as Jeff Crosby follows the course instructions you've given him, I think we'll bag our limit of Milori ships."

                              *   *   *

A taskforce can only travel as fast as the slowest ship, so it took forty-three days to reach the site selected by Jenetta for the confrontation. The ships began deploying their mines and the equipment that would create the electronic grid as soon as they arrived. In three days, they had been able to complete as much as they could until the other ships arrived with their complement of mines.

The arrival of the *Cairo* and *Mentuhotep* a couple of days later allowed the mine-laying groups to almost complete the planned mine field, but it was seven more days before the *St. Petersburg* and the *Buenos Aires* arrived. Still, the work was completed with seven days to spare. Since they knew exactly when the *Ottawa* would arrive, the crews could relax until the final hours, but most gunners chose to use the gunnery simulators to hone their reflexes to an extra sharp edge, while maintenance crews checked, double-checked, and triple-checked everything on the fighter craft.

Jenetta and the ship captains enjoyed dinner together every night, always hosted on a different ship in the taskforce. The talk at the table was always about the upcoming conflict as they sought to cover every possible contingency. With the possible exception of D-Day in Earth's World War II, Jenetta doubted that any single battle had ever been planned and discussed as much in advance as this one.

*   *   *

Surprisingly, no other ships traversed the area of space selected for the confrontation during the weeks that the Space Command ships were in the area, so the *Beijing* wasn't required to engage any shipping. Of course, Jenetta had selected it *because* it was so unlikely anyone would happen by.

As the hour for the battle neared, the ships of the taskforce pulled back four-point-two billion kilometers from the grid area. Being well out of DeTect range, the sensors of the Milori shouldn't see the Space Command vessels until the taskforce began to move in. The ships didn't cancel their DATFA envelopes. Once the Milori ships were stopped, the taskforce was ready to move immediately to a position ten thousand kilometers from the grid-work cage. Sensor buoys, placed within range at the trap, would provide a complete picture of what was happening.

The *Ottawa* appeared on the sensors exactly when expected, and the electronic grid was activated in time to halt the lead Milori ship near the front end of the cage. The temporal envelopes of the lead and trailing Milori ships dissolved as one, and self-guiding mines immediately began moving to block both the front and rear openings of the cage.

Jenetta and her aide, Lt. Commander Ashraf, were on the bridge of the *Prometheus* watching the large viewscreen when the Milori ships came to an instant stop inside the cage. The *Prometheus* was too far distant to see the trapped ships except as a sensor buoy image, but all sensors indicated that fewer than ten meters separated the ships. Jenetta marveled at the electronics that allowed such precision.

"Got 'em," Jenetta heard a young lieutenant at a tactical station exclaim.

"Captain," the lead tactical officer said urgently, "there's a problem."

"What is it, Commander?" Gavin asked.

"There are way too many blips, sir. I'm reading a hundred three ships in the trap."

"A hundred three? Is that a false reading owed to that jamming screen they use?"

"Negative, sir," the officer said as he studied the data carefully. "The Milori force consists of a hundred three ships— mostly destroyers— but there are twenty frigates, fourteen cruisers, and six battleships."

"Dear Lord!" Gavin exclaimed. "It's a full-scale invasion force."

# Chapter Sixteen
~ February 14<sup>th</sup>, 2277 ~

"Com," Jenetta said, "hail Lord High Space Marshall Gulqulk of the Imperial Cruiser *Reguffa*."

"Aye, Admiral."

By the time an image of a Milora filled the front view-screen, the SC taskforce had reached its planned position nearer the cage. Loud shouting was evident on the enemy ship. The Milori were extremely agitated and trying to figure out what they were facing.

The SC fighters, sitting in launch position inside the ships, got the green light and began deploying the instant the taskforce completed its short FTL jump. They would form up in squadrons and wait nearby until called to begin their attack runs.

"I'm Admiral Jenetta Carver of the Galactic Space Command. You've chased one of my ships across two hundred light-years of Galactic Alliance space after making serious threats. I order you to surrender immediately or suffer the destruction you threatened to bring to the *Ottawa*."

"You will not give orders to me in Milori space," the Milora bellowed. "In seconds we'll find out how you've stopped our FTL engines and we'll destroy you and every ship you command. No one can stand against the supreme might of the Milori Empire. The sand in the Galactic Alliance hour-glass is almost gone."

Jenetta set her jaw and stared at the leader of the invading force. "This is Galactic Alliance space. Merely declaring that you rendered our previous claim void when you chose to appropriate our territory doesn't make it so. Since you won't withdraw, you leave me no choice." She added, icily, "You've brought this upon yourselves." She turned to look at the com operator and waved her hand in a cutoff signal. The front screen returned to the view of space. "You have a green light, Captain. Let's do this before they figure a way out."

Gavin nodded to the helmsman and the ship began its planned run past the Milori. In seconds, the *Prometheus* was approaching the trap on a parallel course. In order to engage the enemy vessels properly, it would pass the electronic cage at a distance of just fifty kilometers and at a speed of Plus-One. Ships within the trap were already trying to maneuver. Explosions occurred along the length and breadth of the enclosed space as Milori ships made contact with unseen mines and learned the limits of their cage. The *Prometheus* was distant enough that explosions from the fusion mines wouldn't affect it, but the distance offered no protection from the laser weapons of the Milori ships. Beams of coherent light speared the darkness between the ship and the cage as the Milori laser gunners opened fire. The laser gunners on the *Prometheus*, meanwhile, opened up with their hundred-megawatt phased array laser weapons. So tightly congested were the Milori ships that it almost seemed impossible for the *Prometheus'* gunners to miss.

The *Prometheus'* laser gunners knew that targeting approaching torpedoes took priority over firing on the trapped ships, so they began to concentrate their fire on Milori torpedoes as they approached. The *Prometheus'* own torpedo gunners were firing as quickly as new torpedoes could be loaded into the bow, larboard, and stern tubes. The prodigious number of tubes on the battleship meant that torpedoes were almost always available as soon as the tactical officers achieved a target lock. Steady emanations of torpedo trails were visible leading away towards the Milori ships.

The Milori gunners began to concentrate ever more on defense as the Space Command torpedoes neared their ships, and their gunners were able to destroy a substantial number of the torpedoes. But each time one got through, the fire from that ship diminished noticeably and left it a little more susceptible to fire from the trailing taskforce ships.

Spaced fifteen seconds apart on alternating sides of the elongated trap, the other ships were beginning their runs behind the *Prometheus*. The *Chiron* was in what was normally called the 'cleanup' position with its destructive load of WOLaR torpedoes at the ready.

The *Prometheus* completed its pass in just two minutes, but each of the hundred twenty seconds seemed like an eternity. As the first ship into the fray, it had taken the brunt of the enemy laser offensive. The heavily battered ship moved off and took up a position where it could watch the activity while remaining out of effective laser range. A number of guns on the Milori ships were now silent, but all ships still appeared to be firing. The mines continued to inflict ever greater tolls as the Milori ships probed for a way out of the cage.

As each of the taskforce ships completed its run, it took up a position near the *Prometheus*, twenty-five thousand kilometers from the cage. All eyes on the bridge of the *Prometheus* watched as the *Chiron* fired its normal torpedoes before sending in the special torpedoes from its stern tubes. With the WOLaRs aimed at points between ships rather than at any particular ship, it was hoped that the Milori gunners would be concentrating more on torpedoes actually coming towards their vessel. The WOLaR torpedoes would detonate when they reached a point along the center line of the trap, unless they struck a maneuvering ship first.

The first WOLaR explosion occurred as the Chiron was halfway through its run. The blast temporarily blinded all visual sensors, but as the sensors reset, viewscreens showed that several Milori ships had been destroyed. Other nearby ships, heavily damaged by the blast, had been pushed outward into the surrounding minefield and small secondary explosions filled the area. Incredible explosions continued to annihilate enemy vessels until the *Chiron* reached the observation area where the rest of the taskforce waited.

Milori gunners managed to destroy four of the special weapons before they could detonate, but the six that did detonate decimated the ranks of the Milori warships. As the blinding light from the last of the WOLaR detonations winked out, Jenetta turned towards the com operator and said, "Send in the fighters."

The fighters had moved up from their original positions after launch to a dozen assembly points where they'd be ready when called. They had thus far been exempt from any of the action and the pilots were anxious to begin their attack on the invading horde. When the order to attack came down, the squadrons moved in quickly to engage the Milori ships.

It soon became apparent that the blasts from the special weapons had caused an unforeseen effect. Some mines along the grid had been temporarily 'blinded' by the explosions and their systems had entered a self-test mode, making the mine inactive. The tactical officer aboard the *Prometheus* worked furiously to reboot the mines and reactivate them, but a couple of dozen Milori ships managed to escape from the entrapping barrier before the mines came back on-line. While the network of mines immediately began to reposition themselves and seal the gaps, the fighters moved to engage the freed ships.

Jenetta, watching the action from the bridge of the *Prometheus*, said to the com operator, "Message to all ships. Engage the Milori that have escaped the minefield. Message to fighters. Concentrate on destroying the laser arrays of the ships still inside the minefield rather than perforating their hulls."

Within seconds, the fifteen Space Command ships were once again underway. The fighters outside the minefield broke off contact and moved inside the trap to engage the enemy ships that were still firing from there.

If the Milori ships had been Raider ships, they probably would have broken off and left the area as quickly as they'd come, but the Milori were trained military professionals who didn't run from a battle. They had taken crippling injuries to their ships but they continued to fight on as the Space Command ships engaged them. As Jenetta expected, the battle turned into a real slugfest. The fate of the SC ships was largely in the hands of the helmsmen and the gunners as the battle raged on. Jenetta, feeling a little impotent at this point, could do little but watch as Gavin, sitting in his bridge chair, issued orders to the helmsman. The gunners didn't need any new instructions. They would follow their standing orders to fire on any enemy ship that constituted a threat until ordered to stand down.

There was little the *Prometheus* and the other taskforce ships could do except slug it out head to head with the freed Milori ships. Luck would play a significant role as the two well-trained fighting forces tried their best to destroy the other, but the severe damage already visited upon the Milori while they were in the trap gave a slight advantage to the Space Command ships. The battle would rage both inside and outside the mined area until the guns became silent and torpedoes no longer filled space between opponents.

Gradually, the fighting lessened and then ceased. It was over. The space in and around the minefield was littered with debris and the corpses of ships.

The *Prometheus*, although heavily damaged, was still able to move under its own power. Gavin ordered the helmsman to pull the ship back out of effective laser range in case there was still some life left in any of the Milori ships.

"Damage reports," Gavin said to the com operator.

"Aye, Captain. They're coming in already," the com operator said.

The com chief handed a holo-tube to Jenetta as Gavin took the one from the holder mounted on his chair. They both scanned the list as the ship's computer continually updated the information. It was serious.

At least four torpedoes had hit the *Prometheus*, and huge holes were open in the hull, exposing half a dozen decks to open space. Hits by laser fire were estimated to be in the thousands, and no part of the ship had been spared. The casualty figures at this early stage listed thirty-eight dead and over a hundred wounded.

Jenetta expected that those numbers would climb substantially. The ship had taken a brutal pounding. She turned to the com operator and said, "Contact the other ships and get preliminary assessments."

"Aye, Admiral." The operator tapped a key that sent a prerecorded message to the other ships.

Gavin put down the portable pad and started issuing instructions through his CT. The well-trained crew could do their job without detailed orders, so his instructions mainly involved giving them information they might not otherwise have. He sent Commander Eaton, his First Officer, to personally view the most seriously damaged areas.

"Admiral," the com operator said, "the reports from the other ships are coming in. You can see them on your holo-tube. Just advance the pages.

"Thank you." Jenetta twisted the end of the tube and saw the damage reports from the *Bellona* appear after she reached the end of the *Prometheus'* damage reports. She quickly moved through the pages, reading all the reports. As bad as the damage to the *Prometheus* was, it was far better off than most of the other ships.

"Com, I'm not seeing anything from the *Asuncion, Beijing, Buenos Aires, Cairo, Mentuhotep*, or *Romanov*."

"They aren't responding to hails, Admiral."

Jenetta bit on her lower lip. It could be communications equipment failure, but it might be much worse. Damage to the *Prometheus* was too severe to dispatch anyone to investigate immediately. They would have to lick their wounds and begin the healing process before assisting other ships. Jenetta turned to Gavin. "Captain, may I use your briefing room? I need to send a report to Supreme HQ."

"Of course, Admiral."

Jenetta walked to the large office on the larboard side of the bridge and touched the door sensor. The door slid open silently and then closed behind her. She scanned the damage reports data on the holo-tube once again and then sat down at the captain's desk to record the message.

"Computer, Priority-One message to Admiral Richard E. Moore, Admiral of the Fleet, Space Command Supreme Headquarters, from Admiral Jenetta A. Carver, Base Commander of Stewart Space Command Base, from the GSC Battleship *Prometheus*, with a copy to Captain Michael Donovan, acting base commander, Stewart SC Base. Begin message.

"Hello Admiral. It's my sad duty to report that we have met the Milori and suffered great loss of life. The battle has only just ended, so damage reports are very preliminary. We're currently unable to contact the *Asuncion, Beijing*,

*Buenos Aires*, *Cairo*, *Mentuhotep*, or *Romanov*, and the other Space Command ships have taken a terrible beating. I'm hoping for the best but fear the worst.

"We had expected as many as sixteen ships to arrive behind the *Ottawa* and were greatly surprised when the arriving enemy taskforce turned out to be comprised of sixty-three destroyers, twenty frigates, fourteen cruisers, and six battleships. It appears to have been a full invasion force. My early speculation is that they intended to quickly dispatch whatever ships were waiting to meet them at the border and then move on to destroy Stewart, or perhaps seize it for their own use. Since we know there were only sixteen ships in the Elurra system, the remaining ships had to have joined up with the pursuing Milori force as it traveled through the Frontier Zone. Being outnumbered almost seven to one, we're only still alive thanks to the entrapping minefield we constructed. All Milori guns have now fallen silent, but we're unable to check for survivors, and it may be days before we can even contemplate such an activity.

"I hope that one or more of the additional ships coming to support this sector will arrive soon and be able to assist us. I'll file an additional report as soon as we get an accurate picture of our condition. Know only that we've stopped this invading force and half my taskforce remains minimally functional.

"Jenetta A. Carver, Rear Admiral, Lower Half, from the GSC Battleship *Prometheus*. Message complete. Computer, append a copy of the bridge's video log from the past— two hours."

Jenetta took a deep breath and recorded a second message.

"Computer, new message. Priority one message to Captain Michael Donovan, Acting Base Commander, Stewart SC Base, from Admiral Jenetta A. Carver, on board the GSC Battleship *Prometheus*. Begin message.

"Hello, Mike. You've received a copy of the report I've just filed with Supreme Headquarters so you know that our condition is serious. Keep the information confidential until Supreme Headquarters is ready to release it. Please reply with the current ETA of the ships en route to Stewart. We could use any available help.

"Jenetta A. Carver, Rear Admiral, Lower Half, from the GSC Battleship *Prometheus*, message complete."

Jenetta stood and walked to the food synthesizer where she prepared a steaming mug of coffee. It would take an hour or more for the officers on each ship to assess their situation, so there was nothing for her to do on the bridge right now. Later, she would be able to collect sufficient detail to begin reorganizing her command.

Sitting on the captain's sofa, she went over the battle in her mind, trying to see if there was anything she could have— or should have— done differently. She couldn't think of a thing. They had been fortunate that things had worked out the way they had. Luck had definitely been on their side this day.

Jenetta was still on the sofa viewing incoming damage reports on the holo-tube when Gavin entered the office about an hour later. He couldn't miss the pained expression on her face. She was usually so careful to show only a mask of complete imperturbability and he wondered if she was aware that she had let down her guard.

"Thinking about the people we lost?" he asked softly as he prepared a cup of coffee.

"I let them down."

"Who?"

"All of them. They were depending on me to bring them back alive to their loved ones. I failed, miserably."

"Despite our losses, this battle can't be thought of as anything other than an incredible victory. The thousands that *will* be returning owe their lives to your plan."

"I've been going over the battle in my mind," Jenetta said, almost as if she hadn't heard his words, "trying to determine what more I could have done. They almost caught us cold by adding that invasion force to the pursuit group the way they did. I should have been better prepared. I should have anticipated they wouldn't come to meet us in combat unless they had much greater ship numbers. We had so much time to prepare that they would have expected us to be ready for them."

"I've been thinking about that also. There wasn't any way we could have known. Jeff Crosby and his people certainly aren't to blame. They had to be as surprised as we were. If not for the minefield trap you devised, it would have been the end for all of us. We never could have won a battle against that large a force in the open."

"No, we wouldn't have lasted long. I have to wonder if they had really planned to invade now, or if the appearance of the *Ottawa* in the Elurra system precipitated the event. If we'd had more time, we would have had another nineteen ships as part of the taskforce."

"They probably decided to move up the invasion date for that very reason. Once we knew of their intent, we would naturally begin pulling in every available ship for the engagement. I'm sure they didn't want us to have enough time to get all our forces into play. If we find any of the Milori alive, we'll ask them."

"I'm not so sure they'll allow themselves to be taken alive. The three that the *Ottawa* rescued probably thought we'd just release them on the nearest inhabited planet. And we would have if our SCI agents hadn't turned up that tip about the Elurra system. We must intern any Milora we capture now as a prisoner of war. How's the *Prometheus*?"

"Commander Cameron tells me we'll be as good as new in a few months, but he says it'll take from two weeks to a month just to repair the hull sections where the torpedoes struck us and get the entire ship pressurized."

Jenetta nodded. "I noticed the body count has risen to two hundred sixteen."

Gavin exhaled loudly. "Yes, and we still have many unaccounted for. Some may have been sucked out when the hull was breached. Only about a third of our fighters have returned. We probably won't have an accurate count for hours, but I expect the toll will rise above four hundred."

Jenetta closed her eyes, lowered her head, and shook it slowly.

"You're not to blame, Jen." Gavin said softly.

"I know the Milori are responsible for starting this war, but I should have done better."

"No one could have done better."

Jenetta nodded. "Thanks, Larry. By the way, I've sent a preliminary report to Supreme HQ with a copy to Captain Donovan at Stewart. I've also requested that Donovan send me an updated timetable for the arrival of the nineteen ships underway for Stewart. It's been eight months since they were diverted, and a couple— the ones that were on patrol closest to Stewart— should be arriving any day."

"It will still take at least a month for any of them to get here," Gavin said. "We're only thirty light-years away, but right now it feels like a parsec."

"Yes, we're pretty much on our own for a while. Any word on the six ships we're unable to contact?"

"Nothing yet. I suspect everyone is too busy just getting their own life-threatening emergencies taken care of. Since we and the *Chiron* have the strongest hull plating, we're in better shape than most of the others."

"As soon as Bill Cameron and his people have stabilized the situation here, you should send them out to assist the other ships with getting their emergency situations under control. Once that's accomplished, we'll need to check on the six ships that aren't responding to hails. Assuming it's not simply a communications failure, we'll need to search for crew-members who might be trapped in airtight sections before their oxygen supplies are exhausted."

"I think we can free up some of the engineering people very soon. We've cordoned off the sections where the hull was breached by torpedoes and posted security personnel to keep people from entering the potentially dangerous areas. Bill's people are busy checking the areas damaged by laser hits to ensure we're not losing atmosphere anywhere. Most of them self-sealed immediately, but they all have to be checked to be sure we aren't putting anyone at risk in those areas."

"Of course."

"Should we deactivate the minefield, Jen? It's still live, and Milori ships keep drifting into the mines. Each explosion sends the hulk spinning back away until it makes contact with another mine on the other side or another hulk, so we're seeing an almost continuous series of detonations."

"I suppose we should. I didn't order it immediately in case some of the Milori ships were playing possum. Deactivating the minefield would give them an opportunity to escape."

"I don't think there's much chance of that. The fighters raked those ships over pretty good. If anyone was playing possum initially, I'm sure they're not playing anymore."

Jenetta nodded. "Okay, Larry. Deactivate the minefield. But let's keep a tactical officer scanning for any sign of life from those ships."

"Aye, Admiral," he said, smiling.

Jenetta smiled for the first time since the engagement had begun. Her look changed to one of concern before she said, "I hope this doesn't feel too awkward for you, Larry. I mean, having a former subordinate supervising the engagement might be difficult for some people."

"Not at all, Jen. I'm glad we've had this opportunity to work together again. And I'm elated that you were the one who developed the battle plan. I never would have thought to use a minefield entrapment the way you did. I would probably have just established a 'picket line' or gauntlet of ships and then waded in when the Milori arrived. Perhaps I would have tried using some of the tactics you developed for the Battle for Higgins. But the overwhelming size of that Milori force would have been too much. They would have crushed us to space dust. Your plan saved the day. We're damaged and bloody, but we're alive, thanks to you."

"We were lucky."

Gavin smiled again. "I've heard you use that expression before to explain how you've triumphed over forces of superior strength and numbers. I think Jenetta Carver makes her own luck by always being two steps ahead of her opponents. And I'm not alone, or you wouldn't be wearing those stars on your shoulders. Do you remember our discussion about HQ's plans for you?"

"Of course."

"Well, after they review the battle plan and results, they may start looking for a way to get you to keep those stars.

There isn't any required or recommended length of time in grade for promotions within the flag officer ranks."

"But I'm only a brevetted admiral."

"The brevet status simply gives them a way to take it back without any formal procedure, but you're still a full admiral while you have it, with all the pay, privileges, and responsibilities of the rank. Now that you've accepted flag officer rank, they could permanently promote you to Rear Admiral, Upper, if they wish. All they need is approval from the GA Council. What's the chance they wouldn't get that, given your history?"

"What? They wouldn't dare make it permanent!"

"Just be careful what you agree to or how you refuse it if you ever wish to get command of a battleship."

"Admiral Holt wouldn't let them do that to me."

"Admiral Holt isn't on the Admiralty Board, although he should be. They've wanted him there for a long time, but he's been fighting a battle to stay at Higgins. As bad as permanent assignment to a space station base is, it's still significantly better than being permanently stuck on Earth. He's refused a third star because it would mean leaving Higgins and returning to Earth. You're going to find that the politics in the service, as bad as they are for captains and commissioned officers, are going to affect you tenfold as an admiral. You've been exempt until now, partly because we're out so far, but mostly because Stewart was still being developed as a base. Now that Stewart is commanded by an admiral, a lot of things are going to change."

"Such as?"

"You'll probably get a JAG admiral assigned to the base now and a full level of senior officers to handle a lot of the functions you've been performing. You'll see captains assigned to the Intelligence, Weapons & Research, Communications & Computing, Supply, Logistics, and Port Operations sections."

"That won't be so bad. I've always been swamped with work."

"You'll still be busy, but now you'll be spending more time with diplomats and the representatives of planets in your sectors. That means more state dinners and more involvement in planetary politics. The little fracas on Arrosa was just the beginning."

Jenetta groaned. "I hope you're wrong."

Gavin held up his hand, signaling a pause in the conversation as he listened to a message in his CT. He pressed his Space Command ring with his other hand. "All right. Proceed. Gavin out." Dropping his hand, he said, "Commander Cameron's people have stabilized the *Prometheus* and he's sending some engineers to lend assistance on the *Geneva* and *Plantaganet.*"

"Great, Larry. Things should be getting sorted out about now. If you have no objections, I'd like to make the conference room on this deck into my office instead of continuing to use the office in my quarters. I'd prefer to be closer to the bridge."

"Of course, Jen. You could use this office though."

"No, you need your office space free. The conference room will be fine. I'll have Commander Ashraf get it set up."

"Right. I'll take care of deactivating the mines."

As Jenetta left the captain's briefing room, Lieutenant Commander Ashraf approached her. "Admiral, I've been able to establish direct communications with the eight ships that are still transmitting, and I have a more accurate picture of readiness than the original damage lists give."

"Very good, Lori. We're going to set up the conference room on this deck for our office. Let's go there and you can fill me in."

As they started to leave, a very stressed-looking newsie, the one assigned to the Prometheus, said, "Excuse me, Admiral, is it okay to leave this spot now?"

"Only if you're leaving the bridge. My people are too busy for questions right now."

"Yes, ma'am, I am," he said, as he hurried towards the door to the corridor.

"Probably going to change his shorts," Jenetta whispered to her aide.

"Okay, Lori, fill me in," Jenetta said as she sat down in the conference room.

Looking at her notes, Ashraf began her report. "First, the battleships. The *Chiron's* condition is similar to the *Prometheus'.* It took several serious torpedo hits, lost four torpedo tubes and fifteen laser arrays, but the power systems are intact and the damaged sections have been cordoned off. It's holding atmosphere throughout most of the ship. Your sister is fine.

"The *Bellona*, because its hull is an older design, is a little worse off, but it's stabilized now. They took multiple torpedo hits and those sections have been cordoned off. It's suffered about a thirty percent loss of weapons. Your sister Eliza suffered a concussion when she was thrown against a console on the bridge, but the chief medical officer says she'll be fine in a week.

"The *Thor* is in slightly better condition than the *Bellona* from both a weapons and hull-condition standpoint, but the sub-light engines were damaged. It only has light-speed and thruster power at present.

"The cruiser *Plantaganet*, being of the *Kamakura* class, has a stronger hull than older cruisers. Still, it suffered multiple torpedo hits in the direct engagement with the Milori ships that escaped from the cage trap and is severely damaged. Engineers from the *Prometheus* have shuttled over to help them seal off the damaged areas and seal the holes from laser fire that were too large to self-seal.

"The *Song*, also *Kamakura* class, is in slightly better shape and expects that their own engineers will be able to handle sealing the ship, although they'll need assistance getting their temporal generator and sub-light engines repaired. They're limited to deuterium-thruster power only right now.

"And lastly, the destroyers. The *Ottawa* is in the best shape because it missed the first pass along the trap. Its role in leading the Milori took it so far away that the *Chiron* was already underway by the time it was able to drop its envelope, turn around with sub-light engines, and get back to join us. The damage occurred in the later battle with the Milori ships.

It was struck twice by torpedoes but will be able to handle its own repairs.

"The *St. Petersburg* was badly damaged by torpedoes, but it's stabilized now. The engines are functional and their engineers will soon be available to help other ships. Your brother, Commander William Carver, is fine. He wasn't injured.

"The *Geneva* was badly damaged by six torpedo hits. It's so bad that an accurate damage assessment isn't available yet. Engineers from the *Prometheus* have joined their people and are working to stabilize the ship.

"That's the situation, Admiral."

"Thank you, Lori. Advise all captains that when their ships are stable I want their engineering staffs to shuttle to the six ships that are out of communication and search for trapped survivors. The Marines on all ships will assist in the recovery once the engineers say it's safe."

"Aye, Admiral. I'll get on it right away."

"After that's done, see if you can find out where they've stored the com unit that belongs on this table." Jenetta studied the table casually as she added absently, "It used to have one, and the connection is still here."

"Aye, Admiral."

It took half a day for the combined engineering staffs of the nine ships to stabilize their life support systems, but a few small teams of engineers were working with Marines to look for survivors on the six ships without communications long before then.

Ashraf continually updated her status report with new information as she received it from the various teams, so she was ready when Jenetta asked for it.

"Teams are now working on four of the six ships where we lost communications, Admiral. They've found survivors on every ship so far, but the losses are very high. In those sections where air supplies are low, we're transferring the survivors to the nearest ship with adequate supplies, which happens to be the *Song*. The *Song* is still in the middle of the battle area since its sub-light engines are still off-line."

"Do you have an estimate of the casualty rate?"

"So far it appears that we've lost about thirty percent of the total crew members on the four visited ships. That's only a very rough estimate."

"And the condition of the ships?"

"Multiple torpedo hits on the *Beijing* opened a hole that extends to the center of the ship. One frame section is so badly damaged that it's impossible to pass from the bow to the stern without an EVA suit. Engineers and Marines, entering from bow and stern airlocks, have found at least half the crew alive. All airtight doors were sealed, of course, before we met the enemy, and emergency bulkheads closed in various frame sections when pressure dropped. The sub-light engines appear to be intact, but it will take months to repair the hull damage. Their IDS communications equipment is down, but their engineers are trying to rig something and they should have basic RF communications soon.

"The *Asuncion* appears to be the most heavily damaged of all our ships. The engineers believe it may be beyond repair. It took multiple, serious torpedo hits and the loss of life appears to be as high as seventy percent. The bridge was totally destroyed. The crewmembers who were working in the most interior sections of the ship, such as the weapons control centers or waiting it out in Secure rooms, make up the bulk of the survivors.

"The *Mentuhotep* has been clobbered hard, but it's still better off than the *Asuncion*. The initial estimate is that about half the crew is missing or dead. The bow of the ship split wide open. Damage extends as far back as the bridge. The bridge crew, including most of the senior officers, is missing and presumed lost. The hull breached in several other areas as well. The sub-light engines appear serviceable though.

"The *Romanov* isn't in much better condition, but much more of the crew, including the senior officers, survived. It'll take months of work to get the ship repaired.

"It would be nice if we were closer to Stewart so we could tow the ships back there for repair, but at thirty light-years, it's much too far without a fleet of space tugs. We'll have to remain here to do the work or abandon the ships.

"That's all we have so far, Admiral. The *Buenos Aires* and the *Cairo* haven't been boarded yet because the engineers wanted to visit the most heavily damaged ships first."

"Okay, Lori. Thank you. I'll wait until we have a complete report on the space-worthiness of each ship before I make any decisions about abandoning them, but it doesn't look like we'll be going anywhere soon. We also can't simply leave over a hundred Milori warships here. This cleanup operation could take a year or more— "

Jenetta stopped talking as Ashraf suddenly held up her hand and cupped her left ear. After a few seconds, she touched her ring and said, "Thank you. Ashraf out." Looking towards Jenetta she said, "The *Prometheus* com operator is picking up IDS radio signals coming from the Milori fleet."

"Signals to us?"

"Negative, Admiral. The signals are encrypted."

Jenetta exhaled her breath loudly. "It appears there are survivors. Well, that was to be expected. They're either trying to make contact with other survivors, calling for ships to come to their rescue, or sending a report back to the Empire. Perhaps all three."

"I wouldn't be too worried about options one or three, but option two makes me nervous."

"Yes, we don't know how many ships are in our space. For all we know, they could have another invasion force here larger than the one we fought. And we're surely not going to trap them the way we did the first group."

"I wonder how close their nearest ships are."

"That's the million-credit question. We're going to have to keep a careful watch. Send messages to our observation ships. I was going to recall them to assist with the cleanup, but now we'll need them to keep an eye out for Milori reinforcements. Reposition them directly between us and the Elurra system about a hundred billion kilometers out from our location and close enough to each other that no one can sneak between them."

"But with just six observation ships, we can only cover a small area of space. A Milori taskforce could be coming from a different direction. Maybe we should keep them in closer so they'll be more effective."

"If we keep them too close, we won't have sufficient warning in time to react. Even at a hundred billion kilometers, we'll only have fifteen minute's warning."

"Aye, Admiral."

"We'll need two officers to take command of the *Asuncion* and *Mentuhotep*." Looking at the large monitor on the wall, Jenetta said, "Computer, among the survivors of the taskforce verified alive and well, who are the two most senior XOs on the Promotion Selection List for captain?"

The computer said, "The most senior executive officers are Commander Allen Hollingshead of the GSC Battleship *Bellona*, and Commander William Carver of the GSC Destroyer *St. Petersburg*."

"Computer, voice off. Lori, notify Allen to assume command of the *Asuncion*, and have Billy take command of the *Mentuhotep*."

"Right away, Admiral."

Ashraf sat down in front of the com unit and began issuing orders in Jenetta's name while Jenetta studied the latest damage reports. The total of confirmed dead was approaching one thousand, three hundred, and the total missing was over two thousand. Jenetta saw the images of known officers, NCOs, and crewmembers in her mind as the list scrolled up.

# Chapter Seventeen
~ February 15<sup>th</sup>, 2277 ~

Twenty-four hours after the engagement, search parties had scoured every ship in the taskforce for dead and wounded, and engineers had prepared a basic report on the status of each ship. The *Buenos Aires* and the *Cairo* were the last to be searched and have their condition evaluated. Each had lost a substantial part of their crew, and the ships were so badly damaged that they would be of little use in a fight, not even able to travel at faster-than-light speeds without months of repair work.

The number of confirmed dead had reached four thousand, eight hundred forty-six, with the missing and presumed lost currently standing at three hundred eighteen. A recovery effort devoted to finding bodies floating in space around the engagement area had been undertaken before they could drift too far away, but the task was onerous. They found more Milori bodies than Terran bodies. Enemy bodies were being stored in cargo containers pending final disposition.

Ships lacking the ability to move under their own power were towed to the area where the *Prometheus* had stopped after the engagement, and the ships with functional life support systems were linking up via airlock. Normally, Space Command ships aligned themselves side by side, but because of the damage, all ships with usable airlocks in the bow were connecting to a bow airlock on another ship facing in the opposite direction. This arrangement made the outside surfaces of the ships more accessible to bots and repair crews while also leaving flight bay entrances accessible. To anyone outside, the arrangement looked like something a child would create in their sandbox, and a shuttle pilot could easily get confused if visually searching for his or her ship in the blackness of space. The *Mentuhotep* linked up using stern airlocks because its bow airlocks had been destroyed.

A very weary Admiral Carver sat down at the com unit in the conference room and prepared a report for Admiral Moore at Space Command. She had procrastinated as long as she could, telling herself she wanted as much information as possible before sending the report she knew was anxiously awaited at Supreme Headquarters.

"Priority-One message to Richard E. Moore, Admiral of the Fleet, Space Command Supreme Headquarters, from Jenetta A. Carver, Rear Admiral, Lower Half, Base Commander of Stewart Space Command Base, aboard the GSC Battleship *Prometheus*. Begin message.

"Hello Admiral. It's been twenty-four hours since the engagement and we've stabilized our situation. Most of our engineers are getting some much-needed rest now that shipboard life support emergencies have been dealt with. We'll resume repair activities when they return to duty. We continue to search space around the engagement area and collect the bodies of Space Command personnel and Milori invaders.

"We've picked up radio communication activity from some of the ships in the destroyed enemy fleet, but we've been too busy with other problems to investigate. The messages are encrypted, so we know they aren't trying to contact us. There has been no movement of any of the Milori ships since the engagement ended, but we continue to watch them vigilantly. In the next few days, we'll begin a ship-by-ship assessment of the destroyed fleet as we look for survivors and ascertain that the Milori ships pose no further threat.

"I'm awaiting an updated ETA list of the ships redirected to Stewart so I can reroute some to our location. It appears obvious that we'll be here for some time. The repair and cleanup effort will be massive, and we'll need additional supplies and equipment from Stewart. I've radioed instructions to Captain Donovan to send every available space tug to this location.

"I'm appending a confirmed list of casualties to this message. I extend my heartfelt condolences to the families of each of our deceased comrades. All fought with commendable bravery against an invading force of overwhelmingly superior numbers.

"I'm also forwarding a current damage assessment for each of our ships. I sent a copy of the *Prometheus'* vid log immediately following the battle. Each captain in the fleet will naturally be forwarding their own report at their earliest opportunity and you'll probably receive another copy of the *Prometheus'* log when Captain Gavin submits his report.

"I'll continue filing additional reports every twenty-four hours for the next few days as assessments of our condition become more precise.

"Jenetta A. Carver, Rear Admiral, Lower Half, from the GSC Battleship *Prometheus*, message complete."

Jenetta had sent Lt. Commander Ashraf to get some sleep hours ago and she decided it was time for her to go now. As she entered her quarters, she was enthusiastically greeted by her cats that had been alone in the rooms for almost thirty hours, except for the three very brief visits she had made to feed them.

Jenetta sat on the floor of the bedroom with the cats and brushed their fur while they playfully rubbed against her or climbed over her. She intended to spend a half-hour playing with them and then go to bed, but she wound up falling asleep on the carpeted deck.

Jenetta's cats awakened her early. They seemed to have an infallible internal clock. She stretched, rubbed the cats a little, and then changed into her sweats. Ten minutes later, they were in the ship's gym, currently empty of all other personnel. She spent a half-hour punishing the punching bag with her fists and feet as the cats looked on. They then spent the remaining half-hour running around the track in a flight bay. Returning to her quarters, she showered, fed the cats their breakfast, and then sat down to enjoy hers. Her steward, Chief Petty Officer Virginia Fairsmith, was finally getting used to the cats having the run of the suite. CPO Fairsmith had quickly gotten accustomed to preparing enough food to satisfy Jenetta's appetite and only needed to know what she preferred to eat at each meal.

Ashraf was already at work in the converted conference room when Jenetta arrived.

"Good morning, Admiral."

"Good morning, Lori. Anything that requires my immediate attention?"

"Not too much that's urgent, Admiral. Do you need something?"

"I'd like to visit the sickbays today— all the sickbays."

"Aye, Admiral. I'm sure that most of the things can wait until after you've done that. Oh, one thing I do have to mention. The news reporters are all asking when they'll be allowed to file their stories on the conflict."

"Tell them they can send them in two days. By then we should have everything completely stabilized. That might have more of a positive impact on the stories they file. Things look pretty bleak right now."

"Very good, Admiral, 0800 hours two days from now."

Jenetta quickly took care of the things she deemed urgent and they left to visit the sick bays on every ship in the task-force, beginning with the *Prometheus.*

During the first twenty-four hours after the engagement, sickbay personnel treated and released minor contusion and abrasion cases quickly. Even simple fracture cases were treated and released, leaving the medical staff able to concentrate on the more serious cases. A doctor joined Jenetta and Ashraf as they walked through the sickbay, stopping at every bed so Jenetta could talk with the crewperson if he or she was awake. She told them how proud she was of their performance and asked them if they needed anything. Most asked when they'd be able to send a message home. Jenetta told them that the ban on outgoing messages would be lifted in two days and that a nurse would help them prepare a message sometime during the day that could be queued for immediate dispatch when the ban was raised. It lifted their spirits more than anything else she said.

After speaking to each of the patients in the *Prometheus'* sickbay and several temporary wards, Jenetta and her aide moved to the next ship, the *Song*, and made the rounds in their sickbay and temporary wards. Having commanded the *Song* for a year, she knew many of the injured— if not personally, then at least by name.

That was the way it went for the rest of the morning and into the early afternoon. Jenetta would have called on her sisters during her visitations, but they would have been asleep at that hour since both were on the third watch on their respective ships. Jenetta did look up her brother, though, after they had completed their visits to the sick bays.

Upon entering the *Mentuhotep*, Jenetta returned the salute of the officer at the airlock and asked, "Do you know where the Captain is, Lieutenant?"

"I don't know, Admiral, but I'll find out," he said as he touched his Space Command ring and spoke to the ship's computer. "He's in the Auxiliary Control & Communications Center according to the computer, Admiral."

"Thank you, Lieutenant."

"Would you like me to show you the way, ma'am?"

"Thank you, but that's not necessary. I once commanded a *Kamakura* class cruiser so I'm familiar with the layout. Besides, I wouldn't want you to get into trouble for leaving your post."

"Yes, ma'am. Thank you, ma'am."

"As you were, Lieutenant."

"Aye, Admiral."

Since the *Mentuhotep* was virtually identical to the *Song*, both Jenetta and Ashraf knew the way to AC&C. Upon entering, someone immediately spotted Jenetta and said loudly, "Admiral on the deck." Everyone snapped to attention.

"As you were," Jenetta said.

As everyone relaxed, Billy walked to Jenetta and greeted her formally with, "Welcome to the *Mentuhotep*, Admiral."

"Thank you, Captain. How are you getting on?"

"We're making progress, ma'am. We'll have the ship back in fighting condition as soon as we possibly can."

"Very good, Captain. Is there someplace where we can talk?"

"Yes, ma'am. Follow me."

Billy led the way to a conference room down the corridor. As they entered, Jenetta signaled to Lt. Commander Ashraf that she should wait outside. Lori understood immediately and stood in the corridor in front of the door as it closed.

"Is it permitted for a ship's captain to hug an admiral?" Billy asked, smiling.

"If it isn't, I'll issue a standing order," Jenetta said as she wrapped her arms around her oldest brother and hugged him tightly. When they were young, he had towered over her, but with her height now a bit over five-eleven, he was only a few inches taller.

"I'm glad you're safe," he said.

"We're lucky. All four of us made it through safely. Eliza got a bump on the head, but that's all. She's probably forgotten about it by now, given our recovery rates. How are you enjoying your first command?"

"I've always wanted a ship, but I didn't think I'd have to build it to get one," he said jokingly. "Seriously, things aren't so bad. Everything is repairable; it'll just take time. There are thousands of laser holes in the hull, but most of them have self-sealed and can wait until the bow is repaired. That's naturally our highest priority. I've assembled a temporary senior staff to replace those killed during the engagement, and they're doing fine. You can assign other officers if you wish."

"No, I made you the captain and it's your responsibility to assign people to vacant positions during an emergency."

"Thank you for this opportunity, by the way. I knew I'd get a command someday, but I never thought my appointment would come from my baby sister." He smiled.

"You earned it, Billy. You didn't get it because you're my brother." She paused for a second and then asked in a concerned voice, "Does it bother you very much that I outrank you?"

"I'm happy for you, sis, but I'd be lying if I said my ego didn't feel a tiny bit bruised that my baby sister made admiral while I was still a commander. I promise it won't affect my performance as captain of this ship or as an officer under your command. I've gotten a little ribbing from my friends about it though."

"I've been concerned about how you might feel, but I've never thought for a second that you would let it interfere with your duty. I'm sorry you've taken the ribbing. Perhaps it would make you feel better to know that I envy you?"

"You envy me?"

"Of course. You're on a ship. That's all I've wanted for years, not the rank. I was happiest when I was First Officer on the *Prometheus*. I'd have been very content to remain there for the next fifty-five years, or however long they would have let me serve in a space officer capacity. This taskforce was my chance to get off Stewart for a while and back into the *Prometheus*. I'm just sorry it took an invasion to find a good excuse."

"I thought you were happy with the rank. You're the youngest admiral in the entire history of Space Command."

"I didn't ask for it, or even want it. They just felt the senior officer of the taskforce had to be an admiral. There weren't any handy out here, so they brevetted me into the position because I already had the authority anyway as Base Commander of Stewart. I'm actually the only one out here they could have brevetted while I occupied the position of CO at Stewart. But even though I'm the senior-ranking officer aboard the *Prometheus*, I'm still just a passenger. There are days when I feel as useless as clothes on a Pledgian. The *Prometheus* is Captain Gavin's ship, and I wouldn't even consider usurping any of his authority or responsibilities."

"What will you do when this operation is over?"

"I'll return to being the Base Commander at Stewart, but I was told I'll retain the brevetted rank until the end of my tour. Captain Gavin thinks my duties will change significantly now. He believes that SHQ will create a new level of bureaucracy beneath me. According to him, I'll be required to spend more time engaged in diplomatic activities and supervisory management, and have less direct contact with the daily operations of the base."

"That sounds more like what my idea of an admiral's day would be like. The admiral says, 'Build me a new officer's club,' and it gets built without him or her ever doing anything else."

"That's fine when you're ninety, but not when you're forty-one and want the involvement."

"I'm sure you have plenty to keep you busy right now."

"Yes, until the taskforce is space-worthy again I should have quite a bit to do. But that's not something that should occupy your thoughts. You have plenty of important matters to deal with right now, so I'll go and let you get to them. I'm just glad you're okay. I've lifted the ban on outgoing messages effective two days from now, so you'll probably want to queue up a message to mom and dad about your new command. Good luck, Billy."

"Thanks, sis. You too."

Jenetta and Billy hugged and then Billy headed back to AC&C while Jenetta and Ashraf began the trek back to the *Prometheus* through a dozen ships. Upon reentering the *Ottawa*, Jenetta decided to stop in to see Captain Crosby. They encountered Trader Vyx as they entered a lift for the ride to the bridge deck.

"Hello, Trader. It's good to see you again."

"Hi, Admiral. It's a pleasure to see you again. Permit me to introduce you to Brenda Cardiz."

"Ah, yes. A.k.a. Maria Elena Morales. Hello, Brenda."

"Uh, hello, Admiral. Gosh, you look younger than I do. I'd heard you were young, but I never thought of you as *that* young."

Jenetta smiled. "It's just my appearance. I assure you that I'm almost old enough to be your mother. I'm forty-one now."

Brenda laughed. "Oh, come on, Admiral. Everyone knows you spent eleven years in a stasis chamber aboard a life pod, so that would only make you like, thirty, really."

"Shhh. Don't tell anybody. I'm supposed to be in charge around here."

Brenda giggled.

"Is there anything I can do to help, Admiral? I'm feeling a little useless lately," Vyx said.

"I understand, Trader. There's nothing right now, but stay loose. Something may come up very soon."

"Okay, Admiral. Just give me the word."

"Nice to have met you, Brenda," Jenetta said as the lift door opened on A deck. "Goodbye, Trader."

"Goodbye, Admiral," Brenda and Vyx said simultaneously.

The bridge was very close to the lift, and as Jenetta entered, she received the customary 'Admiral on the bridge!' shout. She responded with 'As you were' and continued on to the captain's briefing room, not seeing Jeff Crosby anywhere in sight. The door opened almost as soon as she stepped in front of it. Crosby, seated at his desk, stood up when she entered.

"Good afternoon, Admiral. Come in, please. Have a seat. Would you care for something to drink?"

"Yes, I could use a mug of coffee."

"I'll get it, Admiral," Ashraf said, moving quickly to the food synthesizer. "Anything for you, Captain?"

"No, thanks. I'm fine."

Jenetta sat down across from Crosby as he also took his seat. This was the first time in many months that they had talked in person.

"That was quite a collection you brought back, Jeff. Good work, by the way."

"I just wish I'd known how many ships I'd accumulated along the way."

"Maybe it's better we didn't know this time. Everyone would have been a lot more nervous. This way we were in the fight before we had a chance to think about it. Thank you, Commander," Jenetta said as Ashraf handed her the coffee.

"That was a clever trap you laid, Admiral," Crosby said. "I don't think the Milori ever wised up to what they were facing."

"It's too bad we can't keep it a secret. Once the news reports are released, they'll change their pursuit tactics, if not sooner."

"Maybe not. If they had been spread out, as we are when traveling, we would have known the size of the pursuing force."

"They could just establish multiple lines," Jenetta said. "You would only be able to see the four or five lead ships, and trapping them in a narrow cage that severely limits their maneuvering ability would be impossible because they would be spread out."

"I guess we'll just have to be prepared for anything."

"The one thing we're not prepared for is another invasion force. I know that if you had seen anything you would have reported it, but have any of your prisoners mentioned anything that might indicate there are other Milori fleets out here?"

"I haven't spoken with them since we first picked them up. There wasn't much to say, and they weren't talking."

"I think I'd like to speak to them. It can't hurt to gloat a little and see if their anger causes them to reveal something."

"Would you like to see them here, or should I have them transferred to the *Prometheus*?"

"Your brig's interview room will do fine."

"Let's go."

Ten minutes later, Jenetta sat in an interrogation room with Crosby and Ashraf as two guards escorted the first prisoner in. Each of the Space Command officers had a translation device clipped to their belt that would send a translated voice message directly to their CT. A guard handed the Milora a translation device adapted to his physiology.

"This is Uthqulk, first deputy negotiator to Commander Acoxxuz," Crosby said to Jenetta. "He's the leader of the group."

"Hello, Uthqulk. I'm Admiral Jenetta Carver."

"I demand that my associates and I be released. You've kept us prisoner on this garbage scow for almost an annual. We've done nothing illegal."

"What is your true purpose in being in the Frontier Zone, Uthqulk?"

Uthqulk stared straight ahead and didn't respond.

"Was it to gather intelligence prior to an invasion?"

He glanced at Jenetta sharply with all four eyes but still said nothing.

"This ship has been to the Elurra system during the past year. You were mere thousands of kilometers away from your brethren."

"Why weren't we transferred?" he asked angrily.

"Tut, tut, you're not playing by the rules. I've given you several pieces of information you didn't know and you've supplied nothing."

Uthqulk glared at her with menace in his four eyes.

"We learned that the Milori Empire was building a base in our territory and we went to investigate. Lord High Space Marshall Gulqulk of the emperor's Imperial Cruiser *Reguffa* informed us that the empire had decided to annex our territory and ordered us out, threatening us with destruction if we didn't comply."

Uthqulk smiled slightly.

"Ah, so you were aware of that. Is Gulqulk a relative by the way? I noticed that your names have the same last syllable. That identifies your clan, doesn't it?"

"He is my cousin."

"Oh, my condolences then. I'm sure he was a very brave Milora. Foolhardy, but brave."

"What do you mean— was?"

"Only that I believe him to be dead. You see, the ships in the Elurra system gave chase to the *Ottawa*. They chased this ship all the way back to this point where we were waiting. I offered Gulqulk the opportunity to surrender, but he felt that his fleet of a hundred three ships could defeat my taskforce of fifteen. I admit they gave us a bit of a fight, but the battle didn't really last very long."

"You lie. No fifteen Space Command ships could defeat so many Milori warships."

"No, I'm not lying. It's quite a mess out there. Too bad you missed the show. Stuck down here in the brig, you probably never even realized a battle was going on, but you should have felt some minor buffeting when this ship was struck by weapons fire. It's only been a day and a half since it ended, so we haven't had much of a chance to clean up the battle site yet."

"How many Milori survived?"

"We don't know. We continued firing until they all stopped shooting. I doubt if any of your ships can move with anything other than thruster power. We've picked up radio signals coming from several ships, but I'm not sending my people in on rescue missions unless I know the survivors won't fire at them. So far, the ships refuse to acknowledge our hails."

"If what you say is true about the battle, you must mount a rescue operation before they run out of air."

"Not until somebody speaks for the survivors."

"I'll speak for them."

"You? You won't even answer my basic questions."

Uthqulk was quiet for a few seconds. "Prove what you've said is true and I'll answer your questions."

Jenetta walked to the large monitor on the wall. "Computer, show an accurate, close-up, sensor representation of the battle area, panning across it slowly." An enhanced image of the Milori ships appeared. It would have been too black to see anything with the naked eye, but the destroyed ships were plainly visible in the representation.

"That could be a simulation," the Milora said.

Jenetta walked over to the table and lifted the com station cover. After pressing a button, the image of the com operator on duty appeared. "Com, one of our prisoners wants to talk with his fellow Milori. Hail the Milori ships on the frequency they're using with his image and let him talk to them. Patch translated exchanges to my, Captain Crosby, and Lt. Commander Ashraf's CTs."

"Aye, Admiral."

Jenetta turned the com unit so the vid lens would pick up Uthqulk's image.

After several hails, the image of a Milora appeared. "This is Yarqill. Who calls?"

"I'm Uthqulk, first deputy negotiator to Commander Acoxxuz."

"Confirm."

Uthqulk held steady and pressed the identify button that would send a retinal scan.

"Scan received and verified. Where are you, sir?"

"I'm aboard one of the Space Command ships. What is your status?"

"I can't reveal that, sir. The enemy will learn."

"Tell me this then: did you engage fifteen Space Command ships with a hundred three of our warships?"

"Yes, sir."

"And the outcome?"

"They trapped us inside some kind of powerful energy cage. If we touched the sides, the ship exploded at that spot. We received orders to fight in spite of being hopelessly trapped, and they commenced an attack on us. They used some kind of unseen bomb that exploded in our midst. Each blast destroyed five to ten of our ships. The entire Third Fleet has been wiped out. I think we might have destroyed one or two of their ships though."

"One or two?" Uthqulk said. He had been acting proud and defiant since being escorted in, but he slumped in his chair now as if someone had let the air out of him. "Who is the senior officer in charge?" he asked the other Milora. "You can tell me. Nothing you say will aid the enemy. They already know they've won this battle."

"Yes, sir. I don't know who the senior officer is, sir. I've only been able to make contact with half a dozen ships. They say that most of our warriors are dead or severely injured. The air is getting stale."

"Listen to me, Yarqill. The Space Command ships will attempt to rescue survivors. But such efforts will cease if you fire upon them. I order you to surrender and to pass that word to everyone you can reach."

"But sir, we were ordered to fight to the last warrior by Lord High Space Marshall Gulqulk."

"The battle is over, Yarqill! There's no reason to throw your life away now. It won't change the outcome. I order you to surrender and save yourself for another day's fight."

"Aye, sir. I'll pass your order along."

"Good. Uthqulk out."

"Yarqill out."

Jenetta waited for several minutes before saying, "Satisfied that I was telling the truth?"

"Yes. How many ships did you lose?"

"None. One ship was damaged by a torpedo. Our engineers are evaluating whether we should repair it here or tow it back to our base and repair it there. The rest were hit by light laser fire, but we're making those simple repairs here."

"It appears that our intelligence was faulty. We were assured that our ships and weapons were on a par with yours."

"Who told you that?"

"Shev Rivemwilth. He will die painfully when my people learn of his treachery."

"You're too late. We took care of that little chore for you. He's been dead for about two years now. He met the same fate that eventually comes to all arms smugglers. His operation had been under investigation for some time, and he didn't have a clue as to what weapons we *really* possess. He only knew what we allowed him to know."

"That pig of an Alyysian. However he died, it was too quick."

"You're not the first to utter that sentiment. Okay, tell me about the Empire's invasion plan."

"I will reveal nothing about the Empire's plans."

Jenetta could see that the Milora was resolute and wouldn't provide information easily, but she had also seen that he was genuinely concerned for the survivors. It was the only card she could play. "Very well." Turning to Crosby, she said, "Captain, have you identified the ships that are broadcasting radio signals?"

Crosby hesitated for a second and then, "Yes, Admiral."

"Very good. Send in the fighters to destroy those ships. There's no sense letting the Milori suffer from hypoxia and then suffocation. This will be quicker and we won't have to care for prisoners."

"You can't do that!" Uthqulk shouted. "They're helpless!"

"I'm not going to send in rescue squads only to see them fired upon."

"But I ordered them not to resist. You heard me."

"I also heard you say you'd answer my questions if I proved we had destroyed your invasion force with fifteen ships. Your word is obviously not to be trusted. For all I know, the order you gave was a carefully coded message for 'kill anyone who enters the ship.'"

Uthqulk glared at Jenetta, who stared back unemotionally. "If I tell you, you'll save my people? All my people?"

"If— and only if— I feel you've been completely truthful, we'll save all who will allow us to save them."

Uthqulk stared at Jenetta with all four of his eyes, then at Crosby, and finally at Ashraf. "Okay. The Empire plans to annex your Frontier Zone. The plan is to push you back to your old border and block you from making further expansions towards our territory."

"We already knew that. Gulqulk as much as told us that, and I informed you of that a few minutes ago. I want the operational plans for the invasion."

"I don't know any more than that."

"Of course you do. You're the first deputy negotiator to Commander Acoxxuz. You came here to solidify your agreements with Shev Rivemwilth and collect whatever new intelligence you could. You know much more than you're telling."

"I've told you what I know."

Jenetta looked at Crosby. "Send out the fighters, Captain. He's not going to cooperate."

This time, Crosby was more aware of the game Jenetta was playing. He lifted the com panel cover without hesitation and began giving orders to his First Officer for the destruction of the Milori ships that were broadcasting.

"Stop! You can't do that!" the Milora shouted.

Crosby ignored him.

"Okay, I'll tell you the rest!" Uthqulk yelled angrily.

"Standby, Commander," Crosby said to his First. "I'll get back to you."

"It won't make any difference if you know," Uthqulk said. "If you can destroy an entire fleet with just fifteen ships and escape almost unscathed, we can't possibly defeat you, especially with a third of our ships already destroyed." Uthqulk slumped even more than he had earlier. "Three hundred fifteen ships were sent for the invasion, divided into three fleets of a hundred five ships. Each fleet had orders to establish re-supply bases within the Frontier Zone first, and the invasion wasn't to start for several lunar cycles yet. I don't know why my cousin chose to launch his part of the invasion so early. I've been out of touch with him since being forced to use the life pod aboard Rivemwilth's ship."

"What was the invasion plan?"

"Phase One was to drive you out of the current Frontier Zone. Phase Two was to drive you back another hundred parsecs to the border established when the Galactic Alliance was first established. Phase Three was to attack your home world and wipe out Space Command Headquarters, bases, your Mars shipyard, weapons production facilities, power generating capability, and telecommunications, leaving your world in ruins and this part of space in total disarray. Privateers would then have free rein until the Empire was ready to exercise full control. I don't have any more details than that, and the Lord High Space Marshall with each fleet has full authority to alter the battle plans if the situation warrants it."

"Where would the Privateers come from?"

"The Raiders, the Tsgardi, and any of our citizens who wished to do it."

"You think you can control the Tsgardi?"

"The Tsgardi are stupid creatures, barely sentient. They do whatever we tell them because they know we could destroy their kingdom easily. We allow them to survive because they're useful at times, and they recognize our natural superiority."

"They recognize your natural superiority? In other words, they fear you?"

"I would not expect you to understand."

"Because we don't recognize your superiority?" Jenetta asked.

"No. Because you expect others to be in awe of yours."

"We only expect you to recognize and respect our territorial boundaries, as we have respected yours. By invading our space and declaring that our prior claim is void, you've only demonstrated your arrogance. Your Empire has embarked on a path that could lead to its destruction."

"You've won this battle. It remains to be seen if you can destroy us."

"It's not our goal to destroy you. But we won't allow you to destroy us either."

"If war was not your goal, you would not have so many powerful weapons. We have conquered innumerous peaceful societies. The half-wits actually believed that if they didn't present a threat to anyone, no one would bother them. They hadn't spent their time developing weapons, as you apparently have. Only warrior races develop such powerful weapons."

"Or those races that will not allow themselves to be conquered by warrior races. We fall into the latter group."

"Are you so sure? Are you so very, very sure?"

# Chapter Eighteen
~ February 16<sup>th</sup>, 2277 ~

Jenetta interviewed the other two Milori, but they refused to divulge anything. She didn't try using the surviving Milori as a bargaining chip again. The information she had learned from their leader was probably as much as she was likely to learn anyway. Her first act after returning to the small conference room that served as her office was to call a meeting of all captains and their first officers.

The large conference room selected for the meeting was capable of comfortably seating the thirty invited officers. Once everyone took their seats, Jenetta began.

"Ladies and Gentlemen, I'm sorry to drag you away from your repair efforts, but I've just learned something of vital importance. A Milora prisoner in the brig of the *Ottawa* has divulged to me that the Milori Empire dispatched three hundred fifteen ships for this invasion effort. The Milori High Command divided this armada into three fleets of a hundred five ships. According to the Milora, the invasion push was not supposed to begin for some months yet, so he doesn't know why this fleet chose to move now. We're speculating that the discovery of their base in the Elurra system by the *Ottawa* was responsible for pushing up their attack timetable.

"I have no way of knowing if the Milora is being truthful, but I don't think we can afford to simply dismiss this information. I can't see where he would have anything to gain by lying, and his story fits with what we knew or suspected. While a hundred three ships is an impressive invasion force, it seems inadequate given their stated intention of annexing our Frontier Zone to their empire. They had to know we would gather all our forces in an effort to repel their invasion, and I'm sure they have a good idea of our fleet size.

"This new information raises a number of important questions. Where are the other two hundred twelve ships? What was their timetable? Did the fleet that attacked us communicate their advancement of the invasion timetable? Have the other fleets also advanced *their* timetable? Where will they attack next?

"We can speculate that the two ships missing from the fleet that attacked us were either left behind to protect valuable resources at established supply bases or were on some mission or other and couldn't link up with the fleet following the *Ottawa*. We have to be aware that they still might show up, however unlikely now that their main battle group has been defeated. It's more likely they'll attempt to link up with the rest of the invasion force. We know that several of the ships in the destroyed fleet have been communicating with each other, and they have probably sent word of the battle back to the Empire and to the other fleets. We'll have to watch for any sign of Milori ships because the other two fleets might already be on their way here. If we assume that progress of the other fleets was synchronized with this one, they would still have been on this side of the Frontier Zone border when they received word of the Third Fleet's defeat.

"Our top priority is to get our ships capable of Light Speed travel as soon as possible. We can worry later about how they look. If two hundred ships suddenly appear in front of us, our only recourse may be to fall back. There's no chance of our trapping them the way we did the Third Fleet."

"Perhaps they'll follow us in a line to a new trap," Captain Yung of the *Song* said. "We could set one up at the border."

"If the ships caught in the trap sent a message to the rest of the fleet, we probably can't count on them falling for that again. Besides, we don't have sufficient mines left or the time to set it up."

"We can't just cut and run," Captain Payton of the *Thor* said.

"Captain Crosby reminded me that Shakespeare wrote, 'The better part of valor is discretion,' after we encountered the Milori in the Elurra system," Commander Upton said.

"We can't possibly defeat two hundred ten Milori warships by ourselves, just as the *Ottawa* couldn't have defeated the sixteen warships by itself. We should fall back and join up with the forces that are coming to support Stewart."

Jenetta let the captains and first officers debate whether to fight or run for a few minutes. Ultimately, she would have to make the decision. She finally held up her hand for silence and then said, "We'll respond to the threat when we know what the threat is. No matter which course of action we decide to pursue, our ships must be ready. I've been allowing each ship to use its engineering staff to work on its own ship now that the emergency repairs have been completed, but that will have to change in light of this new information. We'll need to concentrate our efforts on those ships having the best chance for speedy repair. As soon as those ships are capable of light-speed travel, we'll devote our full resources to each of the others in order of fitness. Captain Gavin, I'd like Commander Cameron to evaluate each ship's present condition and establish the prioritized list."

"Aye, Admiral. I'll assign him to the task immediately."

"We know for a fact that one of our ships is far worse off than the others. I'm sorry Commander Hollingshead, but your ship will most likely be the last to receive repair efforts because the damage is so severe. Half the *Asuncion* engineering staff should report immediately to the *Prometheus* and the other half to the *Chiron*. Keep a few people to maintain the systems that are functioning and to handle small problems that arise, but the majority are needed elsewhere."

"I understand Admiral. Perhaps I should transfer my remaining crew to one of the battleships in case we need to make a hasty departure?"

"Not yet. I believe we'll have at least a few weeks before the other Milori can get here. I'm speculating that the enemy fleets intended to attack at three distinct points, and if they were, it makes sense that the points would be at least twenty-five light-years apart and probably much greater. They would know our forces are thinly spread along the border and believe that a surprise attack by a hundred ships in each fleet would be more than sufficient to meet any threat from us at each selected point. They'd want a wide coverage to take out as many of our ships as possible as they swept through our territory. If this was not the central invasion point, it could take many months for them to reassemble and travel here. Even so, we'll initially operate as if we only have three weeks. This will have to be a maximum effort.

"Captain Gavin, would you and Captain Powers coordinate search and rescue operations on the Milori ships by our Marines? If they offer any resistance, pull out and move to the next ship. We can house prisoners in our cargo bay until we know how many we'll have to deal with. We'll also need medical personnel at the ready. I hope someone is familiar with Milori physiology or can get up to speed quickly by examining some of the Milori cadavers."

"Aye, Admiral," both captains said.

"Thank you, everyone. You've all done a fantastic job and I know that everyone needs rest, but we'll have to push ourselves for a bit longer. Dismissed."

Gavin and Powers hung back as the conference room emptied. As the door closed, Gavin said to Jenetta, "Do you think the Milori will accept being rescued?"

"They're uglier than the Tsgardi, but much more intelligent. I hope they'll understand this battle is lost and we're their only salvation. In any event, I promised our Milora prisoner we'd try in exchange for the information about the invasion plans. He's a proud warrior, but he knows how badly they were beaten. From the brig of the *Ottawa*, we contacted one of the survivors who told our prisoner how we trapped them in an energy cage that caused an explosion if the ship touched the sides. He also said we'd used invisible bombs that exploded in their midst. I'd like to perpetuate those myths. Let's make the Milori think our weapons are far more advanced than their own. If we can create an image of invincibility among the Milori, it will work to our advantage."

"Until they actually attack us and we come up short," Captain Powers said.

"Well, they can't argue that we've destroyed a third of their invasion force. *We* know we don't hold a major weaponry advantage over them, but *they* don't. And that, in itself, will be our advantage."

Repair crews had eased off a little after the emergency repairs had been completed and gotten some much needed rest. Reinvigorated after news of the other Milori fleets flashed through the Space Command taskforce, they were eager to get back to work. Bill Cameron provided rough estimates of the time needed to get each ship capable of travel at FTL speeds, and Jenetta ordered engineering staffs reassigned accordingly.

It seemed like a week had passed since the battle, but in reality it had been less than forty-eight hours. Jenetta received the list she had requested from Captain Donovan showing the ETA for each of the nineteen ships headed to Stewart. As tempting as it was to order every one of the ships to the battle site, she had to consider the safety and defense of Stewart. Some of the ships *had* to remain at the base once they reached it. She agonized over the list for an hour but finally made a decision on reassignments. In a recorded message to each ship's captain, she explained about the battle they had just fought, the imminent threat from the two remaining invasion fleets, and the new orders she was issuing.

Her last pressing matter was a message to Admiral Moore and Space Command HQ. She organized her notes so she wouldn't miss any key points and then made the lengthy recording.

"Priority-One message to Richard E. Moore, Admiral of the Fleet, Space Command Supreme Headquarters, from Jenetta A. Carver, Rear Admiral, Lower, Base Commander of Stewart Space Command Base, aboard the GSC Battleship *Prometheus* in the Frontier Zone. Begin message.

"Hello, Admiral. I have distressing news. During the interrogation of a Milora aboard the *Ottawa*, we've learned that the invasion fleet we destroyed represents only one-third of three hundred fifteen ships sent by the Empire. The Milora claims not to know where the other two fleets intend to attack but did say that the first phase was to push us out of the Frontier Zone, the second phase was to push us back to the original border of the GA, and the third phase was to attack and destroy Space Command Headquarters and bases on Earth while destroying the entire technological infrastructure of our planet. Privateers would then be permitted to run rampant in GA space until the Milori Empire was in a position to exercise complete control.

"I have no reason to disbelieve this information but neither do I have a way to verify it. If the three fleets had intended to cross the border simultaneously, the others will not yet have crossed into 'regulated' space. I'm speculating that the Milori Third Fleet, finding themselves trapped, notified the other two fleets of their situation immediately. I hadn't ordered that communications be jammed because the distance to the Milori home world meant that reinforcements couldn't arrive for several years. Initially, I felt that a message announcing we had destroyed their small taskforce might work to our advantage. Following their arrival and the subsequent battle, I felt that news of an entire invasion fleet being thoroughly beaten by a handful of Space Command vessels would cause the Milori to reevaluate their intentions.

"We're presently concentrating all our repair efforts on the least damaged ships. If the Milori show up, we might have to fall back to the border, destroying our more seriously damaged ships so they won't be of use to the enemy.

"We know that the Milori who survived the battle don't understand how we trapped them and believe the energy cage was responsible for the damage to their ships rather than the unseen mines. They also believe we planted invisible mines in their midst. I didn't correct these misconceptions. In fact, I've deliberately perpetuated the idea that our weapons are so far superior to those of the Milori that they don't stand a chance of defeating us.

"I've transmitted messages to each of the arriving ships, advising them of the situation and amending their orders. I've tried to ensure that Stewart receive adequate protection while making maximum effective use of resources to support our current position.

"The fact that you haven't yet received the first news of the battle isn't lost on me. I wish we were closer so I could rely on the sage advice of the Admiralty Board, but we shall have to get by on just my own judgment and the advice from my captains. I look forward to hearing from you in a couple of weeks.

"Jenetta A. Carver, Rear Admiral, Lower Half, from the GSC Battleship *Prometheus*, message complete."

Jenetta breathed deeply and then released it slowly. She still had other messages to record, including one to Captain Donovan and personal messages to her family— those not present at the battle.

*　*　*

The search and rescue operations aboard the Milori ships yielded hundreds of prisoners. This was just a small portion of the original crews, most of who had continued to fight even as the air around them was evacuating from a multitude of holes in the hulls of their respective ships. Original estimates of two hundred thousand enemy dead were probably not too far off the mark. Thousands of Milori bodies and parts of bodies had been 'swept up' from where they floated in space around the battle area, the victims of torpedoes or mines that had opened huge holes in the warship hulls. Dozens of Space Command crewmembers were still missing despite the best efforts of the 'sweepers' to account for everyone. There might be nothing to find if the bodies had been destroyed in explosions, but they would do their best. Space Command fighters destroyed in the battle were towed back to the assembly area so the pilots' bodies could be extricated for proper interment. Pending their return to Earth or to their home colony, the bodies would be preserved in cold storage.

Jenetta was one of the few who had the time, or perhaps the energy, to work out every morning. She never spent less than an hour punching the bag or loping around the flight bay running track with her cats. She wanted desperately to jump in and get involved, but her position dictated that she sit by and watch as the captains directed the repair efforts aboard their ships. She checked the damage reports frequently throughout the day, watching for updates. With little else to do, she sat and thought about the military tactics and battle plans from ancient wars she had studied. Most terrestrial battles had little direct application in modern conflicts in space, but she never knew where the kernel of an idea would come from. The writings of military leaders and theorists Sun Tzu and Karl von Clausewitz were always a great source of battle strategy information.

* * *

On the fourth day following the conflict, Jenetta sent for Trader Vyx. He arrived at her conference room office mid-morning with the entire coterie of agents.

"Ladies and gentlemen, please come in and sit down. Prepare a beverage for yourself first, if you wish." Pointing to Lori, she said, "This is my aide, Lt. Commander Ashraf."

Vyx introduced the different agents. Jenetta and Lori had previously met all of them except Kathryn.

After everyone had taken a seat, Jenetta continued. "We're about fifteen light-years from the Scruscotto Colony, I believe. I'd like you to undertake a small mission for me."

"Anything you say, Admiral," Vyx said. "It'll be great to feel useful again."

"Is your ship operational?"

"We've had lots of time to get it in prime condition. It was protected in the maintenance bay during the conflict and wasn't damaged."

"Excellent."

Jenetta spent the next ten minutes explaining the mission, and everyone involved discussed it at length before the meeting ended.

"We'll shove off this afternoon, Admiral," Vyx said as the group left the conference room.

"Good luck, Trader," Jenetta said.

* * *

Admiral Moore walked into the enormous meeting hall that the Admiralty Board used for both private and semi-private sessions and took his seat at the center of the large horseshoe-shaped table. The gallery was filled to capacity on this occasion. The other admirals and the dozens of invited

- 226 -

guests immediately halted their conversations and watched the Admiral of the Fleet. He looked at Admiral Platt and nodded. "You may begin, Admiral."

Admiral Platt stood up and began her presentation. "Welcome to this special session of the Board. Everyone in this room, by virtue of their position within Space Command, the Space Marine Corps, or the Galactic Alliance Council, has previously been briefed on the situation with the Milori. Just to refresh your memory, we uncovered a Milori taskforce setting up a permanent base a hundred light-years inside our Frontier Zone. When the GSC Destroyer *Ottawa* approached, a Milora officer ordered the captain to leave the Frontier Zone or be destroyed because the Milori Empire had annexed all space up to our 'regulated' space border. When as many as sixteen Milori warships began maneuvering to leave orbit of the planet where the base was being constructed, the *Ottawa* turned and retreated towards Stewart Space Command Base with Milori ships in pursuit.

"Admiral Carver, the base commander at Stewart and the one responsible for sending the *Ottawa* to investigate the rumor about the Milori incursion, began to prepare for their arrival at the inner border. She formulated an innovative battle plan that would shut down their FTL drive systems and then entrap them in an encircling minefield. The Admiralty Board has been very impressed with Admiral Carver's tactical expertise and resourcefulness in the past, which, along with her administrative skills, accounts for her unparalleled rise within our command structure.

"Yesterday we received a message from Admiral Carver. Rather than reading it to you, I'll show you part of an appended vid log from the bridge of the *Prometheus*. At the start of the vid, the Milori have just entered the prepared trap. Their ACS has shut down their FTL drives. Computer, run the prepared vid log excerpt from the *Prometheus*."

The lower half of a full-wall monitor showed the bridge of the *Prometheus*. The other half showed the front monitor image that the bridge crew was seeing. The tactical officer was heard to say, "Got 'em" as the trap closed around the Milori warships. When the lead tactical officer reported there were one hundred three ships instead of the expected sixteen, there was a sharp intake of breath among the attendees.

The officers and dignitaries watched in absolute silence as Jenetta offered the Milori the opportunity to surrender, then ordered the attack when Lord High Space Marshall Gulqulk finished his tirade. As the *Prometheus* began its attack run, some of the assemblage actually cheered it on as if they were watching a live event.

By the end of the battle, many of the admirals and captains were smiling openly while most of the non-military dignitaries were somber and ashen-faced. The log played until the end. The last scene showed Jenetta entering the captain's briefing room just prior to sending her report.

"This is the report that Admiral Carver sent a few minutes later," Admiral Platt said from her chair. "Computer play Admiral Carver's latest message."

The room became deathly silent again as an eight-foot-high 'head and shoulders' image of Jenetta appeared on the large monitor. She gave her summarized account of the battle and then signed off. Admiral Platt stood up again.

"That's all we have so far. We're expecting another message tonight, but from here on in should only be damage reports, repair estimates, and—" Admiral Platt paused to take a deep breath, "casualty reports."

"Thank you, Admiral," Admiral Moore said. "Ladies and Gentlemen, this concludes the presentation portion of this meeting. Thank you for coming."

"Admiral Moore," one of the Diplomatic Corps attendees said, "is the threat from the Milori over? How are they going to take this defeat? Will there be a non-aggression treaty signed between the Galactic Alliance and the Milori Empire?"

"All good questions, and they'll be taken up now at our regular meeting. Right now, you know as much about the situation as I do. No one was expecting an invasion force, as you saw and heard. It remains to be seen where we go from here. I can't answer any of your questions right now, but I wanted to share this news with you."

The non-military people and the lower ranking officers filed slowly out of the meeting hall, leaving just the ten admirals of the board, their aides, clerks, and a couple of dozen senior officers, including Admiral Holt from Dixon who was afforded a seat at the table. Admiral Moore called the meeting to order and then opened with, "It turned out better than we dared hope, which is astounding considering the size of the force the Milori threw against us."

"It's a miracle," Admiral Hubera said.

"It's not a miracle, Donald; it's Admiral Carver," Admiral Burke said. "I don't know how she comes up with these unique battle plans she develops, but they always seem to work and work very well. There's no precedent in Space Command history for capturing an entire fleet inside an encircling minefield— neither in war games nor tactical scenarios. How many officers do you know who would have devised a plan like that and then executed it so well that an entire invasion force is caught like a net full of fish? Most officers would have followed standard tactics and met the Milori with half their ships, using the other half to attack the flanks and rear once the enemy was halted."

"Admiral Carver is anything but conventional," Admiral Holt said. "I've been telling you for years how brilliant she is. I tend to compare her tactics to those of Alexander the Great because she always does the unexpected and catches the enemy unaware. She's writing the book on space battle tactics. They'll be taught at the War College for years to come."

"She's writing a book?" Admiral Hubera asked.

"Not literally, Donald. I mean that her tactics will surely be featured in future War College training classes."

"She was a poor student and should hardly be used as an example to other students."

"You're just mad because you lost your bet with me, Donald. You know very well that she ranked number one in all her science and mathematics courses— including *yours*, I might add. That's hardly indicative of a poor student."

"She smoked up a zero grav lab while she was a student in my class."

"Don't you think it's about time you forgave a brilliant student for a simple prank committed more than twenty years ago, especially when that student has served Space Command so well and so valiantly?"

"It wasn't simple. That lab was out of service for a week when we needed it most. We had to completely reschedule all the testing for that freshman class."

"Gentlemen," Admiral Platt reminded them, "we have more pressing matters to discuss."

"Yes," Admiral Moore said, "we have the remnants of a taskforce sitting in what I'd have to describe as hostile space, since it's an area where we suspect the Raiders have constructed a new base. Admiral Carver has previously reported her suspicion that it might be as close as twenty light-years from Stewart. If she's correct, it could be between Stewart and our crippled force. Stewart, relatively unguarded at the moment, could be open to attack. Or, the taskforce itself could become a target for Raiders. At the moment, our ships are ill-equipped to defend themselves against an intact fleet."

"When will the additional ships we sent arrive at Stewart?" Admiral Woo asked.

Admiral Platt said, "The first should arrive in a few weeks, but then they're still a month from the battle site. Admiral Carver chose to meet the Milori twenty light-years inside the Frontier Zone, speculating that they'd become more alert as they approached the border. It seems she was right, and the enemy was caught totally off guard."

"My main concern is still with the Milori," Admiral Burke said. "We only expected sixteen ships, but a hundred three showed up. How many more are in the Frontier Zone? Does anyone know the size of the Empire's fleet?"

"The only estimate we have is five hundred warships," Admiral Bradlee said. "That came from a trader who did business with them, so the data can't be relied upon too heavily and the information is at least ten years old. Hominidae-like species aren't very welcome in the Milori Empire, so we haven't been able to get any recent intelligence."

"Ten years," Admiral Platt said as she shook her head slightly. "They could have double that number of ships by now. This might have only been the opening assault on the Galactic Alliance."

"Our own fleet is only three hundred six warships, with another three hundred support vessels such as quartermaster ships, transports, research vessels, and maintenance ships," Admiral Moore said. "And we already need double those numbers just to patrol our territory since the expansion. We can't fight a protracted war and protect our planets, colonies, and space traffic at the same time. The Raiders could just be waiting for an opportunity like this to begin their pirating activities again."

"What can we do?" Admiral Burke asked. "We've already allocated more than ten percent of our ships to Stewart, and half of those haven't arrived yet. How much thinner can we stretch our resources? If the orders were given today to send everything we have to Stewart, it would take three years to assemble them there."

"Stewart is only one part of our border," Admiral Ahmed said. "Granted, its sectors include the most direct path between the Milori Empire and Galactic Alliance space, but the Milori could attack anywhere along our border. We can't concentrate all our forces at Stewart."

"Admiral Ahmed is right," Admiral Moore said, "but it seems clear that we must be better prepared if the Milori intend to continue their aggression. I suggest we immediately begin moving half our remaining warships, about a hundred thirty-five, towards the Frontier Zone border, both to reinforce the sectors adjoining Stewart's sectors and in further support of Admiral Carver. Given the distance to the border, we can't wait until we see an actual continuing threat before we begin moving the ships. Let's send sixty-five to Stewart and thirty-five each to the flanking sectors."

"Who will take operational command of the three new taskforces?" Admiral Burke asked.

"Admiral Carver will remain in command in her sectors. The admirals in command of the adjoining sectors, Martucci and Rhinefield, will assume control of the taskforces in theirs."

"But Admiral Carver is only a Rear Admiral, Lower," Admiral Hubera stated. "Admiral's Martucci and Rhinefield are both Upper Half."

"Admiral Carver is the Base Commander of Stewart," Admiral Platt said. "Since she holds the command position of an Upper Half, she's automatically the commander of all ships in her sectors."

"That was fine for a small taskforce of fifteen ships, but we need a real Upper Half to be in command of a ninety-nine-warship fleet," Admiral Hubera argued. "The Stewart commander is going to control the largest Space Command fleet ever assembled under one StratCom commander. And it takes a week for communications to reach Stewart and another week for a reply. It's too much responsibility for such a young officer."

"I have to admit that I feel a bit disconcerted every time I see an image of Admiral Carver," Admiral Plimley said. "She looks more like a cadet than a flag officer, but her appearance belies her age, experience, and ability. I won't let my envy of her youthful looks affect my opinion of her competency to have this command. She's as suitable for this role as anyone I could name. She's proven that time and again. Donald, you just witnessed a sample of her ability. Would you have done as well? I would probably have used standard tactics and lost every ship to the Milori without stopping them. I sleep a little better knowing Admiral Carver is watching that particular part of our border."

"If the three forces must unite and fight as one in Stewart's sectors, who will command?" Admiral Hubera asked. "The regs assign command to the sector commander, but a one-star cannot be put in command over two Upper Halves."

The admirals at the table looked around to see if anyone had a suggestion for that one. Admiral Moore finally broke the silence with, "We'll cross that bridge when we come to it. We can't possibly unite the forces within two to three years. It will take that long for them to reach Stewart."

The Admiralty Board met again in emergency session two days later, after the message from Jenetta arrived in which she informed Supreme HQ of the two other Milori fleets. They already knew the contents of the vid message, but they watched it again on the large monitor before beginning the discussion.

"This doesn't change things very much," Admiral Moore said. "Orders have already been issued to the fleet immediately reassigning half our warships to the border and ordering them to proceed with all haste."

"Will it be enough?" Admiral Platt asked.

"It'll have to be. We can't release the other hundred thirty-five warships or the very situation Admiral Carver warns against— privateers— will become a reality. They also serve as Earth's last defense if the Milori get past our fleets."

"The real question now is: where are the two Milori fleets?" Admiral Ahmed said.

"We need to get our Intelligence people on this immediately," Admiral Plimley said. "Somebody has to have seen these fleets. Even in the Frontier Zone, a fleet of a hundred ships is going to be noticed by a mining survey crew— a freight-hauler— or someone."

All eyes went to Admiral Bradlee.

"I'm on it," he said. "I sent out a priority message to all my section heads to get their people working on it as soon as I heard the message last night. It'll take time for the messages to reach everyone, but within two weeks every SCI agent in the galaxy will be checking with his or her contacts. We're offering a reward for confirmed sightings of the Milori fleets."

"What more can we do to help Admiral Carver?" Admiral Platt asked.

"There's nothing more we can do in the short term," Admiral Moore said. "They'll either get their ships repaired and return to Stewart or they won't. If the Milori show up before they're ready to evacuate the area, we might lose the fifteen ships in her taskforce. It's unlikely that Admiral Carver can trap any more ships. They won't be blindly following a Judas goat this time."

"What's that? A Judas goat?" Admiral Woo asked.

"Sorry, Lon," Admiral Moore said. "It's an old term from the days when stockyards slaughtered sheep. You see, sheep would just mill around in a pen and wouldn't enter the chute that led to the butchering place, so the stockyards used a trained goat that led the sheep into the chute. At the end of the chute, a special door let the Judas goat out, but the sheep continued down the chute to the slaughter. The term refers to anyone who leads others into a deadly trap as the *Ottawa* did."

"And this time the Milori won't be pursuing a GSC ship," Admiral Woo said. "I understand."

"If Admiral Carver sent out ships as decoys, they might achieve the same thing," Admiral Ahmed said. "As soon as they were sighted, they could retreat. With any luck the Milori would pursue."

"No, the Milori have been alerted now about the entrapment," Admiral Moore said. "They won't fall for it again. Besides, according to the information we received, Admiral Carver cleaned out the armory on Stewart. I've already approved requisitions for replacing the mines, torpedoes, and new WOLaR weapons. Admiral Carver will have to get by with whatever torpedoes the ships are still carrying. Her mines and WOLaR weapons have all been deployed."

"Perhaps it's time again to speak of incorporating the Nordakian Space Force into Space Command," Admiral Platt said. "They've changed a lot of the restrictions that caused us to reject the idea in the past. They treat their women almost as equals now and don't force them to wear outlandish costumes while on duty. Incorporating the Nordakian ships would add twenty warships and thirty-some support vessels to our forces. At least half of their warships have been built since Nordakia joined the Galactic Alliance, and they've included the new technology we've shared with them. They also have a dozen more warships under construction."

"One of the main problems still exists," Admiral Ahmed said. "The Nordakian officers are inadequately trained by Space Command standards. The new Space Command

Academy on Nordakia will correct that in time, but for now it's an incontrovertible fact."

"It'll take generations to slowly replace their entire Space Force with Academy-trained personnel," Admiral Platt said. "We need the ships now. There must be some way we can integrate them into Space Command."

"What if we were to pass a restriction that Academy-trained officers couldn't serve aboard a Space Command ship unless the captain was a graduate of a Space Command Academy?" Admiral Ressler suggested. "It would prevent the frustration an officer might have towards serving under an inadequately trained captain."

"Mixing officers and crews with different educational backgrounds would still be a problem. A captain who doesn't have confidence in his crew would be as bad as the reverse," Admiral Woo said.

"I agree that it wouldn't work," Admiral Hillaire said. "I've given this matter a great deal of thought. The Nordakians who have graduated from the two Academies on Earth occupy regular Space Command posts either aboard ships or on bases, so there hasn't been a problem. Graduates from the new school on Nordakia will also be posted to regular Space Command positions. However, if their old school continues to produce officers, we can never achieve full integration. At some point the old school must be closed."

"I don't think you'll get any argument from the Nordakians," Admiral Moore said. "They've already recognized that a serious problem exists. For ten years, the best and brightest have been entering the Space Command Academies on Earth. With the opening of the Academy on Nordakia, the only enrollees at their old Academy are the ones who couldn't pass our entrance exams. The Academy Board of Governors, headed by Arnold here," he said, gesturing to Admiral Hillaire, "wisely chose to maintain the minimum entrance qualifications used on Earth, so they were only able to fill about half the available freshman class slots on Nordakia this year."

"The sweeping changes they're making on Nordakia will bear fruit in a few years," Admiral Ahmed said. "Embracing technology rather than shunning it, as the clerics had promoted, will bring us a bumper crop of enrollees soon."

"We still have the problem of transitioning the present Nordakian Space Force into a Space Command entity," Admiral Platt said. "If we don't, their military will begin to degrade at an increasing rate as their old academy turns out Space Force officers who weren't able to get into the Space Command Academy."

"It looks like a 'damned if we do and damned if we don't' situation," Admiral Hillaire said. "In order for this to have a chance of working, the Nordakians will have to accept a Space Command officer as the most senior officer of their Space Force during a transition period. All present Space Force officers must be required to attend special classes to learn Space Command rules and regs. Finally, we need to familiarize them with our command structure."

"I can only think of one Space Command officer who has a chance of being accepted as their most senior officer," Admiral Platt said.

"No, don't say it, Evelyn," Admiral Hubera said, covering his eyes with his hand.

Admiral Platt smiled. "See, even Donald realizes it. Admiral Carver is the only one the Nordakians would accept to head their Space Force during a transition. She's officially a captain in the Nordakian Space Force, holds their planet's highest military honor, and speaks Dakis like a native, and she's a citizen of Nordakia. Perhaps most importantly, she's an Azula and a Lady of the Royal House of Nordakia. She's revered on Nordakia almost as much as their king and queen."

Admiral Hubera groaned loudly, his eyes still covered with his hand, causing the others around the room to chuckle. "You had to say it, didn't you?" His comment sent another round of chuckles around the room.

"What about Admiral Yuthkotl?" Admiral Ahmed asked. "He's not going to appreciate being pushed out of the Nordakian Space Force top spot."

"We don't push him out," Admiral Hillaire said. "We bring him here and treat it like a promotion, although he'll only be a Lower Half. The Nordakians are going to need representation on this board anyway and at Supreme Headquarters. Yuthkotl is charming, very intelligent, and speaks Amer."

"Are you suggesting we bring the entire senior staff of the Nordakian Space Force here?" Admiral Ahmed asked.

"Not at all," Admiral Hillaire said. "That decision would have to be made by Admiral Carver."

"Wait a minute," Admiral Hubera said. "You're already assuming that Admiral Carver will be made the senior officer of the Nordakian Space Force. She's just a Lower."

"That would have to change," Admiral Moore said. "She'll need the rank of Upper at least."

"She won't accept it," Admiral Holt said. He had sat listening to the conversation with interest and had said nothing until now. "She'll resign her commission and take a job as a freighter captain or passenger ship captain."

The other admirals stared at him with stunned expressions on their faces.

"She'd refuse the appointment?" Admiral Moore said incredulously.

"She'd resign her commission?" Admiral Hillaire said, even more incredulously.

"Admiral Carver wants to be on a military ship in space," Admiral Holt said. "She'd take a demotion back to ensign if that's what it took. But if that isn't possible, she'd take a job aboard a commercial ship in space."

"But she accepted the promotion to Rear Admiral, Lower Half," Admiral Burke said.

"I'm quite sure she did that only because it's a brevet rank. She'll revert to the rank of captain at the end of her duty tour, and she'll then be eligible to receive a ship. Admiral Carver has accepted posts at two bases and functioned as their base commander because she's a good officer, but how long can you expect someone to put duty over personal happiness? How long can they remain an effective officer?"

The room was silent for a full minute as everyone thought about Admiral Holt's words.

"The matter may be academic," Admiral Moore said. "She's in very real danger of not returning from her current assignment. We've had a brief respite from thinking about the Milori when we got sidetracked on the issue of the Nordakians, but we have to get back to the threat of invasion again. I think we should still consider the appointment of Admiral Carver to Upper Half though. The reassignment of ships puts her in command of almost a hundred warships and an equal number of support ships. As base commander of Stewart, a post normally held by an Upper, we could brevet her with a second star without any formality. May I have a show of hands for all in approval?"

Each admiral at the table— except Admiral Holt who could speak but not vote— raised their hand. Even Admiral Hubera reluctantly voted in favor of the temporary appointment. The words from Holt that Jenetta might resign her commission if the Board assigned her to head up the Nordakian Space Force played over and over in Hubera's mind.

"Good, it's unanimous," Admiral Moore said. "I'll inform Admiral Carver when I respond to her latest message."

*   *   *

Emperor Maxxiloth, enjoying a quiet evening meal with a few dozen guests, stopped eating and listened intently as an aide whispered a message. He excused himself and walked quickly from the dining room. Ten minutes later, he was standing in a special communications room beneath the palace as vid messages continued to pour in from the Third Fleet. Because of the distance, it had taken more than two weeks for the messages to arrive from the battle site.

The communications chief played back the messages from the trapped ships, one at a time, for the benefit of the Emperor and senior ministers who had collected in the room.

On every ship, it was the same story— death and destruction on an unprecedented scale. Some reports had been sent with the last breaths of the com operators and some continued to report until the com operators ran out of things to say. Most messages included data from external sensors and special cameras.

- 238 -

The Emperor watched and listened intently until all the reports had been replayed. By then it was clear that their Third Fleet had been destroyed. All evidence indicated that they had faced just fifteen Space Command warships. The Emperor had known that the invasion schedule had been advanced after Space Command had detected the presence of their ships inside the Frontier Zone, but he had merely felt that the destruction of the Galactic Alliance would occur that much sooner.

Emperor Maxxiloth called an immediate meeting of the war council. It took several hours to convene, and by then he was over his initial shock and was fuming.

"Exalted Lord Space Marshall Berquyth," he screamed at the commander of all space operations, "can you explain this disaster? You have assured me for years that we would sweep through the Galactic Alliance like a broom through a nest of insects. So confident were you that we have changed all the maps of space to show that part of space as being part of our Empire. I had ceased to think of the Galactic Alliance as still being in existence. On your advice, we sent two thirds of our entire complement of warships. You assured us that it would be more than adequate for the job."

"I'm most sorry, my Lord. This has been as much a surprise to me as to everyone else. It will take some time to examine the data we've received. My first impression is that our intelligence has been faulty. The Alliance must have far deadlier weapons than we were led to believe."

"What of our other fleets?"

"We've received no reports of other encounters or engagements."

"They must change course immediately and destroy this Space Command taskforce. We can't afford to have them at our back when we encounter other forces."

"I'm sure Supreme Lord Space Marshall Dwillaak will alter course as soon as he hears of the battle. Since he's much closer, he must already be on his way to destroy the taskforce that surprised our fleet."

"Send him orders anyway. Make him understand how important it is to destroy this force and erase this embarrassment from the annals of our history. And I want the head of whoever is in command of that taskforce."

# Chapter Nineteen
~ March 3<sup>rd</sup>, 2277 ~

Repairs to the *Prometheus*, *Chiron*, and *Thor* should have easily taken over a month, but with the combined energetic efforts of all the engineering crews, they were approaching completion after only two and a half weeks. Engineers had completely rebuilt the hull areas destroyed by the torpedoes and patched the major damage from laser weapons. They would focus on hits that had self-sealed and didn't present a problem to the ship's structural integrity or safety of the crew only after major repairs to the rest of the taskforce were completed. The *Prometheus'* hull was now completely pressurized. They would have the *Chiron* and *Thor* likewise fully pressurized in another day or two at the most. The engineers aboard the *Prometheus* were busy replacing the third, inside layer of tritanium panels after installing new self-sealing membrane in the most heavily damaged areas.

Jenetta was on the flight bay running track completing her morning workout when a com operator notified her that there was a Priority-One message from Supreme HQ waiting for her. She grabbed her towel from the rack by the door and hurried back to her quarters with her cats. Plopping down into the chair in her private office, she called up her messages and selected the one from HQ. She had already received a reply to her original message, so this had to be a reply to the message about the two yet unseen invasion fleets.

"Hello, Admiral," the image of Admiral Moore said.

"The Admiralty Board had already been concerned that there might be other Milori in the Frontier Zone and had formulated certain plans. We've sent out a general alarm and reassigned half the fleet to your border sectors and the sectors on your flanks. It's unlikely the Milori would travel beyond those sectors to launch a surprise invasion. Of the hundred thirty-five reassigned warships, sixty-five have been assigned to Stewart and thirty-five each are being sent to Admirals Martucci and Rhinefield.

"Naturally we hope they won't be needed, but the situation dictates that they be sent. Those reassigned ships closest to the Frontier Zone have already begun their trip. Most will need to stop for provisioning and rearmament before making the long journey. They'll be filled with as much ordnance as possible to replace your exhausted stocks. We've re-tasked ships further away to cover the areas vacated. It will leave us a bit short-handed elsewhere, but we must continue to patrol all sectors.

"Intelligence agents have been notified to put everything else aside and seek information on the two Milori fleets, so by now every agent in galactic space is making contact with their informants in an attempt to locate the enemy.

"With the assignment of the sixty-five ships to Stewart, your taskforce has grown to a fleet of ninety-six Space Command warships, plus the three Nordakian cruisers. Although we previously overlooked the staffing recommendation that a Rear Admiral, Upper, be the base commander of Stewart, the size of this fleet absolutely requires that the most senior officer hold that rank. Therefore, effective immediately, and with the full endorsement of the Admiralty Board, I'm promoting you to the rank of Rear Admiral, Upper Half. This appointment is in accordance with the regulations allowing brevet promotions since you were already the base commander of Stewart.

"A press release has been prepared and is being released today, so don't be surprised when congratulations start flowing in. We are notifying all ship captains in the fleet as part of the regular daily update traffic. The news services have broken the story about your defeating the Milori invasion force with just fifteen ships, so your name is once again filling all the news shows. We haven't yet informed the press about the two other Milori fleets and don't intend to unless the Milori begin new hostilities.

"Congratulations on your appointment, Admiral. You're now one of the top sixty-seven officers in Space Command.

"Richard E. Moore, Admiral of the Fleet, Space Command Supreme Headquarters, Earth, message complete."

When the message ended, Jenetta just sat staring at the Space Commend HQ logo that replaced Admiral Moore's image on the screen without really seeing it. It couldn't be. She had to be asleep. Why else would she be having this nightmare? She pinched herself hard and it hurt. No, she wasn't dreaming.

Jenetta stood and walked to her bathroom. Perhaps a hot shower would make her feel better.

Fifteen minutes later, Jenetta was getting dressed, but she was still in shock. She fed her cats, skipped breakfast for herself, and walked to the bridge. Captain Gavin was usually in his briefing room at this hour. After calling out 'as you were' in response to 'Admiral on the bridge,' she walked to the briefing room. The door opened and Gavin stood up behind his desk.

"You're out of uniform, Admiral," he said, smiling as she entered.

Jenetta looked down at her uniform. Everything looked in place.

"I mean your shoulders. You're wearing your old rank. I can arrange for the proper insignia for you. It'll just take a minute."

"Larry, what am I going to do?"

"Do?"

"About this appointment. We talked about this a few weeks ago. Remember?"

"Ahh, yes, I do."

"I can't accept this promotion. For one thing, I don't deserve it. For another, I don't want it."

"Well, as far as deserving it, you deserve it a lot more than others I could name who've received it in the past. As far as wanting it, you're only getting the pay and recognition for the job you've been doing since capturing Stewart."

"I didn't want that either."

"Well, the only solution I can see is to resign your commission. But would you do that in time of war?"

"No, of course not. You know I couldn't resign with the threat of another Milori invasion force facing us out here."

"They're probably counting on that. My message states they've reassigned sixty-five more warships to your command. With support vessels, the total ship count will be over two hundred, constituting a real fleet. They had to give you another star or assign someone over you, and we both know they don't want to do that."

"I feel like I'm being led around like a prize cow. They yank on the chain and I follow."

"That's part of being in the service. We all give up a measure of our freedom when we elect to serve. But you're hardly like a prize cow. You're holding your own chain and a lot of others. There are tens of thousands of people depending on you. With the new ships, there will be *hundreds* of thousands depending on you."

"Larry, you're not making me feel better."

He chuckled. "Sorry. I'm just trying to show you that *you're* doing the leading. This promotion doesn't mean you'll be stuck behind a desk any more than the last one did. From the way the message I received was worded, I'd say your appointment didn't come from the Galactic Alliance Council?"

"No, it's a brevet appointment like the last."

"So, then there's no problem. They had to give you a second star because they've assigned an enormous fleet of ships to your command. After things have settled down out here, most of the ships will probably return to their old patrol routes. You'll return to Stewart to finish your tour, and then you'll move on to your next posting, which should include getting your own ship— probably a battleship."

"I hope you're right. I just keep seeing myself stuck behind a desk for years when all I've ever wanted was to be in space."

"You're in space right now."

Jenetta smiled for the first time since receiving the message. "I mean as an officer in a ship."

"You *are* an officer in a ship. You're the senior-most officer in *this* ship. You're the senior-most officer in this taskforce. You're the senior-most officer for four hundred light-years. The only higher-ranking officers are all on Earth. And right now, you're more important to us than them and all the admirals that have ever held the rank put together. We're counting on what you always call your luck to give us an edge in the days ahead. I'm really glad you're out here, Jen."

Jenetta smiled again. "Thanks, Larry."

"For?"

"For giving me a place to vent my frustration. For listening to my rants. For giving me the benefit of your sage advice. And— for bolstering my ego."

"Anytime, Jen."

"I think maybe I could eat something now."

As she turned to leave, Gavin said, "And Admiral, you're still out of uniform."

Jenetta looked at him, smiled, and nodded.


After breakfast, Jenetta added a second star to each shoulder of her tunic by removing them from another uniform. Normally, the rank insignia had the two stars positioned on one supporting piece, but this was acceptable under battlefield conditions. She'd arrange for the proper insignia later from the uniform storeroom. They might even have to fabricate them as they wouldn't get much call for admiral insignia aboard ship. As she entered her conference room office, Lt. Commander Ashraf jumped up.

"Good morning, Admiral. And congratulations."

"Thank you, Lori. It's only temporary."

"Of course, Admiral," she said. The tone of her voice suggested she didn't believe it for a second. "Everyone is excited about the sixty-five warships coming to support this sector."

"They know already?"

"I understand that each captain was notified about your promotion and the increase in command size with their regular daily traffic. Naturally, they informed their First Officers, who informed their bridge crews, who informed everyone else. There are probably a few people who haven't heard yet; a lot of the third watch personnel are probably sleeping."

"Those ships won't be here for a long time— perhaps as long as two years. We'll have to get by as best we can until they arrive."

"Aye, Admiral. But you can bring us through. Everyone knows that."

Jenetta looked at her aide for a few seconds without saying anything. "I'll do my best."

"I made copies of the first news reports on the battle. Would you like to view them?"

"Sure. Just let me grab some coffee and we can take a look at what the people back home are seeing."

Jenetta prepared a steaming mug of Colombian and sat down, swiveling her chair to face the large monitor on the wall. Ashraf started a replay of the news reports received on the entertainment channels aboard the ship. For the first story, an image of the reporter placed aboard the *Prometheus* appeared.

"This is Neil Russo, reporting to you from aboard the GSC Battleship *Prometheus* somewhere in the Frontier Zone beyond Stewart Space Command Base. For more than a month, I've been aboard this gigantic ship as it waited for the enemy to arrive. The face on that enemy is Milora. They've invaded Galactic Alliance territory and ordered Space Command to withdraw permanently from our own territory. In an interview with a senior officer, I learned that the Milori Empire issued a proclamation that purports to void the Galactic Alliance territorial ownership rights while annexing our space to their empire. A taskforce of warships, believed to be sixteen in number, pursued a GSC Destroyer, the *Ottawa*, all the way from the Elurra system to the area where we were waiting. That star system is located one hundred light-years inside our outer border, so there has been no doubt from the beginning that this was a deliberate incursion.

"Several days ago, this Space Command taskforce of fourteen ships, under the command of Admiral Jenetta A. Carver, came face to face with the Milori. What follows is actual footage of the meeting and subsequent battle. You'll see exactly what I saw from the bridge of the *Prometheus*. The other ships comprising this taskforce are the *Chiron*,

*Bellona, Thor, Song, Plantaganet, Romanov, Mentuhotep, Asuncion, Geneva, Beijing, St. Petersburg, Buenos Aires*, and *Cairo*. Other Extragalactic News Service reporters were on the bridges of the other ships and most will be reporting their stories shortly. I regret to say that two will not. I dedicate this report to their memory.

"I'll limit my narration during the battle as much as possible. We begin with the scenes on the bridge as the Milori are about to reach our location. The two Space Command officers centered in much of the footage are Admiral Jenetta Carver and Captain Lawrence Gavin. Here, now, is that footage."

The image changed from one showing the reporter to one showing the bridge just prior to the battle. Jenetta heard the reporter say quietly, "Admiral Carver is about to spring her trap. There it is. The Admiral has ordered the energy cage erected around the Milori ships. We've trapped their ships inside. Their FTL drive systems have shut down, and they are powerless to escape. Should they use their thrusters to maneuver and happen to touch the sides of the trap, their ship will suffer an explosion at that point similar to that of a torpedo strike."

The lieutenant at the tactical console was heard saying, "Got 'em," and then there were the remarks about the size of the fleet. The reporter stopped talking while Jenetta hailed the Milori and demanded Gulqulk's surrender, only to have the Milori commander let loose with his tirade. There was a tight close-up of Jenetta as she set her jaw, stared icily at the leader of the Milori fleet, and said, "You've brought this upon yourselves."

The scene changed from one of the bridge officers to an image of what the large main monitor was showing as the battle began. From then on there were no more narration interruptions until the battle ended. The scene cut back briefly several times to show a grim-faced but determined Admiral Carver as she clung tightly to the arm of Gavin's chair for support during the battle and stared at the enormous monitor at the front of the bridge. Ashraf could be seen standing beside her, hanging onto the XO's chair. The image zoomed slowly and dramatically to a tight close-up of Jenetta's face before switching to an image of the reporter again.

"Those large explosions you witnessed after the ships had all completed their passes were made by secret, nearly invisible bombs that Space Command developed a decade ago. This was the first real use of that highly classified weapon, and Admiral Carver decided to use only the smallest size available in her arsenal, hoping not to kill any more Milori than necessary. Her goal was only to stop their invasion and prevent them from firing on our ships. Information about the bomb is still classified but I was able to learn that they are self-guiding. Ordnance specialists seeded them throughout the cage area long before the Milori arrived. Once the Milori had stopped, the bombs were issued a command to locate the largest concentrations of enemy ships and intersperse themselves among them, where they would wait for a signal to detonate.

"All one hundred three ships of the invasion force have been destroyed, but Space Marines have rescued hundreds of Milori survivors from the wrecked ships. The estimated enemy death toll is over two hundred thousand. Laser fire or torpedoes struck most of the ships in the Space Command taskforce during the engagement, but only one ship was sufficiently damaged that repairs may have to wait until the taskforce can return to Stewart. Although outnumbered seven to one, Space Command has clearly demonstrated that its ships and weapons are superior to anything the Milori have.

"This is Neil Russo with ENS On the Scene, reporting from aboard the *Prometheus*, a very long way from Earth. Good day."

Jenetta looked at Ashraf. "That was a rather interesting way he talked about the grid and the WOLaR torpedoes, especially since he was aboard ship while we were deploying the mines."

Lori smiled. "Well, I sort of convinced him to describe it that way. I took the idea from the Milora we reached by the com when we were with the prisoner."

"Sort of convinced him?"

"I happened to mention that there might be a lot more action to occur and that it would help him get a front-row seat. I also explained that it might help to perpetuate those myths in case the information got back to the Milori. It didn't change the real news in any way."

"Is that all?"

"Well, I also told him that if he got the other reporters to go along and report it the same way, you'd give him a full half-hour interview, free from disturbances, once we got back to Stewart. But I think it was his patriotism that won out."

"I'm sure," Jenetta said, in the same disbelieving tone Ashraf had used earlier when Jenetta had said her promotion wasn't permanent. "I'm beginning to see that you're even more devious than I gave you credit for."

"Why thank you, Admiral," she said, smiling.

Jenetta smiled. "Let's have a look at the rest."

\* \* \*

The repairs to the ships continued at a frantic pace. Everyone knew what was at stake and put everything they had into the effort. Supervising officers practically had to have their engineers dragged back to their quarters at the end of each sixteen-hour work shift. But once there they collapsed in exhaustion onto their beds. Even non-engineers had been recruited to assist in the effort. It didn't require specialized knowledge to fetch and carry, although bots did most of that work.

Security people interviewed every single prisoner. They didn't get very much information that wasn't already known, but they had to compile a list of survivors for the records anyway. Space Marines had the grisly job of gathering the dead bodies of the Milori aboard the wrecked ships and collecting their identity disks. They placed the desiccated and frozen bodies— and sometimes just body parts— into whatever large containers were available. In one case an empty cargo bay, once a part of a Milori battleship, held some of the dead.

The work continued like that around the clock. People lost track of time as they concentrated only on the uncompleted tasks. They were either working, eating, or sleeping, and occasionally some fell asleep as they were eating. Jenetta was grateful for each day that passed without word of the Milori fleet. She would have liked to think that the enemy had turned around and headed for home, but that would only be wishful thinking. She knew they were coming.

*   *   *

With the lifting of the ban on personal communications, an avalanche of electronic mail arrived at the ship. Jenetta received her share, of course, and spent some time each evening responding. With the announcement of her latest promotion on the heels of the announcement about the victory, she received thousands of congratulatory messages. She created a sort of personalized response message to send to most people and then just added a very personal sentence or two at the end of each message for the closest of her friends. She exceeded the normal outgoing message limit by a factor of ten, but everyone got a reply. Special individuals, such as the king and queen of Nordakia, naturally received messages composed especially for them. Her message queue contained dozens of messages from Hugh, now out of stasis, and she delighted in viewing those over and over, responding to each one chronologically.

Before responding to her mother's latest message, she viewed it again.

"Hi, honey. Your face is all over the news again. I enjoy seeing it because it means you're alive and well, but I worry about you. I think you're taking on too much responsibility. I'm proud that you're the first two-star admiral in the family, but you looked so unhappy when you had to give that order to attack. I know it has to be taking its toll on you. Now you're going to be responsible for all those people in the fleet also. It just seems like it's too much, and I don't know how you do it. I could never have that many people relying on me. You must get it from your father's side of the family.

"Your father's ship has been reassigned to a different patrol area. He's not coming out your way, but he'll be much closer to home and our messages will reach each other quicker now. I know he's very proud of you because most of his message time is spent talking about you. Mine is also, but it's

- 250 -

because I'm so concerned about you. I know you don't like talking about very personal things in a vid mail, but please tell me what you're feeling.

"There's the timer so I have to finish up. I keep hoping your time at Stewart will go quickly so you can come home for a visit. Take care of yourself. I love you and miss you.

"Annette Carver, Officer Housing, Potomac SC base. End of message."

The months of stress had taken their toll on Jenetta. Since entering the Academy, she had done her best to hide her emotions and always display a look of imperturbability. She firmly believed that a leader should appear to know what they were doing, even when personally filled with doubts. Jenetta was usually far less sure of her actions than subordinates believed. With each new layer of responsibility laid upon her shoulders, she prayed she was up to the challenge and then resolved again that nobody should ever see what she was really feeling, not even family. But she needed a release from the stress of the past weeks. She decided to be completely open with her mother for once.

Jenetta tapped the record button on her com unit.

"Message to Annette Carver, Officer Housing, Potomac SC base, Earth. Begin message."

"Hi, Momma. You want to know what I'm feeling so I shall tell you, but I ask that you not show this to— or talk about it with— anyone else. I cannot afford to have either our own forces or our enemies perceive any sign of weakness.

"I wake up each day filled with dread. I know what's yet to come and fear I won't measure up to people's expectations of me. I fear I'll make an error in judgment and someone else will pay a terrible price. I worry about all the lives I hold in my hands— not just the lives of my crews, but also the lives of the billions who are depending on me to protect them. If I falter or make a wrong move, the enemy might get past us and wreak havoc throughout Galactic Alliance space.

"In December of 1776, Thomas Paine began publishing a series of pamphlets called The American Crises. His opening paragraph in the series was, 'THESE are the times that try men's souls. The summer soldier and the sunshine patriot will, in this crisis, shrink from the service of their country; but he that stands it now, deserves the love and thanks of man and woman. Tyranny, like hell, is not easily conquered; yet we have this consolation with us, that the harder the conflict, the more glorious the triumph. What we obtain too cheap, we esteem too lightly: it is dearness only that gives everything its value. Heaven knows how to put a proper price upon its goods; and it would be strange indeed if so celestial an article as freedom should not be highly rated.'

"I care nothing for glory or triumph, but I care deeply for freedom. Prophetically, Mr. Paine referred to it as a celestial article, but I'm certain he never suspected we'd one day be fighting for our freedom out among the stars. You worry about me, but I worry about you and everyone else on Earth, Nordakia, and all of the other inhabited planets, moons, and space stations in Galactic Alliance space.

"My duty is clear, much clearer than the path I must follow. I feel the weight of these stars on my shoulders throughout every minute of every day. I can feel the pain and anguish of every leader and warrior chief who has ever stood on a battlefield and been forced to send his or her people into situations that will result in almost certain death for many. There are no winners in war. There are only those who lose and those who don't lose as dearly.

"We didn't lose as dearly as the Milori in our last battle, but this war isn't over yet. As we prepare ourselves for the next encounter, my feelings of dread both greet me when I awaken each day and prevent me from falling asleep easily each night. If my face appears grim, it's because it reflects what I feel in my heart. I know my pensiveness won't lessen until this war is over. I'm sorry this message is so melancholy, but you wished to know how I feel, so I've lowered my mask on this one occasion. Please don't share my words with any-one, not even other family members. And always remember that I love you and miss you.

"Jenetta A. Carver, Rear Admiral, Upper Half, from the GSC Battleship *Prometheus*, message complete."

A message from her father was decidedly different. She watched it again before recording her reply.

"Hi, Admiral. Congratulations on receiving your second star. Your battle vid has been replaying almost continuously in the theatre for the past day as every officer and crewman on board studies the tactics you used. I'm sure it'll take its rightful place among your greatest hits in our archives. I think it far surpasses the videos of the destruction of Raider One, the Battle of Vauzlee, the Battle for Higgins, the Siege of Raider Three, and even the Defense of Stewart.

"I suspect my crew wishes they were with a different Carver right now as we perform our routine patrols. I almost wish we were out there also, but it's my job to convince them that our job here is also vital to the safety and security of the Galactic Alliance.

"It looked like your flagship really got pounded in the engagement, so I'd guess you're lying over at the battle site while you make repairs. The massive reassignment of ships to Stewart must mean that this thing is far from over, so get some rest while the engineers do their thing. I love you honey.

"Quinton Carver, Captain of the GSC *Octavian*, message complete."

Jenetta tapped the record button on the com unit.

"Message to Captain Quinton E. Carver on the GSC *Octavian* from Rear Admiral, Upper Half, Jenetta A. Carver on the GSC *Prometheus*. Begin message.

"Hi, Dad. You're correct. Your task is just as important as that of any ship in the Frontier Zone. One fact not yet reported is that the Milori intended to loose privateers in our sectors after destroying Space Command. I said intended, but in truth it may still be their intention. This situation is far from resolved. Even if we should prevail at the border, the Raiders may soon begin to take advantage of the reduced number of ships on patrol to renew their piracy. We've damaged them considerably in the past, but we know they continue to exist. Your crew should understand that their role has become more important than ever.

"I'm sure you're exaggerating the importance of the video, but if I've inspired anyone to develop their battle plan with a little imagination instead of simply employing the old frontal assault with combined flanking positions, I'm happy. Take care of yourself, Dad. I love you.

"Jenetta A. Carver, Rear Admiral, Upper Half, from the GSC Battleship *Prometheus*, message complete."

Jenetta also sent messages to her brothers, Richie, Jimmy, and Andy. Not yet having received a list of the ships reassigned to forward areas, she didn't know if any of them would be moving to her border sectors, but it was likely that one or more would find themselves here since all their ships were of the newer classes.

Her last message was to Hugh. She viewed the most recent message again before composing her reply.

"Hi, honey. If your promotion to Admiral didn't shake me, your promotion to a two-star certainly would have." Hugh made a wry face. "Uh, have you ever thought about pacing yourself? I mean, what are you going to do in ten years if you've done everything before then?" Smiling, he said, "Just kidding. I know you didn't plan any of this and that your goal has only been to again become an officer aboard a ship like the *Prometheus*. It just seems that things around you spiral out of control. I'm not complaining, mind you; I like the excitement. Listening to the stories about you on the news sure livens up an otherwise dull day on a freighter.

"I've sent a message off to Space Command asking them if they're still accepting applications for re-instatement from retired officers. My contract with the freight company will be up at about the time we reach Higgins and I could re-enter the service there. I have just one question: Can lieutenant commanders make love to two-star admirals?" He smiled.

"Love you.

"Commander Hugh Michaels, aboard the freighter *Attar*, message complete."

Jenetta grinned and pressed the record button.

"Message to Commander Hugh Michaels on the freighter *Attar*, from Rear Admiral,Upper Half, Jenetta A. Carver on the GSC *Prometheus*. Begin message.

"Hi, Hugh. I thought I *was* pacing myself. But maybe I set the pace a little too high?"

Changing her expression to a more somber one, she said, "Seriously, at the time of my graduation from the Academy I never expected to even make commander by retirement. If someone had told me I'd become a two-star when I was forty-one I'd have laughed and then referred them to the Psych Department. I look forward to the day when I can take off the stars and replace them with my captain's bars.

"I'm sure Space Command will accept your application for re-instatement in a minute. We're in desperate need of intelligent, experienced officers, now more than ever. Our problems with the Milori are just beginning— not ending, despite what the news broadcasters are saying. Keep this strictly to yourself: we're expecting another major attack by the Milori. The earlier battle was just their opening gambit in this war. Our intel indicates we should expect a far more formidable force in the very near future. My people are working around the clock to get us back in fighting shape to meet them.

"Hugh, if things don't work out like we hope, I want you to know how much I've come to care for you. The month we had on Stewart was wonderful and the memory of that time has really helped to sustain me in recent months."

Smiling, she added, "A two-star admiral can definitely make love to a lieutenant commander. I hope I can prove that to you before too long." She kissed her index and middle fingers and then pressed them to the lens of the screen's built-in video camera.

"Jenetta A. Carver, Rear Admiral, Upper Half, from the GSC Battleship *Prometheus*, message complete."

\* \* \*

With the completion of repairs to the *Prometheus*, *Chiron*, and *Thor*, the engineering crews moved on to the *Bellona*, *Song*, and *Plantaganet*. Having the three large battleships battle-ready meant that the taskforce had little to fear now except from an attack in force by a Milori fleet, but the ships remained connected at their bow airlocks. In the event of an alert, the airlocks would be sealed and the ships separated in a matter of seconds. In accordance with Space Command policy, a junior officer with at least one Marine sentry was always stationed at any open entry point on a warship.

Arriving at her quarters and finding waiting vid messages always brought a smile to Jenetta's face. The one waiting for her this night was from her mother. Tapping the play button on the com unit as she sat down brought an image of her mother to the screen.

"Hi, honey. I received your message a few days ago but I haven't been able to reply until now. The truth is that I was so disconcerted after watching your message that I broke down and wept for hours. A mother is supposed to care for her children and comfort them when they're in pain, but I find that I'm powerless to ease your burden.

"You've always been so very much like your father— strong, silent, and supremely confident of your ability to meet any challenge head on. But you're my daughter as well, and I know that your inner turmoil arises from the traits you've inherited from me. Love and compassion are wonderful qualities, but in time of war they can be a severe handicap for any military leader. You're a Space Command officer, and I know you're up to whatever responsibility you've accepted. I have confidence that you'll find the strength to do what's necessary, and you'll make all the right decisions when confronted with difficult choices. Just have confidence in yourself. I love you and admire you more than I can express. I'm so very, very proud to be your mother.

"Annette Carver, Officer Housing, Potomac SC base. End of message."

Jenetta sat back and stared at the blank screen. She had suddenly become acutely aware of just how long it had been since she'd been home.

\* \* \*

The *Scorpion*, with Vyx at the controls, entered orbit around Scruscotto and established a track that would take it down to the Weislik Space Port. After receiving a pad assignment, Vyx guided the small transport down to the assigned landing spot. As was his custom, he sat in the pilot's chair and relaxed for several minutes before engaging in any conversation.

Vyx had ensured that they had sufficient breathing equipment for everyone on board before leaving the *Ottawa*. Only long-time residents could tolerate the thin atmosphere of Scruscotto without an assist. All others needed the supplemental source of oxygen provided by small units about the size of a newborn infant. The units pulled oxygen from the air and, as the body required it, released it in more concentrated doses through a tube connected to a nose clip.

When Vyx had relaxed sufficiently from the stress of landing on an uncontrolled planet, he said, "Okay, everyone knows our assignment. If we can't get what we need here, we'll move to one of the other colonies and try again. Any questions?"

"Same teams as on Bajurrsko?" Byers asked.

"Unless someone has an objection. It worked out well before."

No one spoke up, so he said, "Okay, let's get to it. We've been sitting on our backsides long enough. It's time to earn our pay."

After Vyx paid the landing fees, they moved out and started working the colony. As he expected, Vyx encountered Ker Blasperra in one of the numerous taverns they visited.

"Hello, Trader," Blasperra said as he reached the table. "Welcome back to Scruscotto."

"Hello, Ker."

"You've been gone a long time. Was your quest successful?"

"Yes and no. I found Rivemwilth's hidden base, but it was full of Tsgardi."

"You obviously managed to get away."

"There was a brief fight and I had to destroy their ship, but I got away."

"And now you've returned for your money?"

"Among other things."

"Looking for a trade perhaps?"

Lowering his voice, Vyx said, "Right now I'm looking for Milori. I've heard that there are two large fleets of warships in the Zone. Have you heard anything about them?"

"Two large fleets, you say?"

"Yes. Each has over a hundred warships."

"Interesting. I heard a few rumors about a large number of ships, but I assumed they were Raiders."

"Where were these Raiders headed?"

Shrugging his shoulders, Blasperra said, "I don't know, and I'm forced to admit that I didn't listen that closely. It didn't appear to be anything I could profit from."

"I would be willing to pay for confirmed information."

Blasperra suddenly grew more interested. "You have something to sell to the Milori?"

"Perhaps. But I would have to know where they are first."

"And what would this information be worth?"

"If it's confirmed, five thousand credits."

"I shall look into it immediately."

"And my five hundred thousand?"

"You shall have that in forty-eight hours. I couldn't leave so much money un-invested, so I loaned it at a very minor rate to someone who has forty-eight hours to produce it upon demand."

"Okay, Ker, forty-eight hours. But no longer! I'm going to need it."

"Of course, Trader. You have always been honorable with me, and I wouldn't think of being any less honorable with you."

* * *

The teams had spent weeks on the planet, and after visiting every large mining camp and town, they returned to Weislik. Vyx and Byers were once again relaxing and drinking ale in the tavern they frequented more often than any other while on Scruscotto. Having collected the five hundred thousand credits from Ker Blasperra, Vyx had spread credits around liberally as they performed their mission. Rumors about Milori abounded, and every low-life on the planet was looking to cash in by providing information— real or fictitious— about their location.

Ker Blasperra arrived at about the same time as the third round of drinks. The tall, thin Hominidae-like creature with a long yellow face and large black eyes stared at Vyx impassively.

"Good day, Trader."

"Good day, Ker."

"I think I may have what you've been looking for."

"Go on."

"A smuggler with whom I'm acquainted was waiting to meet a contact when he was startled by his ship's warning alarms. Thinking that Space Command might have discovered him, he was about to flee when he realized that the numerous ships weren't coming towards him. He watched them on his DeTect scanner as they passed him by at Light-375—"

Vyx had held up his hand. "Light-375?"

"I questioned that point also, but my friend was adamant."

"Continue."

"He didn't count them, but he's sure he was passed by over eighty ships. He said there could have been as many as a hundred twenty, but he can't be any more specific than that because they were traveling in a most unusual fashion. He says they were moving in a single file and he lost track of the count. They came as close as eighty kilometers to his location, but his small ship was hidden among a few small asteroids on the outer edge of a small system and wasn't moving or emitting an energy signature, and therefore apparently wasn't detected."

"Where were they headed?"

"He was nervous and didn't think to get a precise fix until it was too late, but he said they were headed in the general direction of the Nazurz nebula."

"And where was your friend?"

Blasperra produced a piece of paper and handed it to Vyx. "Here are the coordinates of the location where he was waiting for his contact. It's extremely remote, so seeing ships there was quite unexpected."

"Thanks, Ker."

"And my payment?"

"As I said, confirmed information. You'll be paid when it's confirmed."

"How will you confirm my information? The ships are no longer where they were seen."

"That many ships can't hide. Someone else will see them. And when they do, it'll confirm your sighting."

"You never told me what it is you hope to sell to the Milori."

"Nothing. I normally deal in hard goods, but this time I have a buyer willing to pay for information. You sell to me and I sell to them. We both profit."

"And who is your buyer?"

"Ker, that's not how I do business. I didn't ask the name of your smuggler friend, did I?"

"Quite right, Trader. Forgive my solecism."

"Done."

"Now that that part of our business is concluded, I have a most exciting business opportunity for you."

"Really? What is it?"

"I have a client who's looking for someone very dependable and discreet. He has a small cargo he wishes to have delivered to Koppreco."

"A cargo of— ?"

"Aluvian mamots."

"Aluvian mamots carry the Vergun Plague. That's why they're on the illegal import list at Koppreco."

"These mamots have all been quarantined and checked for the plague for two lunar cycles. If they were infected, the plague would have been discovered. I guarantee they're disease free."

"How many?"

"Five hundred."

"Five hundred?"

"The client will pay you a thousand credits for each mamot that arrives healthy on Koppreco."

"A thousand credits for each? That's five hundred thousand credits."

"They fetch a commanding price. For some reason, the mamots that they have on Koppreco won't mate. Each year there are fewer and their value increases. It's not illegal to own them, just illegal to import them because of the plague. The wealthy are desperate to own the noisy little fur balls and the Kopprecon government refuses to revoke its import restriction, making smuggling them in more and more lucrative. Owning one or more has become a status symbol on Koppreco."

"Where are these mamots?"

"In a breeding and quarantine station on Aluvia."

"And I'll get full documentation on their health status?"

"Absolutely. You must be satisfied that the mamots are plague free or you have the right to reject the cargo. If you accept the deal, the client will transfer the funds to me. I'll deposit them in an interest-bearing account and I'll release a thousand credits for each mamot that arrives healthy, returning the rest of the original sum to the client."

"The trip to Aluvia takes a couple of months. Will they hold the animals until I arrive?"

"Of course. By the time you arrive, they'll probably have another two hundred disease free and ready to transport."

"What about food?"

"They'll give you an ample supply for the eight-month trip to Koppreco when you load the mamots aboard your ship."

"Okay, Ker. I'll pick up the mamots, deliver them to Koppreco, and be back here in twenty months to collect my fee."

"Deal. Here's the pickup and delivery information," Blasperra said, extending a hand containing a piece of folded paper.

"You expected me to say yes?"

"It seemed like a contract you'd accept. No slaves and no drugs but with a large fee. And with *your* contacts, I knew that if you accepted it, it would be filled, so I've held it for you for the past two weeks."

Vyx just nodded.

Blasperra stood up. "I'll see you in twenty months."

Vyx nodded again and Blasperra left.

"Drink up," Vyx said to Byers quietly. "I want to send off this information about the Milori as quickly as possible."

# Chapter Twenty
## ~ April 16<sup>th</sup>, 2277 ~

A little over three weeks after repairs to the first group of ships were completed, engineers certified the *Bellona*, *Song*, and *Plantaganet* as being fully battle ready. Most of the engineers had already moved on to the next group of ships and were making good progress. Jenetta called a meeting of all captains and their first officers.

"Good afternoon," she said as she and Lt. Commander Ashraf entered the conference room. "Please be seated."

Jenetta moved to the head of the table and took her seat. "We've received a message from the agents I sent to Scruscotto. They've been able to get a possible lead on one of our missing Milori fleets, and they claim that the source is usually very reliable. Assuming that the informant was telling the truth and assuming that the Milori were headed towards the most likely target along the path indicated by the generalized information we secured, they would seem to have been headed for the Thurews system. If we further assume that they were on the same schedule for crossing the Frontier Zone border as the fleet we met in battle, that they stopped and headed this way immediately, and that their top speed is Light-450, we can expect to see them fifty-six days from now. If they maintain a speed of Light-375, which was their speed when observed, they'll arrive in roughly sixty-seven days. We can really use that extra time."

"Why the Thurews system, Admiral?" Captain Powers asked. "There's nothing there of any military value."

"There's a freight hub there. They've been traveling for quite some time, so the Milori might simply want to restock their food stores before commencing any action. Or perhaps it's nothing more than a convenient navigation point. It's about the same distance inside the border as Stewart. They may have intended to bypass it without stopping if the fleet sent at us was successful. I know I'm making a lot of assumptions, but it's my best guess for a workable scenario. The last of the three fleets, that I'll refer to as the Second Fleet, may be farther away and that would mean that the fleet I'll call the First Fleet would have to wait for them. I'm sure they'll want to combine forces before beginning an attack. It's also possible that both fleets are already much closer, but fifty-six days is the number I've decided to go with for planning purposes.

"The engineers are reasonably sure they can have the *Romanov*, *Geneva*, *Ottawa*, *Mentuhotep*, *St. Petersburg*, and *Beijing* in battle-ready condition by then. The *Asuncion*, *Buenos Aires*, and *Cairo* will have to be moved to a safer location. It's unfortunate that we don't have any space tugs with us, but we needed every square centimeter of space for ordnance. Our engineers have restored sub-light power to the three ships, so they can begin their journey to Stewart under their own power while they wait for a space tug. The tugs from Stewart should arrive before the Milori fleets, so I'm confident our damaged ships will be far from here by the time we re-engage.

"I've moved our six spotter ships to cover the newly calculated approach direction of the Milori fleet. They'll be far enough out to give us an hour's warning time. All we can do now is keep working to repair the damage to our ships and prepare a small trap. We can project an electronic screen thousands of kilometers, even though we only created a one kilometer by one kilometer by two hundred kilometer cage at our last encounter. This time we'll use the maximum range because we can't predict their approach direction exactly. We'll reposition the unexploded mines from our original trap to create a flat-plane defensive minefield where we expect the Milori to most likely attempt a penetration once they arrive. We'll hold position until they begin their attack run and then 'force' them through the minefield like a magician 'forces' a volunteer to pull a certain card from a deck, by shifting ourselves to larboard or starboard. With any luck, they won't try to exit through the sides of this new trap. We don't have enough mines to even begin to establish an encircling mine-field."

"Why don't we just fall back to the border, Admiral?" Captain Payton of the *Thor* asked. "There's no need to engage them here."

"Retreating won't help, Bill. We'd still have to confront this threat, and the border offers no better locations for a battle. By engaging them here, they'll hopefully have to hang around afterwards and lick their wounds, as we've been doing. That will give the ships on their way to Stewart more time to arrive and prepare another line of defense near the inner border. Our job now is to bloody the Milori as badly as we can."

"In other words, we're expendable," Captain White of the *Romanov* said.

"We must do everything possible to prevent the Milori from getting past us here. But there's always a chance we'll survive. We've discovered some of the weaknesses of the Milori ships, such as that they only have two layers of hull plating, and the hull on the top of the ship near the stern is the weakest area on their battleships. Each of you has received a copy of the complete report prepared by the engineers who assessed the damage we caused to the Milori Third Fleet. Make sure your gunners review it and learn it."

"Admiral," Captain Yung said, "you should go with the three ships you're sending away. The rest of the fleet will need you after this battle."

"My place is here, Charles, where I can try to talk the Milori out of taking this action. I didn't have any luck with Lord High Space Marshall Gulqulk, but now they've seen we're not the pushovers they seemed to be expecting. Perhaps the commander of the approaching fleet will be more reasonable. But if he isn't, I'll face the same danger that I ask each of you to face."

With the expected date of enemy arrival established, the days seem to move faster than ever. The three ships that couldn't be repaired in time to meet the Milori threat were stripped of their ordnance and sent off under sub-light power with a minimum crew complement. The job of consolidating the Milori hulls into one group and anchoring them to one another fell to the Marines. Things would be confusing enough once the battle began. They didn't need broken hulls floating into the paths of ships as they maneuvered for position.

Jenetta continued to file her daily reports to Supreme Headquarters and maintained daily contact with Captain Donovan at Stewart. The engineers had plenty to do to keep them busy and the officers found plenty for everyone else to do. Gunners stayed busy studying the reports outlining the weaknesses of the Milori ships or using the simulators in mock combat conditions against Milori ship icons.

Jenetta was studying the latest progress reports from the chief engineers when the computer announced that Lt. Commander Bushnell was requesting admittance. She said, "Come," and the doors opened to reveal a male officer standing just outside the room. He looked exceedingly uncomfortable.

"Come in, Commander," Jenetta said.

He walked in and came rigidly to attention. "Lieutenant Commander Gary Bushnell reporting to the Admiral as ordered."

"Stand easy," Jenetta said as she stood up and offered her hand. "It's good to see you again. How are you getting on?"

He hesitated, then took her hand nervously and shook it gently. "I'm doing fine, Admiral. It's an honor to be serving in your command, ma'am."

"Have a seat, Commander," she said, gesturing towards a chair in front of her desk and then sitting down in her own chair.

He sat down but didn't relax in the chair. Sitting on the very edge of the seat with his back ramrod straight, he said, "Thank you, ma'am."

"It's been a long time since our days together at the Academy."

"Yes, ma'am, a very long time."

"I noticed from your record that you've only been aboard the *Mentuhotep* for the past three years?"

"Yes, ma'am. I was posted there when I received my promotion."

"I wasn't aware that you were in my command until my brother named you as his second officer."

"Is that what the Admiral wished to see me about? I believe I'm ready for the responsibility."

"No, I merely wished to say hello to a former classmate and see how you're doing. Your record for the past ten years has been excellent."

Bushnell seemed to relax a little then. "Thank you, ma'am. I've worked very hard to make up for the stupid mistakes I made as a young lieutenant. I regret those unfortunate incidents and swear they will never happen again."

"I have every confidence in you. I don't believe in holding minor lapses in judgment that occurred during the distant past against someone who's obviously trying hard to be a credit to himself and Space Command."

"Thank you, Admiral. As I said, it's an honor to be serving in your command, a real honor. Your career has been a tremendous inspiration to me and was mainly responsible for resuscitating my own. I took a good, hard look at myself and realized that I was my own worst enemy. I had grown frustrated that I wasn't advancing in rank according to my expectations and turned to alcohol to deaden the pain. After hearing what you did at Raider-One, I gave up drinking completely and dedicated myself to proving to everyone, includeing myself, that I had changed. I have a large print of the Raider-One base explosion hanging in my quarters. I keep it there to remind me what a tremendous difference one dedicated Space Command officer can make."

"Even one voted 'to be an ensign for the longest time?'" Jenetta said, smiling.

"It shows you how silly those titles are. Here you are an admiral, a two-star admiral, while no one else from our class has even made captain yet. You're thirty or forty career years ahead of the rest of us. By the time I make captain, if I do, you'll probably be the Admiral of the Fleet."

"I hope not. I expect you to make captain long before I'd be ready to accept such a position. But it's all up to you. If you continue to apply yourself, the selection board will certainly overlook the very minor, off-duty mistakes of a young lieutenant(jg)."

"Yes, ma'am," he said, smiling. "I certainly will."

*  *  *

Jenetta had dinner with the ship's captains most evenings, but at least twice a week she got together with Christa and Eliza. Billy usually joined them once a week and saw Jenetta at most other evening meals since he was captain of the *Mentuhotep*.

At one of the dinners where it was just the girls, Jenetta asked, "How's your head, Eliza? Any lasting effects from the injury you received during the battle?"

"No, the gash was closed by the next day and there wasn't any sign of the injury a few days later. Your DNA is wonderful, sis."

Jenetta smiled. "It's come in handy a few times, right Christa?"

"Absolutely, Jen. But I don't know if I'll feel that way forever."

"Why not? Because of Adam?"

Christa nodded. "I'm not sure how he feels about my never aging. I've tried to talk to him about it, but he always changes the subject."

"Perhaps he doesn't know how he feels," Eliza offered. "On the one hand it would be nice having a mate who is always young and beautiful, but on the other hand, it might be awkward to pair with someone and then continue to age while they retain their energy, vitality, and sex appeal."

"I think you're right," Jenetta said. "I've worried about the same thing. Hugh looks old enough to be our father because of his premature graying, although he certainly isn't that much older than me in actual years since my birth."

"You haven't mentioned Hugh in a while," Christa said. "Have you heard from him?"

"Yes, I've received a message at least once a week since he was awakened from stasis sleep. The company requires them to sleep half the trip to save on salaries, and since this trip is two years, he'll be going under for another six-month cycle in a few months."

"I can imagine his surprise," Eliza said, "when he learned of your second star. You were just a captain when he went to sleep."

"And I hope to be *just a captain* again in a couple of years. If you calculate the time of my duty tour since Captain Gavin officially installed me as base commander, I've been on Stewart for three years and four months. That means just one year and eight months to go. Supreme HQ has to get my replacement started on his trip soon so he's here when my tour is up."

"Only a year and a half left. I can't believe it," Christa said. "It seemed so long when you first took over as base commander."

"Don't I know it? We could be out here for another five or six months, and by the time we get back I'll be counting the time in months."

"That would be nice," Eliza said, "but we're forgetting the Milori. They may render this entire conversation academic. Long-term relationships and duty tours may not concern us after they get here."

"I'm not going to live my life worrying about the possible calamities that might befall us," Christa said.

"I admit that it has concerned me," Jenetta said. "I'm responsible for all our lives. Us, Billy, and the tens of thousands of others in this taskforce. But speaking selfishly for just a minute, I've always thought there would be one of us three around to carry on my enhanced DNA. Now we're in very real danger of us all being killed out here. I even considered sending one of you on the *Asuncion* so you'd be safe, but I knew you'd never go willingly."

"Darn right," Eliza said. "We've sat in nice safe places while you've been roaming all over Galactic Alliance space fighting Raiders. We're Space Command officers also, and we deserve a chance to do our part."

"Ditto," Christa said. "We'll take our chances the same as you. If these are to be our final hours, let's make them our finest hours."

Looking to change the somber mood that had befallen the trio, Jenetta held up her coffee mug in the manner that one of Alexandre Dumas' famous characters from *The Three Musketeers* might once have held his sword. "One for all…"

"And all for one," Eliza and Christa said simultaneously, clicking their coffee mugs against Jenetta's before the three women broke into a fit of giggling.

*   *   *

By the fifty-sixth day— the date Jenetta had established as the earliest that the Milori fleets might arrive— and the ninety-eighth day since the battle, all twelve ships of the small taskforce were certified battle-ready. Not all of the repairs were pretty, and some areas of the ships were unusable for normal activity. But for warfare, they were almost as functional as they had been in the hours before the first battle. The engineers began to get some much needed rest while the rest of the crew began to grow edgy from waiting. The weapons simulators were being used around the clock, both to further hone skills and as a way to work off anxiety. There hadn't been any more sightings of the Milori since the one report.

When the tugs from Stewart finally arrived, Jenetta made a decision to delay their immediate return to the base with the three damaged ships in tow. At just over fifty billion kilometers into their journey, the three ships had stopped in space and linked up when a problem developed with the sub-light engines on the *Buenos Aires*. Unless the Milori came from the direction of Stewart, they wouldn't be spotted.

The tugs, capable of Light-75, could make the trip from the taskforce to the damaged ships in thirty-seven minutes, so Jenetta decided to use the small craft for transporting engineers to the damaged ships each day. She hoped the Milori would give them enough time to get one or more of the ships battle-ready.

Eight days later, one of the spotter ships sent an urgent message to the taskforce. The Milori fleets were passing their position. They gave the precise location and heading of the

Milori. The taskforce swung into immediate action as General Quarters alerts sounded throughout every ship.

Having information about the Milori allowed the taskforce to move the minefield. They centered it directly between them and the approaching enemy force. An hour's lead-time was more than sufficient for the network of self-propelled mines to reposition themselves once the coordinates were transmitted.

Everything was in readiness when the Milori Fleet came into view on the sensor screens. Jenetta ordered the electronic barrier activated and the enemy fleet came to a stop just short of the minefield. The twelve-ship taskforce was waiting just thirty thousand kilometers beyond the minefield and energy grid.

"Admiral," the com chief said, "the Milori are hailing you."

"Me? Personally?"

"Aye, Admiral."

"Feed our bridge image and the viewscreen image to all ships. Okay, chief, put the Milori on the front viewscreen."

A second later, the close-up image of a Milora filled the enormous screen. Each ship in the taskforce was receiving a split image, with Jenetta on the left and the Milora on the right.

"I'm Admiral Jenetta Carver of the Galactic Alliance Space Command," Jenetta said to the hair-covered visage from which four large brown eyes protruded. "You're trespassing in Galactic Alliance space. I have to assume your intentions are hostile, given the fact that you've arrived here in such numbers."

The Milora chuckled, or at least made a sound the translator software interpreted as a chuckle. The grim-looking face never smiled. "I'm Supreme Lord Space Marshall Dwillaak. And you know very well why we're here. I recognize you from the news broadcasts we've been intercepting. I demand your immediate and unconditional surrender."

"How very interesting," Jenetta said, unperturbedly. "That's precisely what I demanded of your Lord High Space Marshall Gulqulk. Unfortunately for your Third Fleet, he chose to fight. He assumed that simply because he had a seven-to-one superiority he'd destroy us easily. I hope you're smarter, given that you're his superior and obviously much more intelligent. Perhaps you've noticed that your FTL engines have disengaged."

The Milora chuckled again. "We were prepared for that. Our friends in the Raider Corporation have explained how that works. Commandant Mikel Arneu has told us that we merely have to use our sub-light engines to get past the projection and our Light-Speed engines will re-engage."

"Oh, but our grid is much more sophisticated than the simple grid once used by the Raiders. Didn't you hear that it destroys any ship that tries to cross it? Didn't you receive messages from the Milori warriors who tried it during the first encounter?"

"Yes, we did, but those were the wild ravings of severely injured and dying warriors who didn't know what they were saying."

"You said you intercepted our news broadcasts. Didn't you see it for yourself?"

"We saw a clever simulation designed to look like the grid was causing the problem."

"You don't believe your people, and you don't believe the news broadcasts. I have to wonder what it will take to convince you. Perhaps you'll believe your own eyes." Gesturing in the direction of the Milori ships that the Marines had tethered together, Jenetta said, "You need only look at the pile of refuse we've begun to accumulate out here. That growing scrap collection used to be one hundred three of your Emperor's finest warships. And now you bring us another two hundred ships for the scrap heap. Perhaps a demonstration is called for. Select an officer you don't particularly care for and send his ship through the grid. We won't fire as long as it doesn't come closer than twenty-five thousand kilometers— the effective range of your laser weapons."

"Our laser weapons can destroy at ranges far greater than twenty-five thousand kilometers," the Milora said.

"Of course they can," Jenetta said, "as can ours. I said effective range because we both know how such weapons are affected by light-speed lag, diffraction, equipment thermal stresses, and the like. We've had ample opportunity to examine your ships and weapons since we destroyed your fleet. Please, feel free to send one of your ships against the barrier."

The Milora's expression changed. The Terran's challenge was most unexpected. Once Mikel Arneu had explained how the electronic debris field worked, Dwillaak had become supremely confident that his forces would easily destroy the puny fleet opposing his mighty armada. He believed the Third Fleet had been fooled by the Terran admiral's lies and simply allowed themselves to be destroyed where they'd stopped because they feared to cross through the non-existent barrier. The witnessed explosions had to be the result of torpedoes, not some fanciful energy barrier. But why would the enemy now be challenging him to disprove her claim in this fashion? It had to be a bluff. Perhaps she was hoping to have a single warship put into a vulnerable position and destroyed before his forces had a chance to react. Well, he decided, he wouldn't play the enemy's game; he'd send an entire battle group forward. Turning slightly to his left he said, "Send Marshall Talqulk's group forward to a position a thousand kilometers beyond the barrier. No further."

The *Prometheus'* tactical operator changed the view to the front of the minefield but superimposed a much smaller image of the Supreme Lord Space Marshall into an insert area on the front viewscreen.

A dozen ships moved forward slowly under sub-light engine power. It seemed to take forever as all eyes watched their progress. As Marshall's Talqulk's heavy cruiser reached the nearly invisible minefield, two almost simultaneous nuclear explosions ripped apart the bow of the armored hull, whiting out the *Prometheus'* sensors for a second so that only the inset image of Dwillaak appeared on a vast field of white at the front the bridge. The Supreme Lord Space Marshall screamed for the battle group to stop and retreat, but it was too late. Marshall Talqulk, expecting an attack by Space Command forces while exposed in front of the main force, had assembled his group into battle formation instead of using their pursuit tactic of following one after another. His ship had only been a few scant meters ahead of the others, and they'd encountered the barrier at almost the same instant. Huge holes opened in the minefield as fusion mines flashed briefly, but it was at the expense of a dozen prime warships. The destroyed ships spun and drifted beyond the minefield, huge gaping holes in their hulls proof of where the mines had effectively done their job. The tactical station sensor screen on the *Prometheus'* bridge showed that the remaining mines were immediately closing ranks to fill the holes. The Milori shouldn't be able to see that data unless they discovered the special RF frequency the mines used to coordinate with one another.

"You have my condolences for the loss of your brave warriors, Supreme Lord Space Marshall. I assume you believe your own eyes. Or do you feel that this was a clever simulation? Or perhaps the ravings of severely injured and dying warriors?"

Another Milora moved into the picture and whispered something to Dwillaak, then moved back away from the Supreme Lord Space Marshall. Dwillaak calmed and smiled as if again possessing certain knowledge he'd win the day. "Very clever, Admiral. My tactical officer tells me that we have detected mines moving along the grid. We now know how you made it *appear* your grid was causing the damage. I offer you a chance to surrender for the last time."

Although her heart was beating three times normal, Jenetta appeared as calm as if she hadn't a care in the world. It was the ability to appear icy calm in the face of possible disaster that had earned her the nickname 'Ice Queen.' The Milori sensors were better than she had expected, and the number of holes opened in the minefield meant that a lot more had to shift position than she'd anticipated. But she had to appear as supremely confident as Dwillaak appeared. "You still believe that you stand a chance against my forces?" she asked.

"Yes. Oh, I know your ships are well constructed and that your weapons are powerful. But so are ours. A dozen ships, no matter how well constructed or powerfully armed, can't possibly stand up against my force of two hundred six warships— correction, one hundred ninety-four warships. We'll overpower you by sheer weight of numbers."

"A dozen ships? Is that all you think I have available? What if I was to tell you that I have many, many more ships positioned nearby?"

"I told you, we intercepted your news broadcasts. You haven't had time to get more ships here."

"No?" Jenetta raised her left hand and extended her index finger. The com operator pressed a button on the console.

The Milora had watched as Jenetta raised her arm. He continued to watch for some additional movement from her. When no further movement appeared forthcoming he asked, "What does this mean? This one raised digit?"

By Jenetta's calculations, her information exchange credit with the Milora was high enough that he shouldn't be asking any questions of her. Perhaps the unusual system didn't apply to top officials. "It's a signal from me for ships to move up," she said, simply.

Dwillaak's tactical officer hurried over and whispered in his ear. The news shook Dwillaak, but he didn't allow it to alter his outward composure. How had Space Command reinforced their position here so quickly when the news broadcasts all stated that Carver only had fifteen ships under her command?

"So, Admiral," Dwillaak said, "you held back a large reserve force. My tactical officer has detected the nineteen large ships a billion kilometers off your larboard stern quarter. But even thirty-one warships will not be enough to save you. No matter how powerful they are."

"Thirty-one to one hundred ninety-four are better odds than we had at our last encounter with Milori intractability. Just for the sake of argument, how many will it take to convince you to return to your own territory peacefully?"

"You don't have enough for that. The Emperor himself charged me with this mission. I shall not fail."

"No?" Jenetta asked and then raised her arm again, this time extending two fingers. The com operator pressed another button.

After a few seconds, Dwillaak's tactical officer hurried to his side again and whispered something. Dwillaak's expression changed slightly. The arrogant and contemptuous look he'd had until now was gone. "You're full of surprises, Admiral. We see the additional thirty-four ships off your starboard stern quarter. So you really have a force of sixty-five ships. You're not nearly as helpless as you first appeared." Dwillaak was feeling some nervousness now, although he tried to project an image of calm. If fifteen Space Command ships could destroy a hundred three Milori warships, what chance did a hundred ninety-four have against sixty-five? He only had a three-to-one superiority now.

"We were never helpless, Supreme Lord Space Marshall. We originally believed your ships to be much more powerful than they really are, so we brought fifteen ships to the original engagement, as it showed on the news. After a close examination of your ships from the Third Fleet by my engineers, I believe my twelve ships could easily destroy your two fleets. Extra ships will just allow your complete destruction much sooner. We know *all* your weaknesses, and we know you can't possibly survive in battle against us. I would prefer to avoid an action because a few dozen of my people will undoubtedly be injured or killed. So if you need more convincing to withdraw your forces back to your own territory…" Jenetta extended her arm again and raised three fingers.

If it was possible for a Milora to turn white, Jenetta felt that Dwillaak would have done so as his tactical officer hurried over anxiously and whispered to him again. Her words had planted seeds of serious doubt about his fleet's superiority, and with each wave of her hand she conjured up a greater and greater number of ships. This was no enemy trick or sensor malfunction. Those ships were real. But how could she have so many? How could their intelligence data have been so wrong? And how could he possibly hope to defeat an enemy whose ships were obviously so superior to his own? As the number of enemy ships inched closer and closer to parity with the size of his own forces, he knew he didn't have a chance of defeating Carver.

"How many more ships must I call in for battle, Supreme Lord Space Marshall? Do you hold your warriors in such low regard? Would you see them slaughtered in a senseless battle that you can't *possibly* win? Your Emperor has already lost one entire fleet. Would it be serving him wisely to lose an additional two fleets? Surely the Empire could use these fleets back home to squash peaceful dissidents and defenseless insurrectionists. There's no doubt that we would suffer a few casualties in an engagement, and I would like to avoid that if possible, but I'll be even more saddened if you force me to kill so many more Milori. I grieve for the families of the two hundred thousand warriors who will not be returning as a result of our first engagement. Please don't cause me to sadden the families of four hundred thousand more." Jenetta drew in a large breath, then released it quickly in a loud sigh. Almost casually, she said, "But, I will, if that's the only course you leave open to me..."

Jenetta raised her arm again.

"Wait, Admiral," Dwillaak said quickly. "Perhaps our two nations can reach an understanding."

Jenetta slowly lowered her arm. "Will you withdraw from Galactic Alliance space and promise never to return?"

The Milora looked as if he would strangle on his own words. His head shook slightly as he forced the words from his vocal orifice. "Yes, we will withdraw and I will not return."

"Immediately, without stopping anywhere?"

"Agreed."

"How many other ships are in our space?"

"Just six— one at each of the bases we've established."

"You will send them a message and have them immediately withdraw without waiting for you to return. They can wait for you outside our border."

"Agreed."

"Finally, the Galactic Alliance establishes a *new* one-hundred-light-year-wide Buffer Zone outside our Frontier Zone border. It is Galactic Alliance space, and we'll patrol it as we see fit, although we'll not establish any permanent bases there. Your Empire will not try to claim it, nor will any warship from the Empire enter it without first receiving permission from the Galactic Alliance Council or Space Command."

The Milora really struggled to say, "Agreed," to this last condition, which essentially surrendered a wide swath of previously unclaimed territory that otherwise could have been undisputed Milori territory.

"You agree to all these conditions in the name of the Milori Empire and your Emperor?"

"Yes."

"You agree that violating any of these terms will be tantamount to an *open* declaration of war?"

"Yes."

"Very well. Let this be known as the Galactic Alliance-Milori Treaty of 2277."

"Agreed."

"We're holding hundreds of your warriors on our ships. We'll transfer them to one of your ships as soon as your fleets are under way out of our space. What about the bodies of the slain warriors?"

"Their souls have already departed. Dispose of the husks as you wish."

"Very well. Order all ships but one to reverse the course that you followed to get here and continue on that precise course for exactly one hundred twenty GST minutes at Light-375, then turn directly towards the Milori home world and proceed non-stop until they are across the new buffer zone. We have spotter ships watching. Once assured that you're complying, we'll transfer the prisoners to the ship that remains here. It can easily catch up with your fleets using its top speed."

"What about the minefield barrier?"

Jenetta nodded to the tactical officer, who disabled the mines and the electronic barrier equipment, then turned back to the viewscreen. "It's down. You may send out shuttles to rescue any survivors on Marshall Talqulk's dozen ships. Transmit the coordinates of the bases you've established. We'll be sending someone to verify you've indeed vacated them."

"My ship will remain here to accept the prisoners you're holding in your ships after you're satisfied we have complied."

The connection terminated, and the image on the front viewscreen returned to a sensor-simulated view of the Milori fleet. Everyone on the bridge watched as one hundred ninety-three ships turned around and disappeared into the distance, leaving just one lone battleship in position. The conflict seemed to be over without firing a shot.

Captain Gavin turned to Jenetta and said in shock and awe, "I don't understand, Admiral. Where did you get all those warships?"

"I'll explain everything after the last Milora is gone."

An hour later the com operator said, "Admiral, message from the *Piccolo*. A fleet of one hundred ninety-three ships has passed their location headed away."

"Thank you. Com, signal the Supreme Lord Space Marshall that we'll begin sending over the prisoners, and notify Major Visconti to begin transporting them."

"Aye, Admiral."

Jenetta and Captain Gavin continued to sit on the bridge, watching the shuttles move back and forth until all prisoners had been transferred. When the transfer was complete, the Milori vessel turned and left without another word. Jenetta waited ten minutes and then said, "Com, hail Captain Nadealt on commercial frequency 25932.5, please.

"He's on, Admiral," the operator said a few seconds later.

"Put it on the viewscreen."

The image of a uniformed Arrosian officer filled the monitor, making him look much larger than his actual three-foot, four-inch height.

"Hello, Captain Nadealt. You followed instructions perfectly. I'm indebted to you and your crew, the crews of your other ships, the king and queen, and Prime Minister Marueck."

"We're most happy to have been of assistance to you Admiral. We owe you much for bringing peace and stability to our world again."

"I'd like to invite you and the other captains to join us tonight aboard the *Prometheus* for a small celebration. Say 1900 hours GST?"

"Thank you, Admiral. We'll be there."

"I'll look forward to meeting you in person. Carver out."

"Likewise. Nadealt out."

The screen returned to the view of space.

"Com, hail Trader Vyx aboard the *Scorpion* and put it on the viewscreen."

A few seconds later the image of Vyx appeared.

"Greetings, Admiral. It looks like it worked."

"Better than I could have hoped. Thank you, Trader. You may pay off the captains and send them on their way."

"Will do, Admiral."

"We're having a small celebration at 1900 hours. You and your associates are welcome to attend if you wish."

"Thank you, Admiral. I'll tell them, and I'll be there."

"Okay, Trader. I'll see you tonight. Carver out."

"Vyx out."

As the screen returned to an image of space, Jenetta realized that Gavin was staring at her with a confused expression on his face.

"Pay off the captains?" Gavin said. "You used mercenaries? But where did they get all those warships?"

"Let's go to my conference room office and I'll explain."

As Jenetta stood up, Commander Tim Eaton, the ship's First Officer, asked, "Is it over, Admiral?"

"For today, Tim."

The First Officer stood up and started applauding. In seconds the entire bridge crew was applauding, and then cheering, and then hugging one another.

Gavin smiled and said, "I'll notify my crew. Com, put me on ship-wide speakers."

The com chief, carried away with exuberance like the rest of the bridge crew, had to hurry back to his station. "Go ahead, Captain."

"Attention crew of the *Prometheus*. The Milori have turned around and are headed out of Galactic Alliance space. Thanks to Admiral Carver, their surrender and retreat was accomplished without our having to fire a single shot this day. Captain out."

The bridge erupted into cheering again and some people wept in happiness as they released the built-up tension they had been feeling for weeks and months. An hour earlier, they had been sure they were all dead.

"Let's go to the conference room, Captain, and spread the word to the other ships. I'm sure they're anxious to know what's going on."

"I know I'm certainly anxious to know what just happened, Admiral."

Five minutes later, the large wall monitor in the conference room filled with the faces of ship's captains from the other ships in the taskforce, including those of the disabled ships, for the fifteen-way conference.

"The conflict is over," Jenetta said, "for the present. One of our spotter ships has confirmed that the fleet passed their location after one hour, and we're waiting now to hear that the last ship has passed. We have the coordinates of the bases they established and I'll need someone to verify that they've gone, but that chore will be handled by the newly arriving ships."

"I'm dying to know, Admiral," Gavin said. "Where did you find all those mercenaries? And I didn't even know Arrosa had any warships capable of taking on the Milori."

"I sent our agents to Scruscotto with two objectives. One was to learn anything they could about the Milori fleets. It was their information that allowed us to prepare properly for the arrival of the two Milori fleets today. Their second objective was to hire as many ships as possible for a simple job. They were to come here and wait to be called upon, and then move in just close enough for the Milori to pick them up on their DeTect monitors."

"There was a fleet of mercenary warships at Scruscotto?"

"No. The fleet was only to move in close enough to appear as a blip on the Milori screens but not close enough for them to see that the ships were all freighters adjusted in size to appear like battleships, cruisers, frigates, and destroyers."

"Freighters?" Captain Gavin exclaimed loudly. "You hired freighters? You got the Milori to surrender, sign a peace treaty, and retreat by threatening them with a fleet of freighters?"

The captains of all the ships started to laugh, and laugh hard. A couple laughed so hard that they started to choke and their First Officers had to slap them on the back. The laughter was *their* release from the tension of the past days, weeks, and months.

"Essentially," Jenetta said, shrugging. "If it hadn't worked, we would have been no worse off."

"What about the Arrosians?"

"They provided their merchant fleet for free. And all freighter captains had orders to go immediately to faster-than-light speed if I issued the order to 'scram.' They couldn't be harmed once they were moving."

The captains burst out in laughter again.

"Admiral," Captain Payton of the *Thor* said as tears ran down his cheeks, "that's the wildest, and the *greatest*, example of innovative battle strategy I've ever heard. You had that Milora officer soiling himself, and all the time those 'reserve' warships were mere freighters."

"But why didn't you tell *us*, Admiral?" Captain Powers of the *Chiron* asked.

"I didn't want to create any false expectations of hope with what was a last ditch attempt to avoid a battle. If it hadn't worked, there were just the twelve of us against two hundred six enemy ships, less the dozen destroyed by our minefield. I was bluffing all the way from the minute the Milora first hailed me."

"I, for one, am very glad that Admiral Jenetta Carver was here to develop and execute the tactical plan for this engagement," Captain Hyden of the *Bellona* said. "I doubt that anyone else in the service could have routed the enemy today without firing a single shot."

A chorus of exuberant voices echoed the sentiment.

"We were all very lucky today," Jenetta said. "A celebration party for senior officers will be held on the *Prometheus* tonight at 1900 hours. I suspect that your crews are waiting to hear the good news about the Milori retreat, so I won't keep you any longer. After the shipboard expressions of jubilation die down, we can link up the ships. I hope to see each of you later. Dismissed."

Jenetta arrived at the celebration party a few minutes before 1900 hours and was welcomed with applause from everyone who had arrived before her. All of the captains were there, including the three from the damaged ships. They had arrived earlier by space tug. Most first officers were still on watch, but a few had exchanged their duty schedule with their ship's second officer and made it to the party. Most of the intelligence agents had come, and there was a large contingent of Arrosians.

Jenetta moved around the room speaking with everyone. The officers' mess had really outdone themselves when they laid out the fantastic buffet. There was an entire table for salads, another for entrees, and another for desserts. Few people at the party weren't carrying a dish filled with all of their favorite foods. To accommodate the Arrosians, engineering had constructed a temporary raised platform in the front of each table. The taller people at the party could simply lean over it.

Few of the officers were talking with the Arrosians, so Jenetta spent plenty of time with them. She listened to their troubles and praised their bravery and generosity. She had them all eating out of her hand before the party was half over.

Jenetta found Vyx standing against a wall by himself, sipping a drink as she wandered about the room. "Reminds me of the first time we met," she said.

He nodded. "Yes, it does have a familiar feel. But you were just a mere Commander back then."

Jenetta laughed. "Yes, things have changed. At least you're not walking off this time."

"I didn't walk, Admiral, I ran. You scared the hell out of me. I couldn't fathom how the first officer on a ship could know so many details about my supposedly secret investigation. You knew more about my activities than I did."

"I'm sorry I made you so nervous," Jenetta said. "The Alliance owes you a great debt of gratitude for the job you've done for us out here."

"I'm glad I could help."

"I can just imagine what your expense account is going to look like this month."

"It won't be too bad. I mostly used money I earned as a trader. Speaking of which, I'd like you to arrange to get me through Kopprecon customs without being checked."

"Kopprecon? What's up? A little smuggling work?"

"Yes, but nothing harmful or dangerous. I wouldn't do anything that would cause problems. The individual who provided the information about the Milori offered me the job. I have to keep my reputation as a thoroughly disreputable person intact."

Jenetta smiled. "Okay, Trader. Get the details to Commander Ashraf and I'll take care of it."

"Thanks, Admiral."

"Where's Brenda?"

"She went to find out what's happened to Kathryn. Ah, here they come now."

Jenetta stayed and talked to the three agents for a while and then moved on to a group of captains who were laughing loudly. As soon as Jenetta was out of hearing range, Vyx said to Brenda, "Still think Admiral Carver has been mothballed at Stewart?"

"Okay, I was wrong. And I still can't get over the fact that she looks so much younger than me."

As Jenetta approached the group of captains, they parted to admit her.

"Join us, Admiral," Captain Crosby of the *Ottawa* said. "We were trying to see if we could come up with a recorded battle plan even more audacious than yours, but we haven't been successful."

"The Bible talks about Gideon," Jenetta said, "who, with three hundred warriors, defeated the Midianite army. He attacked in the middle of the night, having his men smash jars and blow horns or yell while waving torches. The enemy awoke startled and confused. Believing it was an attack by an overwhelming force, they fled their camp. Gideon's men pursued them and slew many. Gideon was able to slay the Midianite kings, Zebah and Zalmunnah— the people allegedly responsible for the deaths of his brothers."

Captain Crosby smiled. "As I recall, Gideon started with thirty-two thousand warriors and purposely sent all but three hundred home just before the battle. According to the text, God wanted the victory to look spectacular and show that divine intervention was responsible for the victory."

"Still, I think anyone would have to admit that Gideon's plan was pretty audacious," she said, smiling. "Mine was simply a plan born in desperation. I hope I'm never put into such a position again."

"That's what makes it so incredible, Admiral," Captain Yung of the *Song* said. "Unlike Gideon's, *our* situation seemed hopeless. We were all resigned to the fact that this would be our last day. I doubt if there was anyone on board my ship who hadn't prepared a "final" message home. And then, with seemingly nothing left to do except engage in a fight to the death, you bluffed the commander of an enemy force that outnumbered us more than sixteen to one into unconditional surrender and signing a peace treaty. I'd like to watch you play poker sometime."

"I'd like to see the face on that Milora when he learns how you fooled him," Captain Goran of the *Beijing* said. "With so many freighter crews involved, there's no way this will remain a secret for long. I bet Dwillaak throws a temper tantrum that frightens his entire crew out of ten years of their lives."

"We're not likely to see him again," Captain White of the *Romanov* said. "He'll probably be relieved of command as soon as the Emperor learns of his surrender. He'll be disgraced and probably expected to fall on his sword so that his clan can save face."

"Will they abide by the treaty he agreed to?" Captain Remia of the *Plantaganet* asked.

"They'll probably abide by it for a while," Captain Trevor Gillespie of the *Buenos Aires* said. "They'll want to rebuild their fleet before they attack again. Then they'll find some pretext to void the treaty the way they tried to void our prior claim to this territory."

"They obviously have expansionist plans for their Empire and see us as a significant impediment," Jenetta said. "Given the distance from the Milori Empire, those fleets must have been dispatched within months of the Galactic Alliance's Declaration to annex this territory. The Milori probably decided they had to stop us before we occupied even more of the territory they planned to annex. Although their border is five hundred light-years beyond our new outer border, they must have had designs on this space. With luck we'll have several years to prepare for their return."

"So we clearly can't let down our guard," Captain Pope of the *Geneva* said. "By the way, what's happened to those ships that were on their way to Stewart, Admiral? We could have used some help."

"I decided to have the ones that reached Stewart form a picket line one light-year this side of the base where they set up another electronics grid to stop the Milori. Most couldn't have reached us in time for the battle, so they became the second line of defense for the GA. It was my hope that we could damage the Milori so badly that they'd have to stay here for months while they made repairs. If they had decided to push on immediately with just the ships that were still battle-ready, I hoped that we would have whittled their number down by as much as half. In any event, the next line of ships should have had a much smaller force with which to contend. By the time the Milori got past Stewart, they might have only had one-quarter of their fleet still intact. They couldn't continue their invasion plans like that. They would have been forced to wait while they repaired more ships. That would have given the sixty-five additional ships headed for Stewart some much needed time to assemble and prepare to meet them."

"When then *Commander* Carver was promoted to the rank of captain following the Raider attempt to seize Stewart," Captain Powers of the *Chiron* said, "I was honored to stand in for Admiral Holt and pin on her new insignia. At that time, I told her that I couldn't think of anyone who deserved the promotion more. I feel that way about her promotion to admiral as well. I know, as all of you do, that she greatly desires a ship posting, but as Admiral Holt has said, she serves where sent without complaint— and serves spectacularly. I'd like to propose a toast to Admiral Carver. She has served the Galactic Alliance most spectacularly during this difficult period, as she always does."

Everyone raised his or her glass to complete the toast, saying simultaneously, "Admiral Carver."

Jenetta smiled and swallowed the lump that suddenly materialized in her throat. Billy, there as captain of the *Mentuhotep*, was looking at her and smiling. She could tell from the look that he was proud of her. "Thank you for the toast," she said as everyone took a sip and then lowered their glass. "I'm delighted that matters have turned out as well as they have. I appreciate your dedication to duty and the support you've always given me. Steve is correct when he says that my heart is with all of you on board your ships, but HQ sees me in a different role, at least for now. We're Space Command officers and we go where sent and do the job assigned.

"It's been my very great privilege and honor to have served with you during this crisis. I'll be returning to Stewart shortly, leaving most of you here until this mess is cleaned up. We can't very well just leave all these Milori warships here where they can be stripped of their weapons by scavengers. They'll have to be guarded as our tugs tow them to Stewart. A few of you will also have to stand guard over the *Asuncion*, *Buenos Aires*, and *Cairo* as they're towed home. Eventually we'll all meet up at Stewart several months from now because each of the ships in this taskforce still requires months of work to complete needed repairs."

Jenetta paused for a couple of seconds. "I'd like to propose a toast also. This toast is to you, the other officers and the crewmembers who have served Space Command so loyally and who have been prepared to make the ultimate sacrifice in defense of comrades and all the people of the Galactic Alliance. To Space Command."

"To Space Command," everyone said in unison as they clicked their glasses and took another sip of their drinks.

"To absent friends and comrades," Captain Gavin said, raising his glass again.

"To absent friends and comrades," everyone chimed in and then took another sip.

"I think I'll get a plate of food before it's all gone," Jenetta said. "Enjoy yourselves."

As Jenetta selected her favorite foods from the tables, all of which were still overflowing with food, Gavin came up alongside her. "You did good, Jen. Your eyes reflect the sadness you're feeling about losing so many people, but there wasn't anything you could have done to prevent it. Put it behind you."

"I'm not really blaming myself, Larry, because I know I did the best I could, but I am deeply saddened by our losses here. After everyone arrives back at Stewart, we'll have a memorial ceremony. Perhaps then I'll be able to stop thinking so much about the people I lost. I knew most of the officers who were killed, so I'll be preparing personal messages to their families." She sighed. "And I have far too many messages to send."

Gavin nodded. "Have you reported to Supreme Head-quarters yet?"

"No, not yet. I don't know exactly how to tell them about my bluff."

"Just tell them what happened. They can make their own minds up about everything. They will anyway."

"How can I tell them I hired freighters to scare away an enemy invasion fleet that might have run rampant through our space? They'll think I've gone insane. You know, I'm still hoping to get a ship someday."

Gavin chuckled. "It does sound a little crazy when you put it like that, but they'll understand that you took practically nothing and turned it into something. I almost fell out of my chair when all those ships showed up on the DeTect monitors in response to you waving your hand. It was as if you were conjuring them from thin air. I understand how the Milora commander must have felt."

It was Jenetta's turn to chuckle. "I should have told you, but I wasn't sure the freighter captains wouldn't cut and run at the sight of the Milori fleet. Many things had to go right for it to work. We were very lucky."

"As I've said in the past, I've grown very fond of your *luck*."

Jenetta stopped procrastinating the next morning and prepared her report to Supreme Headquarters. She included the bridge vid logs and sensor logs from the *Prometheus* with the report. Each of the captains would also be filing their own reports with all the supporting documentation available, and Supreme Headquarters would create a complete computer simulation of the events that would be studied by the experts for months, or longer. They had already expended thousands of man-hours studying the information from the first conflict and examining the performance of each ship in minute detail.

# Chapter Twenty-One

~ June 23$^{rd}$, 2277 ~

Admiral Moore took his seat at the center of the large horseshoe-shaped table in the enormous meeting hall where the Admiralty Board conducted their sessions and called the meeting to order. The other admirals were all present, their aides sitting dutifully behind them, but the gallery was empty today.

"Now that everyone here has reviewed the simulation data and we have all the reports from our assessment teams, it's time to discuss the performance of our officers during the conflict," Admiral Moore said.

"I agree with the War College findings," Admiral Platt said. "We know that deaths will naturally occur during any major conflict, and although our losses were quite severe in the war with the Milori, the loss of life was significantly lower than anyone could have hoped for given the size and armament of the opposing force. The ship captains performed splendidly, and the battle plan for the initial engagement was nothing less than inspired."

"I concur," Admiral Hillaire said, "but I think that we all agreed on that months ago after Admiral Carver submitted her initial report on the engagement. After all, that's why we gave her a second star. I think we should limit our discussion to the second confrontation now."

"What are you suggesting, Arnold, that Admiral Carver shouldn't be commended for the second confrontation?"

"Not at all, Evelyn. I think she pulled off what can only be described as one of the greatest battlefield stratagems in history. If she didn't already have a Medal of Honor, I'd recommend her for one."

"She did nothing heroic," Admiral Hubera said. "All she did was pull a monumental bluff on an enemy commander.

You think she deserves the Medal of Honor for hiring a bunch of freighters to pose as a fleet of warships?"

"Yes, Donald, I do. Space Command was unable to get a battle fleet to her, so she proceeded to convince the Milori that she had an overwhelming opposing force anyway. They believed it, or the Milori commanding officer would never have agreed to surrender and leave the Frontier Zone, *then* agree to a treaty in which they ceded another hundred light-years of space outside our established border for Admiral Carver's proposed Buffer Zone."

"I wouldn't put too much faith in that treaty, Arnold," Admiral Ressler said. "From what we know of the Milori, they'll be back as soon as they feel strong enough. It will probably be necessary to take the war to their territory next time and have the surrender signed by the Emperor inside his own palace."

"I expect so, Shana, but they're gone for now and we have time to prepare for their next visit thanks to Admiral Carver and her imaginary battle fleet."

"I don't like the fact that she didn't trust her fleet captains enough to tell them about the subterfuge," Admiral Hubera grumbled.

"Since when it is considered improper for a flag officer to keep non-vital information from subordinates?" Admiral Burke asked.

"Non-vital? We're talking about information that was key to the entire plan."

"It was only key once it worked, Donald," Admiral Hillaire said. "It would have been superfluous if it hadn't. Our ship's officers and crews were all fully committed to go into battle on Admiral Carver's command."

Admiral Hubera muttered something under his breath.

"It was a magnificent tactic, even if she didn't advertise it in advance," Admiral Bradlee said. "As an intelligence officer and someone quite used to keeping his cards close to his vest, I admire her ingenuity and audacity. My people are taught to be creative thinkers. Admiral Carver was never trained for that by us, but she has the gift."

"I believe it really justifies the faith we had in her when we assigned the additional ships to her command," Admiral Platt said.

"Shouldn't we recall some of those ships now that the threat is over?" Admiral Plimley asked.

"I'd vote against that, Loretta," Admiral Woo said. "The invasion shows that we're very susceptible to another incursion by the Milori. Unless we begin to see a substantial increase in criminal activity in the sectors where we reduced the patrols, I say we allow them to continue to their new assignments."

"I agree, but let's stick to the topic at hand," Admiral Hillaire said. "What do we do about Admiral Carver?"

"What do you want to do, give her a third star?" Admiral Hubera grumbled.

"No, of course not. She just received a promotion. But she certainly deserves premier recognition for what she's accomplished."

"If not a second Medal of Honor, then she deserves a third GSC Cross at the very least," Admiral Burke said. "Her handling of the conflict saved tens of thousands of lives and ended the problem for the foreseeable future."

"No one has been awarded two Medals of Honor for separate actions since the military fought ground wars on Earth," Admiral Ahmed said.

"No one in Space Command has ever done what Admiral Carver has done during her career, Raihana," Admiral Hillaire said.

"I don't like it," Admiral Hubera said. "It sets a bad precedent. Admiral Carver only did what she was being paid to do. Everyone else in that engagement was ready to forfeit his or her life in the defense of the Galactic Alliance. Should we award everyone who was there with a Medal of Honor?"

"Donald," Admiral Platt said, "it's true that the MOH has usually been awarded to recipients who distinguished themselves in individual combat, often after being severely wounded, but this case is unique. Admiral Carver was prepared to sacrifice herself and her crews to stop, or at least slow, the advance of the Milori. Yes, everyone at the confrontation came very close to sacrificing their lives, but Admiral Carver was the only one with free choice— both about being there and proceeding with her plan. You heard the statements from her captains that they had beseeched her to move to a rear area position from which to direct the battle, but she remained to lead her people and give the Milori an impression of invincibility by her presence. What's more, her actions in preparing to meet the Milori were directly responsible for saving the lives of everyone aboard our twelve warships, some twenty-four thousand officers and crew. The decision to place yourself in imminent danger in order to protect or save others is at the very heart of the justification for awarding the medal and always has been."

"Admiral Carver did save the lives of everyone in her taskforce through the use of her superior intelligence and a monumental bluff," Admiral Moore said. "I see validity in both Donald's and Evelyn's statements. Admiral Carver is very deserving of major recognition for her actions, but I think Space Command's highest honor, the Space Command Cross, is the proper award in this instance. All in favor of awarding Admiral Carver a third Space Command Cross, signify by raising your hand," Admiral Moore said.

Nine hands rose in support of the proposal.

"We have enough to approve the award, but it would be nice to have it unanimous," Admiral Moore said. "Donald?"

"Oh, alright," Admiral Hubera said cantankerously as he raised his hand, "I vote for it simply because she's not getting another MOH."

"It's agreed then by unanimous approval of the Board. Admiral Carver will receive a third Space Command Cross for her actions against the Milori."

"Now, who's going to replace her at Stewart?" Admiral Platt asked. "Her duty tour is up in a year and a half. Whoever gets the job will have to leave for Stewart soon."

"I think she should remain right where she is for another duty tour," Admiral Hubera said. "You're all so captivated by her abilities, let her use them to keep that part of space stable."

"As much as I'd personally like to see Admiral Carver remain on as one of my base commanders," Admiral Burke said, "we have to be mindful of Admiral Holt's warning that she'd resign her commission and take a job as a freighter captain just to get back aboard a ship."

"She'd never resign her commission if she's as good an officer as you all think," Admiral Hubera countered.

"Most of us here at this table have spent much of our lives in space," Admiral Hillaire said. "We know what motivates a line officer to seek such a life, even if we can't really define it easily. We know how powerful the pull of space can be."

"Are you accusing me of being insensitive to the desires of a line officer simply because I spent much of my career as a professor at the Academy?" Admiral Hubera asked.

"No. I simply think you secretly wish that Admiral Carver would resign. It's obvious you don't like her very much."

"She's just another young upstart who's climbed through the ranks too quickly for my tastes. She looks the same as she did on the day she graduated from the Academy twenty-one years ago. Replace the stars with a cadet uniform and she could blend into a group of students so well you'd never be able to spot her. For purposes of calculating retirement, she's only thirty-one years old. I didn't get my first star until I was sixty-eight, and it was the greatest honor I've ever received. I received my second star when I was eighty and approaching retirement. I'm sure it was intended as a retirement gift for my years of service, but the border expansion has allowed me to remain on active duty. I appreciate the trust that the GAC has placed in me, and I've dedicated my life to the good of the service. Admiral Carver doesn't even want the rank. She acts as if we're seeking to injure her when we're only trying to honor her. It annoys me that something so precious to me has been treated with disregard by someone else. I don't have anything personal against her except that attitude. Admiral Holt thinks it's because of a fool stunt she pulled when she was a cadet in one of my classes, but that's not it at all. It's because I don't think she deserves all of the attention that continues to be directed her way."

"That was quite a speech, Donald," Admiral Hillaire said. "I'm sure everyone on this Board understands that you only have the good of the service in mind with every action you take, even if we all disagree with your assessment of Admiral Carver."

"A few months ago we discussed the possibility of having Admiral Carver take responsibility for the Nordakian Space Force as part of our effort to merge them with Space Command," Admiral Moore said. "I've been in communication with the King of Nordakia and he's indicated a willingness to discuss the matter further. In the meantime, he's decided to promote Captain Carver, to the Nordakian Space Force rank of Senior Admiral— the equivalent of our Upper Half. They don't have brevet rank, so the promotion is permanent, but it's naturally not incumbent upon us to match it. Admiral Carver should receive the notification soon.

"On the matter of a replacement, I propose moving Admiral Vroman from Hawking Space Command Base. Admiral Vroman already has his second star and Hawking is only a StratCom-Two base, so we can replace him with a Lower Half. The Flag Officer Selection Board has several candidates on their list. Any of them will do for command of Hawking because it's so far from the border that a new base commander won't be challenged while he gets his feet wet."

"I second the proposal," Admiral Platt said. "Admiral Vroman is a very capable officer, and since he's almost eighty, I'm sure Donald won't have any objection."

"None," Admiral Hubera said. "He deserves the upgrade to a StratCom-One base. He's earned his position by doing an excellent job and has progressed steadily throughout his career."

"My only reservation is that Admiral Vroman has never commanded a fleet in battle," Admiral Bradlee said. "For that matter, he's never commanded a ship in real action, only during simulations and war games. I'm not trying to take anything away from Admiral Vroman. He's an excellent administrator."

"Except for Admiral Carver," Admiral Woo said, "no admiral in Space Command has commanded a fleet in battle.

Admiral Holt did command the forces in defense of Higgins but from the station. And only a few admirals have ever engaged an enemy in battle while they were still ship captains, if you can call skirmishes with the Raiders as being battles. Captain Gavin has twice commanded taskforces in battles against the Raiders, but he refuses to give up his ship and accept appointment to flag officer."

"Lon is correct," Admiral Platt said. "We don't have a pool of battle-experienced flag officers to choose from, and Admiral Vroman has been a very effective administrator."

"All in favor?" Admiral Moore said. Everyone raised his or her hand, and he said, "It passes unanimously. Our next order of business is the award of honors for Admiral Carver's crews."

"I propose we accept the recommendations of Admiral Carver and the captains in her fleet," Admiral Burke said.

"I second," Admiral Bradlee said.

"All in favor?" Admiral Moore said, calling for a vote. As everyone raised his or her hand, he said, "Approved."

*   *   *

Emperor Maxxiloth sat in the conference room watching the report from Supreme Lord Space Marshall Dwillaak. The expression on his face sent chills through the various ministers and aides present. Dwillaak never made an attempt to shift the blame to anyone else.

"...we retreated with most of our force intact, our only losses being the twelve warships destroyed by the enemy mines. I accept full responsibility for this disgraceful retreat, but given the size of the enemy forces confronting us, I knew we would surely be destroyed. We've seen the capability of their ships, and if a mere fifteen could destroy our Third Fleet while only losing one themselves, the numbers we faced could have crushed us easily. Every warrior in the fleet is willing to sacrifice himself for you, my lord, but I felt it wiser to leave Galactic Alliance space for now and preserve our fleets for a future engagement where we have the upper hand. Our recovered warriors are being debriefed to learn every-thing possible about the enemy. We shall begin preparations for a new assault once we've replaced the lost ships, learned more about the enemy's unknown weapons, and studied their tactics for possible vulnerabilities. Report complete."

"Exalted Lord Space Marshall Berquyth," the Emperor said through clenched teeth when the report had finished, "are our forces now in the habit of running away from a fight?"

"My Lord, Dwillaak showed great restraint. It would have been far easier to fight and die than swallow his pride in front of the disgusting hairless Terran by retreating. As he said, he was preserving the First and Second Fleets for another day. We could have struck a blow against the Alliance forces, but at what price? The loss of our First and Second Fleets at so early a point in the campaign would have left us with barely three hundred warships in the entire Empire. We would have accomplished little, and it would have been many, many years before we could mount another offensive."

"And what have we gained? We've not only agreed to leave their space forever, but we've conceded another hundred light-years of my new territory. In the eyes of the galaxy, we've been beaten, and beaten soundly. We have never been beaten before. Not since my great-grandfather started us down this path to our Manifest Destiny have we suffered a loss. When word of this gets out, some of our subjects may begin to think we've grown soft. They may start to think the time has come for them to rebel."

"All the more important to have a strong force, my Lord. With five hundred ships, we can still put down any rebellion or attack from within or without our borders before it gets started. With just three hundred ships, we might have had to pull back to our previous borders. At least we retain the territory up to the Galactic Alliance Buffer Zone. There are still many, many worlds to conquer in our new territory."

"We've smashed all civilizations within our previous territory that had achieved space travel capability and set up puppet governments to control them. The others can wait until we get around to them. Our greatest threat is the Galactic Alliance; they've shown themselves to be a powerful force. Only they stand between us and my great-grandfather's goal to rule the galaxy."

"We must bide our time and rebuild our forces, my Lord. When next we meet this Admiral Carver, we shall be better prepared. You will yet have her head on your trophy wall."

\* \* \*

Jenetta presided over the memorial ceremony at Stewart for the crewmen lost in the battle with the Milori, along with the captain of each ship and the ship's chaplain. The convention center was filled to capacity, and the shops on the concourse were closed for the morning in observance of the ceremony.

Each of the captains delivered a eulogy for the lost comrades aboard his or her ship and then Jenetta stood to deliver a closing eulogy.

"My heart is filled with grief this day, as it has been since the battle. Death is a part of life, but to lose so many who were still in their prime is doubly painful. I personally knew most of the officers we lost, as well as many of the NCOs and crewmen lost from the *Prometheus* and *Song*. The captain, or acting captain, of each ship has eulogized those in his or her command, but I'd like to say a few words about the two captains who are not with us today.

"I first met Captain Joseph Malinowski of the GSC Cruiser *Mentuhotep* seven years ago when he answered a distress signal I sent out from the planet Mawcett, now known as Dakistee. Captain Malinowski never hesitated to answer the call when someone needed assistance. He was a wonderful human being, an outstanding Space Command Officer, and much beloved and respected by his crew. He shall be greatly missed.

"Captain Andrew Novak of the GSC Destroyer *Asuncion* has been a close friend of mine for several years. The *Asuncion* was one of the ships that came to assist the *Colorado* after we had seized this base from the Raiders and became one of the original complement of ships assigned to Stewart. We enjoyed many dinners together over the years. Most ship captains desire little else than to command a Space Command vessel, but I recently learned that Andy hoped his career would take him to a post as a flag officer. I'm sorry he never had a chance to reach that goal. I know he would have performed the duties of admiral as commendably as he performed his duties as a captain. He shall be greatly missed."

Jenetta didn't wish to drag out the memorial with long-winded speeches, but an additional fifteen minutes of eulogy to commemorate the lives of two senior officers who had made the ultimate sacrifice in the line of duty didn't seem excessive. Returning to Captain Malinowski, she spent about seven minutes discussing his career in Space Command and finished by listing the people he was leaving behind. Then she did the same for Captain Novak. When she had finished her eulogies, the chaplains assembled on the dais to offer a series of non-denominational prayers to close the ceremony. Most eyes were at least moist by the end of the memorial service. The ceremony would give closure to the event and now everyone could begin to put it behind them and move on.

Since arriving back at Stewart, Jenetta had spent part of each day preparing personal messages to the families of her lost officers. She had prepared a message of condolence to the family of every crewman, explaining to most that she hadn't known the crewman personally, but from the reports prepared by their captain, she knew they had performed their duty in the best traditions of the service and had died bravely while helping to defend all the peoples of the Galactic Alliance from the invasion force of a merciless tyrant. She had sent all prepared messages just prior to the ceremony.

Jenetta walked sadly back to her office, but it was time to let the unseen wounds heal, so she turned her mind to other matters. Captain Donovan had done an excellent job in her absence, but there were still dozens of small matters that required her personal attention. She had procrastinated about them, putting the matter of completing the messages and planning the memorial ceremony ahead of all else.

Lori made it back to the office ahead of her because Jenetta had stayed behind to talk with her captains briefly. She would see most of them at dinner again this evening and on many more evenings while they remained in port as base engineers fully restored the vessels. The objective of repairs performed before reaching the base had been to get the ships battle-ready. Now, engineers would check every ship thoroughly from keel to sail and repair problems properly. When finished, there would be little evidence of the damage they had suffered. Out of necessity, Stewart had developed a complete repair-dock facility capable of handling almost any problem. It was the only repair facility within five hundred light-years and Supreme HQ had supplied an extra hundred engineers to staff the dock. All newly arriving warships had had their food supplies replenished and had then been immediately dispatched to patrol duty. Normally, crews would receive a period of R&R after such a long voyage, but the current situation precluded such activity. Space Command needed as many eyes and ears out there as possible. That the Milori would return was a conclusion accepted by everyone.

The enemy ships towed back to Stewart by space tugs were brought into the asteroid base. The space along the wall opposite the habitat in the sixty by thirty kilometer cavern was largely unused, so the Milori ships were lined up several rows high and anchored to the cavern wall next to the Raider ships taken in battle.

The weapons research people and engineers wasted no time getting to work on the warships and spent their days examining every square inch of the ships. By the time they were done, detailed ship construction plans would be created and every single aspect of the Milori ships, weapons, computers, sensors, and instrumentation would be known and documented. The bodies of the dead Milori, taken to the heart of the solar system in cargo containers, were ejected towards the star. In time, the sun's gravity would accept the containers, searing the entombed bodies to ashes long before they reached the corona.

Jenetta received notice from SHQ that she was to receive another Space Command Cross, but it didn't excite her the way her previous honors had. Too many good people had been lost this time. She was more excited by the prospect of being the one to bestow some of the medal honors at a ceremony scheduled to be held in one week's time. She would also be awarding promotions to a number of officers, including her brother who would continue temporarily as captain of the *Mentuhotep* until a frigate captain arrived to relieve him. Billy would then receive a destroyer appointment as the destroyer captain assumed command of the frigate. All injured crewmembers would receive a Purple Heart medal, and Jenetta would award numerous other medals for conspicuous service and bravery. Eliza would receive a Purple Heart for her head injury, in addition to the campaign ribbon that every crewmember participating in the battle would receive. The crewmembers who lost their lives would posthumously receive the Space Command Star.

*　*　*

Jenetta was working in her office a few days later when Lori informed her that several Nordakian Space Force captains were requesting to see her. Assuming they were there to present their orders to her, she said to send them in. Three Nordakian cruisers— the *Ezillsuh*, the *Arilalsuh*, and the *Imwellsuh*— had been underway for Stewart since the Milori had first been detected in the Frontier Zone.

Stopping in front of Jenetta, the three captains sank to one knee, placing their right hands, open and flattened, against their chests, their heads bowed. Such behavior was not called for when meeting a senior officer or even an admiral, but being a member of the Nordakian nobility, Jenetta was always accorded this show of respect by Nordakians.

"Kareer a Stewart, Hetrowdi," Jenetta said as they entered her office, the translation from Dakis being 'Welcome to Stewart, Captains.'

Together, they replied, "Zrand Chekkora u Kareerdu," meaning, 'It's my honor to be welcomed here.'

Since there was no one else in the room, Jenetta used Dakis exclusively.

"Please rise, gentlemen. We operate on Space Command military protocol here."

The captain closest to Jenetta said, "My Lady, our king sends you a special message." He held out a thick disk to Jenetta, who accepted it and placed it on her desk. She had seen such disks while on Nordakia. Realizing that the three captains wouldn't stand until she had played it, she placed her thumb lightly on the top surface to begin the playback. A holographic image of King Tpalsh appeared. No wonder the three officers hadn't risen.

"Greetings, Azula Carver. Allow me to congratulate you on your recent stunning victory against the invading hordes of Milori. From what little we know of them, their cruelty and barbarism, we are indeed fortunate to have you protecting our border.

"Three cruisers, the closest of our Space Force to your location, were immediately dispatched to join your forces and assist in repelling the invasion. Although the Milori have already retreated, we've decided they should remain with you as part of your patrol forces. For some time we've been engaged in negotiations with the Admiralty Board regarding the merger of the Nordakian Space Force with Space Command. We've mutually decided that this shall be a first step in that direction. We hope that under your wise direction and tutelage, the three Nordakian Space Force crews will begin to adapt to Space Command protocols. Each of these captains has been required to study and learn the Space Command handbook of regulations thoroughly.

"As a captain in our Nordakian Space Force, you've had complete authority over all civilian Nordakian ships, but for this new direction, you'll need complete authority over all military ships as well. Therefore, by royal proclamation we have appointed you a Senior Admiral. Congratulations, Admiral. We know you'll continue to serve our people with distinction.

"My queen sends her warmest regards and we both hope you'll come to visit us at your earliest opportunity."

The hologram shrunk quickly back down into the base, and the three captains finally rose to their feet.

"What are your orders, Admiral?" the one who had carried the disk asked.

"Tell me your names."

"I'm Captain Tpekera of the *Ezillsuh*, this is Captain Wdelfer of the *Arilalsuh*, and that is Captain Bfruvpax of the *Imwellsuh*."

"I'm pleased to meet each of you. I was privileged to travel from Higgins Space Command base to Nordakia aboard the *Ezillusuh* a few years ago. Is that ship still in service?"

"The *Ezillusuh* was renamed the *Ezillsuh* after a complete retrofit was completed two years ago," Captain Tpekera said. "I was named as its new captain at that time. Our cruisers are now much faster. We can achieve speeds as great as Light-390, although we normally just refer to it as Light-375, a standard designation."

"Wonderful. I'm looking forward to inspecting your ships."

"It will be our great honor to welcome you aboard, Admiral."

"Thank you. I'm pleased that you're here and we welcome your addition to our forces. In the past, because of the Raider problem, Space Command concentrated on patrolling 'regulated' GA space, but we now face a far greater threat from without, so I'm devoting many more resources to patrolling the Frontier Zone than ever before. I think that, initially, it might help to have a Space Command advisor aboard each of your ships. He or she will be available to advise the captain in situations where there might be some uncertainty about GA regulations and protocols."

"Of course, Admiral. I think that would be sensible. We have studied the regulations thoroughly of course, as our king has stated, but further interpretation would be helpful in certain situations."

"The problem may be in finding someone fluent in Dakis. It will be difficult enough explaining some things without having to overcome a language barrier."

"That should not be a problem, Admiral. Since Amer has become the de facto standard throughout Galactic Alliance space, Space Force Command advised all officers to begin studying the language ten years ago. Five years ago, it became mandatory at the Space Force Academy that all officers be fluent before they could graduate. At the same time, serving officers were told that promotions would be contingent upon the candidate's ability to speak Amer. It has been a great incentive, and most officers now speak Amer fluently."

"That's wonderful. I've been away from Nordakia for much too long. I hadn't heard of that change."

"The service has changed greatly since you returned the True Word of the Almuth to our people, and we have tried to emulate Space Command. Most officers are quite anxious to integrate the services. The increases in our ship speeds are thanks to technology given us by Space Command."

"That's excellent news. I'd love to hear more about the changes taking place back home, but I have another meeting in a few minutes. Perhaps we can get together at dinner to discuss it further. I host a very informal dinner party for ship's captains several times a week. You're welcome to join us tonight."

"Thank you, Admiral. We'd love to."

"Wonderful. Come to my private dining room immediately next to the officers' mess at 1900 hours. My aide can give you directions to the dining area."

"We'll be there, Admiral."

"Then I'll see you this evening. Captains," Jenetta said as a goodbye, nodding once to indicate their dismissal. The three Nordakians saluted with the Nordakian salute and left after Jenetta returned it.

* * *

The awards ceremony was conducted in the convention center a week later. A newly designed campaign ribbon awarded for participation in the battle had already been presented to everyone who had been aboard any of the fifteen ships. It was only the fifth such ribbon created since Space Command had been founded. The others were for participation at the Battle of Vauzlee, the Battle for Higgins, the Battle for Dixon, and the Battle for Stewart. The latter ribbon came in several variations, commemorating different aspects of Stewart's acquisition and defense. The medals awarded at the large ceremony were for acts of conspicuous gallantry or for injuries sustained in battle. Eliza received her Purple Heart medal for having sustained a concussion, even though she was fine a day later because of her recuperative powers. Jenetta also awarded all of the other purple hearts. Prior to the ceremony, she had toured the wards in the base hospital and awarded all the medals to the injured recipients who were unable to attend the ceremony.

Captain Gavin stood in for Admiral Moore and awarded Jenetta's third Space Command Cross after all of the other medals had been distributed. He read a short speech from Admiral Moore commending Jenetta's role in the war with the Milori and then added his own comments about Jenetta's short but superb tenure as an admiral and the leader of the taskforce. At the conclusion of the speech, the convention center erupted in applause that lasted a full two minutes.

Following completion of the medal awards portion of the program, Jenetta bestowed promotions on a number of officers, working her way up from the lower ranks to the higher. When she pinned on Billy's new bars, he smirked at her. She scowled at him in her best 'Admiral Holt scowl' impression and he stopped. Billy was the last to receive his new rank, being one of only two captains promoted at the ceremony. Captain Hollingshead was the other.

All of the news services covered both the memorial ceremony and the medal ceremony. Jenetta was seldom off camera these days. She longed for a return to the days before the reporters had arrived, but those days were past forever. With the arrival of the diplomats, Stewart was becoming a newer and larger version of Higgins Space Port.

# Chapter Twenty-Two
~ September 30th, 2277 ~

"Trader Vyx to see you," the message from Lt. Commander Ashraf said as it scrolled up on Jenetta's com screen.

"Send him in, Lori," Jenetta said. The computer automatically transmitted the instruction to Lt. Commander Ashraf's screen.

"You may go in, Trader," she announced.

Jenetta was sitting at her desk when he entered the office. "Come in, Trader, and have a seat. Beverage?" she asked, pointing at the food synthesizer.

"I'm set, Admiral," he said as he sat down.

"You can't have completed your business on Koppreco this quickly," Jenetta said.

"No, I've just returned from picking up my cargo on Aluvia and I'm on my way to Koppreco now. I wanted to make sure you had arranged the clearance."

"I have. They're expecting the *Scorpion* and will clear you through customs without a search of your ship."

"It's nice to have friends in high places."

"How many mamots are you bringing in?"

"Who said anything about mamots?"

"Isn't that your cargo?"

Vyx smiled. "You always seem to be a step ahead of me. I forget that you were in Intelligence."

"Only temporarily; Captain Kanes had me assigned to his section while I was waiting for my ship to arrive back in port at Higgins."

"But you figured out that I picked up mamots?"

"It was a logical deduction. I know you wouldn't bring anything harmful to Koppreco so I thought about all the harmless but restricted things. Mamots are in short supply and their increasing value has made them the most obvious cargo for smugglers. If the Kopprecon government was smart, they'd make them legal again so they could quarantine all the incoming animals instead of dealing with the problems from diseased smuggled animals."

"The mamots I'm carrying were quarantined for months, and each has been checked for the plague. They've been certified free of infection."

"I'm sure you've taken all precautions. If I didn't trust you I wouldn't have arranged for you to bypass customs."

"We should be back this way in about fifteen or sixteen months, Admiral. This little job will pay for a lot more freighter time if you need it."

Jenetta smiled. "I appreciate what you did for us and I've sent a full report to Captain Kanes at Higgins. We can't honor you openly, but you and your team have each received a written commendation in your files and a Space Command Star that you will receive— some day."

"I wasn't fishing for a compliment or a medal, Admiral, but it's nice to get some recognition, even if I can't wear it on my chest as other Space Command officers can. It would be nice to think we've seen the last of the Milori, but I fear we haven't."

"I share your trepidation, as does Supreme HQ. But as far as Stewart is concerned, it'll be someone else's problem next time they come. I don't even expect to be here when you get back."

"You're being fired? After saving the Alliance's butt?"

"No, not fired. My tour of duty here ends in about a year. Some other officer will be coming to take my place here and I'll be sent somewhere else."

"They can't do that. You made this base. We only have it because of you. You've defended it against attacks by the Raiders and now an invading alien force. They can't just take it away from you. Other admirals keep their command until they retire, unless being promoted. Are you being promoted again?"

"I've grown sort of attached to Stewart, but I'm hoping to get a battleship for my next command."

"Two-star admirals don't get command of battleships, except as overall command of taskforces or fleets."

"They do if the Admiralty Board takes back the stars. My promotion was only brevetted to deal with the crisis."

Trader Vyx shook his head. "Damn. When they made you a two-star, I thought the Admiralty Board had finally gotten some good sense kicked into its collective head. I suppose your replacement will be some eighty-year-old rear echelon brass-polisher who's just looking for a soft place to finish out his career or someone using the position to try landing a cushy spot at SHQ, when what we really need is a younger free-thinker who can deal with the unique problems that must be faced on a regular basis at a very forward base like Stewart."

"I'm sure my replacement will be fully qualified to handle the job, even if he or she doesn't look like a recent academy graduate."

"I doubt if it will be somebody who could have brought the Arrosians and Selaxians back together the way you did. Oh, by the way, I ran into somebody on Scruscotto who knew a little something about those terrorist attacks. I pumped him as much as I could."

"Really? Well don't keep me in suspense; what did you learn?"

"The attacks were made by a criminal group of Arrosians for strictly mercenary reasons. They've no ideology drum to bang so they haven't claimed credit for any of the bombings. They were trained, funded, and armed by Shev Rivemwilth's people."

"Rivemwilth? He was behind the attacks?"

"None other. I guess our long dead friend figured a nice, dirty little war would be good for his business. He wouldn't be the first arms merchant to foment trouble with the intention of selling to both sides once things got rolling."

"His motivation might have been much deeper than that."

"Deeper?"

"I interrogated the Milori who ejected from the Tsgardi ship you destroyed. One of them talked after I promised to rescue any Milori survivors trapped in the destroyed ships. I convinced him that the invasion force didn't have a chance against all our new secret weapons, and I imagine he considered himself a patriot by telling us about the Empire's plans so we could try to prevent further loss of life."

Vyx chuckled. "I would have liked to have been there for *that* interrogation."

"He told us that Rivemwilth was the one providing them with intelligence about Space Command's weapons and our ability to defend ourselves against an invasion. It now seems clear that the attacks on Arrosa were merely a diversionary ploy. Rivemwilth probably hoped we'd be so preoccupied that we'd never notice the Milori until it was too late. Perhaps he hoped to get his old base back as part of the deal."

"That which we call Arrosa, by any other name would be as foul," Vyx said.

"Excuse me?"

Vyx grinned. "Just a little play on words. I was paraphrasing Shakespeare, Admiral."

"It sounded like part of the balcony scene from Romeo and Juliet."

Vyx smiled and nodded. "Act II - Scene II. Juliet says, 'What's in a name? That which we call a rose, by any other name would smell as sweet.' Shakespeare was, of course, saying that a person's name shouldn't make a difference. My meaning is that the planet didn't make a difference. Rivemwilth just needed a little war to distract your attention away from the Frontier Zone. Which solar system suffered through the death and destruction a prolonged war of his making brought didn't make any difference to Rivemwilth."

"The situation between Arrosa and Selax was ready-made for his purposes. He just had to heat things up a bit more. Did you happen to get any names of the terrorists on Arrosa?"

"I heard a few names, but some of them are only partials and I don't have any proof that the facts are correct."

"I'm sure the Arrosians would appreciate any leads we can give them. A lot of people were killed in those *terrorist* bombings."

"Okay, Admiral. I'll make a list if you'll give me a pad."

Jenetta leaned forward and slid a portable viewpad towards him on the desk. He grabbed it before it could fall off the edge and entered all the names he'd heard.

"That's it, Admiral," he said as he slid the viewpad back to her.

"Thanks," she said, looking at the list. "I'll see that Arrosian Intelligence gets this information." Jenetta paused for a couple of seconds as she put the pad on her desk. "If I don't see you again for a while, it's been an honor knowing you. I want you to know how valuable your services have been to the Galactic Alliance. We're indeed fortunate to have such individuals as yourself and the other members of your team."

"Ditto, Admiral. The small hunk of metal they've hung on your tunic will never come close to expressing what a difference you've made to this part of the galaxy and the entire Galactic Alliance. I hope they do right by you with your next posting."

"Thanks, Trader. Goodbye."

Vyx then did something very unexpected. He stood up and came to attention, then saluted. This was the first sign of military behavior Jenetta had ever seen him exhibit. As Vyx stood rigidly in front of her, Jenetta couldn't know that it was the first time he'd felt the urge to salute any officer in many years, but she knew it was special. She stood up and returned his salute. He smiled, then turned and left her office.

After he'd gone, she moved to her SimWindow and stared at the activity in the asteroid's port. Perhaps it was because of Vyx's words, but for the first time she realized she was going to miss the base when it was time to move on in a year. Her cats must have sensed something in her mood because they came over and stood at her side, something they never did when she was alone in the office.

~ finis ~

*Jenetta's exciting adventures continue in:*

\*\*\*  ***Castle Vroman***  \*\*\*

,

# Appendix

This chart is offered to assist readers who may be unfamiliar with military rank and the reporting structure. Newly commissioned officers begin at either ensign or second lieutenant rank.

| Space Command | Space Marine Corps |
|---|---|
| Admiral of the Fleet | |
| Admiral | General |
| Vice-Admiral | Lieutenant General |
| Rear Admiral - Upper | Major General |
| Rear Admiral - Lower | Brigadier General |
| Captain | Colonel |
| Commander | Lieutenant Colonel |
| Lieutenant Commander | Major |
| Lieutenant | Captain |
| Lieutenant(jg) "Junior Grade" | First Lieutenant |
| Ensign | Second Lieutenant |

The commanding officer on a ship is always referred to as Captain, regardless of his or her official military rank. Even an Ensign could be a Captain of the Ship, although that would only occur as the result of an unusual situation or emergency where no senior officers survived.

On Space Command ships and bases, time is measured according to a twenty-four-hour clock, normally referred to as military time. For example, 8:42 PM would be referred to as 2042 hours. Chronometers are always set to agree with the date and time at Space Command Supreme Headquarters on Earth. This is known as GST, or Galactic System Time.

## Admiralty Board:

| | |
|---|---|
| *Moore, Richard E.* | Admiral of the Fleet |
| *Platt, Evelyn S.* | Admiral - Director of Fleet Operations |
| *Bradlee, Roger T.* | Admiral - Director of Intelligence (SCI) |
| *Ressler, Shana E.* | Admiral - Director of Budget & Accounting |
| *Hillaire, Arnold H.* | Admiral - Director of Academies |
| *Burke, Raymond A.* | Vice-Admiral - Director of GSC Base Management |
| *Ahmed, Raihana L.* | Vice-Admiral - Dir. of Quartermaster Supply |
| *Woo, Lon C.* | Vice-Admiral - Dir. of Scientific & Expeditionary Forces |
| *Plimley, Loretta J.* | Rear-Admiral, (U) - Dir. of Weapons R&D |
| *Hubera, Donald M.* | Rear-Admiral, (U) - Dir. of Academy Curricula |

| *Ship Speed Terminology* | *Speed* |
|---|---|
| **Plus-1** | 1 kps |
| **Sub-Light-1** | 1,000 kps |
| **Light-1** (*c*) *(speed of light in a vacuum)* | 299,792.458 kps |
| **Light-150** or **150 c** | 150 times the speed of light |

| *Hyper-Space Factors* | |
|---|---|
| **IDS Communications Band** | .0513 light years each minute (8.09 billion kps) |
| **DeTect Range** | 4 billion kilometers |

| Strat Com Desig | Mission Description for Strategic Command Bases |
|---|---|
| 1 | Base - Location establishes it as a critical component of Space Command Operations - Serves as home-port to multiple warships that also serve in base's defense. All sections of Space Command maintain an active office at the base. Base Commander establishes all patrol routes and is authorized to override SHQ orders to ships within the sector(s) designated part of the base's operating territory. Recommended rank of Commanding Officer: **Rear Admiral (U)** |
| 2 | Base - Location establishes it as a crucial component of Space Command Operations - Serves as home-port to multiple warships that also serve in base's defense. All sections of Space Command maintain an active office at the base. Patrol routes established by SHQ. Recommended rank of Commanding Officer: **Rear Admiral (L)** |
| 3 | Base - Location establishes it as an important component of Space Command Operations - Serves as homeport to multiple warships that also serve in base's defense. Patrol routes established by SHQ. Recommended rank of Commanding Officer: **Captain** |
| 4 | Station - Location establishes it as an important terminal for Space Command personnel engaged in travel to/from postings, and for re-supply of vessels and outposts. Recommended rank of Commanding Officer: **Commander** |
| 5 | Outpost - Location makes it important for observation purposes and collection of information. Recommended rank of Commanding Officer: **Lt. Commander** |

## Sample Distances

| | |
|---|---|
| **Earth to Mars (Mean)** | 78 million kilometers |
| **Nearest star to our Sun** | 4 light-years (Proxima Centauri) |
| **Milky Way Galaxy diameter** | 100,000 light-years |
| **Thickness of M'Way at Sun** | 2,000 light-years |
| **Stars in Milky Way** | 200 billion (est.) |
| **Nearest galaxy (Andromeda)** | 2 million light-years from M'Way |
| | |
| **A light-year** (in a vacuum) | 9,460,730,472,580.8 kilometers |
| **A light-second** (in vacuum) | 299,792.458 km |
| **Grid Unit** | 1,000 Light Yrs² (1,000,000 Sq. LY) |
| **Deca-Sector** | 100 Light Years² (10,000 Sq. LY) |
| **Sector** | 10 Light Years² (100 Sq. LY) |
| **Section** | 94,607,304,725 km$^2$ |
| **Sub-section** | 946,073,047 km$^2$ |

The following two-dimensional representations are offered to provide the reader with a feel for the spatial relationships between bases, systems, and celestial events referenced in the novels of this series. The mean distance from Earth to Higgins Space Command Base has been calculated as 90.1538 light-years. The tens of thousands of stars, planets, and moons in this small part of the galaxy would only confuse, and therefore have been omitted from the image.

Should the maps be unreadable, or should you desire additional imagery, .jpg and .pdf versions of all maps are available for free downloading at:

`www.deprima.com/ancillary/agu.html`

The first map shows Galactic Alliance space after the second expansion. The white space at the center is the space originally included when the GA charter was signed. The first outer circle shows the space claimed at the first expansion in 2203. The second circle shows the second expansion in 2273. The 'square' delineates the deca-sectors around Stewart SCB, and shows most of the planets referenced in Books 4 through 6 of this series. The second image is an enlargement of that area.

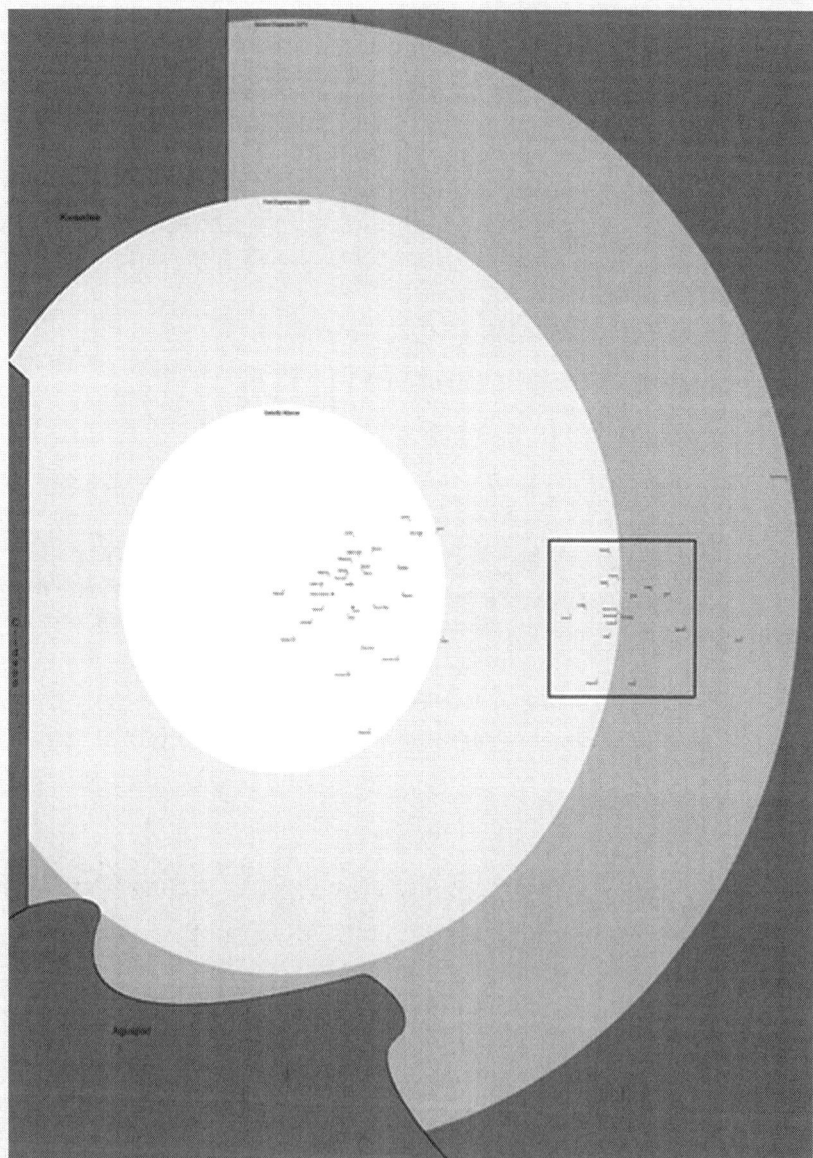

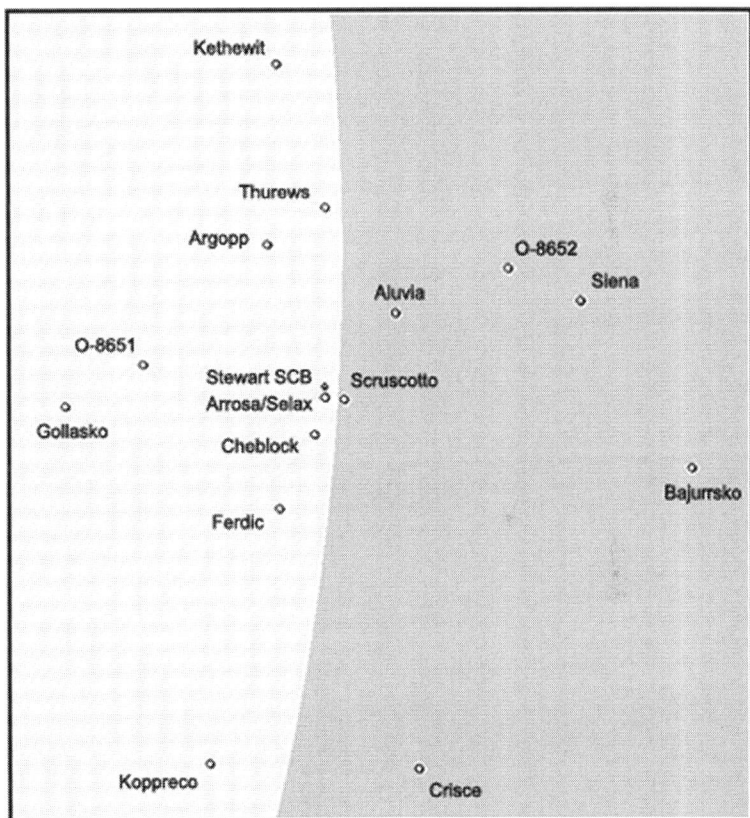

3482701R00180

Printed in Great Britain
by Amazon.co.uk, Ltd.,
Marston Gate.